I0762156

The Armageddon Diaries

Alice and Julie

David Powers

The Armageddon Diaries – Alice and Julie

First Edition - June 2025

Library of Congress Cataloging-in-Publication Data
Powers, David.
The Armageddon Diaries – Alice and Julie/David Powers.
362 p. 22 cm.

978-0-9985447-8-6 (hardcover)
978-0-9985447-9-3 (paperback)
979-8-9925863-0-5 (ebook)

1. Fiction. 2. Adventure stories, American.
3. Armageddon--Fiction. 4. Apocalypse--Fiction. 5. End of the world--Fiction. 6. Pandemics--Fiction. 7. Nuclear warfare--Fiction. I. Title.

Library of Congress Control Number: 2025908702
Printed in the United States of America

Eerie Forest
www.eerieforest.com

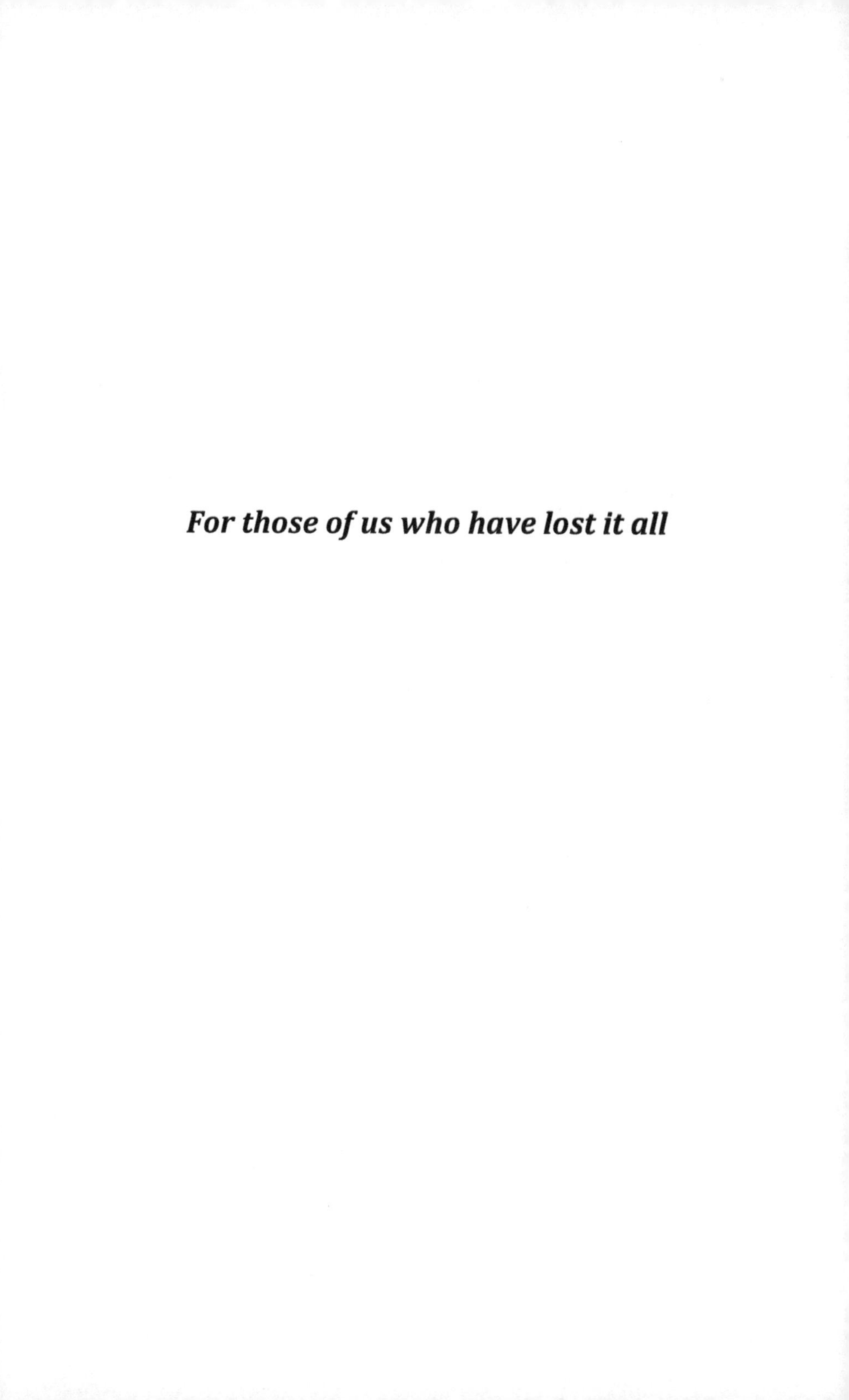

For those of us who have lost it all

ALSO BY DAVID POWERS

UNBURIED MEMORIES
TIDINGS FROM THE ABYSS
THE MAN FROM BUZZARD ROOST
THE TANDOORI BOX
PROTECT THE FLOCK
KIN AND CLAN

Winter 2039

Dear Reader,

I found two diaries belonging to my adoptive mother, Julie Werner, and her best friend, Alice Jenkins. Julie and Alice rescued me at the age of seven. I shall always be indebted to these remarkable women for taking me in and loving me as their own.

My biological parents died when I was merely an infant in the 2024 pandemic. Sadly, I have no memories of them.

I merged the well-worn diaries chronologically for easier reading without changing or deleting any text.

Tina Werner

Alice – June 16–22, 2029

6/16/2029

Dear Diary,

I just killed David with my bare hands. I can still hear his rasping breaths crowding the tent as I clamped my fingers around his throat and squeezed with all my strength. I couldn't bear to see my betrayal reflected in David's pale gray eyes, so I shut my own.

The man resembled a skeleton, sick and weak as a baby. I had nothing against Dave. In fact, I had come to love him during our brief time together. He made a good traveling companion since I met him four months ago in Chicago. With no food and a single gallon of water, I had to make a choice—me or him.

Will people see what I did as an act of mercy? Or would a jury of my peers condemn me to death?

I can't dwell on these thoughts now, or ever. Survival is the only thing that matters and the one task I have to focus on. I must find food or die like all the others.

6/17/2029

Dear Diary,

I have set up the two-person tent beside a stone wall, seeking shelter from the howling wind. The sky is growing dark, but with no meteorologists to deliver the seven-day forecast, I can only guess if a bomb cyclone is brewing over the next hill. I just drank the last ounce of water.

As I lie inside this nylon cave, the four-by-seven-foot space feels too big for me—an emptiness vaster than the Grand Canyon. The air carries a mixture of David's scents, a bittersweet memento of his presence. His musky body odor mingles with the foulness of the disease that ravaged him.

Today marks my second entry into Samantha Mathews' pink diary. I will walk down the hill tomorrow, hunting for food and water. They say you cannot last three days without a drop to drink. Tonight, I shall pray for David Carter's soul—a man with an open heart and a wry sense of humor. I won't ask God for anything for myself. I learned years ago that the Big Kahuna has more pressing issues on his mind than me.

My wristwatch claims it's 8:35 p.m. The candle is melting to its base, and my penlight has dimmed to near-uselessness.

6/18/2029

Enough of the "Dear Diary" nonsense. Who is Diary, anyway? I had a terrible night's sleep due to the wind and thunder. Thankfully, David Carter did not star in my nightmares this time. Instead, my father, Richard, stood on the hood of his broken-down Ford F-150, shouting, "Allie, don't forget to drain your hot water heater!"

A few hours ago, the lightning highlighted the silhouette of a man waving a club against the thin wall of my tent. I unzipped the door and peeked out. My heart crawled back from the pit of my stomach when I realized that a dead tree had created the shadow, and not David rising from the grave to devour my brain. Still, I had to be certain, or there'd be no rest for the weary. I slipped on my boots and hiked half a mile to a railroad culvert. Dave lay beneath the mound of ballast gravel where I left him. "So sorry I didn't have a shovel or the strength to bury you properly." David gave no response, not even a moan, which was for the best. The downpour began on my return to the tent. I'm shivering through my wet clothes.

It rained all day. I collected water in a plastic bag and tipped it into my canteen. Although five years have passed since Election Day, I still worry about radioactive fallout. No food in any of the houses or buildings.

6/19/2029

It's 7:20 a.m. Starving. Stomach cramps.

The soil is soaked. My weather prediction for the next twenty-four hours is hot and humid, with a chance of showers—just a typical summer day in Alabama. According to my watch, today is Tuesday, June 19th, which I believe was a federal holiday.

Dear God, please let me find edible food and potable water. Hello? Can you hear me up there?

6/20/2029

Montgomery! I am in McGehee/Allendale inside an upscale house on Boxwood Drive. The leather La-Z-Boy chair I'm sitting in is designed for napping. I'm gorging on a FAMILY SIZE box of stale Cheerios (BEST IF USED BY 08 MAY 2022) and guzzling a bottle of Gatorade Blackberry Wave (do sports drinks ever go bad?). Whole grain oats and artificial sweat aren't the greatest food and drink combination, but beggars can't be choosers.

Despite my diary's limited number of words, I take pride in my writing. Dunno why. Self-therapy for a former literary agent? Do I hope to leave this diary for future generations to display on a shelf in the Smithsonian? Will museumgoers read my sentiments and wish they had known me, or would they rather use the paper to wipe their asses? And who can say—extraterrestrial archeologists might excavate my journal after humanity vanishes into the ether and waste millenniums translating my nonsensical ramblings.

I spread my damp tent on a couch to dry. The green material reminds me of a giant cocoon, which you could say is its primary function. This morning, I emerged from the silky envelope, a butterfly ready to take flight. David's absence has left a heaviness in my heart. But am I also relieved? Waves of guilt, guilt, and more guilt.

I discovered a sewing kit in a kitchen drawer and stitched up a rip in the tent's nylon fly. The sun damaged the fabric. How much longer will this shelter withstand the elements? Like me, the waterproof seams are coming undone, thread by thread. On my own, with no lack of vacant houses and apartments to select from, I sleep within walls as often as possible. Not a lover of the "Great Indoors," David disliked the scent of decay. He also believed that camping off the beaten path was safer.

I once asked David for his opinion on the present-day population. Not knowing how many Americans had survived the catastrophes troubled me. He worked as a statistician for the U.S. Department of Labor on projects related to the economy. Dave scratched his scraggly beard before ping-ponging the question back to me, as was his tendency. "Alice, what do you think?"

I'm bawling like a prepubescent schoolgirl! Weep water is smearing the ink. I suppose I truly loved David. Now, I'm completely alone. ALONE! ALONE!! ALONE!!!

I took a stab at the current population. "A million? Ten million? More?"

David smiled without mirth. "Can you guess the number of people you've encountered since we met?"

We had journeyed from Illinois to Alabama in the last three months, passing through Indiana, Kentucky, Tennessee, and Georgia. My feet throb thinking about all that hard pavement.

Chicago had a sizeable population. Ten thousand? The majority of the buildings on the South Side were still standing. Some residents considered the fish swimming in Lake Michigan edible. The North Side wasn't as blessed. Bombs had leveled the entire way to Milwaukee. David referred to Brew City as an ashtray when sharing the horrors he witnessed.

Chicago, Indianapolis, Louisville, Nashville, Huntsville, Birmingham, and the small towns in between? How many people did Dave and I set eyes on?

Indianapolis had an extensive population of ex-military and civilian militias. Eight thousand? After such prolonged disobedience, the thought of law and order encouraged us. But then, General Custer's rallies at the Speedway filled us with fear. We observed scenes of skinheads engaging in violent fights and firing guns into the air. Every day, there was another public execution. Oftentimes multiple. So-called thieves, rapists, heretics, anarchists, and whoever didn't toe the line swung high in the noon-time sky. One night, we evaded the roadblocks and headed south to Kentucky until we hit the outskirts of Louisville.

The Gateway to the South had transformed into a ghost town. Someone had erected warnings around the city's perimeter. They were not your typical DANGER DO NOT ENTER or RESTRICTED AREA AUTHORIZED PERSONNEL ONLY signs. Instead, exhibitions of men and women strapped to lampposts or nailed to wooden crosses assaulted our senses. What breed of monster mutilates children? The stench of death hung heavy, as if the very essence of life had been snuffed out.

I developed a toothache while stepping over the Tennessee border. In downtown Nashville, ex-medical personnel had pieced together a clinic at a middle school. Dr. Phillips used forceps to yank out my infected molar. He handed me the rotten tooth and a bag of dusty dental supplies. "Stay away from sweets, and remember to floss!" Phillips' chest bore a curved DO NOT RESUSCITATE tattoo. He wouldn't accept a cent, not that I had anything worth trading. Nashville had fifteen hundred people? Three thousand?

Oh, I nearly forgot to mention that Music City had held on to its music scene! David knew I loved country tunes, so one day, he surprised me with a trip to the Grand Ole Opry. A trio of talented musicians played "Take This Job and Shove It" on guitar, fiddle, and snare drum in front of the burned-out auditorium. I'll never forget that pleasant afternoon.

We spent a month in Huntsville. For reasons unknown, the enemy had left the arsenal alone. Unaffected by the bombings, the largest city in Alabama drew a diverse populace from near and far. Did a resident quote a population of twenty thousand? Not exactly wall-to-wall bodies compared to the half million in metropolitan areas before the war, but plenty more than the other places I'd been to. A farmer's market operated on a barter system, and the provisional government opened a school—fiery beacons of normalcy amidst the reign of terror.

One hundred fifty miles away in Tuscaloosa, ex-Army engineers made a refinery operational again. The team "re-energized" the remaining oxidized fuel in automobile gas tanks and filling stations. Eventually, roughnecks pumped crude oil from the ground, refined the petroleum into gasoline, and shipped the valuable commodity to nearby communities. Vehicles, mainly vans delivering essentials, navigated Huntsville's patchy roads.

Something had happened in Birmingham. The Big Bad Thing. Five thousand living in The Magic City?

So, kids, dust off your handheld chalkboards, abacuses, or slide rules, and let's do basic math. 10,000 + 8000 + 3000 + 20,000 + 5000 = Not enough people to fill MetLife Stadium. Go, Giants!

I told David that I figured the number of inhabitants in the towns we had passed through to be around fifty thousand.

He nodded approvingly and removed a *Rand McNally Road Atlas* from his backpack. "Gimme a sec."

I dozed off while he circled cities on the U.S. map and notated the page margins. Just as I was falling into a deep sleep, Dave shook me awake. "I estimate four to five million survivors in the United States. Without current verifiable data, one hundred and fifty million worldwide?"

I doubted it then and still doubt now that so many souls roam the earth. If there were, we would have picked up more promising news on our shortwave radio (until the innards shorted out). Surely, out of five million Americans, someone had the ability to turn on the lights?

That's enough for now. I must finish searching these houses before dark.

Good haul today. I decided to sleep inside the home on Boxwood Drive. Nobody died here, so the vibes are positive, and the rooms haven't been ransacked. I cannot say that for the other buildings on this block. You'd think I'd get used to the thousands of dead bodies I've seen—some funky-fresh, most dried-out husks or piles of bones after exposure to the climate for so long. I still get the willies whenever I happen upon the remains of adults or children.

One memory that refuses to die is the Pittsburg family of four who group-hanged themselves in Saint Paul's Cathedral. The

Cunninghams stood on the same bench until the bravest member kicked it over. My money is on the father, given how heavy the pew looked. Or they all pushed at once. "Come on, guys! All together now! One, two, three!" The Hamiltons also strung themselves up in a house of worship. What's with churches and suicides?

I scrounged batteries for my flashlight and swapped out my clothes, which is simpler than finding soap and water to wash out the dirt. Right now, I'm using a candle to be able to write—the tall, fat kind you set on the fireplace mantel or bathtub rim for decoration but never actually light because you've got electricity and *don't have to worry about tripping over bloated corpses.* There are cartons and cartons of candles stacked in the bedroom closet. Somebody clearly had talked the lady of the house into buying a metric ton of wax at a candle party. Recall the days before GoFundMe when your next-door neighbor or closest friend guilted you into emptying your wallet for Amway, Tupperware, or Mary Kay? It's always the same old story with crowdfunding. "My cat needs an operation," or "My daughter doesn't want to be the only girl not going on the senior class trip to Cancun." These big fellas are too bulky to pack more than one, though they last forever and smell amazing.

Thank you, God, for the food you brought me.

6/21/2029

I woke up refreshed! These 1000 thread count sheets feel luxurious, a stark tactile contrast to the coarseness of my fleece sleeping bag. And the goose-down pillows? Heavenly. I slept until the sunlight shined through the curtains, casting a homey glow across the carpet. Living this way could become habit-forming.

Is it Thursday? Time to shower, slip into my best dress, pick up a coffee at Starbucks—I deserve a super-sized Trenta today—and drive to Inkwell Literary Agency. Sid, my overbearing boss, will shoot me that familiar "you're late again, Alice" sneer, then drag me into his corner office to rag about his gold-digger wife, Brianna. A year ago, I came upon a Starbucks cup in mint condition. I pretended to sip Caramel Macchiatos for days until the paper bottom dropped out. I often play make-believe to improve my mental fitness, which is a dismal negative two out of ten if I'm forced to rate it. And that's on a sunny day.

I ate a whole box of strawberry Pop-Tarts. The pastries may fill my tummy and provide a sugar rush, but they're far from nutritious. I require protein in my diet. David Carter taught me to forage for nuts and berries in the woods. And mushrooms. "Alice, you must learn to exist on your own." I patted him on the head and laughed. "Why, David, when I have you to fulfill my every hunger?" In hindsight, I wish I had paid closer attention. I remember to avoid green, yellow, and white berries and only eat fungi if it's found floating in a jar of spaghetti sauce.

David also showed me how to hunt and trap. Unfortunately, tracking game is becoming more challenging with dwindling animal populations. Pigeon and squirrel would taste prime grade to me now. General Custer's bullies confiscated our firearms in Indianapolis. Huntsville had an armory with decent deals. David acquired a Remington rifle, and I had a sweet little Taurus handgun until Birmingham. Fucking Birmingham.

Going out again.

I saw someone this afternoon—a tall woman around my age. What am I now, thirty-seven? She exited an upper-story window on Fernway Drive, three houses from where I was behind a car stowing canned soup in my backpack. I doubt the woman spotted me. She climbed down the extension ladder, collapsed the rungs, and took off through the backyards. I debated calling out, "Hey, you!" but held back. David always warned me to study strangers before making contact. I didn't follow her. Scared? Yeah, she scared me. Maybe I should have tagged after her. Being alone sucks.

6/22/2029

This old house, which initially seemed ideal, now feels spooky. Even with secured doors and windows, every tiny squeak and creak freaks me out. During the night, I heard faint footsteps echoing from upstairs. I hid under the comforter instead of investigating.

It's bizarre how a new day improves my outlook. Under the protection of daylight, I was able to poke my head into the attic, peering for vampires hibernating in their coffins or black widows spinning ginormous webs, reassured to only find mouse droppings. I ended up sitting on a bed in one of the kids' bedrooms, which may have been a boy's room with its racing car wallpaper and fighter jet models hanging from the ceiling.

I wept for Kenneth. He also had a passion for planes, especially those WWI aircraft with two wings—the ones Snoopy flew to battle the Red Baron. Today wasn't a blubberfest as in previous years when I went catatonic, incapable of eating or drinking for days. Just the usual cry my eyes out until I am out of tears. I miss my son so much. A bit of that salt loss was for David Carter as well.

Biplanes. Why couldn't I remember that word? Biplanes. Biplanes. Biplanes.

I assembled an assortment of Campbell Soup cans: Cream of Mushroom, Tomato, Vegetable Beef, Creamy Chicken Noodle, and, yuck, New England Clam Chowder. I'll save that tin for last. The pre-cooked soup can be eaten cold by adding seasoning to enhance the culinary experience. Many rural areas have installed propane furnaces and stoves where heating or cooking is not a problem as long as a few pounds of Hank Hill fill the tank. However, in suburban Montgomery, the kitchen cooktops run on natural gas or electricity. I have kindling to start a small fire, but I don't want the smoke to attract unwanted visitors.

Dear Diary, I can smell your brain overheating. "Alice, aren't there any outdoor barbecues?" And you're right. Some houses have propane grills. I might bump into the elusive Ladder Lady while checking the backyards.

Julie – June 22, 2029

6/22/2029

Jules is correct. This Alice chick is batshit crazy! "Julie, who, in their right mind murders their own boyfriend?" Not that Jules hasn't taken care of business before. And it sounds like this David Carter guy was a dollar short of buying the farm, anyhow.

Now, I'm writing in *her* diary—Alice's diary. She wrote how this pink diary once belonged to someone named Samantha Mathews. Who is this Samantha, and how did Alice get her hands on her journal? And why, may I ask, were the front pages torn out? At first, I resisted swiping the damn thing. Personal shit should be kept private. Nevertheless, I eventually gave in to temptation and shoved the reading material into my backpack.

Yesterday, we burgled a doctor's home office for meds. As we were leaving, I spied a woman carrying canned goods out of a McMansion on the end of Fernway. We followed her to another lavish house on Boxwood. Driven by curiosity, I returned this morning. After Alice left, Jules and I used our aluminum ladder to enter a bathroom window. We rummaged through her belongings, only running off with the diary. I don't know why this book called out to me. Jules is still sore at me for not letting her steal the soup cans.

I printed my name, JULIE WERNER, with a black Sharpie on the diary's front cover.

A laugh escaped my lips as I read Alice's nickname for me. "Ladder Lady." Jules found no amusement in the comment. Unlike me, Jules came into this world without a funny bone. I chose not to divulge Alice's impulse to call out to me. Jules doesn't need to know every minute detail. Besides, she's shown little interest in reading the diary. Yet. I haven't determined if I'll let her. But anyone who's had the pleasure of meeting Jules quickly learns she can be pretty persuasive when she wants something.

Alice - June 23, 2029

6/23/2029

Yesterday, while I was out, someone broke into the house on Boxwood Drive and stole my pink diary. I returned from a long day of scavenging to discover my diary was missing. I distinctly remember leaving the book on the kitchen island when I locked up. Panic set in as I scoured the lower floor for signs of intrusion. Every window and door remained firmly shut and secured. However, muddy shoe prints in an upstairs bathroom led me to a jimmied window. I ran outdoors and spotted ladder marks in the wet soil. The thief had to be the woman I saw on Thursday. Ladder Lady.

I'm writing in a school composition notebook with marbled covers—a Mead, though the brand doesn't matter. Books were stacked on the boy's desk, each designated for a different subject. I selected the MATH workbook and tore out the pages where BRADLEY SCOTT scrawled a handful of elementary algebra equations. "Find the value of T if T + 15 = 30." Oh, Brad, T is not and never will be 20.

Am I nervous? More pissed off than scared. Ladder Lady invaded my personal space. The image of her drooling all over my intimate feelings sickens me to the core.

Is she dangerous? Lacking a weapon, I am as defenseless as a deer in a clearing, waiting for the hunter to send a bullet through its pounding heart. Last night, I pitched my tent on the 9th hole of the Montgomery Country Club. I'm now lying on an air mattress, scribbling these words in the early morning light.

It's unreal how humans cannot restrain themselves from poking their noses into other people's belongings. Without question, I search the drawers, closets, and medicine cabinets of all the homes I stay in, even crouching on my knees to sweep my hands under dressers and beds. Now and again, a desirable item pops up. More often than not, I uncover artifacts from a bygone era—worthless trinkets that only bring forth melancholy. At one point, I collected jewelry, believing that the bigger gems could be traded for food. Such a foolish notion! Diamonds have always been nothing more than sparkly rocks.

The distinction is that I take things abandoned by deceased individuals. I don't steal from the living. That statement isn't entirely true—I've stolen from the living when absolutely necessary. And I take food or ammunition, not some dopey diary.

Ladder Lady left me the canned soups. Which is what? Considerate?

I packed my gear and started walking, desperate to put distance between Montgomery and myself. Boxwood Drive could have been my sanctuary for months if Ladder Lady hadn't interfered.

My green REI backpack, puffy with extra provisions, chafes my shoulders. Every five or six miles, I've had to stop to rest.

I'm comfortably seated in the front of a sporty red 2019 Ford Fiesta parked at O'Reilly Auto Parts. I know the year of manufacture from the registration docs in the glove compartment. Harvey Abernathy never installed the four Champion Double Platinum Power spark plugs sitting on the passenger seat. The key is in the ignition. Today is my lucky day! Unable to turn a deaf ear to the call of the road, I place my foot on the brake pedal and crank the starter. The roar of unbridled horsepower hurts my ears. *Vroom! Vroom!* And we're off to the races. Gone are the days of achy ankles and blistered feet for Alice Jenkins! Well, at least in my dreams. When did I last experience the thrill of tearing up the tarmac? Three years ago?

I shall keep the comical keychain. YOU'RE AN ASSHOLE BUT I LOVE YOU!

A block or two away, a man recites verses from the Book of Revelation. "And I beheld when he had opened the sixth seal, and, lo, there was a great earthquake, and the sun became black as sackcloth of hair, and the moon became as blood." A "sackcloth of hair"? *Blech!* It is amazing how far sound travels during the End Times.

When I first met David Carter in Chicago, he was preparing to head south. "I'm going to the Gulf of Mexico, Alice. Care to join me?" February in Chiberia with only a mummy sleeping bag for warmth is brutal, so I agreed to his proposal. Edward, David's brother, had sent a letter through the "Pink Pony Express"—women delivering messages by off-road motorcycles. "Dave, New Orleans is great! Come on down!"

Without David, I don't have a specific destination in mind. Long-term goals aren't my forte. Others decide for me. Food, water, shelter. Safety is numero uno—it's the Wild West out there. New Orleans is three hundred miles away. I'm two-thirds of the way from Chicago, so why quit now? Where else can I go? What else is there for me to do?

If I walk ten miles a day, I can arrive at The Big Easy in a month. That is, if all goes well—a colossal "IF." A bicycle is faster and will allow me to carry more rations. David and I rode mountain bikes covering hundreds of miles from Indianapolis to Birmingham—my happiest period in the five years since Election Day. Then we hit Brummie, and everything rapidly changed. David never blamed me for what happened, an act of kindness for which I bless him.

I'll hoof it until I find a working bicycle further down the road.

I heard a motor on Old Selma Road and hid in the brush. To my surprise, a silver-bearded man wearing a coonskin cap zoomed across the Catoma Creek bridge on a red, white, and blue electric golf cart. A tattered American flag fluttered from a pole mounted at the rear. The electric company's transformers are toast. How does Davy Crockett charge the lithium batteries? Maybe the 21st-century frontiersman installed racks of solar cells wherever he slips off his moccasins at night.

After a string of churches of all denominations (so long as they are Christian), the landscape transitioned from backwoods to acres of fallow fields. The windows in the few standing homes reflect my slow passage. Are people with ill intentions leering at me from behind the dark panes of glass?

I reached a railroad crossing and turned south onto Wells Road. Another two lanes of nothingness. The tar and chip surface unrolled as straight as an arrow. I walked down the center of the broken yellow line, able to see for miles. Despite the openness of the terrain, my scalp itches, and I feel as though a red and white target is painted on my skull. I am powerless to stop myself from scanning the countryside. I wish I had eyes in the back of my head like that woman Dave and I met in Chicken Bristle. Stephanie's "Spidey Sense" shielded her from threats. Since I left Montgomery, I haven't been able to shake the idea I'm being followed.

Paranoia, of course. My mother always complained I was high-strung. Barbara chastised me whenever I got overly excited. “Alice, don’t be such a drama queen!” *Pugh!* She was the born neurotic.

Meanwhile, my father’s days of running his plumbing supply business and nights of “working late” consumed his every waking moment, leaving little room for his family. Which is worse—being ignored or enduring relentless criticism? Why didn’t I seek mental health care when psychotherapists were still available?

I have never enjoyed highways, and Selma Highway is no exception. Endless fencing leaves me nowhere to run and hide if bandits were to appear. In such a harrowing situation, my only option is to lie in a swampy ditch, praying for them to pass without detecting me.

I am currently eating lunch at Suburban Propane. SPAM. Hickory Smoke Flavored, to be precise. BEST BY OCT 2027. Fresh! Not in a million years did I think I’d grow to love this pink crap. Although I no longer possess a camping stove, I had hoped that this distributor would stock small propane cylinders. The two submarine-sized supply tanks and the dozens of mini-sub-sized tanks are too big to cram in my backpack. Propane, propane, everywhere, nary a drop to burn. The Peterbilt delivery truck’s wide bench seat is perfect for a catnap.

I walked farther than planned today. Fifteen miles, more or less. A discarded road sign claims I’ve arrived in the one-horse town of Burkville.

I’m inside Rock Creek Baptist Church. I hiked up a steep hill to get here, a trickle of water flowing in the roadside stream. I peered into the windows of the preacher’s house out back, not feeling the urge to try the door. Too tired? Bad juju?

My exploration ended at a sacristy supply cabinet containing a half-case of Concord Altar Wine and a box of Broadman Gluten-Free Communion Wafers.

While the vino's deep purple hue and saccharine taste won't win any international awards, and the crackers are as dry as Jesus' bones, the Eucharist items make for a fabulous cocktail hour. It's a sin that I lack a can of Cheez Whiz to squirt on these round relics.

The ground outdoors is free of footprints, and there aren't any tracks in the carpet of dust indoors. Nobody has stepped into this place of worship for months, maybe even years. With a wooden bench as my bed and a kneeling pad for a pillow, I raise a toast to you, dear Diary. "To the road that stretches before us. May our glasses be ever full!"

Julie – June 23, 2029

6/23/2029

Jules and I tailed Alice to Burkville, a gloomy little town most likely named after a plantation owner using slave labor to harvest his cotton. On our way here, we noticed a grave-shaped marker. The stone honored Viola Liuzzo, a courageous White civil rights worker who was mercilessly gunned down by the KKK.

Jules had her reservations about following Alice. "Julie, why are we chasing that skinny White woman? When did you become a stalker?" She usually gets her way. Sometimes, if I stand my ground, I win. I told her to piss off. Is Jules jealous? Or is she afraid I'll run away with the "dumbass with the pink diary"?

I sleep with one eye open, constantly aware of Jules watching me.

Alice clearly hasn't traveled much on her own. She is clinging to the main roads, taking a southwestern route. The woman must have relied heavily on her man to tell her what to do. Jules' tracking expertise, inherited from her woodsman father, has been invaluable. She foretells Alice's next move even if she's half a mile ahead. The woman is too far west for Mobile to be her destination. Jackson, Mississippi? Ages ago, Jules taught me the art of wilderness survival. I still cherish the day she gifted me my very own Buck knife.

Why did Alice leave Montgomery? She had a roof over her head and access to food. Was it because I took her precious diary? And what's so important down south? Family? She won't last long on her own. Without Jules by my side, I wouldn't stand a chance.

We are in an apartment above Clyde's General Store. The faded sign atop the entrance boasts FRESH PRODUCE, though the merchant himself is far from edible. As we settled in, Jules rolled Clyde in a blanket, towed him down the back stairs, and flipped him into the ice machine. She kept his shotgun, a Benelli SuperNova pump, and a carton of 12-gauge shells. Our apartment's front window has an unobstructed view of dead-end Rock Creek Road, the only way out from the Baptist church Alice is staying in.

Vandals have emptied the shop, unless you count the shelving and the sickly-sweet smell of leaking refrigerant. Oh yeah, and a stack of Georgia scratch-and-win cards. While I'm busy fixing dinner—smoked rabbit, dandelions, and wild strawberries—Jules amuses herself with the lottery tickets. Every few minutes, she exclaims, "Another winner!" Having her out of my hair is nirvana.

Jules wants the bed. Even with a clean set of sheets, I can't bring myself to lay my head where Clyde gave up the ghost. With an inch of mold encasing his whole body, the man resembled the Creature from the Black Lagoon. She's welcome to stare at a ceiling full of buckshot and blood tonight—I'll be on the couch in the living room.

I lie in the shadows, questioning why I feel compelled to document everything. Writing about others has always been easy, but writing about myself is a painful chore. Each word I press to paper is like squeezing blood from a stone. A bloodless stone. I can't help but think that Jules is a stone, a hardened hunk of granite.

I penned a lot of poetry before the world, as I knew it, ended. My love for literature began when I was young. Was it fifth grade? I also wrote short stories about my family or made-up fantasies about others. Academically, I excelled as a straight-A student, particularly in my favorite subject, Creative Writing. During the summer between my junior and senior years, I attended Loyola Marymount University's Beginning Screenwriting Program in Los Angeles. Professor Kennedy encouraged me to apply to LMU. He said I had a knack for expressing myself.

Fuck Robert McKenna and the red Dodge Charger he rode in on.

Alone

Darkness came as a knock on the front door—
"Pack your things, girls,
and leave what's precious on the floor."
Jules, I split in two the day I met you,
and now we're together forever
like flies stuck on glue.

Sometimes I hate Jules. There are days I wish she were dead.

Alice - June 24, 2029

6/24/2029

My head is killing me—a vice squeezing my skull harder and harder with every beat of my heart. Instead of going to bed early, I drank an entire bottle of altar wine. I uncorked another because I found an empty bottle of Holy Hangover in the baptismal font. All the communion wafers are gone. Did I black out? I haven't been this drunk since my wild college days at the University of Rochester. I dropped two Excedrin into my palm, but I returned the pills to the container. I'll keep the acetaminophen for one of those rare, excruciating migraines.

I'd give five years of my life for a vitamin B12 intravenous drip.

Less headachy, I walked to the stream to wash up and slake my thirst. The water tasted okay. I'll wait and see if I get vomirrhea or die from dysentery. Wish I had a LifeStraw to filter out the nasties or at least a bottle of iodine tablets. I need to eat. The mere thought of slurping cold soup raises bile in my throat. I hope the convenience store has something stomachable. Although I intended to start my day at sunrise, I'm crawling back into bed.

It's nearly one thirty in the afternoon. I'm resting against a gas pump outside Clyde's General Store. Regular is $18.32 a gallon. Premium? If you have to ask, you can't afford to drive. There is nothing in the shop besides roach and rat shit. The place stinks like rotten fruit. I am done in. Depressed. No ambition. At all.

According to my *Rand McNally Road Atlas*, Hayneville is three hours away by foot. The route is flat as a board with not much in between. The sky is a brilliant shade of blue with fluffy white clouds. An eight-mile walk is achievable if I take my time.

As the lyrical poet Eminem once freestyled, "Don't ever try to judge me, dude. You don't know what the fuck I've been through." A woman from Huntsville mentioned seeing Slim Shady busking on the streets of Detroit.

I stopped at a long brick house with a NEED A MASSAGE? – MELLOW OUT sign out front. A deep tissue massage is precisely the indulgence I crave. And a mani-pedi. The backyard pool is green with algae, but the outdoor furniture has held up well to twenty seasons of atmospheric abuse. I'm sunbathing on a chaise lounge, watching a flock of crows peck for earthworms. The largest one just flew south with a lizard dangling from its beak. I should get off my butt and check inside the home.

I almost crushed my big toe breaking the doorknob off the back door with a cinderblock. There's nobody here, either alive or zombified. The kitchen pantry only has three jars of Vlasic pickles and an open box of Wheat Thins. I shot a few balls on the rec room's pool table until I snapped the cue stick over the "Happy Days" jukebox. Playing games alone is no fun at all.

Whenever I search a vacant house, I wonder about the owners. Did they fall victim to Crunk and meet their demise at home or in a hospital bed? Maybe the National Guard bussed them to a COVID quarantine zone, or the family headed north to outrun the pandemic.

A blockade of bullets had greeted me and my fellow refugees in our ill-fated attempt to cross the Canadian border. Seth Lenke saved my bacon by throwing me into a trench filled with dead bodies. Wherever you are, Mr. Lenke, I am eternally indebted to you.

Was that a gunshot? It sounded nearby. Is somebody hunting in the woods? I just heard a second boom.

I'm hiding behind a torched Dollar General to catch my breath and get my bearings. People live in Hayneville! Dogs bark. Children scream. Or is that laughter? I'm turning onto Cemetery Road, knowing exactly where I'll sleep tonight.

I am back to the safety of my tent from skulking around the dark town. Warm gusts of wind shake the nylon flaps, but none are powerful enough to whisk me away to the Land of Oz. I've camped in big boneyards, small boneyards, and atop mass graves. My only recollections are the way I feel reading the headstones. Mortal.

My grandfather loved telling me his favorite joke whenever we drove past a graveyard—the only rib-tickler I remember. "Allie, how many dead people do you think are buried in that cemetery?"

I'd play along. "You got me, Grandpa Charles. A hundred?"

"All of them, Allie," he'd reply with a straight face. "They're all dead. Every fucking last one of them."

Did I laugh as hard as my granddaddy? Perhaps. He did not say, "fucking." I included that swear word to add punch to the punchline. Grandpa Charles never cussed in front of children.

Two hundred people live in Hayneville? Three hundred? Some houses are illuminated with candles and lanterns. As night fell, men and women set up lawn chairs by the courthouse. A bluegrass band performed on a low stage. I didn't recognize any songs, but the singer had a melodious voice.

I plan to venture into town tomorrow. The streets seem safe. I need to talk to someone above ground before I go bananas.

Julie – June 24, 2029

6/24/2029

Footsteps jolted us from a nap. Jules aimed the Benelli pump at the stairway until the intruder left. I peered out the window. Alice, looking out of gas, was slouched against a fuel dispenser. I hope she's not ill.

The next town on Route 21 is eight miles away. With half the afternoon in the bag, I doubt Alice will make it beyond Hayneville.

Jules gets grumpy when she's forced awake.

Alice left Burkville dragging her feet. Jules and I have to be careful not to overtake her.

I heard barking at Tallawassee Creek. Searching for the source of the noise, we slid down an embankment to a small encampment. A woman wearing a rose-colored housedress stood by while a bearded man whipped a dog chained to a tree. The animal abuser turned as Jules racked a round into her shotgun. Without batting an eye, she blasted him in the chest. "Ma'am, I am counting to ten, then pulling the trigger. Run away as fast as you can! On your mark, get set, go! One, two. . . ." I treated the canine's wounds with Neosporin. The cuts weren't as bad as they first appeared.

Now, there is an additional mouth to feed. The tag on the collar says OSCAR, so that's what we'll call him. Oscar is as good a name as any.

Oscar prefers Jules to me. He sticks to her like a shadow, which is unsurprising since Jules plays better with four-legged animals than with two-legged ones. Oscar's physical appearance is unique. His white snout contrasts with his floppy orange ears. Orange spots cover his muscular white body. Bobbed tail. Kinda cute! Jules gave me the lowdown on Brittanys, a breed from the Brittany region of France. "Julie, now we have a bird dog to help us hunt." How does she know so much? I miss Wikipedia.

We explored an animal clinic located a mile north of Hayneville. I found a bottle of chlorhexidine to clean Oscar's lacerations. A slice on his hindquarters is deeper than I had initially thought. Let's see how long the bandage lasts before he tears the tape off. By happy chance, the clinic stocked a supply of pet food. Oscar sniffed at the fossilized puppy chow but gobbled the canned food as if the chicken was still clucking. It is a pleasure to have Jules talk to someone other than me.

I get why Jules killed the dog whipper. Humans should never mistreat an animal. Would I have shot the woman? What if she had no alternative other than to be with that creep? My distress perplexed Jules. "The bitch had it coming to her!" This kind of crap keeps me up at night. Wherever I look, I see a creek stained with the colors of her floral dress.

Alice is camping in Hayneville Cemetery. Her glowing green tent is visible from the abandoned house we're squatting in. She's reading, or maybe she has a new journal.

Jules kept calling me. "Julie, put down your stupid pink diary and come to bed!" The pooch is in the bedroom with her. I can't tell if it's Jules or Oscar snoring. Or both. That dog sure farts a lot.

Today has been long and eventful. I'm too tuckered out to add another word.

Alice – June 25, 2029

6/25/2029

I got up early, packed, and headed toward the tallest structure in town, the white HAYNEVILLE water tower. Along my path, I passed NAPA Auto Parts, Family Dollar (across-the-street competition to the incinerated Dollar General), Ace Hardware, QP Gas, Subway, a post office, a library, and a couple of banks. The New Salem Christian Church and the Lowndes County Courthouse have striking antebellum facades.

These words were inscribed on a historical marker behind the domed courthouse: ON MARCH 29, 1888, A MOB OF AT LEAST 200 WHITE MEN LYNCHED THEO CALLOWAY, A 24-YEAR-OLD BLACK MAN, NEAR THIS COURTHOUSE IN LOWNDES COUNTY, ALABAMA. MR. CALLOWAY WAS ACCUSED OF KILLING A WHITE MAN AND INSISTED HE ACTED IN SELF-DEFENSE, BUT HE NEVER HAD THE CHANCE TO STAND TRIAL.

To paraphrase the rest of the written description, the county sheriff colluded with the bigots who abducted the prisoner hours before his scheduled court date. The mob hanged Theo from a chinaberry tree, leaving his corpse riddled with bullets. Revoltingly, the governor supported the arrest of all Black individuals who sought justice. Those responsible for the lynching faced no consequences.

The reverse side of the sign revealed how White gangs committed countless acts of brutality against Black Americans, spanning from the end of the Civil War until the conclusion of World War II.

I sat on an iron bench in the village square, dwelling on this line from the marker: THE LOCAL NEWSPAPER HEADLINES APPLAUDED THE MOB'S ACT. "TAKEN FROM JAIL IN THE APPROVED STYLE, AND JUDICIAL EXPENSES SAVED."

An older man walking his golden retriever greeted me with a friendly gesture. I smiled and waved back. From my observations at last night's bluegrass concert, all the attendees were African American. Why didn't these oppressed people say, "To hell with this town"? I suppose uprooting oneself is difficult, even when the roots are planted in such bloody soil. How I hate the South and everything it stands for.

I passed ACE, a large building still specializing in hardware and lumber, to reach what used to be the Family Dollar. A vinyl sign, PEARL'S TRADING POST, swung above the entrance. A yellow Post-it note on the glass door read, AT LUNCH—BE BACK AT 12:30.

At 12:29, a slender Black woman arrived to open the store. A notice required all outsiders to wear masks. I slid a white N95 over my nose and followed a family of four into the dimly lit interior. A wide selection of merchandise stocked the shelves and hung on the walls. After browsing the expired packaged goods, my nostrils lured me to the fresh fruits and vegetables section.

My backpack held nothing of value, so I approached the proprietor to offer my assistance. She looked me over from head to toe, questioning my health.

"I feel fine," I assured her.

She touched my forehead before motioning for me to remove the mask. "I'm Pearl. And you are?"

"Alice. Alice Jenkins."

Pearl called another woman from the back room to take over the counter. She led me past a fishpond to a tennis court-sized field. I spent the afternoon beneath the scorching sun, pulling weeds. Digging my hands into the rich earth made me feel needed for a change. When five o'clock rolled around, Pearl rewarded my efforts with a paper sack filled with beets, carrots, collard greens, peaches, nectarines, and pears—items I didn't have to cook. She commended me on a job well done and invited me to return tomorrow.

I eagerly accepted her proposition.

Pearl asked where I was sleeping. I pointed at my tent bag. "Hayneville Cemetery."

In response, she gave me a key. "North Washington Street. The white house with the attached garage belonged to my mother until, you know. . . . It isn't the Waldorf Astoria, but the sheets are clean, and there's a water well in the back. The bed is much more comfortable than lying on a pile of somebody's old bones. You're welcome to stay as long as you want. I'll inform the neighbors to look out for you."

Maybe the South ain't so bad after all.

This home is delightful! I opened the windows to let in some fresh air. The bed in the main bedroom is made, and the water splashing out of the hand pump is sweet. A silver Tesla Model 3 is parked in the garage, its battery as dead as its inventor. Little did Elon Musk foresee a planet depleted of electricity before he could attain his trillionaire status. From the backyard, I have a lovely view of the fishpond and the field where I labored. I'm currently in a hammock, watching the sunset and listening to chirping crickets. Ouch! I had better go indoors before the tiny, winged vampires drain me dry.

Julie – June 25, 2029

6/25/2029

Prior to entering Hayneville, Jules hid the Benelli SuperNova shotgun and shells in the nearby woods. Despite our darker skin tones, I can't ignore the sensation that we stand out more than Alice does. Jules believes that a guy and his dog gave her the stink eye. He seemed like a nice old man to me.

Alice roamed the town before disappearing into a market. When she didn't come out, we circled around the back and spotted her weeding a farmer's field. Eventually, Alice emerged from the store carrying a bag of groceries. We followed her to a home on North Washington Street.

We are in an empty house across the lane from Alice. Jules discovered a set of keys under the doormat. The amount of dust blanketing the furniture proves that no one lives here. No dead pets. No mummified bodies stacking the closets or bathtubs. The refrigerator is cleaned out and left open. Rooms devoid of personal paraphernalia, such as family photographs or vacation souvenirs, give off the sterile vibes of an Airbnb.

I read the historical markers while exploring the town. Too much bad shit happened in Hayneville, some not long enough ago to call ancient history. Jules glared at the signs, her hands clenching and unclenching. My vigor to write a poem or start a short story tonight has disintegrated.

Alice – June 26, 2029

6/26/2029

I spent the morning picking pole beans, packing them into bushel baskets, and carrying them to Pearl's Trading Post. The afternoon sped by as we washed vegetables for the market. Pearl Jackson and Caddy Lee, who also works at the store, joke and laugh with each other. Their cheerful banter uplifts my spirits. So far, the ladies haven't grilled me on who I am or why I'm in their town. I want to open up to Pearl and Caddy, but my lips remain sealed tighter than Sister Nancy's hoo hah.

My break is over. Let's shuck more corn.

I'm in the hammock again. Red-winged blackbirds swoop above the fishpond. Goodbye, mosquitoes! Although my hands are shredded from peeling back the husks of hundreds of ears of corn and my lower back aches, my mind feels clearer than it has in months.

Pearl has invited me to join her and Caddy at the courthouse for the "Nightly Concert." "Regular performances give folks an incentive to leave their dark houses." She chuckled. "No more binge-watching *Game of Thrones*."

I returned from the village square, where a man introduced as Wilbur King strummed an electric guitar wired to a battery-powered amplifier. Caddy mentioned that the musician played bass for Wilson Pickett. I feigned familiarity with the name.

As we folded our seats, I asked Pearl, who appeared to be in her sixties, how long she's lived in Hayneville. "My whole life. I was born the same day Ruby Sales almost died. August 20th, 1965."

Intrigued, I urged her to share the story.

"Civil rights protesters picketed Whites-only businesses in Fort Deposit a week earlier. As a result, the county police rounded up all thirty-one activists and threw them in jail." Pearl gestured over her shoulder. "Just down the road from here. Fortunately, the jailers got a look at my mom's pregnant belly and let her and my dad go free. The warden released the other demonstrators on the 20th. Hot and thirsty, the men and women walked to Varner's Cash Store for drinks, one of the few places serving non-Whites. As they approached the building, a White deputy sheriff named Tom Coleman aimed a shotgun at Ruby Sales, a seventeen-year-old Black girl. A White man leaped before the blast to shield her. Jonathan Daniels bled out on the street. If my parents were still part of that group, they could have been seriously injured or even killed." She studied her fingernails. "I may never have existed."

"What happened to the girl?"

"Ruby became a famous civil rights activist."

"And the deputy? Was Coleman found guilty?"

"What do you think?"

I found maintaining eye contact with Pearl difficult as I conveyed my deep sorrow for her community's pain and suffering.

Julie – June 26, 2029

6/26/2029

People often ask me how I met Jules Turner. They express unease when I take so long to answer. You see, I cannot recall the exact date. I do remember she walked into my world after a drunk driver took my parents' lives.

A month after my sister Julia and I separated, I heard three loud knocks while watching TV in the living room of my foster parents' house. The Johnsons were in the backyard building a snowman with their son. I got up and opened the front door, surprised to find a Black girl around my age standing on the icy stoop. Interstate 81 acted as a geographical barrier dividing Syracuse, NY, into two halves. The Office of Children and Family Services moved me from the west side of the city, University Hill, to the predominantly White southeast—the affluent Country Club town of Dewitt. Oh, how I missed my friends and our tiny apartment on Monroe Street!

Despite no Girl Scout uniform or order forms, I suspected the teenager sold cookies or magazine subscriptions. She held up a blurry photo. "Hi, I'm looking for Oliver. Have you spotted any orange and white dogs running around your neighborhood?" She shifted from foot to foot, her fingers deep in the pockets of her purple parka. The outside temperature hovered at ten degrees—cold even for January.

I had always wanted a puppy, but the apartment manager strictly prohibited pets. "Sorry, I haven't seen your dog. It's freezing. Come inside and warm up."

The visitor stood in the center of the spacious room as brightly dressed contestants on *The Price is Right* screamed for Drew Carey's attention. She took in the modern furnishings, her gaze landing on the artificial Christmas tree standing in the corner. "The holidays are over. When will you take down that ugly thing?"

Her comment was rude, yet I also despised that tree. Its droopy plastic branches reminded me of the day Robert McKenna plowed his Dodge Charger into my parents' Honda Odyssey. Regardless of his alcohol level being .16%, twice New York's legal limit, I knew the justice system wouldn't convict a White off-duty deputy of vehicular manslaughter. As predicted, McKenna walked out of that courthouse grinning from ear to ear. The Christmas tree, especially the winged Gabriel tree topper, symbolized that tragic event.

I shrugged. "This is the Johnsons' favorite time of year. Little Stevie loves crawling under the tree to sleep beneath the colored lights. Can I help you find your dog?"

She beamed. "I'd appreciate that." This made me smile for the first time since December. "Do you need to tell your parents?"

"No." I laughed. "I'm almost seventeen." Remembering that I was a new family member, I reconsidered my decision. The Johnsons were a lovely couple who genuinely cared about my emotional state, which remained bleak. "I'll let Bill and Diane know I'm going out. What's your name?"

The girl hesitated before extending her right palm. "Jules. Jules Turner."

"Nice to meet you, Jules!" I babbled excitedly, "Do you live nearby? I'm new here and unfamiliar with the area. I started attending Jamesville-DeWitt High School, and it's been a struggle fitting in with all the—"

"Palefaces? Yeah, I go there, too! JD is an excellent school. Maybe we can study together?"

Jules and I spent the rest of the afternoon searching for her lost dog, but we never found him. The next day and the day after, we checked the cages at the local animal shelter—no Oliver.

I didn't see Jules for several weeks, which left me confused and disappointed. Jamesville-DeWitt wasn't wholly Caucasian. Whenever an African-American girl rushed by, I'd call out, "Hey, Jules!" an embarrassment for me and whoever I mistakenly addressed.

Around Martin Luther King Jr. Day, I caught Jules alone in the girls' restroom. In a moment of vulnerability, I opened up to her about the pain of losing my parents, only to discover that she, too, was an orphan. Desperate for companionship, I pleaded with her to be my friend. As Jules embraced me, swearing that she wouldn't leave me, an enormous weight lifted off my shoulders.

Diary, that is how Jules Turner and I met. We've been inseparable, except for a brief period in my early twenties.

Now that I mull it over, Jules wasn't always this mean. Her personality underwent a drastic transformation after Election Day. Can't blame the woman for trying to cope. I imagine we have all, in some fashion, mutated into monsters.

Sisterhood

Good and Evil—
they are intertwined
like Saint and Devil.
Let me tell you, sister—
you take the former,
and I'll take the latter.

Alice – June 27, 2029

6/27/2029

I awoke to the melodic chirping of birds. The sweet perfume of climbing wisteria and wild camellia drifted through the open windows. This Wednesday morning felt normal, pre-Election Day. As soon as I hopped out of bed, a torrent of horrid memories washed these pleasant sentiments down the drain.

Nosy, I toured the house before heading to work. Framed photographs cluttered every corner, capturing moments frozen in time. Among them were shots of Pearl's parents, Pearl as a toothless child, and a cute boy I assumed was her younger brother. Family photos hung proudly above the fireplace. Apart from the three wrestling trophies in the garage awarded to Landon "Hitman" Jackson, I found no other possessions that could have belonged to Pearl's dad. He may have passed away, or her parents' marriage ended in divorce.

In contrast to the absence of her father's belongings, my new friend Pearl had left all of Athena B. Jackson's possessions untouched, giving the impression that her mother had just stepped out to pick up the daily paper or a gallon of milk. This place is a shrine to yesteryear. Bric-a-brac tops every available surface, and framed needlepoint covers the walls. An open November 2024 *TV Guide* rests on the living room coffee table with several prime time shows circled in red. The bedroom dresser overflows with neatly folded underwear, shirts, and pants. Church dresses hang in the closet.

Not a speck of dust anywhere. How strange.

The bathroom's medicine cabinet contains prescription medicines, oral hygiene products, and beauty items. I considered taking the Ambien, knowing its value for trade, but I can't pilfer a pill from Pearl.

This town is nice. The people are friendly, and I feel safe. I haven't decided whether to stick around or bid a tearful farewell to Hayneville and continue to New Orleans. What still draws me there?

I noticed women and men patrolling the outskirts of the town. One of them was Wilbur King, the electric guitar player. On our lunch break, ham on homemade bread smothered with creamy mayonnaise and tangy mustard, I questioned Pearl and Caddy about the armed guards. We sat on lawn chairs under a gigantic elm. This was our conversation.

Caddy wiped a dab of mayo from her mouth. "We must safeguard everything we've built. Occasionally, one of the townsfolk requires overnight confinement for drinking too much moonshine. Overall, our citizens abide by the law, a modified version of the Ten Commandments."

Pearl clarified. "Just the most important two—thou shall not steal or kill. In the early days, we banished a few troublemakers, largely those released from the county jail. Crunk spread like wildfire, and no one wanted anything to do with them."

"We had a murder case a couple of years back," Caddy added. "A domestic dispute turned violent. We conducted a trial in the courthouse and—"

"Found him guilty," Pearl interjected, her lip curling in disgust. "He faced a volunteer firing squad. Abbott Boone and his wife, Dolly, are buried in the cemetery you slept at, Alice."

The town's governance aroused my curiosity. "Does Hayneville have a mayor?"

Pearl answered. "Doc Callaway held that position before he died of heart disease last March. The city council oversees all matters until we elect a new candidate. My brother Ardy serves as the chairperson. He attended Columbia and had dreams of becoming the next Obama 'til," she mimicked playing on a drum set, "*ba-dum ching*—no more Washington, D.C.!"

I remembered the handsome young man from the family photos. "What about outsiders? Pearl, you welcomed me into your tight-knit community without asking any questions."

"I'm pretty good at reading people. It's sort of a sixth sense, Ardy says. Travelers coming through this part of Alabama are few and far between, and the majority only pass by on their way north or south. The Carsons and the Buckleys are the only families who stayed because their relatives live in Hayneville. Shirley Carson is the principal of our school."

"Do you trade with neighboring towns?" There had been little on the way down here.

Pearl nodded. "Mosses and Gordonville are seven miles to the west. Not too far to walk. Fort Deposit is to the south, and White Hall is to the north. Both are sixteen miles away—close enough to reach by bicycle or horse. Montgomery is twenty-five miles as the crow flies. We have three functioning trucks and a dozen motorcycles, but we only use these vehicles for essential projects. Out here in the sticks, locating fresh fuel and repair parts is challenging. McGill's Hill is also north, but like Benton, we rarely trade with them."

"Why not?"

Pearl glanced at Caddy, who grumbled, "They're not, er, very friendly."

I recalled the historical signs and envisioned White people parading around in white sheets burning wooden crosses. "I just came from Montgomery."

Caddy leaned forward expectantly. I knew that itch all too well in an age with no cable news or internet. "How was The Gump?"

I pictured Tom Hanks on the big screen, running so fast his leg braces fell off. "You mean, like, Forrest Gump?"

Caddy chuckled. "Forrest Gump grew up in Greenbow, Alabama, a fictional city based on Montgomery. A local hip-hop group, Deuce Komradz, popularized the term after the movie. I had their second CD, *Still Ridin Smokin*."

I failed to visualize this respectable citizen, now a plump woman in her mid-forties, as a rebellious, weed-toking youth. "Montgomery, ah, The Gump, was okay. Not too many inhabitants. I stayed in a house in McGehee/Allendale until I sensed someone watching me. They stole something of mine. A diary."

Pearl raised her eyebrows. "I see you scribbling in a composition notebook whenever you can."

"I found a new journal. Writing helps me to organize my thoughts."

"Where else have you been?" Caddy rubbed her arms. "I haven't set foot over the Lowndes County line since Crunk hit the fan."

Pearl spoke as I wordlessly unearthed the places and people I had tried to keep buried. "Ardy and I drove our mother to Montgomery at the beginning of COVID-24 to get vaccinated. Downtown was chaotic with all the looting and shootings. We got out of there in a hurry and went to Selma to buy vials of Moderna mRNA on the black market." She frowned. "I lost my husband, Curtis, during COVID-19. He declined the injections."

I confessed, "The man I traveled with from Chicago was an anti-vaxxer." Vaccines became a chronic topic of disagreement between us. "Sickness changed David's attitude. We had no food or water. He was dying, and I had no choice but to—"

I cried the rest of my story onto the women's shoulders.

"Hush, child." Pearl patted my back. "I've done terrible things, too. Saint Peter might slam the Pearly Gates shut in all our faces."

"You're the only people I've told." I dried my eyes. "David wasn't a right-winger. After all the misleading media coverage ahead of Election Day, he just didn't believe in the 'fake news.'"

Pearl shook her head, a mix of anguish and understanding shining in her eyes. "You can lead a horse to water. . . . Curtis declared a week before he fell ill, 'If the Dear Lord sends the Grim Reaper to harvest my soul, nothing you stick in my vein shall stop Him from flying me up to Heaven or dragging me down to Hell.' I called for an ambulance when he couldn't breathe. But the ornery old fool refused to go to the hospital, afraid the 'demon doctors' would sell his body parts." Her voice cracked. "In the end, I had him cremated at Belford Funeral Home and scattered his ashes into the water around my house. Some nights, I sit by Trevor Lake and yell at my husband for being such a bonehead. Most of the time, though, I ask God why He had to take my Curtis."

Caddy's atypical silence and grievous expression concerned me. "Caddy, are you all right?"

Pearl touched her friend's arm. "She won't talk about her family. Still too painful."

Caddy swallowed. "July will mark three years." She sat straight in the slatted chair. "I don't know what happened to my husband and kids. One morning, I woke up, and Percy and my two daughters, Mazie and Lettie, were gone. At first, I figured the three had walked into town for food. When they didn't return, the sheriff formed a search party. We found no trace of them, not a single footprint. No note or missing clothes. It's as if my family vanished into thin air. I can't sleep wondering if they're alive or dead."

Now came my opportunity to comfort these brave women. After blotting our tears on our sleeves, we continued to shell cowpeas, more quietly than before.

Julie – June 27, 2029

6/27/2029

Jules and I walked Oscar along the streets of Hayneville today while Alice worked at Pearl's Trading Post. We passed by the building every few hours to check on her. She'd be either out back washing mountains of vegetables, stocking shelves in front of the store, or helping customers.

Jules hoped I had lost interest in the "weird White woman." She wants us to move on, but she's not defining where to go. I haven't responded to her request yet, but I've gnawed on our bone of contention long enough to give myself a dull headache. And a complex sensation of sadness. . .or loss?

Armed men and women patrolled Rebel Field, a football stadium running wild with puffballs. I caught snippets of their discussion from behind the landscaper's shed.

A man complained. "We shoulda dealt with McGill's Hill when we had the chance!"

"Only six roads lead into Hayneville," a woman chimed in. "At Monday night's security meeting, Ardy and Wilbur said they were posting lookouts."

Jules has become more determined to leave town after digesting these worrisome words.

I noted on my *AAA* map that McGill's Hill is seven miles north of our current location. Four churches, two cemeteries, a row of plantation houses, a post office, and McGill Academy line the town's country lanes. This place must have been a slave master's paradise in the pre-war days. Hayneville clearly has something McGill's Hill needs. Is it food? Access to medical supplies? Guns?

Alice – June 28, 2029

6/28/2029

At the end of the day, Caddy asked Pearl a question I didn't want to overhear. "Are you gonna tell her?"

When the storekeeper nodded, I noticed the dark circles under her eyes.

"Come with me, Alice. I'll fix you something to eat." Pearl pushed her green mountain bike as we walked a mile from town to, of all names, Streety Road.

Water surrounded the fenced-in estate on three sides. We approached the enormous house with an empty inground pool, a guesthouse, and a boathouse. Although the property had fallen into disrepair, I exclaimed, "Wow!" while taking in the spectacular view.

Pearl smiled self-consciously. "Curtis and I did okay before the coronavirus hit. My husband and I leased land to Family Dollar and Dollar General. We also owned NAPA Auto Parts. Curtis managed the front of the shop. I handled all the ordering and bookkeeping. We had a good life until the gas stations shut down."

As Pearl opened the front door, an animal ran into the yard.

"You have a dog?" I bent to rub the canine's orange and white back. "What's its name?"

"Oscar. My brother asked me to take care of him. Not sure for how long."

For dinner, Pearl and I enjoyed a "ploughman's lunch" of bread, cheese, hard-boiled eggs, and apples. After we were done, we strolled to the boathouse and sat on the dock in Adirondack chairs beneath a large green umbrella. To the west, a giant peach hovered above a windbreak of longleaf pines. Trevor Lake shimmered as if on fire.

I breathed in the beauty, wondering if I was about to lose my job and get kicked out of town. Outside of Pearl loaning me the keys to her mother's residence to shelter me and giving me bags of groceries to fill my stomach, nothing of material significance had changed hands. I still felt overpaid by this generous woman. Nowadays, some say an ounce of kindness is worth more than a ton of gold.

I ended the silence. "Pearl, what's bothering you? You can tell me anything."

Pearl gazed at the lake, its smooth surface mirroring the silver clouds. "There's darkness on the horizon. McGill's Hill is just a two-hour trek north of here."

"You said you don't trade goods with them?"

She faced me. "Alice, I have nothing against White folks. My mom's mom was Irish. Nana Deirdre raised me while my mother cleaned houses. And you should know I have no ill will toward you. In fact, you've been a joy to work with."

My abdomen churned with dread as I waited for the big "BUT."

Pearl clenched my wrist so forcefully I wanted to pull away. "But you have a tough decision to make. I can't imagine how I'd react if in your shoes. Or if I could answer honestly." She let go of my arm and sighed. "We have friendly ears in McGill's Hill. Not everybody's bad. My brother received information about an upcoming attack."

I shuddered, picturing an army charging forward at full tilt. "We're the target? When will it happen?"

"In the next few days. Ardy says the leaders are preparing. We may get an advanced warning, but I doubt it."

"Why? What does McGill's Hill want with Hayneville?"

Pearl drew a comparison. "Have you watched *Survivor*?"

Surf, sand, palm trees, and your fellow exiles banding together to vote you off the island. "With Jeff Probst?" I remembered that reality TV show well. I had quickly wearied of all the mudslinging.

"Jeff was the host. On *Survivor*, the castaways always stuck to their original tribes no matter what. My dad called their fear of exclusion 'Human nature at its worst.' The people of McGill's Hill treat their neighboring communities, Mosses, Gordonville, and White Hall, which are principally Black, as," her fingernails dug into her palms, "inferior."

"How can you be sure I'm not a mole for the other side? Isn't it more than a coincidence that I rolled into town just before this raid?"

Pearl's laugh released the tension. "Because of your backpack! That ratty old thing you won't put down because you're afraid of losing it."

I spun the green nylon bag on my knee, examining the patches I had sewn onto the sides. Every emblem represented somewhere I've been: NIAGRA FALLS – NEW YORK, WINDY CITY BULLS, NORTH CAROLINA – THE TAR HEEL STATE, NASHVILLE STRONG.

"What am I looking for?" My eyes landed on the white words embroidered on the upraised black fist—BLACK LIVES MATTER. The protests took place in the spring of 2020. Peter and I had taken the Greyhound bus to Washington, D.C. "I'm not going anywhere. How can I help?"

Pearl stood to unlock the door to the boathouse. The twilight cast an angelic aura around her head and shoulders as she reappeared carrying two hunting rifles. "Ever shot one of these, Alice?"

Julie - June 28, 2029

6/28/2029

Jules and I are inside a holding cell in the Lowndes County Courthouse. They took Oscar! At least for now, our jailer let me keep my diary, which is why I can record today's events.

We were standing outside Pearl's Trading Post at noon when two armed men cornered us.

"Where are you from, and why are you here?" the bigger one demanded.

As I explained we were passing through town, Jules sneered and shouted, "What's it to you, G.I. Jane?" As you can expect, her retort didn't land well. I worried "Jane" would slap Jules silly. Instead, the stoic man called someone on a walkie-talkie, from where a male voice ordered him to bring us to the courthouse.

Honestly, it's not so bad. The bed is clean, and, an hour ago, a woman wearing an N95 mask delivered lunch—our first decent meal since Montgomery.

"Way to go, Julie." Jules dug into a plate of grilled venison and boiled potatoes. "Three hots and a cot."

As Jules tosses and turns on the lumpy mattress, I'm trying to stitch together a plausible story to explain why we were loitering around the store. Should I tell our captors we wanted to shop but had nothing to barter with? I could say we were waiting for a handout. Was I afraid Oscar might bite a customer?

The air in this room is stifling. I'm going to shut my eyes for a minute. Racking my brain makes me drowsy.

Going back to earlier, after we were locked up, a man sat in a chair beside our cell. The interrogation transpired like this:

"I see they fed you." His words echoed in the imposing courtroom. "Need anything else?"

"Where's Oscar?"

"Your dog is safe with my sister. I'm Ardy. What's your name?"

"Julie." I pointed to the bed. "And that's Jules."

He looked up from his notepad. "Is it Julie or Jules?"

I could sense Jules scowling at me. "Julie," I stated firmly to avoid further confusion.

"Last name?"

"Werner." I glanced at Jules, who remained uncommunicative.

"Coming from?"

"Montgomery."

"On your way to?"

I lifted my eyebrows at Jules, silently requesting guidance. "Uh, nowhere in particular."

Ardy aimed the red dot of an infrared thermometer at my forehead. "You feeling all right? Any dizziness, congestion, or coughing?"

"No. Last winter, I built up antibodies during a mild case of COVID. Plus, I got the Pfizer shots while the vaccines were still available."

"98.6. Normal." Ardy put the temperature gun in his pocket. "When did you arrive in town?"

"Sunday night."

"Today is Thursday. What have you been up to for the last four days? And where were you sleeping?"

My mother, God rest her soul, had raised me to be truthful. "Our first night, we stayed in a house by the cemetery. Now we're bunking on North Washington. The place with the picket fence and the nice front porch."

Ardy nodded as if he knew the address. "Broke in?"

"There were no doors at the graveyard home. Washington had a key underneath the doormat."

Ardy underlined several words with a pen. "I appreciate you being so upfront with me, Julie." His facial appearance changed from indifferent to suspicious. "Why were you at the Trading Post?"

A door clicked open, and an older, uniformed man entered the white room. He set my blue backpack on the floor and whispered into Ardy's ear.

"Very interesting." Ardy shared his notes with the officer. "Julie, we've poked through your bag. Anything you want to divulge before Wilbur checks the two houses you occupied? Is there something or someone that might cause harm?"

"A shotgun is all. For our protection."

"You referred to somebody else. Jules. Where is she now?"

Jules covered her head with the blanket. I shrugged.

Ardy exhaled. "It'll be better for you and your friend if you tell us where she's hiding."

"Are you going to jam bamboo shoots under my fingernails?"

My questioner ignored my flippancy, the tightness of his jawline exposing the pressure he was under. "Be careful out there, Sheriff."

Wilbur patted his sidearm, a pearl-handled cowboy revolver, and hurried off.

Ardy opened the top of my pack and peered inside.

My heart sank when he pulled out a pink book. "That's mine!" I rushed forward, my arms stretching past the iron bars. "Give it back!"

Ardy pressed a finger to his lips and continued reading. Each stroke of his ballpoint on the pad tripled my agitation. After what felt like forever, my jailer laid the diary on his lap. "Who is Alice Jenkins?"

Jenkins must be Alice's last name. What could I say? He had read every single word. "Who?"

"Based on all I've read, this woman doesn't know you. Did you take her diary in Montgomery and follow her to Hayneville?"

"Am I under arrest?"

Ardy smiled wearily. "For stealing a book? We're just ensuring that you and your partner aren't threats to our community. Is Jules still on North Washington?"

When my interrogator realized I had no more to add, he handed me my diary and walked out.

Jules gazed at the skylight high above the barred ceiling. "That asshole will bring your girlfriend." From the length of her shadow, I reckoned we'd be spending the night incarcerated. "We are so fucked."

I, too, worried that Alice would appear at any moment. And I also realized we were screwed, blued, and tattooed—especially yours truly. "Even if Alice comes here, what can she do? She has no proof we broke into her house."

"Proof?" Jules scoffed. "Her diary was in your backpack. Prosecutors use the term 'damning' for hard evidence of guilt."

Desperate to distance myself from the imp chewing a hole in my nerves, I crossed over to the jail cell window. "I'll give Alice the diary. She'll thank me."

"That woman will read everything you wrote about her!"

"Nothing terrible!"

"Still pretty creepy, eh, Julie?"

"Piss off, Jules!"

We hurled insults at one another until the sky turned the blackest of blacks.

Alice – June 29, 2029

6/29/2029

I conked out in Pearl's spare bedroom last night. She cautioned me that walking back to the village unaccompanied wasn't safe in the current conditions.

After a hearty breakfast of ham, eggs, and buttery biscuits, we carried our deer rifles to the backyard. Pearl positioned paper targets at varying distances on the lawn. My marksmanship impressed her. "Alice, you're a regular Annie Oakley!" I told her how my father took me to the shooting range, the only activity he enjoyed doing with his daughter.

As we tore down the bull's-eyes, a uniformed man peddled up the driveway on a blue bicycle. I recognized him as the guitar player from Tuesday's concert. He spoke with Pearl, who acted surprised.

Pearl called out, "Alice!" as they approached me. "This is Wilbur King, our sheriff."

The sheriff hadn't ridden out here for Coffee with a Cop. "Do you know a Julie Werner?"

I shook my head.

King showed me a pink book with JULIE WERNER printed in block letters on the cover. "Does this belong to you?"

I opened the diary, skimming past my entries to text penned by a different hand, feminine yet more steady. "Jules is correct,"

I read out loud. "This Alice chick is batshit crazy! 'Julie, who, in their right mind, murders their own boyfriend?' Not that Jules hasn't taken care of business before. And it sounds like this David Carter guy was a dollar short of buying the farm, anyhow."

The sheriff confronted me. "You wrote how you strangled a man traveling with you?"

I nodded, my heart thumping in my chest as I read further. "Jules and I tailed Alice to Burkville, a gloomy little town most likely named after a plantation owner using slave labor to harvest his cotton."

"We are holding a female claiming to be Julie Werner in the courthouse." He threw up his arms in frustration. "A posse is sweeping the town for this Jules, but we haven't enough staff for such an extensive area."

Pearl defended me before I could clarify how my actions were more of a "mercy killing" than "malicious murder." "Alice told Caddy and me about David. He was dying, and they had no food or drink. She's all torn up about it! We've been relatively safe in Hayneville. I cannot picture what this woman endured on the road."

King insisted I come into town. Pearl seemed distant as she took my rifle and lent me her bicycle.

We propped our two-wheelers against the courthouse wall and ascended one of the dual staircases to the second floor. The sheriff unlocked the door, revealing a white-paneled chamber resembling the interior of a church, except for the iron cage in the back corner. A Black woman rose from a cot to grasp the white bars with both hands. Her eyes met mine with a mix of fascination and, perhaps, a hint of fear.

King gave the pink diary to the woman before speaking into his walkie-talkie. "Ardy, we have Miss Jenkins."

"10–4. Be right there," crackled from the tiny speaker.

Julie Werner and I mutely appraised each other while we waited. The fit woman stood several inches taller than me. Near my age, she wore clean jeans and, odd for this hot and stuffy room, a tattered gray LMU SCHOOL OF FILM AND TELEVISION sweatshirt. Despite the long scar marring her left cheek, the woman's beauty and poise rivaled that of a successful runway model.

A door opened, and a man dressed in a pair of black pants, white shirt, and red necktie hurried into the courtroom. This younger, masculine version of Pearl led the sheriff out of earshot. After a brief conversation, he came over to me. "Hey, Alice. I'm Ardy Jackson." Ardy's grip was firm, his warm touch reassuring. "Pearl told me all about you. Do you recognize this woman?"

"I read what she wrote in my diary." Julie's facial muscles undulated with conflicting emotions as I spoke. Disappointment or satisfaction? Rage? Joy? Or did the morning sunlight filtering through the shutters create this illusionary effect? "I was scavenging a house in Montgomery when a woman crawled out of a window across the street—too far for me to get a good look."

The prisoner wedged her face between the bars, her right hand coaxing me to come closer. "I stole your diary, Alice!" She held out the pink book to me. "Here, take it." Her remorseful tone and expression swiftly mutated into animosity. As I reached for my journal, she retracted her offer. "Bitch!"

Ardy yanked me away from the raving woman and guided me out of the courthouse.

We left Sheriff King and walked five minutes to the brick Hayneville Town Hall/Police Department/Fire Department building. Inside Mayor Paul Callaway's old office, the town council chairperson pulled out a seat for me and sat behind a desk piled high with papers. Keys labeled COURTHOUSE (SPARE) and ARMORY dangled from a wooden rack.

I asked, "Does Julie have a mental illness? She acted so normal, and then she changed into somebody else."

The chair squeaked as Ardy leaned backward. "I studied the medical journals in our library. I'm no shrink, but after interviewing Julie, I think she suffers from dissociative identity disorder. If that's even her real name."

Sybil, a 1970s miniseries starring Sally Fields, flashed onto my mental TV screen. "She has a split personality?"

"DID is a rare affliction, possibly induced by childhood trauma."

"You don't believe this Jules character she writes about exists?"

Ardy raised his shoulders.

"Is Julie dangerous?"

He rubbed his chin. "She attacked you."

"What will you do with her?" I foresaw a firing squad binding Julie to a telephone pole, sticking one last Marlboro between her lips.

"Our guest is fine where she is. She has food and shelter. Wil's people are watching her."

"Did you read my diary?"

Ardy crossed his arms. "I had to."

"Do you think I'm a bad person?"

"I am very sorry for your loss."

"Is Pearl mad at me?"

Ardy showed me his walkie-talkie and then set it on the table. "I spoke to my sister. She says you're staying for the fireworks and are an excellent shot."

"But do you trust me?"

"My primary concern was that you were spying for McGill's Hill. Your diary proves that you have no affiliation with that community."

"So?"

"If Pearl vouches for you, we're good." He unfastened his necktie and handed me the strip of red cloth. "Tie this on your left arm."

"What for?"

"Alice, you're the only White woman in this town. I'll let our people know you'll be fighting for our side. That armband may be the one thing preventing you from getting shot."

After leaving Town Hall, I hopped on my bike and rode to Pearl's Trading Post. I filled Pearl in on Julie Werner and my meeting with her brother. She didn't question the red tie knotted around my wrist.

The afternoon ticked by as I restocked the shelves and scrubbed the floors. I kept returning to my white-knuckled interaction with the prisoner. Why did Julie follow me? What are her true intentions? If the woman meant me harm, she had plenty of opportunities to slit my throat while I slept.

At closing, I disinfected the butcher table with white vinegar (Caddy slaughtered and plucked chickens) before rinsing the sharpened implements in a bucket.

Pearl came out the back door as I finished hanging the washed towels on a clothesline. "Ready?"

"Sure." I massaged a crick in my neck. "You never lock the store. Aren't you worried a thief will clean you out?"

"Hasn't come to pass." She strapped a sack bulging with food onto her bicycle rack. "If someone's that desperate, they can have anything they want."

"For I was hungry, and you gave me food. I was thirsty, and you gave me drink. I was a stranger, and you welcomed me."

"Alice, you know your scriptures!"

"My mother was ultrareligious." I needed this woman on my side. "Pearl, you realize I'm alluding to you taking me in?"

"The Golden Rule: Do unto others as you would have them do unto you."

We walked through the empty parking lot to the sidewalk on Hayneville's main drag, East Tuskeena Street. I stopped at North Washington Street, unsure of her mood. She already knew I strangled my boyfriend—a top-ten sin. And now my questionable connection to Julie Werner? "Pearl, is sleeping at your mom's house still okay? I understand if, after today, my presence makes you uneasy."

"Of course. But until we resolve our troubles with McGill's Hill, you're coming home with me." She adjusted the bag on her bike rack and smiled. "Guess what's for dinner?"

"Pepperoni pizza?"

Pearl smirked.

"I couldn't do what Caddy does." I grimaced. "Killing all those poor chickens."

"Yeah, you could." She watched a gray tomcat pounce on something small and furry. "We do whatever it takes to survive."

Supper was a nutritious delight. We had grilled chicken and corn on the cob. I asked Pearl where she gets gas for the barbecue. The Hayneville city council arranges for a tanker truck to drive eleven miles to Suburban Propane. My host dreads the day the tanks will run dry.

We washed the dishes and utensils. Pearl's residence has running water and even features the most modern amenity—a flushable toilet! Rooftop solar cells power a pump. We moseyed down to the lake to sit beneath the green umbrella. This evening, Pearl carried two wine glasses and a bottle of Merlot out of the boathouse instead of loaded firearms. Her laughter bounced off the hills when I told her of my wild night guzzling altar wine at Rock Creek Baptist Church.

Pearl disclosed how she and her high school chums used to sneak sips from her parents' secret stash of port and cream sherry, refilling the bottles to the marked line with water. Ardy once caught them red-handed and extorted a swallow of wine for his silence.

The ethyl alcohol did an outstanding job of obliterating any bothersome brain cells. "Pearl, did you also read my diary?"

She emphatically shook her head from side to side. "Nuh-uh. None of my beeswax. That's between you and your maker." Pearl thrust her hands to the heavens in resentment. "Who appears to be taking an extended vacation in a galaxy far, far away."

"Ardy read every word."

"Alice, remember when I told you about the execution? I failed to mention that I was one of the six volunteers putting a slug in Abbott Boone."

"Administering the punishment must have been horrible, Pearl."

"Shooting him didn't faze me one bit. I've known Dolly, Abbott's wife, since the Pioneer Girls. When I heard that my friend was stabbed and that Sheriff King captured Abbott with blood on his dungarees, I had to have vengeance. I testified at his trial to seeing bruises on Dolly's face and arms during my visits. She used to roll down her shirtsleeves and layer on heavy makeup to conceal the discolorations. Dolly brushed me off whenever I questioned the marks or tried to arrange for domestic abuse support. 'Clumsy me bumped into a door.' Or, 'I tripped on an uneven sidewalk.' She confided in me only when her neck turned black and blue. 'Pearl, it's so hard being a woman.'"

I envisioned my ten fingers imprinting an ugly ring into David's throat. "The victims need to accept help."

"That may be true, but with the bloodstains on Abbott's clothes and my testimony, the jury found him guilty and sentenced him to death. My hand shot up the day Judge Armstrong asked for volunteers to carry out the capital punishment."

"You stood up for Dolly. Didn't that bring some gratification?"

Pearl let out a lengthy sigh. "There's an old Chinese proverb about getting even. 'He who seeks revenge digs two graves.'"

Confucius was a wise man. My own burial place awaits me, double-deep and filled with earthworms. "Abbott Boone murdered your friend. You had every right to be angry."

"Abbott didn't kill Dolly. Months later, I learned the assailant's true identity."

"What? Who?"

"Dolly had an older brother. Silas."

"Pearl, how did you find out it was him?"

"Wilbur King discovered the murder weapon in Silas' house while investigating a burglary. The dimwit hid the stolen goods along with the bloody knife below the floorboards. The sheriff thrashed him to a pulp until he confessed to stabbing Dolly."

"Why on earth would he do that to his own sister?"

"Wil said I'd sleep better if I didn't know the specifics."

"What happened to Silas? Another firing squad?"

My new friend groaned as if every muscle in her body ached. "Can't say for sure."

The moon's cratered face reflected on the water's dark surface. Our bottle of wine stood empty, red liquid staining the bottom of both glasses. I resisted the urge to press any further.

Julie – June 29, 2029

6/29/2029

I've caught a case of the jitters after only two days in this tiny jail cell. Jules' moans, groans, and stinky sulfur farts are wearing away at my sanity. I'm furious at her for trying to assault Alice. I worry about Oscar. Why won't they let me see my dog?

The woman who brings our meals hasn't told us her name. I have a hunch that she is the sheriff's better half since he affectionately calls her "Sugar." She and Wilbur let Jules and me out long enough to take a cold bucket shower in the judge's chambers, which contains a full bathroom and a thousand law books. Sugar keeps her distance from us. I think she's scared of Jules.

> Diary,
> When will they release us from this cage? Do you even know? Jules is losing control. If Wilbur hadn't confiscated our belts and shoelaces "for safekeeping," she'd probably use them to host a necktie party, with me being the guest of honor. All we do is sleep, watch people pass by on the street, and await our fate. A spa day or an all-expenses-paid trip to Hawaii isn't in the cards, that's for certain. If I tear my sweatshirt into a hundred

narrow strips, I can fashion a rope to solve everyone's problem.

Your friend,

Julie

Could I hang myself? Am I suicidal? An intriguing question.

Leap of Faith

We stood on the edge of a towering cliff—
I nodded north, and she stared south.
One little nudge, and down she goes,
falling, falling, falling
to the Land of Woe.

Pretty cheesy, don't you agree, Diary? It's not Emily Dickinson, but slapping together this short rhyme killed ten minutes that would otherwise have been spent pulling out my own hair.

As for taking the easy way out, paddling my carcass up the River Styx doesn't rank high on my list of lifetime achievements. What are my Top Ten Goals? The woman in the cage scratches her thinning scalp. "Hmmm."

1. Find Julia or die trying.
2. Make a million bucks. Better aim for a billion, considering inflation.
3. One of my wildest dreams is to build a luxurious home on a Caribbean Island with an Olympic-sized swimming pool and a personal chef.
4. I want to speak French fluently, like the legendary Josephine Baker. *Parlez-vous Francais?*
5. Exploring the world's seven wonders, particularly the Egyptian pyramids, might be thrilling. Oh, and there's that haunted house in San Jose where

malevolent spirits warned Sallie Winchester to keep adding rooms or suffer a gruesome fate.

6. Finding my life partner is something I yearn for. Does he exist? Is it too late?
7. The desire to raise children with my "once in a lifetime" warms my heart, even if it's just one boy or girl.
8. Get my novel published. Seeing my book on library and bookstore shelves would bring me a sense of accomplishment.
9. Win an Academy Award for writing and directing a blockbuster movie. I'll swing the golden statue above my head, yelling, "How do you like me now?"
10. Make a real friend.

Julia holds the utmost importance of all these tasks. I'll never stop searching for my sister.

Drawing lines through 2, 3, 5, 8, and 9, as these items are impossible to attain. Much obliged, World War III! Number 4? I took two years of high school French. In my spare time (I have oodles of that now), I could study a *French for Dummies* textbook or dig up a Sony Walkman and listen to *Learn French in Your Car* cassette tapes. Unless I backstroke to Paris, *bonjour, au revoir, oui,* and *non* are all the words I need to know. Let's face it, today's "City of Light" hardly compares to the "Gay Paree" of old. I may as well take up Latin. X-ing out 4. What about 6 and 7? Meeting a boyfriend or husband is challenging, what with a shrinking XY chromosome pool and no more dating apps. Kids? How many eggs do I even have left? Aunt Flo hasn't come to visit since August of last year. Aren't I a little too young for menopause? Stress—my hormones must be out of whack. I am crossing those off as well.

What remains?

"Find Julia or die trying" and "Make a real friend."

Concise and clear-cut, but are they DOABLE?

I ask myself about the second one. Making a real friend is tricky with Jules watching my every move. With her constantly at my side, why am I so damn lonely? Is Alice the key to my happiness? Can she help me locate Julia? I followed her here, and what did it get me?

Diary,
Fuck you!

Luv,
Julie

Alice – June 30, 2029

6/30/2029

I awoke to the sound of rustling and peeked out the bedroom window. My benefactor crisscrossed the backyard, shoving things into the shrubs. When I went outside to inquire about what was going on, Pearl explained that she was hiding her valuables in case marauders descended upon Hayneville. Oscar nipped at our heels as we carried Pearl's belongings outdoors, distributing bags and boxes across her property.

The walkie-talkie chirped during breakfast. Ardy informed Pearl that he was holding a town meeting later that evening to address the "rodent problem"—the code word Haynevillers use to refer to the issue with McGill's Hill. Ardy specifically requested my attendance, but he abruptly signed off before I could question why. Pearl and I walked to work with our Mossberg Patriot rifles slung over our shoulders.

I asked my boss if I could go to the courthouse at lunchtime. She stared at me as if I had a KICK ME!!! placard swinging from my neck. "You want to visit that deranged woman?"

I nervously nodded yes. Pearl radioed Ardy, who gave me his permission under one condition: "You must not approach the jail cell." He also relayed the sheriff's findings. "Wilbur found no evidence of a second person living in the two houses Julie said she slept in." This report concluded that Jules either doesn't exist in bodily form or has left town.

The minutes crept by as I washed crates of dirty radishes. I rehearsed my upcoming conversation with Julie, with each iteration intensifying the twitch in my eye. What if I set her off, and she goes berserk, her razor-sharp talons reaching for my throat through the iron bars?

It baffles me why I feel obligated to talk to Julie. After all, that crazy bitch stole my diary.

I am recounting my dialog with Julie. The following is not an exact transcript though, as it took place five hours ago.

Julie's lack of surprise as I entered the courtroom hinted that Ardy or Wilbur must have notified her of my noon appointment. Randy Spalding, a strapping guard I hadn't yet met, positioned a chair for me six feet away from the cell. He sat in the corner, using a combat knife to carve a fox from a block of wood. Curled woodchips scattered the floor between his polished military boots.

Julie and I locked eyes until she broke the ice. "Thanks for coming, Alice. I feel awful about our initial meeting." She patted her chest. "My confinement put me on edge."

I should note that Julie's facial expressions during our twenty-minute exchange startled me. An internal struggle was clearly playing out with her alter ego, Jules, I assume. Didn't Sybil possess sixteen personalities?

"No biggie." I wondered if she detected the tremor in my speech. "How are you being treated?" I immediately realized the foolishness of my query, seeing the starkness of her environment—a ten-by-ten-foot cage furnished with a small cot and partially concealed camping toilet.

Julie's smile was both beautiful and disarming. "We've, I mean, I've stayed in worse places. Have you seen my dog?"

I made the association. "Oscar?"

"Yes. How is my furbaby?"

"Oscar is well. He's with me at Pearl's house. That's Ardy's sister."

She clasped her palms with hope. "Can you bring Oscar by?"

"I'll do my best. Julie, why were you tracking me?"

"That's the million-dollar question, isn't it, Alice? There's nothing else to do in this cell but think." She held my pink diary up to the vertical bars. "I created a list of personal goals. Most are laughable, except for two. See the second one?"

I strained to read the tiny cursive script flowing across the rectangular pages. Only two of the ten lines were not crossed off: "Find Julia or die trying" and "Make a real friend."

"Who's Julia?"

"Julia is my identical twin. We were sixteen the day our parents died in a car crash. Child Protective Services split us up, forbidding any communication between us. I haven't seen my sister in twenty-two years."

"That is unnecessarily cruel! I'm so sorry."

Julie sniffled. "One day, we'll be together."

"And the item at the bottom of the list. You're seeking a friend?"

"Alice, I need *you* to be my friend."

What is this woman's motive? Why would she choose to be close to someone she only saw briefly on an empty street in Montgomery? My cheek muscles quivered in defiance of my efforts to maintain a poker face. "Julie, that is very flattering. But why me? I am nobody special."

"Alice, that's where you are mistaken."

I didn't know what to say. Despite my limited stay in Hayneville, I already regarded Pearl and Caddy as my friends. We had shared life-altering moments. Ardy, Wilbur, and his wife Charlene? For now, the three were just acquaintances, but I genuinely liked them. Instead of probing deeper to find out why she believed I was special, I turned the spotlight back on her. "Julie, where did you grow up?"

"Syracuse, New York."

I tried relating to her. "Really? I grew up south of you in Paramus, New Jersey. Lots of malls and shopping centers."

"Did you enjoy living in New Jersey?"

I remembered my high school days and the congested highways. "Can't say I miss it. Bergen County is an endless parking lot. On the drive to the University of Rochester, I used to stop at the Syracuse McDonald's to grab an Egg McMuffin or Big Mac. What was your city like?"

She gripped her temples and groaned.

"Hey, hey! It's okay if you don't want to bring up the past. You've experienced a great deal, especially with losing your sister."

Julie sighed. "We're not used to small talk." There she goes with that "we" again. Did she slip up? "Alice, I've been on my own since. . . ." She shuffled to the cot and slumped onto the thin mattress. "Forever."

Have you ever held yourself back from saying something that might hurt the other person, but your mouth shoots the poison-tipped darts regardless? Even as you speak, you question why your tongue is betraying you. I took a deep breath and blew. "Julie, you said 'we' a few times. Ardy mentioned somebody named Jules?"

The woman's head swiveled toward the toilet area. She seemed about to call out to someone hidden behind the screen, but her mouth quickly snapped shut.

I dared to ask, "Julie, is Jules with us now?"

The detainee stood up, beckoning with her right hand.

The guard intervened as my seat's metal legs scraped the planked floor. "Ms. Jenkins, please step away for your own safety. Ardy gave me strict orders."

"Sorry, Mr. Spalding."

Julie slid a pen from her pocket and jotted something in the diary. She tore out the page, crumpled up the paper, and tossed the ball at my feet.

I flattened out the sheet and read the scrawled words. A band of hot and cold steel clamped my rib cage.

She's always here.

When my eyes met hers, she mouthed, "ALICE, HELP ME!"

The town held the "McGill's Hill Rodent Problem" meeting beneath the Hayneville water tower's lengthening shadow. People gathered in the assembly hall of the New Salem Christian Church, their anxious faces illuminated by gas lanterns. Pearl spotted Caddy and waved her to a saved seat in the front row. She clenched her friend's hand. "Looks like everyone's here!"

Ardy, with his head bowed in concentration, and Wilbur, with his chin held high, hurried to a low stage in the front of the hall. Ardy's outreached arms directed those still standing into the stackable chairs. "Please be seated. We have much to discuss." The smokey room quietened. "Pastor Clarke will begin with a prayer."

The rail-thin minister, garbed in a traditional black robe and white clergy collar, stood behind the oak eagle lectern. He unfolded his notes and cleared his throat. "Luke, Chapter 10, Verse 19. 'Behold, I have given you authority to tread on serpents and scorpions, and over all the power of the enemy, and nothing shall hurt you.'" Clarke tucked the note in his pocket and elevated his palms. "Those who willingly spread evil in God's land are destined to be destroyed."

Ardy returned to the reading stand, his eyes sweeping over his rapt listeners. "There is news," he said, "and it's not good." A murmur rippled through the assembly. "We've received reports of an imminent attack on our town."

A beefy man in the fifth row stood up. "And what you gonna do about it, college boy?"

Pearl sprung to her feet. "Carver Dixon, show some respect! Sit your ignorant ass down, or I'll do it for you!" The hall echoed with laughter as the humiliated heckler plopped back into his chair.

Ardy settled the crowd. "Carver's right. I'm no general. I didn't serve in the armed forces. However, many here tonight fought valiantly, some as far back as the Vietnam War." He pointed at a row of seated women and men. "Sheriff King and I met with Captain Calhoun and his team of veterans to devise effective strategies. We are confident we can defend ourselves against any external aggression."

A man and a woman, both with paler complexions than mine, entered the room from a side door. Ardy welcomed the pair to stand beside him. "Pastor Underwood and Mrs. Underwood kept us informed along with other McGill's Hill residents."

A voice croaked from the rear, "Satan sent these tricksters to deceive us!"

Wilbur positioned his sturdy frame before the apprehensive couple. "Charlene and I have known Emmett and Rosalynn for years. Emmett served with me in the Marines. They've risked their lives to be here with us. Cash Peyton, without their help, you and the missus might end up buried in a mass grave like those poor folks in Tuskegee."

A petite woman used a cane to rise from her chair. "When are they coming for us?" She brandished a century-old six-shooter. "I'm itchin' to blow their motherlovin' heads off!"

The room erupted with a chorus of bloodthirsty threats. I worried the mob would fire bullets through the church's roof.

Ardy motioned for Pastor Underwood to speak. The man of the cloth held up a Bible in his left hand. "First, I apologize to the good people of Hayneville for my neighbors' lack of compassion. The Apostle Peter said, 'For the eyes of the Lord are on the righteous, and his ears are open to their prayer. But the face of the Lord punishes those who do evil.'" He laid the worn book on the lectern. "A devil going by the human name of Corbin Holt slithered into McGill's Hill under the cloak of darkness. He claimed to be a faith healer, but I have never believed a word that has slipped off his forked tongue."

The presiding pastor exclaimed, "False prophet!"

"Amen, Brother Clarke!" Underwood's arm snaked through the air, his hand contorting to simulate a fanged mouth. "The ancient serpent walks amongst us. This demon took joy in circulating fear and distrust throughout our community. Rosalynn and I exposed his lies, but few listened. Mayor Wayne went missing under suspicious circumstances. Corbin moved into his house days before Chief Perry called off the search parties."

"Why us?" Caddy cried out. "We donated supplies whenever you asked! Both food and medicine."

Underwood brought his palms together in invocation. "'In his arrogance, the wicked man hunts down the weak caught in the schemes he devises.'"

"Pastor, are you implying that we're the weak ones?" Caddy swung the leather-handled Estwing hatchet she used to behead fowl. "The first of your people who sets foot in Hayneville is getting Littl' Miss Maurine right through their thick skull!"

Ardy tried to placate the growing outrage. "Hold on, everybody! The Underwoods are on our side." Perspiration beaded the chairman's brow as he summoned a distinguished silver-haired gentleman to the stage. "Captain Calhoun is heading our operation. He'll fill you in with the details."

The captain's steely eyes gleamed like those of a bald eagle swooping in on unsuspecting prey. "All sources indicate the invasion will occur tomorrow, at night."

Almost in unison, the citizens declared their concerns.

"So soon?"

"We're not ready!"

"I don't own a firearm!"

"What about the kids and old folks?"

Calhoun's meaty fist pounded the lectern for order. "This raid is a shock for us all! We are very aware you haven't had time to prepare. But we know who they are, and we shall be equipped! Sheriff King and I will organize all able-bodied men and women into defensive units. The police department's armory is open to those who need weapons and ammunition. At first light, Principal Carson will guide the children and the infirm to a secure location outside town."

Ardy signaled me to the platform. His sister encouraged me to step forward. "You may have seen Alice at Pearl's Trading Post. She's new to our town and wants to fight alongside us." He whispered, "Show them your wrist." I lifted the arm wrapped in Ardy's red necktie. "Pastor Underwood is shepherding those wishing to join our cause to Hayneville. Our allies wear the same armbands as Alice. Do them no harm."

A middle-aged woman, a frequent customer at Pearl's, shrieked, "The Lord commandeth, 'Thou shall not kill!' I cannot be an accomplice to murder!"

Captain Calhoun scowled at the outburst. "Let me remind you, the people of McGill's Hill are instigating the violence." He fingered the gold crucifix hanging around his throat. "'As surely as I live,' declares the Lord, 'I take no pleasure in the death of the wicked, but rather that they turn from their ways and live.'"

The ex-military officer scanned the hall. “Emma, or anyone else who wants to desert their brethren, can walk out of here right now. We don’t need you. The rest of us will wipe our enemies from the face of the earth!” He shook his fist. “Hayneville is our home!”

The crowd rose in solidarity, roaring with approval. How many of those present would answer the call to action?

I waited for an assignment, hoping to be in the thick of the fray.

Pearl pulled me from the line. “You’re with me, Ardy, and Wil. We’re not waiting for McGill’s Hill to come to us. Tonight, we chop the head off the snake.”

Julie – June 30, 2029

6/30/2029

Alice came to visit me today! She asked me about Jules. I should have kept my stupid mouth shut.

I am at the window of my jail cell, watching people stream into an old church. The town must be having some kind of meeting.

Alice, Wilbur, Ardy, and another woman left the event early and jogged up the street. Where are they off to in such a big hurry?

P.S. Diary, I was frustrated during my last entry, but I had no right to belittle you. I promise it won't happen again.

Alice – July 1, 2029

7/1/2029

I walked in at 3:35 a.m. I can't stop sobbing, so sleep is out of the question. Everything turned to shit. Wilbur is dead. And now the whole town of McGill's Hill is coming for us.

I managed a little shuteye, if only for an hour. Now is the time—perhaps the only time—to jot down what happened last night. I am sitting at Pearl's dining table, a single candle illuminating my diary.

Ardy, Pearl, Wilbur, and I left the town meeting and rushed to Hayneville Town Hall, which houses the police and fire departments. Wil unlocked a metal door, permitting us access to the armory. The room was stocked wall to wall with firearms. Pearl and I had our scoped rifles, but the sheriff strapped our hips with sidearms, both Glock 22s.

After a brief debate on whether we should take the quickest or safest route, Ardy decided on the most direct path: seven miles up AL-97. Wilbur rolled out four blue mountain bikes, and we set off on the half-hour trip. I got the shakes crossing the Highway 80 intersection, especially when I learned why they brought me along for the ride.

Picture this, dear Diary. A White woman in a White town walks up to a White house and knocks on the front door. No matter how late the hour, the White homeowner will unbolt the door for a White damsel in distress. "Sir, I'm lost. Can you help me?"

Did I feel deceived at the time? Absolutely.

To make matters worse, Pearl broke the news to me. "We'll grab the ringleader when he opens the door for you."

"And then what?"

"The demon disappears."

The "ringleader" they referred to was Corbin Holt, the "demon" who had taken over McGill's Hill armed with nothing more than a wink and a smile. I understood "disappear" to mean "dead." And I got why Pearl needed me for this job and why it was so important. With one rap of my knuckles, I could save countless lives in Hayneville.

At around 9 p.m., we stowed our bicycles under the hedge of a white Greek Revival-style plantation house centered on lush acreage. Warm amber light flickered from a room on the first floor.

Ardy gave my Mossberg rifle to Pearl and tucked my Glock into his belt. "Alice, Pastor Underwood described Corbin Holt as a bald man with a black goatee. He's short and has a beer gut."

Pearl crept behind the residence to intercept our target in case he escaped from the back. Wilbur and Ardy waited on either side of the front double doors as I walked along the circular gravel driveway, up the five marble steps, and onto a portico supported by six pillars. When Ardy nodded, I lifted the brass ring and struck the lion head knocker three times. I wished I still had the handgun, or at least a blade.

The door cracked open, exposing a blue eye—a female eye! Wilbur shouldered the oak door, slamming the adolescent girl onto the floor. Ardy returned my Glock and followed the sheriff. I stood in the doorway, watching as

Pearl just hobbled into the kitchen to brew tea. She looks as ghastly as I feel. Her eyes are red, and her face is puffy. I don't remember Pearl falling. She might have injured her foot when running away. Pearl set a steaming cup in front of me, picked up a rifle, and limped into the yard. I should talk to her, but not before I complete this entry.

I aimed my Glock at the trembling girl while the men searched the main level of the house. There was nobody there. Wilbur tapped his ear and pointed upward. As the sheriff neared the top of the staircase, a baldheaded man with a Van Dyke beard sprang onto the interior balcony holding a pistol grip shotgun with a flashlight attached to the barrel.

I witnessed the entire sequence of events as if in slow motion—the ear-piercing blast, Sheriff King tumbling down, his blood spattering the white wainscoting, and the fat fuck two-stepping down the stairs. BAM! The second shot blew out the sidelight next to me. I wouldn't be writing this if Ardy hadn't seized my arm and thrown me out the front door.

A knotted string of unpleasant flashbacks rips through my mind.

> Me racing to the backyard rose garden, where Ardy found his sister crouching beneath a water fountain.
>
> The three of us running through the forest, hopping over decaying logs like frightened rabbits.
>
> Ardy bawling to the stars, "Damn you! Why didn't you take me instead?"
>
> Pearl forewarning the sheriff's wife, "Charlene, you may want to sit down."
>
> The new widow pushing her aside. "Get out!"

> Ardy leaving us at Pearl's house to report our failure to Captain Calhoun.
>
> Pearl and I sitting at this very table, unable to fathom that Wilbur is dead.

Pearl just ordered me to go to bed. She'll wake me if she hears anything. Today will undoubtedly require every ounce of our energy.

Voices dredged me up from the dismal depths of a dream.

Ardy and Pearl stood on the patio under a giant oak tree. Oscar lay by their feet, panting. A red ball of fire licked the crowns of majestic longleaf pines. After enduring such a tragic night, the beauty surrounding me stung like a slap on the cheek, a graphic reminder of the contrast between life and death.

"Hey," Ardy greeted me as I crossed the grass. Worry lines creased his handsome face. The weight of responsibility had aged him overnight. Politicians with a conscience are rare. I wonder if this quality might get in the way when push inevitably comes to shove.

"Shouldn't we be digging foxholes or rigging trees with booby traps?" I didn't intend to sound sarcastic, yet I felt let down. Even resentful.

Pearl moved to stand beside her brother. "Alice, Ardy and I apologize for not including you in our plan." She studied her sandaled toes. "Exploiting your skin color to lure Corbin Holt into the open was my idea. I knew using you was wrong, but I did it anyway. I'm sorry."

Would I have done the same thing if I were in their place? I chuckled, surprised to find that I had chuckles left in reserve. "All is fair in love and war. Something needed to happen. I am honored that you chose me to be your Trojan horse." I checked my watch. 6:03 a.m. "Any news?"

Ardy dropped onto a lawn chair. "Pastor Underwood sent me a message. Corbin Holt held a rally after we left. Everyone in McGill's Hill is demanding revenge."

"They *all* want bloodshed?"

"Alice, a handful of dissenters may be the only ones preventing Holt from bulldozing Hayneville to the ground as we speak."

"Tell me the truth. Do we have enough people and ammunition to defeat them?"

Ardy weighed my question. "Hayneville outnumbers McGill's Hill. We're on our turf and are willing to fight to the finish to survive. Invaders fear heavy losses. Some shall turn and run." Ardy gazed at his sister with a mixture of love and concern. "Even so, casualties are a factor. I'm considering evacuating our town."

"Guys, I've traveled this country. It's no man's land out there! Hayneville is as secure as anywhere you'll find."

After a nourishing breakfast, Ardy appeared revitalized—a man in control of his thoughts and actions. "Let's get ready to rumble!" Pearl locked Oscar in the house, ensuring he had enough water and food. Her brother made several calls on his walkie-talkie as we hurried to town.

We arrived at the courthouse. Captain Calhoun divided people into groups as they approached carrying guns, axes, and baseball bats. Randy Spalding (the guard whittling a fox in the upstairs courtroom) distributed weapons and ammunition to those in need. I noticed Julie watching me from the jail cell window and elected not to wave back.

The captain addressed his troops from halfway up the courthouse's stone steps. "We sent a small team to McGill's Hill to capture Corbin Holt. Our mission failed. Holt shot and killed Sheriff Wilbur King."

The crowd gasped.

A man rattled a machete, the glint of sharpened steel catching the sunlight. "I'm gonna skin that scumbag alive!"

Shrouded in widow's black, Charlene King flaunted a gun that matched Wilbur's pearl-handled cowboy revolver. "Let's bury them all!"

The throng, driven by an unquenchable thirst for revenge, shook fists and screamed curses.

Calhoun restored decorum. "We can't win this battle if we cannot control our emotions." He held up a piece of paper. "We've assigned you to defensive units, each led by someone with military training. A and B will cover 97 North. Although the 97 is the shortest road here from McGill's Hill, our enemy could approach from any direction. Stay vigilant! C can guard 97 South. D defends the highway from Montgomery. E handles 21 South—the way to Gordonville—and F will patrol the eastern section of town and the 26."

There were ten groups in total, with the remaining four allocated to individual buildings and crossroads. I'm going to facilitate communications with Pearl, Caddy, and Ardy. Calhoun called Pastor Clarke to come up the stairs.

Clarke likened us to David versus Goliath (shouldn't we be Goliath if we have superior forces?) and prayed for our deliverance from the "evil oppressor."

Captain Calhoun stood tall, his charisma cutting through the tension. "I understand you're scared. It's normal to break into a cold sweat when death is on your doorstep. But hear me loud and clear! The people in McGill's Hill aren't supernatural. Corbin Holt isn't the bogeyman. God created them of flesh and blood, the same as us. If a trespasser is in your sights, pull the trigger. Whether man, woman, or child, they won't think twice about harming your family. Turn to your neighbor. Show your love and pledge your protection." He drew his firearm from its holster, revealing a gleaming Desert Eagle pistol. "Now go! And as the Widow King so wisely said, 'Bury them all!'" Calhoun concluded his motivational speech by firing the elephant gun into the sky.

We are inside the Hayneville police department. Lanterns and candles form small, flickering pools of light. There have been no reports of activity from the combatants on the frontline. Captain Calhoun presumes that Holt is preparing for a nighttime assault. It will be dark in an hour. I asked him if the Underwoods were escorting other sympathizers to our town.

Our commander's eyes landed on my red armband. "Emmett is not responding on the radio."

I hope they are safe.

Captain Calhoun and Randy Spalding, a former Marine lieutenant, huddle over a desk in the officers' briefing area. They pore over topographical maps and draw strategic diagrams on a whiteboard. Ardy uses the handheld transceiver to relay commands to the team leaders out in the field. I always imagined warfare to necessitate thousands of uniformed soldiers. Even on a smaller scale, the image of a dozen rabble-rousers wielding clubs and pitchforks scares me.

Pearl is assisting Ardy. She'll use a bicycle to run ammunition to shooters or, if the distance is too great, a trail bike. Caddy and I helped a trauma nurse, Eloise Simmons, set up tables in the report room to treat the wounded. Eloise brought cartons of pain medications, topical antibiotics, and bandages from the Hayneville Health Center. We carried intravenous fluid bags and rolled IV stands up East Tuskeena Street. Saline solution bulges the IV bags, not blood.

My specialization? I wasn't given one. I suppose I am an all-around girl Friday, eager to jump in wherever needed.

Ardy delegated me to keep watch on the police department's flat rooftop. My loaded rifle is propped against the waist-high parapet. Sundown is merely minutes away. The elongating shadows along West Tuskeena hinder my ability to spot potential prowlers on adjacent properties. I'm so hungry I could eat an entire woolly mammoth. A long-dead wartime philosopher wrote, "War is extended periods of boredom punctuated by moments of sheer terror." I'm parched, too. I resist the temptation to lay my head on the roof and close my dry, itchy eyes. I radioed Ardy about a black plume growing above the southern hills. He instructed me to notify the team of any noteworthy changes.

The wind picks up as dusk nears. Western clouds glow in a spectacular sunset. Open fields and trees lie between us and Fort Deposit, the largest town in Lowndes County. Are wildfires causing the smoke? Did somebody from McGill's Hill intentionally strike a match?

A week after David and I waved *adios* to Chicago, we crossed the Wabash River into West Lafayette. It wasn't a nuclear bomb that laid the home of Purdue University flatter than an Indiana cornfield. Thermite-spewing drones had. Gray fumes drifted from the ashes. There was not a drop of water leaking out of the yellow fire hydrants' open valves.

A one-armed child with blistered cheeks ran to us. He pressed his hand on the fractured sidewalk. "Still too hot to touch. Where are the fire trucks?"

I asked David if the boy could come with us, already knowing what his answer would be.

The smoke is all too coincidental. I updated Ardy, but he did not seem as stressed as I am.

A sudden movement caught my attention, as if someone darted across the street from the old Presbyterian Church. There's nothing to see in my rifle scope. Ardy sent Randy out to investigate the area. No people. No cats or dogs. Ghosts? I convince myself that my nerves are playing tricks on me.

At 9:15 p.m., Pearl climbed the steep stairway to the roof to bring me some refreshments and assess the situation. Orange lights were visible on two of the taller ridges.

She set her elbows on the parapet to steady a pair of binoculars. "How far is that?"

I peered into the powerful glasses. "Ten miles? Five? Hard to say. Might be a lot closer."

Pearl rubbed her forehead. "Fort Deposit Creek runs through Hayneville. The canyon is a tinderbox this time of year."

I returned her binoculars. "Did they start the fire?"

"McGill's Hill?" Pearl stared at the inferno. "I oughta tell Captain Calhoun." She sped down the stairs.

If the flames hit town, our only escape is north to our fine friends in McGill's Hill.

Julie – July 1, 2029

7/1/2029

No one's guarding me! Sugar, the lady who usually brings us breakfast, was a no-show. My hungrometer is pegging at twelve stomach pangs per second. Jules is complaining that the portable toilet smells pretty ripe. I agree with her. Shit stinks.

It's midmorning. They confiscated my wristwatch, so I'm unaware of the exact hour. Jules and I observed people assembling by the courthouse—no kids or old folks. Alice arrived with Ardy and the woman from the previous night. Was that his sister? Alice saw me in the courtroom window. I raised my palm, but she turned away without acknowledging me.

A gray-haired man mounted the steps, puffed out his chest, and spoke. I strained my ears, unable to catch any words from this distance. A man flashed a machete, and a woman—*Sugar?*—showed off a handgun. Where's Wilbur? The townspeople wanted vengeance. Those shouts were loud enough for me to understand. "Kill him! Kill him! Kill him!"

After General Grant (Jules' nickname) gave further instructions, everyone bowed their heads as a clergyman folded his hands. Dramatic arm gestures brought energy to the general's closing statement. As the zealous crowd chanted, "Death to McGill's Hill!" he fired his massive pistol into the sky.

The men and women split into small units, dispersing in different directions. Alice and her friends accompanied General Grant toward the west part of town. The police station, maybe?

Something's going down, and we're stuck in this stupid cell.

> Diary,
>
> Have I told you what Jules did to a man in Ithaca, New York? This incident occurred several years after I graduated from Syracuse University, where I earned my Journalism Degree. I was twenty-five and had landed my first real reporting job in Ithaca at a nonprofit online newspaper, *Ithaca Voice*. Despite chicken scratch for pay, I learned tons from the editor, a Korean woman who had worked at the *New York Times*.
>
> I submitted my last article for the day about a bird flu outbreak and joined my colleagues for happy hour at the Starlight Tavern. We laughed and traded stories as discount beer filled pitcher after ice-cold pitcher. My amiable evening hit an unexpected speed bump when a member of THE DREAM KILLERS, a local softball team, insisted on buying me a drink. I politely declined, but Mr. Macho wouldn't take no for an answer. Uncomfortable, I waved goodbye to my coworkers and slipped outside.
>
> To my alarm, the man followed me into the parking area. Concerned for my safety, I reached into my purse and grabbed my bear repellant. I held the canister in my left hand, clutched the keys in my right, and rushed to my parked Toyota. As I opened the door, he thrust me onto the front seats, hiked up my skirt, and yanked down my panties.

What happened next is a blur. I suddenly felt the man being pulled off my back. When I looked up, Jules stood atop my attacker, discharging the can of pepper spray into his eyes. Mr. Macho squealed like a swine led to slaughter until Jules slashed his throat with my car keys.

I lay on the hard concrete, gasping for breath as Mr. Macho's blood pooled around me. "Jules, what have you done?"

"I defended you from being raped." She unlocked the Camry's trunk. "Help me throw this bag of garbage in here."

We carved up Mr. Macho with a knife I kept in the glove box, gift-wrapped the fish food-sized portions in weighted sacks, and sank the whole clusterfuck into Cayuga Lake. I cleaned up at a gas station and drove home.

To this day, I don't know why Jules was in Ithaca. She never gave me a straightforward answer. I had lost touch with her after leaving Syracuse. Whatever the rationale for her return, Jules has protected me ever since.

Your friend,

Julie

Late. Nobody brought Jules and me lunch, and it's now dinnertime. Did they forget about us in here? All we have is a jug of water. The thick walls deaden our desperate pleas. Jules paces back and forth like a caged tiger.

I awoke again in this dimly lit room, having dreamed of fire. The images dissipate like smoke as I splice together the bubbling celluloid scenes.

Is it ten o'clock at night or two o'clock in the morning? When the sun is shining on the opposite side of the planet, dark is dark with no shades in between. My stomach grumbles louder and louder with each passing moment. "Shut up!" I scold it. "You only missed three meals!" My throat is scratchy, and my eyes burn. Do I smell smoke? Is the courthouse on fire? Jules attempted to pick the ancient lock with the inside of my pen, but the plastic ink chamber was too flimsy. I'm telling myself over and over not to panic.

My cellmate is ready to snap.

Alice – July 2, 2029

7/2/2029

Five or six gunshots from the east awakened me at 2 a.m. I notified Ardy, who said he'd radio Group F for assistance. Unable to see a thing through the rifle scope, I hopped onto the parapet. Indistinct figures scurried past the courthouse, their intentions screened by inky darkness. Are they friends or foes? Flashes brighten the night, closely followed by thunderous reports.

The battle has begun.

Pearl came to the rooftop holding her hunting rifle. She informed me that Group F carried the school principal, Shirley Carson, to our location on a stretcher. Caddy and Eloise had to dig a bullet out of her leg.

Sporadic gunfire resounds everywhere around us, each volley louder than the last.

Pearl stationed herself back to back with me on the south section of the roof. A sudden BANG! made me flinch. She fired her Mossberg again before griping, "Did I get that motherfucker?"

A letup in the fighting has allowed me to write this. The silence is disquieting. What are those motherfuckers up to?

At 4 a.m., Pearl relayed the latest news. The blaze has overrun the trailer park by the horse racing track, a mere half mile away. The wind already feels hotter on my face. I picture my diary and me getting incinerated to ashes, our white flakes snowing upon the people of McGill's Hill.

At sunrise, Ardy hurried to the rooftop with an urgent message. "Time to pull out. Downtown is burning!"

Pearl and I descended to the main floor. In the briefing area, Captain Calhoun packed the portable CB radio into a duffel bag. Caddy and Eloise gathered medical kits and prepared Shirley for transport by re-bandaging her stitched calf and transferring her into a wheelchair. Randy unlocked the armory. Pearl, Ardy, and I hastily grabbed additional ammunition.

The captain distributed Motorola two-way radios and instructed us to use channel 8 as he guided us out of the rear door. "Based on recent reports, Hayneville has suffered significant losses." Red embers swirled above Calhoun's head. "And the fire is out of control. I will join my troops where most of the fighting is. Guys, I can't force you to come with me. If I were you, I'd follow Old Swamp Road and enter 21 at the Water Authority. Go south to Mount Willing, then take the 45 to Fort Deposit."

Pearl disagreed. "If Fort Deposit is where the flare-up originated, nothing might be left." She lifted her deer rifle. "I won't abandon my neighbors."

Ardy stood alongside his sister. "I am with her until the end."

Caddy gripped the principal's wheelchair. "Eloise and I are pushing Shirley out of town. We'll come back once she's safe."

Randy cranked up his middle finger. "Fuck Corbin Holt. I'm with the captain!"

The group turned to the one silent individual among them.

Pearl opened her arms to hug me. "Go with Caddy and Eloise. They need help with their patient."

David's face floated in the shadows. He had been eager to get to New Orleans, and, for a time, so was I. A woman's face overlaid his spectral image, splitting in two before fading.

"I am staying," I avowed, "but I have to do something first." I beelined to the mayor's office, barking my shin on Ardy's desk as I pocketed the ring of courthouse keys.

When I returned, Captain Calhoun, Lieutenant Spalding, Caddy, Eloise, and Shirley were gone. I had missed my chance to wish them luck.

Pearl, Ardy, and I edged down Lafayette Street, stopping at a drugstore overlooking the village square. Powerful gusts of wind whipped the hair off my head. The air felt dry enough to spontaneously combust.

Ardy pointed toward W&C Insurance. A White man clad in an ALABAMA CRIMSON TIDE sweatshirt had a young Black woman in a chokehold. I toggled the Mossberg's safety and centered the enraged face in the scope.

Pearl tapped my shoulder. "Over there."

Three more White men exited Long Valley Bank, dragging a Black man by the leg. I motioned for Pearl and her brother to handle them before pivoting my muzzle back to my target. Bracing myself, I aimed and squeezed the trigger. The insurance office's whitewashed wall turned crimson with the college basketball fan's brains. The woman rose to her feet and staggered away.

Ardy fired his AR-15 at a hoard of McGillians galloping across the square. "Run! Split up!"

Pearl and Ardy dashed along South Commerce Street, with Pearl veering into a field near the Subway sandwich shop. The flames would drive the siblings either east or west. I sneaked into the bank's narrow alleyway, resisting my instinct to stay with my friends.

I waited by a tow truck before crossing the intersection to the back door of the courthouse. Sweat trickled down my temples until the last key on the ring unlocked the latch. I swung the rifle over my shoulder and chambered a bullet into the Glock.

Once inside the lightless building, I felt my way up the stairwell to the second floor and opened a door in Judge Armstrong's robing room. I peered around the magistrate's armchair into the courtroom.

A woman stood in a cage, irradiated by an eerie orange glow seeping through the windows. She called out from behind the bars, "Who's there?"

"It's me—Alice. Julie, are you alone?"

"Just me and. . .please get us out of this thing!"

I sheathed the gun, sprinted down the aisle of bench seats, and fumble-fingered each key into the cell's antique lock.

"Look out!"

As I turned my head, Julie tore the handgun from my holster and fired four times. Two men collapsed by the podium. The flak-jacketed duo must have tailed me into the courthouse. I swung the metal gate open.

Julie bolted from the enclosure, passing the Glock 22 to me. "Give Jules the rifle."

My psyche wrestled with the sheer weirdness of her unyielding request. "What?"

"Do it!" I relinquished the Mossberg to the newly free woman. She rushed to a window and pushed up the sash. Julie, Jules—or whoever currently had physical domination—shot at people on the street. Her voice deepened and roughened as she demanded more ammo. I slid a box of Winchester cartridges across the tiles. "Alice, guard the doors!"

The courtroom had five entryways for public and restricted access. As I opened the wooden door behind the judge's bench, smoke billowed in through the doorframe to blacken the ceiling. I filled my lungs with oxygen and crept to a window. New Salem Christian Church, where the town meeting had taken place, blazed to the heavens. "Julie, ah Jules, we need to go!"

Jules popped off a final round (henceforth, I shall refer to Julie as Jules if in character—telltale signs are gruff expressions and enunciations) and slung the rifle on her back. She snatched her pack, pried a pistol from one of the dead men's hands, and exclaimed, "What are we waiting for? Let's go!"

With the courthouse's rear annex aflame, Jules and I ran into daylight, down the front steps, and across the pavement strewn with Black and White bodies. I shouted at her back, "Where are we going?"

She led me under the QP gas station's canopy and behind Brothers Mini Mart. "We're finding Oscar and getting out of this hellhole."

"I can't leave my friends."

"Alice, you've only been in Hayneville for a week—it's too soon to become attached to anyone."

Jules had a point. I have left so many people floating in my wake since Election Day five years ago. "You don't think much of me, do you?"

"Traipsing after you wasn't my idea."

My brain bled trying to imagine the conflict that must be raging inside her head. I walked Jules to a picnic table shaded by an elm tree, a peaceful setting if not for the gunshots and soupy air. "Sit." She lowered onto the planks, her discomfort at being ordered around revealed in a scowl. "Jules, may I speak to Julie?"

A muscle spasm rippled across the side of her face. "Why? What for?"

I traced a triangle in the smog with my forefinger. "I'd like the three of us to be friends."

"Bitch!" she spat out. "You're not taking Julie from me."

Jules recoiled when I touched her hand. "Even if I wanted to, I don't believe I can." I visualized Siamese twins fused at their skulls. "You and Julie are," I paused to choose my next word, "conjoined." I hooked my two index fingers together to symbolize their bond and smiled.

Julie smiled back. "This town locked me up for no good reason." She licked her chapped lips. "I'm not exactly thrilled to be here."

"Julie, tell me about your relationship with Jules. Do you see Jules or just hear her?" Julie's eyes fixed on something behind me. I turned—there was nothing but a pile of milk crates. "Jules is here, isn't she?" The hair on my neck stood up as Julie slowly nodded. "Does she intend to hurt me? Am I safe?"

"Jules is cognizant that her actions affect me." More gunfire. A block away? "She'll give her life for you, providing you pose no danger."

I couldn't comprehend Julie's obsession with me. "You asked me to be your friend when we first met but never explained why." Though I had experimented with women, I always found myself more drawn to men. *And how well has that worked for you, Alice?* I hesitated to ask, "Julie, are you, um, in love with me?"

"Love? Alice, I am not sure I know what true love is. I was sixteen the day my mom and dad died in a horrible car accident. Jules appeared on my foster parents' doorstep a month later, and she's stayed with me ever since—apart from a few years in my twenties."

"We all need somebody to lean on. I had someone before I reached Montgomery, but he's. . . ." I trailed off, realizing she had read my diary and knew the truth.

Julie laid her palm on mine. "Both of us have made questionable choices to survive." She squeezed my fingers. "Alice, why did you endanger yourself to rescue me?"

I duplicated her response to her motive in pursuing me to Hayneville. "That is the million-dollar question, is it not?"

Julie smirked. "What happened to Ardy and Wilbur? And that woman who fed us? The sheriff's wife."

"Corbin Holt started this bloodbath by killing Wilber. I cannot tell you where Charlene is. I shot a man who was assaulting a girl, and his pals chased after us. Ardy and his sister, Pearl, are on the run."

"Can you find out if Pearl and Ardy are okay?"

I pushed the radio's talk button. "Ardy?" The air sizzled with static. "Ardy, are you out there?"

Captain Calhoun's baritone timbre came through clearly. "Who is this?"

"It's Alice. Have you seen the others? We got separated."

"No. We're low on ammunition, and the enemy has us hedged in. The fire claimed everything south of Tuskeena Street." Gunfire in the background. "Can you help?"

I glanced at Julie. "Where are you?"

"Do you know Mount Zion Church?"

"Negative."

"It's near the Hayneville Cemetery. . .on Academy Lane. In a building at the end of a—"

More gunshots. "I've been to the graveyard. What should we do?"

"From Belford Funeral Home, go up Academy. Once you're across the pond, keep to the right. Creep along the trees to the blue house. Units A and B are with us. We can't hold out much longer."

"Hang on, Captain. We're close to you."

The canopy of the QP gas station had caved in from the intense heat, flattening the gasoline pumps. We cut behind the senior center and post office, turning north onto Academy Lane. The brick funeral home lay in ruins. Screeching metal filled the air as we crossed a shallow water basin via an old stone bridge. The Hayneville water tower squeaked, wobbled, and, with a painful shriek, toppled. An earsplitting crash sent up a cloud of black soot—a spectacular sight if we hadn't been ducking from small arms fire.

"This way!" Jules hissed, pulling me past a MOUNT ZION CHURCH sign into a grass field. She handed me the Mossberg.

I added cartridges into the rifle's detachable five-round magazine and rammed the box into the well. Walls of undergrowth made seeing nearly impossible.

Jules grunted in exasperation. "We need a higher vantage point."

"I'll pick them off from the church's roof. Can you two check the back of the house?" (I cannot believe I had to reference more than one person.)

Jules fist-bumped me before slipping into the trees bordering the driveway.

I raced to Mount Zion, climbed a willow tree, leaped to the church's rooftop, and crawled up the mossy incline. Once in position, I propped the long gun on the peak and pressed my eye to the magnifying optics. From this elevation, I could see six men and two women firing their weapons into a one-story residence.

My walkie-talkie squawked, "Alice!"

I ducked. "Pearl?"

"Where are you?"

"On the roof of Mount Zion Church. Captain Calhoun is pinned down in a blue building on the north side of the road. He's out of ammo."

"Mount Zion?"

"Affirmative. The woman Ardy locked up in the courtroom is with me. She's flanking the attackers from the woods."

"We'll look for her. Be there in five."

I peeked over the rooftop. Should I shoot? Pulling the trigger would expose me, but the captain did not have time on his side. Besides, Jules was a wildcard. Her moves were so unpredictable.

As I analyzed the situation, a youngish woman with what appeared to be a DIY flamethrower strapped to her shoulders drew my eye. Was she responsible for the fire that consumed half the town? I aimed my rifle at the red cylinder, held my breath, and unleashed 180 grains of leaden death.

The fuel tank's explosion sent shockwaves, saturating the air with gasoline. Flames engulfed the girl and the two men struggling to extinguish her. I swept the property with the scope—the remaining five targets had vanished. The three whirling torches keeled over and lay still as the danse macabre winded down for a smoking finale.

Jules chased a long-haired man around the left side of the house. A single shot placed a bullet in his back. Jules crouched over her fallen prey, posing like a hunter photographed on a big game safari. Four enemies now, their whereabouts unknown.

The two-way radio crackled to life. "Alice, we're at the cemetery. We caught a man and woman fleeing. What is your status?"

The sound of gunfire prompted me to press my cheekbone against the asphalt shingles. "Pearl, several people are on the loose." I peeped past the ridge. A pair of men were sprinting in my direction. I leveled the Mossberg, zeroed the scope's crosshairs on the closest one, and punched a hole in his black NRA – NO LIVES MATTER T-shirt.

Heavy panting behind me spun my head. Before I pulled the trigger on my handgun, the assailant lost his grip on the shingles and slid over the edge. I stretched my neck across the rain gutter to see a blond man sprawled on his posterior.

Jules discarded the emptied Springfield XD and scooped up the howler's Sig Sauer P320. "Alice, someone's coming!"

I recognized the newcomers' clothing. "Hold up—that's Pearl and Ardy!" I shinnied down the tree trunk. "How about him?"

"Blondie's not going anywhere with that bone sticking out of his leg."

We hurried to the parking lot.

Ardy kept his AR-15 trained on the two prisoners as he asked if we were injured.

I brushed off the black granules embedded in my elbows. "Just a few scrapes. Pearl and Ardy, I'd like you to meet my friend, Jules."

The siblings masked their confusion better than I had ever dreamed—no gaping mouths, arched eyebrows, or triple blinks in sight. Pearl seemed pleased as Ardy shook Jules' hand.

Captain Calhoun, Lieutenant Spalding, three men (a blood-speckled patch covered the youngest's right eye), and two women (a sling supported the taller one's left arm) plodded through the dust.

The captain praised us for our heroism. "Rambo couldn't have accomplished what you did!" Gun magazines swelled his pockets. "We searched the dead for ammunition. Corbin Holt isn't here."

Ardy's face reflected the disappointment we all felt. "We've not seen him either."

Pearl squinted at the female captive. "Karen Fuller? You used to shop at my market every Thursday. I always slipped extra produce into your bag. What did we do to deserve your hate?"

Karen's jawline tightened, but her mouth remained shut.

Ardy jabbed the AR-15 into the man's kidney. "Where's Holt?"

Karen exclaimed, "Leave Jim be!"

Jules came closer. "Are you two married?"

Jim tucked his wedding ring into his pants, but not before I noted how the five embedded diamonds matched Karen's gold band.

Jules unfolded her Buck knife and waved the shiny blade in Jim's face. "If you don't tell us where Holt is, I will hack off your wife's nose and force-feed it down your throat. Jimmy, if that's not enough to loosen your tongue," she held the sharp tool to Karen's crotch, "I'll gut her like a rainbow trout."

I had zero misgivings about Jules being able to follow through with her threat.

"Don't touch her!" A thread of drool hung from the corner of Jim's mouth. "Karen and I wanted no part of this mess. Holt and his gang intimidated our entire town into voting for the takeover. Pastor Underwood got beat up trying to stop them." He turned to his wife for corroboration, but she looked away. "We will help you find that thief and put an end to him."

I pointed at the church. "One of Holt's men fell off the roof. He has a broken leg."

Randy strode over to Blondie. "Well, well, well! If it isn't my old friend Walter Hubbard! Remember how we used to carpool to Montgomery Bowlero on Tuesday nights? You and I were on the same team! The Pin Ticklers. We always pulled into the Waffle House on South Boulevard for a T-bone and hash browns before the long ride home. Those were fun times." He swatted at the black flies dive-bombing the man's open wound. "Compound fracture. Excessive bleeding. Walt, you need immediate surgery. The problem is our doctor died a few months ago. And our trauma nurse, who had steadier hands than Doc Callaway, escaped town with a patient that you assholes shot." Walter yowled as Randy squeezed his thigh. "The positive news is, I served as a combat medic in the Marines.

Two tours in Afghanistan. I can heal you," the lieutenant applied more pressure to the punctured flesh, "if you tell me where Corbin Holt is."

"Randy," Walter wailed, "you can't fix me! I'm all busted up!" His eyeballs twisted toward the wall of fire. "Don't leave me here to die!"

Randy cocked his Smith & Wesson.

Walter screamed, "The one you're after is at the big house on Trevor Lake!"

Pearl kicked the man who attempted to kill me. "That's my place! How many of you are there?"

"T-t-ten. T-twelve? I told you what you want to know. Now get me the hell out of here!"

Randy terminated the interrogation with a bullet to Walter's abdomen. He deftly twirled his pistol before sliding the carbon steel back into its leather sheath. "Lead the way, Pearl!"

Thirteen of us, with Karen and Jim bound with rope, left the gut-shot man behind to moan, groan, and call out for Jesus. Pearl picked a northern route along Cemetery Road to evade the encroaching flames. Our two-hour trek to her house took us over rural lanes, fire trails, and cattle paths. As we side-stepped clumps of cow pies, I asked Randy if he could have mended Walter Hubbard's splintered femur. I assumed that major surgery required an operating room with sterilized equipment and an anesthesia machine. Not to mention an economy-size box of titanium rods and screws.

Randy chuckled. "Nah, my mother begged me to be a doctor, but the thought of slicing into somebody's skin makes me queasy. I served in the Corps in the Judge Advocate Division. Mom was happy to have a lawyer in the family."

We followed a power line access road southward to Rebel Field, where a scoreboard advertised: HOME OF THE MCGILL ACADEMY REBELS.

One of Captain Calhoun's team members traced the sign of the cross on her forehead and chest.

Black scavenger birds spiraled into the russet sky as we approached male and female bodies hanging from a yellow goalpost, naked except for the red cloths wrapped around their throats. Someone without a dictionary had incised TRAITER into the Underwoods' stomachs.

"Cut them down!" Ardy commanded. "Now!"

The pastor's and his wife's purple faces and swollen tongues revealed that they'd been dead for hours.

It's late, almost eleven o'clock. Two hours have passed, and I am not yet done updating my journal. Julie is at the table, hunched over her own diary. I wish I could read her version of events. Would I want Julie to see what I wrote?

Hope glimmered today amidst the tragedy and loss. Around 6:30 p.m., a storm rolled in from the north to extinguish the flames.

I asked out loud, "Did the Hand of God intervene?"

"There's no such thing as God," Jules muttered, before wandering into another dimension.

Is Julie's more violent half hovering above me now, misconstruing my every word?

Ardy and Pearl are sitting by the lake underneath the green umbrella. Captain Calhoun and Randy are upstairs, sleeping in a spare bedroom. Calhoun's teammates, Bonnie, Gage, Regina, and Cooper, are bunked in the guesthouse. Arthur is in the garage, wrapped in plastic sheeting.

Though I'm running on empty, I am determined to complete today's journal entry out of respect for those no longer with us.

We laid the Underwoods in the gardener's shed at Rebel Field. Ardy said a few kind words in their honor. Captain

Calhoun drew the thirteen of us (always an unlucky number!) into a huddle. "Streety Road runs parallel to this football field. Before Lieutenant Spalding sent his buddy to bowl gutter balls at Limbo Lanes, Walt told us that a dozen men and women are holed up at Pearl's house. The two-faced maggot coulda been lying, but with his pain, I doubt it. The smart move is to wait until dark."

Bonnie Bowman, the tall woman with the incapacitated arm, glowered. "Those cockroaches hanged the preacher! I vote to go in before they crawl back into the cracks."

Gage Caldwell, the young man with the eye patch, gestured at her bleeding shoulder. "You're wounded, Bonnie. I think you should stay here."

Bonnie one-handed a pistol fitted with a sound suppressor. "My shooting arm is solid as a rock, Mr. Caldwell. You're blind as a bat. How are you gonna aim that scatter gun?"

"I just point the business end in their general direction and set off the spark." Cage winked his good peeper and pumped a shell into the chamber. "Don't worry, Miss Bowman. I got you covered."

Bonnie's and Gage's banter sounded more like flirting than squabbling. I had the impression that the two knew each other intimately—or desired to.

Jim from McGill's Hill held up his trussed wrists. "Holt killed our pastor. If you give us weapons, we'll help you capture him."

Cooper Conrad, a large man, clenched his hands. "Jimbo, you're lucky to be still talking."

Randy tossed a length of hangman's rope to Cooper. "Tie the Fullers to the goalpost. Gage, help him."

Pearl gazed beyond the longleaf pines to the darkening sky. "A lake surrounds my property. All that water will shield Holt from the fire. We have just an hour or two until we'll be forced to withdraw northward."

Jules turned to Pearl. "Any food in that house?"

"Yeah, if those lowlifes didn't ransack the pantry."

Jules stood next to Bonnie. "Then I'm with her. Julie and I haven't had a crumb to eat in two days."

Those not in the know swiveled their heads in search of this "Julie."

Calhoun chewed his lip. "Let's vote on it. Raise your hand if you want to attack now instead of at nightfall."

Eleven arms shot up, two of them attached to Jules.

The captain crouched down at the football field's end zone, scratching a map in the soil with a twig. He outlined Trevor Lake, the horsehead-shaped peninsula, and Pearl's house. "Only one way in." He drew a long line to the box topped with a triangle. "The problem is that our enemy will see us from a mile away."

Randy took the stick and poked a few dots at the entryway to the estate. "Those fools are bottled in. If some of us advance from the lakefront and force them down the driveway, the rest of us can open fire." He aimed his rifle at a black-feathered bird perched on the landscaper's shed. "It'll be easier than shooting crows in a cage."

Pearl etched a cove hidden by trees. "My husband built a dock for townsfolk to use for fishing. The Buckleys and Pastor Clarke have rowboats tied there."

Captain Calhoun smiled with approval. "Perfect for an amphibious assault!" The eagle's cold, crafty eyes evaluated each of us like pawns on a giant's chessboard. "Bonnie, Gage, Regina, and Arthur will entrench themselves on Streety Road across from the main entrance. The drainage ditch will conceal you from all angles." He marked a straight section on the opposite bank of Trevor Lake. "From this earthen dam, Pearl's and Alice's rifles have clear shots of the house. You others are with Randy and me in the boats."

Jules moved to my side, uncharacteristically concerned for my safety. "We're staying with Alice."

I tried my best to reassure her. "Don't worry, Jules. I'll be on the far side of the lake."

She frowned. "What about the fire?"

Pearl propelled her arms. "We can swim away."

The captain tapped his wrist. "It's 6:30. Who has watches?" Randy, Cooper, and I put our hands up. "Coop, give yours to Gage. It will take our group ten minutes to get to the boats and the same amount to paddle to the rear of the property. Pearl?"

"Um, fifteen minutes to the dam. Couple more to set up."

"Gage, Bonnie, Regina, and Arthur, listen up. At precisely 7 p.m., start shooting at the house to attract their attention. Pearl and Alice will spot targets and take them out. Keep changing positions to create the illusion of a greater force. Conserve your ammunition and beware of crossfire." He rapped on his breastbone. "Try not to hit one of the good guys."

"Be careful, Alice." Jules hugged me before shifting to Calhoun. "Sir, we'll go with you and Ardy!"

The captain welcomed Jules with a handful of extra ammo. "This is a surprise attack. Switch off your walkie-talkies. Once our rowboats land at the boathouse, we'll use every capability to make Holt fall back." The military man rubbed his palms together. "Let's turn Pearl's driveway into a goddamn meat grinder."

Regina gasped. "Is that—?"

"Lightning!" Arthur gaped upward. "Those are thunderclouds, not—"

"Smoke!" I completed his sentence as a drop wetted my face, followed by a bigger one. The downpour was upon us as Pearl and I climbed the earthen dam.

Julie closed her diary and pocketed her pen. Right after we entered Pearl's front door, Jules devoured half a loaf of white bread and half a pound of cured ham. She washed down the starch and protein with a quart of carbohydrates and fat—fresh goat's milk. With Jules occupied elsewhere, Julie is watching me write. Like clockwork, she methodically plucks a pecan from a ceramic bowl, inserts the hard shell into Nutty the Squirrel's metallic jaws, and pulls the bushy tail. I listen to her molars pulverizing the nutmeat into a paste.

Does Julie's intensity bother me? Will I grow accustomed to her constant scrutiny? I am gradually adjusting to Julie's unique personality, or should I say personalities. Hints of whom I speak with lurk behind Julie's and Jules' brown irises. If Leonardo da Vinci claimed the eyes are the windows to the soul, then this woman is blessed with two. She possesses opposing yet connected forces—hot and cold, light and dark, the yin and the yang.

Julie's eyes are inviting and affectionate. Is "loving" too strong an adjective? Does that particular emotion unsettle me? On the contrary, the hooded orbs below Jules' furrowed brows are as warm as a cup of frozen hot chocolate on a frigid winter morning. Hateful? Quite often, but no antagonism has been directed my way since the day she tried to strangle me at the Hayneville Courthouse.

Has Jules surrendered to Julie's will? Has she agreed to coexist with me, or is she scheming to rub me out?

Perhaps Julie can answer these hot topics tomorrow. I also want to learn more about her parents and how she got that scar on her cheek. But now, I must finish this story before I zonk out.

The rain fell in buckets. Pearl and I took longer than planned, slip-sliding on the sodden roadway to Trevor Lake's earthen dam. We clawed up the rocky embankment and rested our rifle forestocks on a fallen tree trunk. Sparks of gunfire were scattered here and there. Bonnie and Gage had already engaged the enemy.

I wiped off the scope's wet optics with my thumb. "I don't know if I can hit anything at this distance."

Raindrops glistened on Pearl's face. "You'll be fine. Do like your daddy taught you at the shooting range." I stared into the heartless eyes of a trained assassin. "We have a job to do. Let's get 'er done."

An aluminum boat emerged from the cove. Cooper was rowing while Randy covered the shoreline with his assault rifle. The second rowboat came into view a moment later, carrying Ardy and Captain Calhoun. "Pearl, I see your brother, but where's Jules?" The four men stepped over the gunwales and slithered up the reedy banks.

We watched intently as the captain guided Randy, Ardy, and Cooper through the backyard. A sudden hail of deadly projectiles flew from the house's rear windows.

Pearl fired first. She has sharper vision than me because I never saw who she aimed at or if they were struck. I scanned the yard for movement.

A Herculean man wearing a too-small flak jacket lumbered out the door, holding a long rifle. I increased my tension on the trigger, pausing when my scope vibrated out of focus. Pearl sent Hercules to the golden gymnasium in the sky with a single shot to his brawny neck. I nailed the woman who crawled out to help him in the side.

Then I spotted the demon himself. Corbin Holt dropped from an upper window to the roof above the garage. I had the creature responsible for all this misery right in my crosshairs. Just as I readied to let loose, he tilted his head sideways as if listening to a voice. I turned to locate the source of the distraction and promptly lost Holt.

Pearl and I aimed our weapons toward the kitchen and dining room, firing whenever we saw a muzzle flash. Our guns were deafening from this side of the lake, but we only heard their muffled pops.

I was too preoccupied to notice someone scrambling up the slick slope but caught the unmistakable BANG-BANG! of a double tap. Pearl and I dropped our Mossbergs, rolling onto our sides to draw the Glocks.

As we readied ourselves for self-defense, a recognizable voice called, "Alice, don't shoot. I'm climbing up!" Jules crested the dam, her larger-than-life "I'm back!" reminiscent of a line from a 1980s movie hero.

I sat up in astonishment. "Shouldn't you be with Captain Calhoun?"

"I was, but somebody came after you, so I," she kissed the smoking handgun, "helped him to see the error of his ways."

I beckoned to her. "Come here and get down!"

Jules got behind the horizontal tree as Pearl fired one last round at a topless man in stained overalls. He took three unsteady steps before belly-flopping into the lake. A few more gunshots reverberated across the water, soon replaced by the calm pitter-patter of raindrops and rustling of leaves.

I surveyed the land around Pearl's home. Five forms lay on the back lawn, the deluge obscuring their identities. I lowered the rifle. "Is it over?"

Pearl reloaded the Mossberg's box magazine. "Let's go see."

We hastened past the eyeless corpse and up the muddy road to Pearl's guesthouse. The wavering beam of a flashlight cast shifting shadows within the main residence.

Jules elevated her Sig Sauer. I pushed her arm downward. "Listen! Are those voices?"

"That's my brother!" Pearl tiptoed to her living room windowsill. She stood upright, signaling for us to advance.

Captain Calhoun marched out of the back door. Lieutenant Spalding followed, prodding the now-gagged and fettered Corbin Holt onto the patio with the tip of his rifle. Next came the young woman who had opened the front door for me at Holt's plantation house. Ardy, Regina, Bonnie, and Gage trailed behind them.

Pearl embraced her brother. "Where's Arthur and Cooper?"

"Coop is bringing back the Fullers." Ardy sighed. "Art didn't make it."

"Oh, so sorry to hear that!" I indicated Holt and the teenager. "What are you going to do with them?"

Ardy contemplated the oak tree towering above the pool, its mighty limbs reaching for the flickering sky. "I have plans for the leader. He held the girl against her will. Olivia Dawson is free to go."

Pearl and Regina lit a ring of tiki torches on the patio. Jules and I dragged Holt's gang out of the house and from the front driveway to lie with the other casualties on the flagstone tiles. There were six men and three women. I stood by the man Pearl plugged in the neck (not looking so Herculean now) and the woman I shot in the ribs coming to his aid. Were they a couple? Strangers? Either way, now they're together forever. The bare-chested country boy Pearl blasted had drifted too far offshore to snag without wading into the water.

Cooper escorted Karen and Jim Fuller into the backyard. He handed the manila rope used to execute the Underwoods to Ardy. Pearl's brother fastened a horseshoe to the cord and flung the weight over the oak's stoutest branch. Randy untied the metal plate, looped a slipknot, and slid the noose past Corbin Holt's ears.

Karen drained of color as Ardy tossed the end of the rope to her husband. "Pull. Both of you."

Jim released the braided line. "You can't force us to do this!"

Ardy extended three fingers. "You have three options. One: If you hang Corbin Holt, we'll accept you into our community. Two: You are free to leave Hayneville, but only after you eliminate your leader. And I'm certain you can figure out number three."

Karen didn't lift a finger as Jim tugged the rope hard enough to tighten the noose around Holt's pudgy neck.

Regina waved her palm. "Shouldn't the condemned get a last word?"

"Screw him." Jules pretended to tow a line. "String 'em up, buttercup."

Ardy yanked the gag from the doomed man's lips. "We're all tired. Make it quick."

Corbin Holt pleaded for reprieve. "You don't have to—"

Ardy jammed the rag between Holt's teeth and cranked his hand at the Fullers.

Jim strained to raise the obese ringleader off the patio. "Karen, don't just stand there!"

Karen and Jim's combined strength boosted Holt an inch above the flagstone tiles, where he hung like a piñata stuffed with carnitas. Olivia Dawson took hold of the rope, her tears mixing with the rain. We joined the collective effort, huffing and puffing to hoist three hundred pounds of human offal three yards above the hard surface. Once Ardy knotted the cord to a lower bough, we, the executioners, stepped back to enjoy the show.

Corbin Holt's fleshy body, bathed in the radiance of thirteen flaring torches, twisted and turned, his bare feet kicking at something only he could see.

Julie – July 2, 2029

7/2/2029

Gunshots woke me from a fiery nightmare. I joined Jules at the courtroom window, both of us coughing from the smoke. Irate White people marched up the street.

"Julie, we need to leave!" Jules kneeled to examine the cot. "We can use these legs to pry open the door. Shit, they're bolted on!"

At least the posts supporting the cot were sturdy steel, not flimsy aluminum. "Jules, let's pick up the whole bed."

We threw off the mattress, slid the cot across the cell, and tipped the frame on its side. The metal leg twisted and broke in half when we tried to use it as a lever against the heavy gate. The other three followed suit.

Jules hurled a bent brace at the lock. She gripped the cage's iron bars and hollered for help.

Bloodcurdling screams drew me to the window. A White man tossed a flaming liquor bottle through the library's main entrance. Two shots. The firebug spun and collapsed to the sidewalk. As he crawled behind the book drop box, a bullet with his name on it found him.

Our noses are pressed against the cold floor to evade the hot fumes.

Hold on. I hear noises.

Diary, feel free to quote me: *Miracles are real!*

Is it before or after 10 p.m.? I'm at Pearl's, sitting next to Alice. I could request the hour, but I don't want to interrupt her. We're both updating our diaries. My belly is full from the ham sandwiches Jules made earlier.

I should mention that it's pouring outside. Alice asked Jules if God had quelled the fire to save us. Jules, a Jean-Paul Sartre-certified atheist, wagged her head and shuffled to the couch. A few moments without her breathing down my neck is better than sex.

Ardy and Pearl walked to the lake to unwind. Captain Calhoun (General Grant) and Randy, the whittler who was guarding me, climbed the stairs to the guest bedroom. Bonnie and the other three are in the guesthouse.

Arthur, a member of Calhoun's team, was killed during the firefight. We carried his body off the street and laid it in the garage. The thought of Art alone in the dark depresses me.

There's so much more to write.

The door behind the judge's raised bench creaked open. I knew Alice wouldn't forget me!

Two White males barged into the courtroom as Alice unlocked the cell gate. I borrowed her handgun and shot both in the chest. Alice gave her rifle to Jules to snipe at rioters, then went to identify an escape route.

Just as the smoke thickened and the heat became unendurable, Alice shouted, "This way!"

I stuck one of the dead intruder's pistols in my belt. Jules strapped the Mossberg to her back. We ran down the front steps, crossed the lane, and sought shelter behind a convenience store.

Alice seemed befuddled. "What are we doing?"

"Once we find our dog," Jules said, "we're outta here."

Alice expressed her reluctance to leave Hayneville. She reached for Jules' hand—a big, no, no. "You and Julie are conjoined." WTF did she just say? "Can't we all be friends?" My heart was beating so hard I feared it would throw a valve.

Alice questioned if I could see Jules. Of course I can see her! Why would Alice ask me that? She wanted to know if Jules might hurt her.

Black cotton candy whirls inside my skull, its sweet stickiness gumming up all logical thoughts.

Alice explained how Corbin Holt shotgunned Sheriff King in McGill's Hill. Holt's troublemakers had pillaged and plundered Hayneville. Alice tried to contact Ardy and his sister on the radio. Rather than hearing The Jackson 2 singing "Blame it on the Boogie," Captain Calhoun reported that he and his fighters were trapped in a house.

We rushed to a church. Alice climbed onto the sloped rooftop with her hunting rifle. I approached where Calhoun and his team had barricaded themselves. A fireball erupted into the sky, flushing a hippy dude out of hiding. I bird-dogged Jerry Garcia across the grass, putting an exclamation mark between his tie-dyed shoulder blades. Two more men came after Alice. She got one with her Mossberg, and I yanked the other one, a fair-haired tree monkey, off a branch. Jules confiscated Blondie's weapon before delivering a crushing blow to the remnants of his thigh bone. YEE-OWWW!

Ardy and Pearl arrived at the church parking lot with two White prisoners in tow, Karen and Jim Fuller. Captain Calhoun, Randy, and five other fighters exited the blue building, grateful to be alive. Ardy confronted the Fullers, demanding to know where Corbin Holt was. Jules warned Jim that if he didn't give up his boss, she'd slice off his wife's schnoz and serve it to him with a side of lady bits. Taking Jules at her word, Jim swore he had nothing to share but promised to help us pin down Holt.

We hurried over to the fella with the smashed-to-smithereens femur. After Blondie told us that Holt was livin' it up at Pearl's lake house, Randy shot his old bowling league partner in the tum-tum. Diary, remind me never to get on Randy's wrong side!

We hiked through the countryside to Rebel Field—*the war is over, General Lee!*—the same football field where Jules and I heard rumors of a raid five days ago. A dyslexic with a Ginsu knife had hanged a White man and woman from a goalpost. Alice told me that the pastor and his wife kept Ardy apprised of the goings-on in McGill's Hill. RIP, Mr. and Mrs. Underwood.

Captain Calhoun advised a sundown offensive. Jules and Bonnie wanted to charge guns a-blazing. Everyone, aside from the captain and the Fullers (Cooper tied Jim and Karen to the goalpost), voted to finish the fight ASAP.

The captain sketched a map in the dirt. Wishing to stay with Alice, I objected to Calhoun's intention of bringing me and Ardy on a boat. Alice assured me she would be safe with Pearl. I hesitantly relented, aware that, as a sniper, she'd be out of the line of fire. As the six of us pushed through the dense thicket to access rowboats, I saw someone shadowing Alice and Pearl. He would have gotten to them if Jules hadn't blown both of his eyes out (I'd never have believed the accuracy of her shots if I hadn't witnessed the wounds myself!). In my opinion, Jules' Schwarzenegger-esque "I'm back!" deserved a laugh from Pearl and Alice.

We hurried to Pearl's house after the hostilities ceased. All the familiar faces were accounted for, except for Cooper. He went back to the football field to get Karen and Jim Fuller. And Arthur, of course, who had died. I had felt a sense of camaraderie with Art that could have blossomed into something more.

I spotted Pearl lighting tiki torches. "Did you see my dog?"

She shook her head. "Oscar will come back once it quiets down."

A loud moan directed my attention to the patio, where a young female poked a hogtied adult male with a sharpened stick. "Pearl, who's the girl?"

"Olivia Dawson." She shot a withering glare in the man's direction. "And that's Corbin Holt, the pig who held her hostage in his plantation house."

Cooper returned from Rebel Field with the Fullers. Alice, Jules, and I arranged the fatalities in a neat row. Jules, always the prankster, positioned an older man and a younger woman in a compromising position. Diary, I wasn't entirely accurate when I told you that Jules lacked wit. She was born with a funny bone, but the calcium binding the tissue is seriously fractured.

The real party started now. Randy slipped a noose around Holt's throat. Ardy passed the rope to the Fullers and ordered them to pull. Jim gave it his all, yelling for his wife to lend a hand. Holt resembled a Bolshoi ballet dancer executing a clumsy pirouette as the tips of his toes kissed the stone stage. Olivia Dawson added her two tons of revenge, followed by Jules, Alice, and me.

Corbin Holt sure looked stupid swinging by his dumbass neck.

I rock back in my chair, watching Alice furiously craft sentence after wordy sentence. Typically, my journal entries incorporate eloquent adjectives, adverbs, and all the other literary elements necessary to bring a story to life. Tonight's narrative has been scribbled as if under a strict newspaper deadline.

Alice's question echoes in my mind: Would Jules ever hurt her?

Alice – July 3, 2029

7/3/2029

Early in the morning, Julie and I searched the grounds for Oscar. We found no live dog, but no dead dog either. I tried to comfort her.

Someone had cut Corbin Holt from the oak and cleared the flagstone patio. Physically and emotionally sapped, I did not ask who had performed this unpleasant task or what happened to the bodies.

Pearl and Ardy cooked breakfast, and then the thirteen of us (still a luckless number) carried our plates of eggs and sausages to the lake. We lined up along the edge of the dock, sitting with our toes dipped into the tepid water. The scent of carbonized wood lingered in the damp air.

When Regina voiced concerns about the fate of her home, Bonnie, in a lousy mood, responded curtly. We remained mum until Ardy got up and said, "Time to bury the dead." We followed him to the garage, where a tarpaulin lay over a row of corpses. Ardy grabbed a shovel from the rack and turned to his sister for guidance.

"Arthur shall be laid to rest by the lake with a pleasant view of the hills." Pearl nodded to herself in sudden remembrance. "Emmett and Rosalynn Underwood can also be placed under the shagbark hickory tree. As for Holt and the others, cart that trash away and burn it."

Gage and Bonnie pushed a wheelbarrow to the football field to collect the Underwoods.

Captain Calhoun, Randy, Regina, and Cooper took spades and a pickax to dig a hole for Arthur, Emmett, and Rosalynn.

Jim, Karen, and Olivia volunteered to remove Holt and his goons. Pearl loaned them a small four-wheeled wagon to haul the ten bodies down the lengthy driveway to a nearby farmer's field.

Julie and I waded into the murky water, the thick muck clinging to our toes. We floated Pearl's victim to shore using his Dickies overalls strap. Then I rowed the boat to the earthen dam with Julie sitting on the left side of the rear seat to accommodate Jules. We dumped the slimebucket Jules drilled in the eyes into the rowboat. Why does dead weight always feel twice as heavy?

By the time we paddled back to the house, the kid-sized wagon stood ready for our use. Julie and I, accompanied by Pearl, Ardy, Bonny, Gage, and the three McGillians, transported our two bodies and a gallon of kerosene off the property. Cooper, Regina, Randy, and Captain Calhoun stayed behind to finish the grave.

We stacked up our enemies in a wild blueberry field. Ardy doused their torsos, limbs, and heads with the lamp oil. No eulogies were verbalized during this low-tech cremation. Olivia touched a lit match to the base of the putrid pyramid. Flames crackled and danced—Corbin Holt blazing the brightest.

We gave Arthur and the Underwoods a proper burial. Cooper, who I learned attended seminary before Election Day, conducted the service. Each of us, even the Fullers, shared anecdotes about the deceased. I spoke of the pastor and his wife's incredible courage in standing up for the citizens of Hayneville.

Julie entwined her fingers and bowed her head. "Jules and I didn't get to meet Emmett and Rosalynn, but we shall pray for their safe crossing to the afterlife." A single tear rolled down her scarred cheek. "Even though I only met Arthur yesterday, I already miss his smile and unwavering positivity."

Cooper scooped up a handful of clay and tossed it into the communal grave. Once we filled the hole, Pearl laid a bouquet of white wildflowers on the mound.

Randy and Captain Calhoun departed in search of injured personnel. Karen and Jim, anxious to see how many neighbors survived the conflict, borrowed Pearl's bicycles to ride up to McGill's Hill. Ardy spit on the ground as the two peddled away. Regina, Cooper, Bonnie, and Gage left to check on their friends and relatives.

After lunch and an aborted attempt at a nap on the patio (the Sandman passed me by, as he did Julie and Olivia), the three of us rowed the bloodless boat around Trevor Lake. We would have been sitting ducks if any marauders remained in the reeds.

I took in Olivia's glumness, realizing she must be experiencing symptoms of PTSD. While I deliberated ways to console her, Julie let go of the oars. "Olivia, the abuse you suffered can't be undone. But you're safe now—as safe as anyone."

I caught a whirligig and watched the black beetle swim in my palm before releasing it back into the water. "Will you return to your hometown? Where are your mom and dad?"

Olivia's chest hitched, and a tremor racked through her body. "They've been missing for two months. I know Corbin Holt murdered them."

Julie's eyes followed a formation of geese flying overhead. "A drunk driver killed my parents when I was your age. The state placed me in a foster home. Do any of your aunts or uncles live close by?"

"Uh-uh." Olivia wiped her eyes with her forearm. "I won't step foot into that shitty town ever again. Nobody helped me. Not even the police chief."

Old newsreels of Nazi Germany, Hitler, and the Holocaust flickered through my mind. "Olivia, people act irrationally if they fear a tyrannical ruler. There must be somebody in McGill's Hill who's willing to take you in now?"

My insensitivity kicked off a fresh wave of sobs.

Julie practiced more compassion. "Olivia, you're not alone. You have us."

I nodded in agreement. "Pearl gave me the key to her mother's home. She'll let us stay with her if the house is gone."

Julie pushed on the right oar to reverse the boat. She took her time paddling to shore.

At 4 p.m., Pearl, Ardy, Olivia, Julie, and I ventured into town to size up the damage caused by the fire. Captain Calhoun had informed us that everything south of West Tuskeena Street had either been destroyed or needed significant reconstruction, including the town hall building. Oddly enough, the neighboring Presbyterian Church, founded in 1842, stood unscathed.

We entered downtown Hayneville. A scene from a disaster movie greeted us. Men, women, and children wandered through the aftermath of the previous night, their dirty faces haggard with shock and disbelief. Stray dogs (none of them Oscar) roamed the village square, gnawing on things I hadn't the stomach to look too closely at. Further along, masked men used a horse and makeshift travois to drag decomposing bodies to the cemetery.

All that remained of the historical courthouse was its 1856 cornerstone. The fallen water tower had smashed the New Salem Christian Church in completely. Next to the torched library, the brick post office stood proudly in another perplexing display of Mother Nature's whims.

Going past the now-razed funeral home, Pearl urged us to hurry. We chased her into the Family Dollar and ACE Hardware parking lot. The polyester banner of PEARL'S TRADING POST flapped from a light pole, its vibrant colors starkly contrasting with the surrounding devastation.

Pearl rummaged through the debris, picking up dented cans of chicken soup and cracked canning jars. She tossed the worthless items aside.

Ardy embraced his sister. "Don't worry. We'll rebuild."

Her sooty hands smudged his white shirt. "How? Look at ACE! Our town used to have enough stored lumber and hardware for basic repairs. We no longer have the inventory to fix a single building, let alone hammer together a new one. Without diesel fuel and repair parts for the construction machinery, we are. . . ." Pearl slumped onto the buckled vinyl flooring, her fingers releasing a handful of melted batteries into the ashes. "Ardy, I can't go on like this. I'm done."

Her brother kicked a hole in the last standing wall.

Pearl used a shelf support to right herself, her face shifting from resentful to rage. "We're taking it all!"

Ardy glared at the skeletal trees. "Take what? Everything is ruined!"

Pearl pitched a hard-nosed solution. "Let's relocate everyone in Hayneville to McGill's Hill. Their houses and businesses were untouched by the flames."

Pearl's quick fix made perfect sense to me. "Olivia, what's your perspective? Do you think that's feasible?"

"Some old-timers are bound to put up a stink." The teenager watched the black horse struggling to pull the carrion-laden travois. "But by day's end, the worst of them will be covered with dirt."

We toured the residential areas. Ardy's place on Miller Circle was just a pile of bricks. I stood before the home I lived in on North Washington. Athena B. Jackson's cast iron water pump rose above the rubble as a last vestige of happier times.

Julie – July 3, 2029

7/3/2029

Alice, Jules, and I searched everywhere for Oscar this morning. I pray he is unharmed and will return to us.

Everyone had breakfast by the lake. The scrambled eggs and pork sausages reminded me of the Sundays my foster parents drove Stephen and me to Mother's Cupboard in East Syracuse. Stevie and I always looked forward to those Family Combo meals.

To clarify, when I say "everyone," I am referring to the participants in last night's hanging: Me and Alice, Pearl and Ardy, Captain Calhoun and Lieutenant Spalding, Bonnie and Gage (is it just me, or are those two doing the horizontal mambo?), Regina (runs her mouth but is funny as hell), and Cooper (he's on his knees a lot, so he must be religious). Did I forget anyone? How could I miss Olivia Dawson and the lovely couple hailing from the charming white-bread town of McGill's Hill, Alabama? The Fullers sat at the end of the dock, Karen acting like a bug had crawled up her bum and laid a jillion eggs. Alice, Jules, and I took Olivia under our wings. Fucking Holt. That child molester did a number on the poor girl. I'll need to spend some one-on-one time with her.

Regina attempted to spark a conversation with Bonnie but was given the cold shoulder. Bonnie's attitude is understandable. The past twenty-four hours were pretty freakin' awful.

As we got up this morning, Jules turned to me. "How are you?"

Strange of her to ask such a personal question. "Fine. And you?"

"Not good." She clammed up as I dug deeper.

The tiny fish nibbling on my toes darted away when Ardy stood. "Let's tend to the dead." We stretched our achy joints and dragged ourselves to the garage. Blood-soaked canvas concealed eleven bodies. Once we add the one in the lake and the one on the earthen dam, we'll have a baker's dozen.

Ardy grabbed a shovel. "Pearl, what should we do with them?"

His sister deliberated the matter at hand. "Bury Arthur by the water. The same goes for the pastor and his wife. Corbin Holt and his bootlickers don't deserve everlasting peace. Rid my land of that filth and reduce it to ashes."

While Calhoun, Randy, Cooper, and Regina dug a grave underneath a hickory tree, Gage and Bonnie fetched the Underwoods from the football field using a wheelbarrow. Pearl rolled out a small green John Deere wagon for Olivia and the Fullers to convey the "filth" to a field near the entrance to her gravel drive. Given the cart's one-corpse capacity, the three had to make multiple trips. I believe Mr. Deere designed the toy wagon for kiddies eager to tow their doggies and kitties around the house, not cadaverous adults.

Alice, Jules, and I retrieved the scrawny dude who fell in the water (Pearl sniped him in her backyard) and the guy Jules caught creeping up on Alice and Pearl at the dam. The floater was a breeze to slide up the muddy shoreline and into the garage. Because of his patched overalls and 1950s duck's ass hairstyle, Jules thought he could pass for Jethro from *The*

Beverly Hillbillies. I pictured Pruneface in *Dick Tracy.* Alice rowed Jules and me across the lake. Despite our combined strength, we had difficulty tipping "Norman No-Eyes" into the rocking rowboat. That sightless tub of lard weighed a ton.

Back at Pearl's, we borrowed the toy hearse for the final two runs to the berry field. We piled the carcasses high, with Corbin Holt the cherry on top of this stomach-churning sundae. Olivia tossed a match upon the pyre, shouting, "Burn forever in Hell!" A woman's blonde hair flared, followed by a man's blue jeans, a plaid shirt, and so on. When the stench of frying flesh grew more nauseating than a week-old bucket of KFC, I held my nostrils shut to avoid upchucking my breakfast.

At the lake, Calhoun and his crew used ropes to lower Arthur and the Underwoods to the bottom of a grave. Seeing those three lying in the dirt saddened me. Art's death, in particular, hit me extra hard.

Under the hickory's shady leaves, Cooper called upon us all to speak. Alice praised the Underwoods' bravery. I shared how I missed Arthur. Jules appeared bereft, but she didn't utter a word.

Captain Calhoun and Lieutenant Spalding walked into town to confirm whether the fighting had indeed ended. Jittery Jim and Krabby Karen borrowed bicycles to go back to McGill's Hill. Ardy muttered, "Good riddance to bad rubbish," as the Fullers pedaled away. Cooper, Regina, Bonnie, and Gage had kinfolk to attend to.

After tomato and cheese sandwiches for lunch, Olivia, Alice, Jules, and I went to catch some z's on the flagstone patio. The chaise lounges were comfortable, but I couldn't help but fixate on what Jules now calls the "Hanging Tree." I finally drifted off, only to jolt upright when Olivia screamed in her sleep, "Don't you fucking touch me!"

Alice, also wide awake, proposed taking the boat for a spin. I offered myself for rowing duties. Alice and Olivia sat behind me in the stern seat, with Jules on the bow. As we glided over the lake's glassy surface, the tranquility of the scene clashed with the horrors we had endured. Birds soared above, and fish swam below as if nothing terrible has ever happened on this blue orb we call Earth. Diary, I've paddled canoes and kayaks before, but rowing a boat takes some getting used to since, like life, you can't see where you're heading.

I noticed Olivia's despondency and assured her that everything would be fine. I wasn't overly surprised to learn the heart-wrenching truth. Corbin Holt had permanently subtracted her mom and dad from the family equation, leaving Olivia with zero kin. She vowed never to return to McGill's Hill. I empathized with the teenager and shared the sorrow of losing my own parents at her age.

Tears flowed freely as Alice and I extended heartfelt invitations for Olivia to come stay with us.

The other desirable news? I figured out how to turn the boat around to get us home.

Later in the day, Ardy slid into his work boots with an air of determination. "No more putting it off. Let's see what remains of our town."

The six of us approached the once-lively downtown. All the wanton destruction and senseless violence disgusted me. Bodies littered the streets, grim tokens of man's inhumanity to man.

Each fallen animal increased my panic. *Is that Oscar?*

The mournful melody of "What a Friend We Have in Jesus" reached our ears. Four somber men, three singing and one playing the trumpet, carted the dead away using a rig harnessed to an old black mule.

After spending most of my time in Hayneville locked inside the county courthouse, I felt no displeasure seeing our iron cage squashed flatter than an IHOP pancake.

Pearl raced to her place of business with Alice on her heels.

Ardy stopped in the parking lot, his eyes welling up and his throat muscles tightening. "My sister invested so much of herself into that market. We haven't the resources to restore any of this."

I patted his arm. "Pearl's a born survivor. She'll come up with a plan."

Pearl sifted through the wreckage, her search yielding little of value. I rescued a teddy bear resting between blackened sardine cans. Theodore had singed fur, but his satin I LOVE YOU heart shined bright red. I gave the stuffed animal to Olivia.

Ardy reassured his sister. "Our town can be rebuilt!"

Pearl's outcry startled Ardy. "McGill's Hill is ours for the taking! I shall crush anybody that stands in my way!"

I have to admit, that woman's got bigger balls than any of the men I know.

Alice – July 4, 2029

7/4/2029

I reflect upon the "good old days," realizing how much things have changed. We used to have eleven U.S. federal holidays. Americans anticipated this time off, especially those precious three-day weekends when we escaped to the mountains or the beach.

In order by date, you had:

New Year's Day
Martin Luther King Jr. Day
Washington's Birthday
Memorial Day
Juneteenth
Independence Day
Labor Day
Columbus Day
Veterans Day
Thanksgiving Day
Christmas Day

No one celebrates any of these holidays anymore. The atmosphere is devoid of the excitement that once filled us with joy. The sights, sounds, and smells of families picnicking in the park are distant memories.

This sunny Fourth of July commemorates the day the former United States declared independence from the grip of mad King George. I wish this day of remembrance brought back fond thoughts of my parents taking me somewhere special. Perhaps we'd embark on a ferryboat cruise across the Hudson River, followed by an elevator ride to the top of the Empire State Building. Or, if we had to stay nearby, watching the lions gobble raw meat at the Zoological Park could be educational. How about going to Garden State Plaza to catch a movie? *Transformers*, anyone? I'd even see *Ratatouille*. The dazzling fireworks display at Memorial Field would be the perfect finale for a fun-packed day.

Alas, none of these Fourth of July dreams ever materialized, not so much as a twenty-minute jaunt to my grandparents' house to grill hotdogs and lick ice cream cones. Instead, Richard always spent the morning on the links with his golfing buddies and the afternoon at the Arcola Country Club, downing martinis with women he shared beds with but not wedding rings. Barbara also wasted the holiday drinking. In the kitchen. Alone.

Until I mustered up the courage to leave home, I spent much of my youth in my bedroom with my closest friends—a pile of library books. Without the company of Jane Austen and Toni Morrison, I'd have slit my wrists before jumping in front of an express train with a plastic bag pulled over my head.

Everything changed when Kenneth arrived. Resolute not to become my parents, I turned major holidays, Thanksgiving and Christmas, into grand celebrations. Minor occasions like Mother's Day, Father's Day, Groundhog Day, Festivus, and Kwanzaa became cherished rituals. When times were good, Peter and I observed them all. Halloween, in particular, held a special place in my husband's heart. One year, he spent a small fortune on a twelve-foot-tall skeleton to outdo the neighbors.

This stopped when an unwanted guest entered our household. Our son got sick. Really sick. Kenny had pulled through COVID-19 with no more than a fever and a cough, but Crunk landed the little guy in the hospital on a ventilator. And, as you know, few walk away from COVID-24 once they're infected. Kenneth died five years ago today. July Fourth is my least favorite holiday.

During breakfast, Julie noticed I wasn't eating. "Alice, are you feeling okay?"

"I'm just tired." I faked a smile and scooped poached eggs onto my plate. "Didn't sleep well because of the heat." At 8 a.m., the outdoor thermometer already registered ninety-one degrees. No lie there.

We devoted the early hours to calling for Oscar and cleaning Pearl's property. We swept up any broken glass and sealed the window openings with cardboard. However, the bullet holes in the exterior siding were not easily patchable.

Julie and I finished swabbing the bloody garage floor. We walked to the lakeshore to lay fresh trout lilies on the newly dug gravesite.

Julie touched my arm. "Alice, unless I'm mistaken, today is the Fourth of July. Did something happen on this day?"

I sat beneath the hickory tree, the peeling bark jabbing me in the back. "I had a son. Kenneth would be ten years old."

"Is today his birthday?"

"No, it's the day he passed away."

Julie joined me on the grass. "I am so sorry, Alice."

"The doctors couldn't save him."

"During the pandemic?"

"Yes. My husband, Peter, left me a month after the funeral. We fought over who was responsible for Kenneth's death. It tore us apart."

Julie took my hands in hers and shut her eyes. Her lips moved as if in worship or quiet consultation with someone unseen—was it Jules? Julie loosened her grasp as she opened her eyes. "Did I tell you that I have a twin sister?"

"Yes, Julia. The state separated you after your mother and father were in a car crash?"

Julie wiped the perspiration from her brow. "An intoxicated driver, Robert McKenna, drove down the exit ramp onto the wrong side of the highway, causing a head-on collision. Julia and I were trying on our Christmas gifts when the police notified us of the accident. Our parents' minivan caught fire."

"That's horrible! And this occurred on Christmas day?"

"Christmas morning. Mom and Dad asked us to go with them to bring their elderly friend to our house for dinner. I wanted to see if my new clothes fit me, so I convinced Julia to stay behind. Our parents left later than planned. My selfishness was the reason they never came home."

"Julie, you were only sixteen. Their accident wasn't your fault! All teenagers crave independence."

She smoothed the maroon letters on her too-tight LMU SCHOOL OF FILM AND TELEVISION pullover. "I was wearing this sweatshirt when the cops knocked on the door."

"Why didn't the authorities put you and Julia with the same caregivers?"

"Remember how you said Peter blamed you for your son's illness? My sister held me responsible for what happened to our parents. Julia requested for the dependency judge to place me in a different foster home. She threatened to run away if they didn't comply."

Julie and I have both suffered crippling losses, though my grief hasn't driven me to spawn an invisible friend. "Does Jules ever talk about Julia to you? They haven't met, right?"

"No, Jules entered the picture after Julia left." She picked up a flat-shaped rock and skimmed it across the water. The stone skipped five times before sinking. Julie leaned closer, her voice dropping to a whisper. "Jules is afraid I'd abandon her if I found Julia."

I cupped my fingers to my mouth. "Would you?"

"Did you love your husband even after he left you?"

"I had mixed feelings—I became a real mental case. The guilt consumed me entirely. Should I have forced a playful five-year-old boy to constantly wear a mask and gloves? Although COVID-24 vaccines for children remained in phase 3 clinical trials, I could have enrolled him. And why didn't I drive my son to the doctor the day he showed symptoms? When Peter emptied our bank accounts, I got wind he was shacked up with a coworker, a woman I had welcomed into our home multiple times. My affection for him quickly degraded into hatred."

"Is Peter still alive?"

I shrugged. "I quit thinking about that prick years ago."

Liar, liar, pants on fire.

During the noon-time meal, Ardy discussed organizing another town gathering. "We'll perform a head count and speak to the current state of Hayneville."

Pearl rapped her knuckles on the kitchen table. "What of my intention to shift the survivors to McGill's Hill?"

"Just two days have passed since the attack." Ardy buttered a second slice of bread. "Bringing up such a life-changing decision while we're still grieving isn't wise. Plus, I haven't had the chance to evaluate McGill's Hill."

Olivia's arm sprang up. "I'll go," she gestured at Julie and me, "if they come with me."

Jim and Karen Fuller hadn't yet returned the bicycles, so the four of us (including Jules, as this is the way my brain functions now) walked for two hours in the afternoon sun. The landscape transitioned from charred stumps to flourishing foliage with every mile we traveled north. We took regular hydration breaks under any available shade.

Beneath the BP gasoline station's green and yellow canopy, Olivia told us how she grew up in a town with few people of color. "I attended McGill Academy from preschool to sixth grade when—"

"Segregation school!" Jules blurted. (I've yet to break down Julie's alter ego to Olivia.)

Olivia nodded. "You're right, Julie. Only two Black students were enrolled in our school: Tennie and Declan. I used to hang out with Tennie after class. Her mom sorted mail at the post office."

Ardy said Hayneville had a thousand citizens prior to 2020. The coronavirus outbreak and Election Day decimated this number by two-thirds. "What's McGill's Hill's present population?"

"Our town had a hundred locals. During school hours, McGill Academy attracted twice that amount. After doomsday, our community expanded as families from other regions sought refuge here."

"White flight!" Jules flapped her arms. "White people fleeing from Black areas."

Olivia winced at the uninhibited outburst of animosity. "My guess is McGill's Hill's population is similar to that of Hayneville. Before all the fighting, of course."

On South Broad Street, we passed the plantation house where the sheriff met his end. I wondered if we could recover Wilbur's remains for Charlene. Soon, the largest facility in town came into view—McGill Academy.

I surveyed the rows of classrooms and the boxy structure I assumed to be a gymnasium. "Is this still a school?"

"It was," Olivia replied, her wistful tone tinged with pride. She singled out a building overlooking an overgrown baseball field. "All the kids, including myself, were taught in that room. We focused on the three Rs—reading, writing, and 'rithmetic. No history or foreign languages, and very little science. Headmaster Strauss claimed I have a tenth-grade education. I read any textbooks I can get my hands on from cover to cover."

Julie gestured to the vast campus. "These schoolrooms are perfect for housing Hayneville's homeless."

"That's a terrific idea!" I scanned the area. Hayneville had a small downtown. As far as I could see, McGill's Hill had no businesses at all. "Olivia, where do people shop?"

"Before Election Day, we drove twenty minutes to Montgomery. Now that Hayneville and Fort Deposit are burned to the ground, I don't know where the residents can buy provisions."

An older gentleman approached us, prompting Julie to draw her Sig Sauer. "Olivia!" he called out. "Is the fighting over? Are you all right?"

"As well as can be expected, Mr. Baskin. How is Mrs. Baskin?"

His eyes were glued to the cocked pistol in Julie's dark hand. "My wife is terrified that Hayneville is coming to wipe us out."

"Corbin Holt is gone," Olivia stated matter-of-factly. "I helped stretch his neck."

The man struggled to select his words. "Oh. That's. . . ."

Olivia unfolded a slip of paper. "I listed everyone who conspired with that psychopath. As you can see, Mr. Baskin, your name is not here. I've scratched off half the raiders. Your input is required for the rest."

"We shouldn't be out in the open." Baskin crossed the street to a grand plantation house. "Bessy!" he hollered from the front porch. "We have visitors!"

I clutched my Glock, uncertain if "visitors" was a code word for something sinister.

A woman brandishing a long knife squinted out of an upstairs window. "Earl, who's that with you?"

"Olivia Dawson and her two friends. May I ask your names?"

"I'm Alice, and she's Julie."

Earl beckoned for his wife to come down. "Darling, can you fix tea for our guests?"

We sat at the kitchen table with our backs to the wallpapered wall. Bessy placed a kettle on a camping stove. The hissing gas triggered unwanted flashbacks to Birmingham.

Earl plucked a pencil from a A DAY WITHOUT COFFEE IS LIKE A DAY WITHOUT HOPE cup. "Let's see your list."

Bessy's eyes narrowed in suspicion as she peered over his shoulder. "Why are Arnold Baxter and the other names crossed off?"

Julie tapped the paper with her finger. "These people invaded Hayneville and are now dead. We need to determine which of your neighbors colluded with Corbin Holt and where they are now—alive, wounded, or deceased."

Bessy gasped. "So you can shoot them?"

Olivia's face hardened, aging her beyond her sixteen years. "Do you have a problem with that, Mrs. Baskin?"

I opened my hands in an offer of peace. "Ardy Jackson simply wants to talk with those who participated in the aggression. It'll benefit everybody if they come forward willingly."

The shrill whistle of the teakettle startled Bessy. She set five delicate teacups onto saucers and placed them on the silk tablecloth. Her hands shook as she poured steaming hot tea into each one. "Oh dear, I forgot the hoecakes!" Bessy rose from her ball and claw chair, returning with fried cornmeal cakes arranged on a china dish. "My apologies for the lack of syrup and butter. We used to buy groceries at Pearl's Trading Post. It was so sad to hear about her store."

Earl circled one name on the paper, added three more, and x-ed two of those off. "That's all that I know of." He slid the sheet toward his wife. "Darling, are there any others still in town?"

Bessy studied the lengthy list. "Althea told me her son is missing. And this one here is on his last leg." She drew a question mark next to Rufus Aiken and put a line through Sterling Walton Jr.

I took a sip from the floral teacup. "Mrs. Baskin, this tea is delicious! What's in it?"

"Thank you, dear. It's wild chamomile with a pinch of rose hips. Pearl gave me the herbs to plant in my garden. Alice, didn't you work at her market? I think I've seen you there."

"Yes, Mrs. Baskin, for a short while." I motioned at the list in her hand. "By the way, how many people live in McGill's Hill?"

She looked into the distance, calculating in her mind. "We had two hundred and thirty. Now, I'd say we're down to one hundred fifty." Liquid shame trickled down her face. "Not all these folks were evil. Corbin Holt was a fiend."

Olivia's cheeks flushed. "Then why didn't you and Mr. Baskin rescue me? You used to play gin rummy with my parents!"

Visibly shaken, Earl pushed his antique chair back and stepped outside. I watched from the kitchen window as the once-wealthy man got on his hands and knees to weed the garden.

A leaden lethargy replaced our animated chitchat as we returned to Pearl's house. I felt no satisfaction in seeing the disgrace etched into those old faces.

After dinner, Ardy inspected Olivia's modified "Invaders" list. His interest switched to disgruntlement at counting the number of McGillians he had considered close friends or at least benevolent acquaintances. "Eighty-two dead, twenty-five injured, and eight unaccounted for. Alice, how many people did Mrs. Baskin say are left in her town?"

"A hundred and fifty, including the wounded. Her husband figured that twenty more live in rural isolation."

Ardy pinched his stubbled chin. "We won't know the amount in Hayneville until the town meeting."

I invited Julie to speak. "Julie has a suggestion regarding our housing shortage."

Julie swiveled to the side. "Jules actually came up with it."

Her response took me by surprise, and I had to correct myself. "*Jules* has a solution for our homeless."

"Great, Jules!" Ardy exclaimed. "Let's hear it!"

Julie's intonations and mannerisms changed, captivating everyone's attention. Jules looked so. . .content? Jubilant, even? "I can't take full credit. Julie and I put our heads together. McGill Academy is empty. Anyone in Hayneville who needs a place to live can move into the classrooms. And, from what I've been told, the town's water tower is still operational!"

Olivia explained how solar panels powered the water station pumps. "The waste flows into underground septic tanks. Beds and extra clothing might be a complication, though."

I gazed out the dining room window, my mind wandering to the Trading Post, where I had spent so many enjoyable hours. "What about food?"

Pearl spoke to herself as if she was thinking out loud. "The fire destroyed most of our crops. However, fresh nutrients have enriched the soil. The town stored seeds in airtight drums at various locations. All but the southernmost containers are unharmed. If the farmers plant immediately, we can harvest vegetables and fruits in three months. For now, rationing our supplies is mandatory."

Ardy reclined in his easy chair. “I’m encouraged after hearing your ideas on restoring normalcy. Let’s call it a night.”

Julie – July 4, 2029

7/4/2029

The morning slid by in a flurry of activity at Pearl's house as we searched for Oscar and cleared Corbin Holt's mess. The blood-splattered floors presented a challenge to scrub without the help of Mr. Clean and his bulging muscles.

I remarked to Alice that she hadn't touched her breakfast, gently probing further as we washed the gore off our shoes with lake water. She confided that her son, Kenneth, had succumbed to Crunk five years ago on this very day, July 4th. Alice feels at fault for the way she handled her boy's illness. Sadly, her hubby, Peter the Prick, left her alone to deal with her heartache.

The conversation shifted to what had happened to my mother and father on Christmas morning. Apart from Julia and Jules, not a living soul knows how I refused to go with my parents to pick up Mrs. Sullivan. My disobedience led to their car ending up in the path of Robert McKenna's oncoming headlights.

I reassured Alice that Kenny's death wasn't negligence, pointing out that billions of others were lost to the pandemic as well. She accepted the reason I wear my Loyola Marymount University sweatshirt as penance. I am well aware that this filthy old rag is repulsive, but wearing sackcloth is my way of repenting for my sins.

Alice inquired whether Jules ever mentions Julia. I wasn't sure. Maybe in years past? Then came the killer question: Would I be free to leave Jules if I found Julia?

At lunchtime, Pearl resubmitted her plan to relocate Hayneville's displaced to McGill's Hill. Ardy proposed another town assembly, but he simultaneously did not want to overwhelm the attendees until we had more concrete information. Olivia volunteered to report on McGill's Hill's housing situation and wanted Alice, Jules, and me to accompany her. With the "Leaving Jules" dilemma at the top of my mind, this diversion arrived at the perfect time.

We walked at a snail's pace up the 97 in the sweltering heat. Every hundred steps, I'd call into the woods, "Oscar! Come here, boy!"

Jules and I are losing hope.

Olivia shared that her school, McGill Academy, had few Black students.

Naturally, Jules couldn't hold her tongue. "White supremacists!" "Gentrification!" To steady my nerves, I envisioned Corbin Holt's swollen corpse swinging from the Hanging Tree.

We entered McGill's Hill. Jules studied the numerous buildings scattered across the McGill Academy campus and held up her palm. Her poised recommendation stunned me. "The people of Hayneville can fill these vacant classrooms."

Is Jules finally coming out of her shell?

A White senior citizen appeared in the distance. Olivia recognized him as I instinctively reached for my gun. Earl led our group to a stately plantation house where his wife, Bessy, greeted us with the biggest carving knife I've ever seen.

I have to give Olivia kudos. She's prepared a list of the McGillians who were influential in Corbin Holt's rise to power.

Earl and Bessy read the names, drawing lines through the deceased. Olivia totaled the number of living and injured individuals to one hundred and fifty, incensed that none of her neighbors attempted to free her from Holt's grasp. I don't blame the girl for itching to strike every name off that list.

Alice raved about Bessy's "flavorful" cup of tea. Those homegrown herbs tasted way too bitter for me.

The slog back to Pearl's felt endless. The others seemed pooped or lost in thought. As for me, the soles of my feet hurt from treading on blacktop hot enough to fry an egg.

After supper, Ardy assessed Olivia's DEADER THAN DEAD, ALL FUCKED UP, or ALIVE AND DANGEROUS list. The number of people who had looked Hayneville's council chairperson in the eye but secretly wanted to stab him in the back was astounding!

Pearl spoke about farming. Nobody would starve if farmers planted seeds immediately.

Alice announced I had a brilliant idea to assist those who lost homes in the blaze. While she kindly gave me the credit, I redirected the recognition to Jules.

I admired how Ardy treated Jules with respect, considering that she'd been nothing but mean to him so far. "Tell us, Jules!"

When Jules smiled back, she appeared to be an entirely different person. "The good news is we can repurpose the classrooms, gym, and administrative offices at McGill Academy into living spaces. And with the water tower running on solar energy, access to drinking water won't be an obstacle."

Holy crap! Jules is reminding me of. . .me.

Meeting over, we hit the hay.

P.S. Though I do feel a part of this "family," I'll never find peace until I'm with my sister. Julia, where are you?

Alice - July 5, 2029

7/5/2029

I woke up at 8:45 a.m. Julie no longer rested on the queen-sized bed beside me. Olivia wasn't in the next-door bedroom either. I went downstairs to find the kitchen, living, and dining areas unoccupied. The door to Pearl's master suite remained closed. Ardy is bunking in the guesthouse now that his home can fit in an ashtray. I grabbed a hunk of stale bread, poured myself a glass of tap water, and walked into the backyard.

Julie called from the lake, "Hey, sleepyhead!"

Olivia smiled and waved.

A dog barked and dashed up the hill.

"Oscar!" I squatted to comb my fingers through his matted fur. "Where were you, boy?"

Julie laughed joyfully. (Or was that Jules? It's getting tougher and tougher to tell.) "I heard a noise this morning—Oscar scratching at the back door! Aside from sore paws, he seems fine."

We settled by the water's edge, the sun still too low for the green umbrella to provide UV protection. Today promised to be another scorcher, but sunburn and heat exhaustion were the last things on my mind. For the moment, we were together, and that was enough.

Olivia's spirits had lifted. "What's up for today?"

"We'll find out when Pearl and Ardy rise and shine." Completely bushed, I needed a day off. Better yet, I deserved an entire month off on a Fijian beach. However, with Hayneville in shambles, I knew that lounging in the shade of a palm tree with a pitcher of kava and a good book was just a pipe dream.

Ardy shuffled down the slope wearing blue shorts and a bold DON'T MESS WITH ALABAMA T-shirt. "Mornin', y'all." He spotted Oscar on my lap and couldn't contain his excitement. "Oh, my lord! Look who's back!" The dog trotted up to Ardy, showering him with affectionate licks.

Jules stood up. "What's the plan, Bossman?"

"Got any ideas, Jules?" (Ardy is more proficient than me at ascertaining who he's speaking with.)

"There is only one thing to do." She sliced her fingers across her throat. "Cross off some lines on Olivia's list."

Ardy raised his palm. "Captain Calhoun and Lieutenant Spalding are developing—"

Jules cut him short. "Let's find the attackers before they slip away!"

Ardy sighed. "Would that really be so bad?"

Jules' jaw clenched.

Olivia held up a sheet of paper. "Here's an updated tally. After accounting for the deceased, I added home addresses for the wounded. That leaves us with Corbin Holt's inner circle. Those assholes might have skipped town, but I suspect they're nearby."

Jules and I exclaimed simultaneously, "Where?"

Olivia's eyes gleamed. "Something had been nagging me from the moment we left McGill's Hill. Remember the one-room schoolhouse at McGill Academy? Corbin ordered the instructors to stay at home during the time my parents went missing, and he moved me into his house."

"Why?" I asked. "What reason did he give?"

"Corbin claimed a new COVID mutation was mushrooming throughout Alabama. 'I shall do everything in my power to protect our children!' Yesterday, I noticed trampled grass around the classroom's front steps. No one should have been in that building for at least two months."

Ardy arched his eyebrow. "Olivia, that's not much to go on."

"There's more. All the window blinds were shut. Headmaster Strauss loved lots of sunlight. He believed vitamin D grew strong minds and bodies."

The sound of squeaking planks caught our attention. "Welcome home, Oscar!" Pearl strolled along the wooden dock, holding a coffee cup. "Ooh, I haven't slept that long since. . .I dunno when. Are you discussing dietary supplements?"

Ardy angled the umbrella against the rising sun. "Olivia thinks Corbin Holt's surviving men are at McGill Academy. Holt had closed the school, warning of a supposed new virus strain. But one classroom looks recently occupied."

Pearl snuggled the squirming pup. "We'll tell Captain Calhoun."

Julie (is she back?) stroked the scar on her cheek. "Should we get him involved?"

Pearl blinked twice. "Why wouldn't we? With Sheriff King gone, Calvin and Randy keep the peace."

Olivia urged Julie to speak. "There is a name on Olivia's 'unaccounted for' list that requires," she touched the facial mark again, "special consideration."

The young girl's knuckles whitened as she clenched her fists. "Tyrell Ryker is a rapist. He needs to pay for what he did to me."

Pearl kissed the top of Oscar's orange head. "The hunger for revenge is consuming your soul from the inside out. Do you really want that man's blood on your hands?"

Olivia stared each of us down. "If none of you help me, I will find Ryker on my own."

Our firearms are cleaned and loaded. Five borrowed bicycles lean against the side of the garage. We should be in McGill's Hill thirty minutes from now. Please, God, let us all return unharmed.

9:30 p.m. My heartbeat regulates as the adrenaline dissipates from my bloodstream, yet my fingers won't stop quivering. Ardy and Pearl are with me in her kitchen. Julie and Olivia are upstairs. Thank God everyone in our group is safe.

The bike ride to McGill's Hill took longer than expected. A thorn punctured my tire, forcing me to dismount every few miles to use Ardy's hand pump. Despite the delay, the western sky still held remnants of a fiery sunset by the time we reached McGill Academy.

Our squad crept across the weedy baseball field. Olivia pointed out the room where she thought Tyrell Ryker and his accomplices were hiding. Pearl and I positioned ourselves as snipers on opposite sides of the small building. I scaled a ladder onto the gymnasium's rooftop, fearful I'd crash through the crumbling surface. Pearl's rifle barrel protruded from the third-base dugout.

Our plan was simple yet risky—Smoke 'em Out. Here's what we were going to do:

1. Olivia pours kerosene on the classroom's rear wall.
2. Julie lights the fuel, and they fall back to a dumpster enclosure.
3. Ardy shouts, "Come out with your hands up!"
4. Pearl and I cover everybody from a distance.
5. Holt's men walk outside peacefully, and we tie them up.
6. TBD.

What actually happened?

Olivia splashed a gallon of lamp oil along the modular classroom's foundation. Julie's Zippo lighter failed to spark, and nobody had thought about bringing matches. So, instead of the "burn 'em out, buckaroo" scenario we had so carefully planned, Olivia and Julie threw rocks at the windows.

Ardy screamed, "This is the police! We know you're in there. If you do what we say, you will not be hurt!"

Silence for eight seconds.

"I'm coming outside!" a voice rasped through holes in the glass. The door opened a crack.

Somebody I couldn't get a bead on yelled, "Drop your weapons!"

The door slammed shut. Julie and Olivia started shooting at something. Pearl's rifle flashed twice. I joined in by firing four rounds into the entrance.

Silence.

The hoarse-sounding guy waved an American flag from the window. "I am unarmed!"

Ardy called, "Is anybody else inside with you?"

"Only me in here. Henry went to take a piss."

"Then come out slowly. Put both hands up!"

The bullet-ridden door swung open, and a white-haired man staggered down the steps. Olivia and Julie steered him out of my line of sight. Pearl emerged from the dugout, prompting me to climb down from the roof and hurry over.

Ardy exited the classroom. "All clear!" He rolled a lifeless body onto its back. No gun. No knife. "Is this the man who assaulted you?"

Olivia inspected the bloodied face. "Ryker had long hair."

Ardy dragged the graying man to stand in front of her. "How about him?"

She shook her head. "He's way too old."

"Were these two men associated with Corbin Holt?"

"No, Ardy. I've never seen either of them before."

I just left Olivia's bedroom. Julie is staying behind to comfort her. All I hear are the wails of penitence.

Julie – July 5, 2029

7/5/2029

Barking awoke me. Jules opened the back door, and Oscar padded in as if nothing had happened. I hugged our furry companion as tight as I could, whispering sweet nothings into his ear. Jules playfully scolded Oscar for causing us to worry, then fed him a big bowl of meat scraps. I'm still emotional despite the immense sense of relief.

Olivia joined us by the pool. Oscar rolled onto his back for a belly rub. As Jules wandered off, Olivia and I walked to the dock. The morning luminescence painted the landscape with a soft glow. Doves cooed, and carp broke the water's surface—representations of nature at its finest.

Olivia's head tilted upward, her blonde curls cascading over her shoulders. "Do you remember how airplanes sounded?"

"Ugh! Never a peaceful moment with those dirty birds. The propeller-driven planes droned around like giant bumblebees sniffing for sunflowers. And those mile-high jets polluting the skies? But the helicopters had to be the noisiest of them all. An Apache flew over my head a year ago in Boston."

"Julie, did you see the rockets on Election Day?"

"The ICBMs? I lived in Ithaca, two hundred miles from New York City, Philadelphia, and Washington D.C. Jules and I felt the ground shake three times, like massive earthquakes." A tadpole swam past, the amphibian's slimy body resembling a jumbo spermatozoon. "We ran for the hills, convinced the world was ending."

"Why do you think they stopped launching?" When Olivia yawned, I glimpsed the little red dangler in the back of her throat—another tadpole.

"Are you referring to the Russians, the Chinese, or us Americans?"

"Uh-hum." The girl wiped the soot from her legs. "None of the politicians did us any favors. Why didn't their militaries finish the job?"

I thought about Election Day, unsure whether I felt happy or sad to have survived. "Maybe the generals mutinied. Only an omnipresent being can answer that. 'The eyes of the Lord are everywhere, watching the sinful and the good.' The Big Cheese knew exactly what was happening down in those missile silos and still let those half-wits push the launch buttons."

"My mother and father often quarreled over God's existence. Dad said God doesn't give a damn about us. Mom swore God was dead."

"We're still here, Olivia. But, yeah, both your parents could win that debate."

She changed the conversation to a subject of a more disturbing nature. "Ardy called you Jules last night. Is that your middle name or just a nickname?"

"Neither. I am Julie. And Jules is. . .Jules." *Why couldn't I answer her simple question?* I changed the topic. "Olivia, how old were you on Election Day?"

"Eleven. I remember that Tuesday all too well. My mom and dad stayed glued to the television. They were watching. . .CCN?"

"CNN. CNN, MSNBC, and FOX were the main cable news stations."

"My parents, all worked up, dismissed me whenever I asked questions. Uncle Jeremy and Aunt Adelaide came to our house. My cousin, Caroline, went to college in Los Angeles. Aunty called her dorm but received messages that the telephone circuits were fried. When the government announced that the radiation levels had decreased, my aunt and uncle drove to the West Coast."

"Did they find your cousin?"

Olivia slumped. "Nobody heard from them again. My mother learned that her two younger brothers had also died and completely lost it. She'd stare out the window for hours, mumbling their names. Dad took Mom to a clinic in Montgomery. Even with a pocketful of pills, she was never the same."

"How did you end up in Corbin Holt's custody?"

"Chief Perry suggested I stay with a neighbor after my parents disappeared. 'Olivia, the department is doing everything possible to track down your mother and father. Can you think of any reason why they left town?' The chief dropped me off at the Palmers, and a week later, Corbin knocked on their door. 'Mr. Palmer, we're concerned that someone might harm Olivia. I have my own security detail. She'll be safer living with me.' The Palmers were happy to send me packing. Corbin forbade me from ever leaving the plantation house. 'For your safety,' he said."

"Alice told me how they attempted to assassinate Holt in McGill's Hill."

"A night I wish I could forget. After Corbin shot Sheriff King in the head, he and his cronies got blind drunk. Even with my bedroom door locked, one bashed his way in." Olivia shut her eyes. "I'm so ashamed."

I embraced the sobbing teenager. Oscar rested his snout on her lap. "There was nothing you could do. Those wicked men are dead now."

"No." Olivia wiped her face. "Not all of them."

"What do you mean?"

"Mr. Baskin circled a name on my list as 'unaccounted for.'" She grimaced. "Tyrell Ryker."

"The man that assaulted you is still in McGill's Hill?"

Olivia shrugged. "Julie, what will Ardy do with the people who attacked Hayneville?"

"We'll have to ask. Did Tyrell Ryker reside in your town, or did he arrive with Corbin Holt?"

"I knew everybody growing up. Keeping track became impossible with all the transients streaming in and out."

"Olivia, do you want us to help you find Ryker?"

I heard heavy breathing and spun around. Jules stood on the dock, swinging a rusty machete.

A few hours later, Alice came trudging from the house, her fatigue somersaulting to elation as she realized Oscar had safely returned.

After our talk, Olivia appeared less tense and more eager to know the Jackson's plan for the day. As if on cue, Ardy came out of the guesthouse and ran over to Oscar. You can judge a man's character by how well he handles dog slobber. The big guy accidentally sat on a splinter sticking out of the dock, and I had to choke back a giggle.

Jules was raring to round up Corbin Holt's co-conspirators. "Those murderers are getting away!"

Ardy said Captain Calhoun and Lieutenant Spalding were determining the best way to manage the situation. "Enough people have been hurt."

Olivia shared her corrected McGill's Hill list. She believed that Holt's men were sheltering at McGill Academy, evidenced by the footmarks outside her old classroom and the closed window shades.

Pearl came down to the water, thrilled to reunite with Oscar. Ardy relayed Olivia's theory about the gang's location. His sister also advised us to keep Captain Calhoun informed.

Olivia permitted me to speak. "One of Olivia's abusers, Tyrell Ryker, may be at the school. If so, he must be punished for what he did to her."

Pearl's efforts to deter the girl from "taking an eye for an eye" fell on deaf ears.

Olivia shook her fist in defiance. "I'll kill that piece of shit myself!"

Jules and I are upstairs, in Olivia's bedroom. We've returned from McGill's Hill. The poor girl is not doing well. Nor am I. We made a huge mistake rushing to McGill Academy with no forethought.

I took another innocent life.

Henry's chest had more holes in it than a slice of Swiss cheese. Any of our bullets could have stopped his heart—except for Ardy's because his back was turned to the weaponless man. Nevertheless, I must shoulder the blame. Why wasn't I more cautious? Why didn't I slow things down?

Ralph informed us that he and Henry had been on the move since Election Day. They traversed the country together, working in various towns as handymen, hopscotching north in the summer heat and south in the winter cold. Grievously, both men lost their families to the coronavirus in early 2024.

The stranger's voice commanding us to discard our guns echoes in my ears. I see Ardy's hands raised in surrender as the shadowy figure draws closer. Olivia confirmed his identity.

"That's him. Ryker." I counted nine shots. Bam! Bam, bam, bam, bam. . .bam, bam, bam, bam! Who fired the first shot? Was it me?

Jules examined my Sig Sauer P320. Only four rounds remain in the ten-round magazine.

Ralph pleaded for answers as he turned Henry's pockets inside out. "Why did you murder my friend?" He dumped his traveling partner's knapsack onto the grass.

Pearl transferred Henry's belongings to Ralph's bag and pointed northwest. "There's a town within walking distance. You'll be in White Hall by morning if you leave now."

Alice – July 6, 2029

7/6/2029

Pearl and Ardy left early to attend meetings at the still-standing Presbyterian Church. They first met with farmers to schedule seed plantings and then with carpenters to coordinate a street-by-street damage assessment. Once Ardy shares the survey results with the other council members, he will hold a town get-together to weigh the pros and cons of moving Hayneville's surviving population to McGill's Hill.

Oscar and I played fetch on the back lawn. The sound of clanging pans drew me to the kitchen, where Julie was cooking cheese omelets on the stove while Olivia stared out the open window.

"How did everyone sleep?" My question sounded stupid even to me, but the intolerable silence ached like a cavity that needed filling.

Julie slid a yellow half-moon from the pan, twisted a pepper mill, and placed the speckled plate before Olivia. "Like a baby on codeine. And you?"

I chuckled. "Me too. I dreamed I hit the jackpot but couldn't decide what color Ferrari to get. Such a nightmare!"

"Rosso Corsa is my preference. You can't go wrong with traditional red." Julie handed me an omelet. "Be sure to order the retractable hardtop option for summer beach cruisin'."

I tapped Olivia's arm. "What would you buy if you won a billion dollars?"

The girl glared at her cooked eggs. "A time machine."

Julie sat across from us. "Wise choice. I'd set the date to the exact moment Robert McKenna took his first gulp of air and then jam my big, fat thumb down his tiny, little throat."

Olivia's eyes sparked with interest. "Who's Robert McKenna?"

Julie stabbed her fork into her spongy omelet and spoke with her mouth full. "The drunken fool who killed my parents." She tapped her temple. "Messed me up big time." Julie grinned at the empty chair. "As you might have noticed."

Olivia pushed away her untouched food. "I am losing my mind thinking about that man—Henry. What am I supposed to do now?"

Jules shoved the dish back. "Eat what Julie made for you. Life goes on whether you like it or not."

"But I feel—"

Jules' plate flew over Olivia's head, shattering against the cabinets. Yellow free-range eggs and orange cheddar cheese clung to the white enamel. "You haven't even experienced real pain."

"Jules!" I held up my hands. "Get ahold of yourself! She's just a kid!"

Oscar ran around the table, barking.

Julie rose to the surface, her voice shaking with remorse. "Wh-what happened? You know I'd never intentionally harm either of you!" Her arms stretched out to us, seeking forgiveness.

Confusion surged through Olivia's face. She grabbed a cleaver. "Who the hell is 'Jules'?"

"Calm down!" I hooked Olivia's free arm and towed her outdoors.

When we reached the pool, she angrily pulled away from me. "Take your hands off me!"

"Have you heard of dissociative identity disorder?"

Olivia swiveled to see if Julie had followed us. "Uh-uh."

"Julie and Jules share the same head—disconnected personalities, each experiencing separate thoughts and emotions."

Olivia looked at me uncertainly. "Alice, are you making this up?"

"No, I wish I was." Julie watched us from the dining room window. "Ardy did some research. DID is incredibly rare. He thinks Julie created an imaginary friend, Jules, to help her cope with the loss of her parents. They died in a violent automobile accident, and Julie's twin sister, Julia, blamed her for it. Julia then left Julie to fend for herself."

"Man, that's—" Olivia's bewilderment grew. "Sweet Jesus, how does that even work? Do Julie and Jules know about each other?"

"Julie speaks to Jules as if she sees and hears her, but I sense that Julie suspects their relationship isn't normal. Still, I'm no expert. She needs professional psychological counseling."

"So Julie is good, and Jules is. . . . Alice, is she dangerous?"

"Jules is stronger-willed and lacks moral scruples. She'll defend Julie tooth and nail."

Olivia's breathing quickened. "You saw Jules attack me. What did I say to make her explode like that?"

"Let's find out." I guided Olivia into the kitchen, her fingers clutching the sharp blade.

The foresty scent of Pine-Sol made me sneeze as Julie finished scrubbing the gooey mess from the cabinets. I clapped my hands. "Jules!"

Jules wrung out the cloth and hung it on the faucet. "Olivia, taking out my stress on you was inconsiderate of me. Julie says I have anger management issues related to unresolved grief."

Olivia returned the cleaver to the knife block before crossing to the cupboard and picking out a clean dish. She divided her breakfast in half. "Here ya go, Jules. There's enough for both of us."

Jules sat at the table, staring at the omelet but not touching her cutlery. "The things I've done are reprehensible." She squeezed Olivia's arm. "You reacted reflexively, pulling the trigger when you heard me shoot. I checked the bullets in our guns. You may have hit Henry once, but I shot him six times."

Was Jules being truthful, or was she trying to shift the guilt away from Olivia? Regardless, I admired her for the effort and its effect. The teenager straightened her back and forked the eggs into her mouth. "Thanks so much for breakfast. This omelet is fantastic. Maybe one day you'll teach me how to cook?"

Delight transplanted from Jules' face to Julie's. "Be glad to, anytime. Cooking isn't the difficult part. The challenge is finding ingredients without local supermarkets."

Although the food was cold, the atmosphere had substantially warmed up.

Julie hesitated. "Alice, where were you going after you left Montgomery?"

"The man I was traveling with, David Carter, had an older brother living in New Orleans. With nowhere else to go, I figured I'd continue onward and," a knot tightened around my stomach, "tell Edward what I did."

Julie nodded, removing papers from her jeans pocket. She handed the thin bundle to me. "This is all I have."

I unfolded the first worn sheet to see Julia Werner's Facebook profile.

478 Friends

Global Markets Analyst at EEHG

MS Applied Economics at William Carey University

Went to Oak Grove High School

Lives in Hattiesburg, Mississippi

From Syracuse, New York

Any doubts I harbored concerning Julia's existence dissolved as I studied the profile photograph. Except for the shorter hair, radiant smile, and absence of a facial scar, Julia Werner was a carbon copy of Julie Werner. I smoothed out the second page, a water-stained printout of the Whitepages website.

Julia Ann Werner

AGE: 30s

CELL PHONE: 601-555-0112

CURRENT ADDRESS: 198 Treasure Point, Hattiesburg, Mississippi, 39402

RELATIVES: Julie Elaine Werner

OTHER ADDRESSES: Syracuse, New York

I returned the papers to Julie. "You know where she lives?"

"When the World Health Organization declared COVID-19 as a pandemic, I couldn't bear the thought of dying without seeing my sister again. As COVID-24 cases multiplied across North America, I searched for her online. I often dialed Julia's listed phone number but never pressed the call button."

"Why not?"

If Julie had an answer, she kept it to herself. "Hattiesburg is on the way to New Orleans. Alice, will you help me find Julia?"

My spontaneous response surprised me. "I may not proceed to Louisiana. I like it here in Hayneville. Pearl, Caddy, and Ardy are my friends."

Olivia sprang up from her seat. "I'll go with you, Julie! Maybe, along the way, we'll uncover what happened to my parents."

As I write these words hours later, I realize that, even then, I had no choice. Life is funny that way.

"Even if I agree to accompany you to Hattiesburg, have you considered the outcomes? Julia might have moved, or, I hate to say it, she may be dead. Let's be realistic, Julie. If Julia is alive, your sudden appearance could be disruptive after so many years apart."

Julie tugged at the frays holding her gray Loyola Marymount University sweatshirt together. "I still need to know."

"What if Julia isn't there?"

"I'll keep looking." She fluttered her hand. "You can continue to New Orleans or backtrack to Hayneville."

Olivia gripped my wrist just as my son Kenny did when excited. "So, are we going?"

I pulled the *Rand McNally Road Atlas* from my backpack and opened it on the dining room table. "If we were to leave for Hattiesburg, we would take the 21 and then the 28." I tapped the map. "At Camden, we'd stay north to Coffeeville or turn south toward Grove Hill. Two hundred miles on either route." A vivid image of David wasting to skin and skeleton flashed before my eyes. "It's a three-week hike if food and water are available. Olivia, what's the word on the towns along our path?"

"I haven't been outside Lowndes County since Election Day, but we pick up news from the few wanderers coming through McGill's Hill." She frowned. "Benton is one place you want to avoid."

I remembered Pearl's warning. "Ardy's sister mentioned the people there aren't friendly?"

Olivia pursed her lips. "Unfriendly is an understatement. They'll shoot you on sight. Benton has a UFO cult headed by a crazy woman. Empress Paulina believes a flying saucer will shuttle them to planet Nibiru."

"Hmm, so many crackpots out there." I traced my forefinger along a series of side roads on the map. "What about Mosses and Gordonville?"

"Most of their residents relocated to Hayneville after a tornado destroyed their towns."

"And Camden?"

"Camden has a sizable population, at least compared to here. My parents drove there before the quarantine. It's an hour by car, I think? My dad liked Tru Value hardware, and Mom loved the state park."

I closed the atlas, hoping that joining Julie and Olivia wouldn't be my biggest mistake.

Pearl returned home at 3 p.m., while Ardy stayed in town to assist the carpenters with the damage assessment. I invited her to the lake. "From the look on your face," she said, "what you're about to say won't leave me jumpin' for joy."

Pearl listened intently as I explained Julie's long-standing mission to locate her sister and Olivia's desire to start a new life.

"I'm going with them."

"Alice, when you first arrived in Hayneville, you spoke of New Orleans. Was it to find someone's brother?"

"Does the Pink Pony Express come this way?"

Pearl twisted her right hand as if revving a motorcycle engine. "The shotgun-slinging messengers riding pink Hondas?"

"Those ladies are unstoppable. David Carter's brother sent him a communication at the beginning of the year." Despite having Edward's handwritten note tucked in my pack, I had committed the optimistic words to memory. "Dave, I pray you are well. Come to New Orleans. The streets are safe to walk at night, and the economy is booming! I'm in the French Quarter, at the Hotel Saint Pierre. I'll leave a forwarding address if I move. Hurry, little bro. I miss you! Edward."

Pearl nodded thoughtfully. "We've heard updates about New Orleans on the police department's shortwave radio. The citizens petitioned to rename the city 'Newer New Orleans.' Ardy and I wondered if the reports were legitimate or just scams designed to entangle the gullible in a spider's web."

"David recognized his brother's longhand, so I am confident his invitation, at least, is authentic."

"Alice, I understand your desire to confess your sins. But will you truly be helping or just acting out of selfishness? Wouldn't Edward be happier believing that David is alive?"

"Once we confirm whether Julia is in Hattiesburg, I'll reconsider my journey to New Orleans. I enjoy living here."

Pearl gazed at the blackened hills. "After the fight and the fire, your perception of this place has changed. Am I right?"

"You and Ardy will rebuild Hayneville."

"Alice, I'm sixty-five. I am dog tired, my bones ache, and I'm afraid this old girl is short on second chances. We've already lost too many good people, and now we're losing you, too."

A groundswell of self-condemnation crashed over me. Should I return to Hayneville? Every time I peer into the future, all I see is the troubling past. I want to circle back to Pearl and Ardy, but what if something better awaits me?

Julie – July 6, 2029

7/6/2029

Jules woke up on the wrong side of the bed this morning, as cranky as a two-year-old with a diaper rash. She complained about everything under the sun.

"It's too hot."

"I'm hungry."

"My back hurts."

Whenever Jules starts an argument—that woman knows how to push my buttons—I visualize my happy place.

> August 2001. Two weeks before the terrors of 9/11. The Jersey shore. Point Pleasant. Beach access at Ocean Avenue. The lovely lady in the floppy hat pins yellow "Daily" badges on our brand-new pink swimsuits. "Have fun today, girls!" Julia and I dash straight into the churning surf. Mom cautions, "Slow down, Julie! Be careful, Julia!" The numbing cold is soon forgotten as we jump above each cresting wave. Our parents lounge in rainbow beach chairs, shaded by a matching umbrella. Mom giggles at Dad's corny jokes. My sister and I dig a cozy nook into the dunes, our backs against a white picket fence. Tropical winds carry peaceful thoughts. We hide from the swirling sand beneath

> a *Shrek* beach towel. Julia—my best friend in the whole wide world—and I laugh and laugh some more. The golden sun sinks lower and lower over the boundless expanse of blue and, after a green flash, is gone.

I cooked breakfast for Jules, Olivia, and Alice. The cheese omelets I so lovingly made splattered across the kitchen cabinets when Jules blew her stack. "Eat your food, Olivia! You don't know the first thing about real life!"

On the contrary, I think this sixteen-year-old girl has experienced far too much pain and agony. She threatened Jules with a meat cleaver—a brazen move! Alice dragged Olivia outdoors. Whatever Alice said to her worked wonders, because Olivia eventually put the knife away and shared half her eggs with Jules.

Jules apologized to Olivia and took full responsibility for shooting Henry. It was a gracious gesture that appeared to be beneficial. Olivia wants me to teach her how to cook!

I asked Alice where she was headed when we followed her from Montgomery to Hayneville. The man she euthanized after they ran out of food, David Carter, has a brother in New Orleans. She expressed her need to complete the journey and 'fess up to Edward.

I showed Alice my sister's Facebook profile and the Whitepages entry. She questioned why I hadn't already made the trip to Hattiesburg to see Julia.

My actions baffle me—specifically, my apathy. I had sixteen years before the pandemic and Election Day to track down Julia and beg for her forgiveness. My inadequacy perplexes me, especially given the countless nights I've spent praying for her well-being. I even lit votive candles for her after Sunday Mass.

I invited Alice to come to Hattiesburg, but she did her best to discourage me. "Julia could be elsewhere, or she's dead." And the jab that stung the most—as the truth always does—"What if your sister doesn't want you to find her?"

Olivia jumped right on board. "When are we leaving?" She's champing at the bit to say *"Hasta la vista"* to all her heart-rending memories. Let's hope the girl has better luck escaping her past than me.

Alice and I brooded over the map. It's three weeks to Hattiesburg, whichever route we choose. Pitfalls and pratfalls await us at every turn.

Alice – July 7, 2029

7/7/2029

We got off to an early start. Julie and I stuffed our backpacks with supplies. Olivia used Arthur's knapsack, which Pearl had kept, to pack clothes and necessities.

Caddy and Eloise had returned to town with Shirley, who was on the mend. Along with Pearl and Ardy, they organized our big send-off, their voices brimming with hope and concern.

After much hemming and hawing, Julie left Oscar behind. "He'll be safer with you, Pearl." We heard his sad howls until we reached the far side of Trevor Lake. While I do miss Oscar, I agree he's better off in a stable environment. On a more selfish level, I prefer not to share my food with an animal when on the road.

We're having lunch at Mount Olive Church. I reread what I wrote earlier about leaving Hayneville. The sentences are short, the words abrupt. They give the impression that I don't care. The fact is, I care a whole lot. Only an hour has passed, and I already want to turn around and run home.

Is Hayneville really "home"? That sentimental word releases swarms of emotions I squash before they bite me and begin to itch.

I have called nowhere "home" in years. My parents' house in Paramus, New Jersey, was my childhood home until I fled from their nonstop quarreling and faultfinding. The Bergenfield condo where I lived with Peter had been home before Kenny died and my husband ran off with Harmony "The Whore" Henderson.

Pearl's expression filled my entire being with guilt and despair when I waved for the final time. Ardy seemed to be angry at me.

We hit a roadblock just a mile past the GORDONVILLE CITY LIMITS signboard. Someone should have scouted ahead on the 21, but the high humidity and serene sounds of nature had lulled us into a false sense of security. Around a bend, at a sign for WALL STREET (no wall, not much of a street, and definitely no stock exchange), two men and one woman stood behind a wooden barricade. All were equipped with assault rifles.

The woman, clothed from neck to ankle in blue calico, shouted, "Halt!" It was too late for us to escape into the woods. We froze like opossums. "Where are you coming from?"

Julie cupped her palms around her mouth. "Hayneville! My friends and I are on our way to Hattiesburg!"

"What's your business there?"

"We're looking for my sister."

The woman scowled. "Didn't you see the signs? You're trespassing on private land. Throw down your weapons."

My father, a huge fan of action films, often berated the characters on the TV screen for complying with the villain's demands. "Bruce, don't give her your gun! Now you ain't got a pot to piss in!" Be it Willis, Eastwood, Thurman, or Chan, my dad always provided free scriptwriting lessons.

Unfortunately, life on the street isn't as comfy as your living room couch. We laid our rifles and handguns on the hot macadam.

"Drop your backpacks and put up your hands. Line up in a row, facing away from me. Then come toward my voice so Maurice can pat you down."

"It's an encouraging sign they didn't just shoot us," Julie observed as we stepped backward.

Olivia spoke from the side of her mouth, "Apostles of Eternal Love."

I tilted my ear to hear her better. "What?"

"See their shaved heads? They're from Benton."

The young man wearing a black PINK FLOYD T-shirt bound our wrists behind our backs with nylon ties and frisked our pockets. The older man led our group up a pathway while the woman prodded us forward with her Colt M4 carbine.

"Javier, wait out here." She pushed us into a dilapidated shack, shut the door, and pointed at the concrete floor. "Sit."

Light filtering through a gap in the roof illuminated a rusty diesel engine and pumping equipment covered with blue tarpaulin. I prayed Jules was cooking up a strategy to free us.

"I am Sister Aurora. On behalf of Empress Paulina, I welcome you to Nibiruville. May I have your names?"

"I'm Alice. This is Olivia, and that's Julie. Could you please untie us? We're passing by your town and pose no threat."

Sister Aurora's stained and frayed prairie dress grazed the dusty floor as she squatted to our eye level. A ray of sunlight highlighted a pinkish N branded on the top of her scalp. "All trespassers are required to pay a penalty."

I nodded at our bags. "Take what you want. We've nothing of material value."

"One of you," the woman whispered ominously, "shall stay with us."

Jules grinned the fangs of a she-wolf. "We appreciate your offer," her voice dropped an octave, "but the four of us are walking out of here together."

Sister Aurora missed Jules' reference to the size of our group. "Empress Paulina preaches that selflessness of sacrifice is essential to colonize planet Nibiru." She unlocked a small black box with a red N painted on the side and removed a revolver. "If you can't choose between yourselves, perhaps a simple game of chance will help." She inserted a bullet into the chamber. "Who wants to play first?"

Jules shot me a sideways glance. Although I hadn't an inkling of what Julie's wilder half had planned, my muscles tensed to spring. "Let's get this over with," she said. "Give me the gun."

Did Jules intend to finish the "game" by shooting me?

"Show me your hands, Julie." Sister Aurora snipped the zip tie with a wire cutter. She slid the revolver across the hard floor. "Close your eyes, spin the cylinder, pull the hammer, and put the muzzle to your head. Say a prayer, then squeeze the trigger. If that thirty-eight moves a millimeter in my direction," the Apostle of Eternal Love leveled her M4 at Jules' chest, "I'll end the competition for you."

Jules picked up the handgun, her hands unwavering as she hefted its deadly weight. "Dear Lord, cleanse me with the blood of your son Jesus and absolve my sins. Glory be to the Father, the Son, and the Holy Ghost. Amen." With her eyelids clamped tight, Jules spun the cylinder, the ticking ratchet far too loud for the airless room. She pressed the two-inch barrel against her right temple, cocked the hammer, and, without faltering, placed her finger on the trigger.

I braced myself for an earsplitting BANG!—Jules' grey matter spraying the side of my face—or a quiet click followed by her eyes flying open in relief. Both scenarios sent my heart racing into the red zone.

To my shock, neither occurred. Jules held out the revolver to me. "Alice, I changed my mind. You owe me."

As Sister Aurora's widening eyes tracked my shaky hand, and her lips parted in startlement, Jules side-armed the gun into the distracted woman's open mouth, just as Julie had skillfully skipped the stone across Trevor Lake on the Fourth of July. I dove under the long forestock, head-butting the now-toothless woman in the gut. Jules ripped the assault rifle from Sister Aurora's grasp and smashed the buttstock into her forehead.

Lights out.

Olivia mouthed, "Did they hear us?" as Jules severed our bindings.

The door hinges screeched. "Everything good, babe?" The tip of a rifle poked through the crack. "Delilah?"

"I'm fine!" Olivia called out in a surprisingly excellent imitation of the woman lying before us.

The rifle barrel lowered.

But Olivia pushed her luck too far. "Be there in a minute, Javier."

Javier stuck his nose in the doorway, gasping as his eyes fell upon the crumpled form in the blue dress. "Maurice! Come here, Maurice!"

I searched the room, dismayed by the absence of windows or loose wallboards. A lofty ceiling loomed above, and a solid floor lay below. The entrance also functioned as an exit, so our options were finite. Once Maurice summoned the cavalry, we would be trapped like rats in a clogged drainpipe. I grabbed the Russian roulette revolver, opened the cylinder, and rotated the single cartridge to be behind the hammer.

My dad's gravelly voice channeled Dirty Harry, "Do you feel lucky? Well, do ya, Allie?"

I snapped the cylinder shut, hoping Javier wouldn't risk shooting into the pumping station after calling Sister Aurora "babe."

Jules examined the Colt's magazine, her mouth agape. "It's empty!"

Olivia patted down Delilah's cotton frock for ammo. "Nothing here!"

Did Jules launch Sister Aurora into the great beyond? "Is she still alive?"

Olivia's fingers pressed against Delilah's wrist. "Alice, her pulse is slow, but it's steady!"

"Try to revive her!"

"How?" She raised her palm. "Should I slap her?"

"That could make her condition worse! Just tell the bitch to wake up!"

Olivia pleaded with the unresponsive woman as I wriggled forward on my stomach. "Javier! This is Alice. We've got a gun. We'll release Delilah if you let us go. Do we have a deal?"

A frantic voice hollered through the door. "Lilly! Baby, talk to me!"

I peered behind me. "Is she awake?"

Olivia's face portrayed the pictorial definition of "woe is me."

"Javier, is Delilah your wife?"

"Empress Paulina united our hearts beneath the Divinity Tree during the last blood moon. Please don't hurt her."

"Javier, I'll be upfront with you. We struck Delilah to be able to break free. She's breathing but unconscious, and she may need stitches. If you and Maurice give us your weapons, we'll carry your wife out so you can take her to a doctor."

He choked up. "Benton had a doctor, but she run off with the smithy."

"Then check on her yourself. She'll likely be in pain when she opens her eyes. Your face is the only one she'll want to see."

"I put down my rifle. If anyone hurts me or my lady, Maurice is gonna radio headquarters for backup. You don't want Empress Paulina's panties twisted in a knot."

I sat on the cement, resting Delilah's hairless head on my crossed legs. Blood flowed onto my knee from a four-inch gash above her eyebrow, but her flaring nostrils reassured me she was still with us. I held the revolver against the woman's fractured skull. "Come in, Javier!"

The man who directed us to the shed stood in the doorway. His eyes zeroed in on the gun pressed to his wife's ear.

Jules twirled her finger. "Pull up your shirt. Show me what's in those pockets."

Javier complied, having nothing more to hide than a pair of love handles. I readied for any shenanigans as he kneeled to kiss Delilah's cheek. "I'm sorry, baby, I never meant—"

Delilah's eyes fluttered open like a heroine from the Hallmark Channel (the *Lost Letter Mysteries* converted me into a hopeless romantic). "Oh, Javier!"

I added the "Oh, Javier!" for dramatic impact. In truth, the concussed woman retched before blacking out again.

Sister Aurora's improving health could be our ticket out of this insane asylum. "Javier, let Maurice know Delilah is recovering."

"Maurice, Lilly is alive!"

Olivia uncovered the pumping machinery. "We can carry his wife outside on this tarp."

We slid Delilah onto the plastic sheet, with me one-handing the rear. My other hand aimed the single-shot revolver at her torso.

Javier went to the door. "Maurice, are you alone?"

"Yeah, Javier!" a nasal voice exclaimed. "It's just me!"

"We're coming out! Don't shoot!" Delilah's firmly sealed eyelids alarmed Javier as much as they alarmed us. Was the woman asleep, braindead, or already stiffening from rigor mortis? Only God had the answer.

We emerged from the darkness, squinting at our surroundings.

Maurice had lied.

Dear Diary, as you read this, you've deduced that I am among the living at the time of writing. What about Olivia and Julie/Jules? Are they alive, dead, captured, or free? You'll never guess what happened next.

Ten armed men and women moved in on us. Shaved and branded scalps marked their allegiance, except for one distinguished Black woman with gray roots threading her long dreadlocks.

Empress Paulina.

I made my intention crystal clear by shoving the revolver closer to Delilah. "Let us pass, or I'll kill her."

Empress Paulina's face tilted to the sky as if invoking the godship. "The Creator of All Things has winged Sister Aurora to the land of milk and honey. Nibiru."

Her followers echoed her last word, "Nibiru!" three times.

If Delilah's waxy complexion hoisted a red flag, her motionless chest sounded a klaxon. Javier cried out, accidentally releasing his corner of the tarpaulin. His wife slid off the plastic, hitting her bloody head on the ground.

I pointed the gun at Paulina. Even if I shot her squarely in the heart, the others would finish us lickety-split.

Unexpectedly for us, the leader began chanting in a language resembling Klingon from *Star Trek*. *"Bang visopmeh miw visovchu. . . ."*

Paulina's disciples swayed in rapture, clapping to the rhythm and harmonizing with the chorus. Much like participants in a party game of musical chairs, I feared we three might be seatless once the melody ceased.

In retrospect, I should have singled out the least euphoric cultist. Now that it's over, I can describe the woman as Asian, in her older teens, tall but very gaunt, and, of most importance, having vengeful brown eyes.

The girl gripped the cold steel of an AK-47, the extended banana clip adding to its lethality. Despite her emaciated appearance, her movements were swift and precise, a testament to her mastery of quick draw. The Apostles of Eternal Love cascaded like life-sized dominoes as she mowed them down in a blur.

Two remained standing.

Empress Paulina lifted her palms in surrender. "Sister Sophie, I've always been good to you! Remember how I pulled you from the depths of Mordor?"

"Mordor is from a book—a fictional world that doesn't exist!" Sophie waggled the assault rifle at Javier. "Run, Mr. Gomez!"

Delilah's head lolled back as Javier cradled her, a mask of mud and leaves sticking to her wet face. "I can't leave my baby all alone."

"Your funeral." The Angel of Death danced in Sophie's eyes as she upraised the scuffed and scratched Kalashnikov.

Olivia positioned herself between Sophie and the grieving man. "Get up, you fool! No one else has to die today!"

Javier struggled to his feet. He gazed forlornly at Delilah before shuffling down the lane.

Empress Paulina's authoritative voice pierced the electrified air. "Sophie!"

I must say, the head of the Apostles of Eternal Love suffered no lack of allure. What was the source of her power over others? How did she speak with such conviction? What demon concealed itself behind those penetrating eyes? How did it differ from those possessing Jim Jones, Marshall Applewhite, and David Koresh, all self-appointed demigods who commanded absolute devotion from their susceptible worshipers? I've crossed paths with many cults since Election Day. All were helmed by delusional rulers who had descended into madness.

I scanned the dead, spotting a black THE DARK SIDE OF THE MOON T-shirt. Had Maurice's spaceship safely landed on planet Nibiru?

Sophie's rifle swung back to Paulina. "It's you and me now." She used the stubby barrel to indicate us. "Nobody else to lord it over. Or sacrifice to your false gods."

"Sophie, I love you like a daughter. Together, you and I can discover new worlds."

I had the handgun. Who should I spend the single bullet on? The unarmed cult leader or the heavily armed ex-follower?

Olivia, once again acting as a human shield, bravely protected Paulina. "Sophie, what did this woman do to you?"

The AK-47 shook as Sophie trembled. "Four months ago, my mother and I walked from Selma to Montgomery to track down my aunt. Same as you, we encountered an AEL roadblock." Her eyes darted toward the shack we narrowly escaped from. "Mrs. Gomez made us shoot each other with a revolver loaded with one bullet. She babbled about Empress Paulina and her plans to colonize planet Nibiru, claiming that only human souls possess enough biofuel to charge their starship's impulse engines. My mom kept pulling the trigger until the gun went off. She sacrificed her life to save mine."

"Dear God!" Olivia turned to Paulina. "How many souls have you collected?"

The maniac held up nine fingers.

"Is that enough to fly your spacecraft to Nibiru?"

"We need six thousand one hundred and seventy-four," Paulina replied confidently.

Olivia blanched with horror. "Did you just—?"

Paulina orated as if lecturing a classroom full of future rocket scientists. "Also recognized by mathematicians as Kaprekar's Constant. We must harvest an additional six thousand one hundred and sixty-five souls to embark on our eight-year space exploration." She stuck up her chin proudly. "At Harvard, I titled my doctorate dissertation *The Positive Effects of Strong Religious Beliefs on Interstellar Travel.* I taught advanced trigonometry at Auburn University. My flight path calculations are accurate to within one one-hundredths of a degree, with the condition that the amassed spirits remain unadulterated."

Sophie let loose a chilling laugh. "Paulina told us, 'For an individual's vital force to generate maximum kinetic energy, their loved ones must deeply mourn them.' That's why the mutant didn't kill me along with my mother." Sophie aimed the automatic rifle at Olivia. "Get out of my way."

Our youngest stood firm with her hands up. "Sophie, a man in McGill's Hill murdered my parents and held me captive. His accomplice attacked me, and I sought revenge without considering the consequences for me or my friends. Knowing the wrong person paid the price is—" Olivia's eyes swept over the ring of lifeless bodies. "Thank you for helping us, but please let her go."

Has Olivia given up her lust for blood?

This Shakespearean play could end in a few ways. A floodlight shines down from the heavens as Paulina gets on her knees and begs for leniency. Sophie takes pity on her captor, setting her free with a strict warning to never harm another living soul—*or face the music.* Picture me entering stage right, quoting a line from *Breaking Bad*, "What kind of pizza do you like, Paulina?" and then using my "N" revolver to drill an "O" in her worm-infested brain. Alternatively, with both parts portrayed by the EGOT-winning Viola Davis, Julie and Jules act out a scene rated Extreme Violence (the E and V are always capitalized). Or did Paulina solve the problem herself by swallowing a cyanide pill hidden inside the silver flying saucer locket hovering on her neck?

Dear Diary, you've noticed I omitted a key member from my cast list. Every memorable plot needs a twist.

A sudden thud broke the silence as Olivia's fist connected with Paulina's mouth, sending her sprawling. Fueled by an inner strength, Olivia pounced on the fallen woman, repeatedly slamming her skull against a rigid pipe. The battered empress crawled over her slaughtered believers to escape, her blood mixing with theirs. Halfway up the path to the shack, the Apostles of Eternal Love's leader rolled onto her back. As she huffed out her last words, "Nathan, don't forget to pick up Chloe after school," I wondered if Paulina saw planet Nibiru through the thick clouds.

Does our modern reality truly brim with peril, or do I perpetually thrust myself into precarious predicaments? I pledge to tread more cautiously.

Julie – July 7, 2029

7/7/2029

Olivia killed a woman today—not the most auspicious way to launch our expedition to find my twin sister. Empress Paulina got what she deserved, but can we trust Olivia?

The town of Mount Willing is just another widening of the road. There's a convenience store/gas station, and that's it. Oh, and a U-Haul dealer with no trucks or trailers to rent. Our lodging is a rustic log cabin tucked away at the end of an unnamed, dead-end street. Olivia and Sophie climbed into the bunk beds in the kids' room. Alice and I share the main bedroom. I'm writing and she's snoring. Alice worked on her diary as soon as we arrived. I was too pumped from all the activity to concentrate.

Jules is patrolling the wooded property. Tonight, nervous tension isn't the cause of her insomnia. She discovered a working stove and jar of Maxwell House Original Roast. Jules brewed a gallon of jitter juice and drank it all, down to the last drop. I will sleep soundly knowing my caffeinated angel is out there watching over us.

Alice proposed packing up and leaving Hayneville this morning. I hadn't planned to take off so promptly. Perhaps she's not into long farewells. Neither am I. Still, I felt sad saying goodbye to Pearl and Ardy. Decent people are rarer than five-leaf clovers.

Olivia, however, was bursting with excitement. I don't blame her for wanting to wipe Corbin Holt and McGill's Hill from her memory. And poor old Henry. Yet, her mood swings raise concerns about her mental stability. One second, Olivia is defending Empress Paulina from Sophie's wrath. The next, she's pulverizing the screwball's cerebellum into gray goop. But hey, who am I to judge? I sometimes feel a duality within myself, one part Mother Teresa and the other part Elizabeth Bathory.

We ran into a roadblock manned by the Benton loonies, who are also known around the galaxy as the Apostles of Eternal Love (or AEL, if you can't live without acronyms). Javier and Delilah Gomez and their sidekick, Maurice, held us captive in a shack. Mr. Gomez and Maurice stood outside while Mrs. Gomez jibber-jabbered on about Empress Paulina's ambitions to rocket her flock to an exoplanet that's orbiting Proxima Centauri: Planet Nibiru. Or was it Nibaru? Naburu? Forget the spelling. What matters is the wacko loaded a revolver with a bullet and presented us with an ultimatum. One in our group would not be allowed to exit the shed vertically.

On a side note, one time when my mother went for a girls' night out at Electric Avenue, my father allowed Julia and me to watch *The Deer Hunter* on HBO. Mom came home right in the middle of the nail-biting Russian roulette scene featuring Robert De Niro and Christopher Walken. Dad spent the rest of the night on the couch. I can't tell you if my sister slept. My eyes did not shut for a week.

So, back to today. With no specific course of action, I accepted the gun. I didn't want Alice or Olivia to shoot first. Is that right? Was taking the firearm an act of generosity or a sign that my own life holds such little importance? Jules chewed me out for volunteering. "Julie, you'd leave me alone in this world?"

I saw an opening and winged the revolver into Mrs. Gomez's face. *Hope this lady has good dental insurance,* I thought, as her teeth flew down her throat. Alice dove into our captor's solar plexus as Jules tore the rifle out of her hands and put a divot in her noggin. KAPOW!

Mr. Gomez heard the commotion. "Delilah! Delilah! Are you okay, baby doll?"

Uh, baby doll is not okay—at all.

Alice urged Javier to, "Come in and help your wife!"

Delilah was still sucking air when we lugged her boney ass outdoors. And who did we find waiting so patiently for us? None other than the CEO of the AEL and her ten minions. Our mouths hung open as Sophie Chen, one of Empress Paulina's own, used a machine gun to reap her cohorts' souls. BRRRRRT!!! They toppled to the earth like scythed stalks of corn, except for Javier and Paulina.

Sophie offered Javier a choice. "Leave your dead wife behind or join her on Nibiru." He decided with his mind rather than his heart, probably realizing that plenty more fish swim in the sea.

Sophie was gearing up to waste the woman who ventilated her mom's head when Olivia stepped between them. Here's the part that confounds (and worries!) me. Olivia related the story of McGill Academy and Henry's needless demise. "Sophie, take it from me. Seeking revenge will never bring you peace, blah, blah, blah. . . ."

The words were barely out of her mouth when, in a sudden role reversal, Olivia split Paulina's melon open on a drainage pipe.

The cult leader uttered a cryptic one-liner before shutting her mouth forever. "Ethan, remember to pick up Zoe after band practice."

Alice is moaning "Birmingham" in her sleep. Experts strongly advise against waking someone from a nightmare, so I'll let her be.

Alice – July 8, 2029

7/8/2029

Julie shook me awake at 6:15 a.m., her finger against her lips. I understood her need for silence and followed her past Olivia and Sophie's bedroom. A child's playset awaited us in the backyard, its colorful surfaces damp with morning dew.

Julie gripped the swing's two chains and pushed with her feet. "Yesterday was a total disaster."

The hangers screeched as I swung back and forth. "Yeah. We can't let that happen again."

"Alice, why didn't Sister Aurora load her rifle?"

Tempted to respond with "Only God knows," I bit my tongue. I doubt even He would have the answer. "Weird, huh? Was it a mistake?"

Julie frowned. "It's not just that. The girls. . . ."

I knew there was a problem, but I didn't want to admit that I had no solution. "Olivia and Sophie?"

"They're," she bit her lip, "misbehaving."

I scoffed. "Misbehaving" was one way to put "mass murdering" mildly.

"Do you agree that Olivia is acting irrationally? And what do we really know about Sophie?"

Last night, the angels on our shoulders prevented the devils from ditching Sophie Chen between noplace and nowhere.

Olivia Dawson has been with us since Corbin Holt swayed and swiveled from Pearl's oak tree. Her distress is fathomable. Yet the question persists: Will Olivia bounce back?

"Julie, we're all on the hook for McGill Academy. Henry's wrongful death traumatized Olivia, and rightfully so. If Sophie hadn't taken care of the Apostles of Eternal Love, we wouldn't be here with our toes in the air."

"Somebody needed to remove Empress Paulina from power." Julie's jaw twisted. "I just wish it didn't have to be Olivia. She defended that zealot! What triggered her to do a complete one-eighty?"

Olivia and Sophie emerged through the back door, yawning and rubbing their eyes.

My braking boots created a little cloud of dust. "I guess now's the opportunity to find out."

While Olivia settled on one side of the rusty seesaw, Julie asked, "How did you guys sleep?"

Sophie added her weight to the opposite end of the plank, lifting Olivia above the grass. "Off and on. I hoped the bad dreams might disappear after we left Benton."

"Sadly," I tapped my head, "that's not how the mind works." My remark dredged up a recent dream—my lips kissing David's neck hard enough to dissolve the thick makeup concealing a ring of ugly finger-shaped bruises. "What about you, Olivia?"

Revulsion crossed the girl's face as she inspected her fingernails. On the way to Mount Willing, Olivia had painstakingly scrubbed Empress Paulina off her hands in a nearby brook. "I'm going to Hell for what I've done, aren't I?"

An image of Ukobach, the demon responsible for stoking the hellfire, flickered like an old silent movie in my visual cortex. I pointed downward. "If the nether world truly exists, we'll be dancing the Hokey Pokey in the flames right beside you."

Olivia's bottom lip quivered. "The idea of spending time without end with Corbin Holt is unbearable."

"That monster is roasting with Empress Paulina in the lowest level of Hades for their treachery." I squeezed her shoulder. "What you did to that woman doesn't warrant even a minute in Purgatory."

"But I never wanted to hurt her!" Olivia burst into tears. "I just went—"

"Bonkers," Julie muttered under her breath.

Sophie lowered Olivia to the lawn and dismounted the seesaw. "If you hadn't killed that nutcase, I'd have cut out her heart. Paulina punished us mercilessly if we didn't comply with her absurd rules. She withheld food and water and locked 'Satan's sinners' in an underground cellar called the 'redemption room.' I had to lie in my own filth for three days straight."

Julie hopped off the swing. "Tell us more about yourself, Sophie."

Sophie picked a deflated soccer ball out of the weeds. "Not much of a story."

"Still wanna hear it. How old are you?"

"Eighteen." She smirked. "Old enough to vote."

"Where did you grow up?"

"Northern California. Know where Humboldt County is?"

"The Emerald Triangle?"

Sophie's forefinger traced the raised N on top of her shaved head, flinching as if the healed brand still hurt. "My parents migrated from the Bay Area to grow marijuana near Garberville. We lived in mountain country, so COVID-19 and '24 hardly touched our remote community. Then Russia nuked San Francisco, Los Angeles, and San Diego, sending radioactive clouds up the coast. My parents threw my younger sister Megan and me into the rear of their Jeep and raced east. Steam started blowing from under the Wagoneer's hood a mile outside Reno. My dad was checking the radiator when a military Hummer pulled next to us. Instead of helping, the soldier hit my father on the head with a billy club. Mom and I fought him off, but the brute dragged my sister out of our car and into his truck. That was the last time I saw her."

Julie's expression mirrored Sophie's sorrow. "What happened to your dad?"

"The hospitals were overflowing with the injured and sick. A triage nurse examined the crack in my comatose father's skull and handed my mother a vial of morphine with a syringe. 'Give him the whole dose.' Mom's fingers trembled so much that I had to administer the injection. The crematoriums ran out of gas, so we had to bury him in someone's pumpkin patch. We wandered from town to town until the goddess of bad luck lured us to Benton."

Julie grimaced. "Beshaba and I are well acquainted. So, Sophie, it was just you and your mom?"

"Yep. We attached to various groups, leaving when things got sketchy. My mother and I spent a year harvesting alfalfa in Salt Lake City. Then the First Presidency issued a final notice to join the Mormon faith or get lost."

Julie swatted a mosquito that landed on her forearm. She smeared the blob of blood and guts with her finger. "I heard the Prophet executed the unconverted."

"The Latter-day Saints treated us like equals until the Third Plague—The Big Drought. When the rainmakers failed to produce a single drop, President Rasmussen pinned the 'blight' on the gentiles. We split the day the protests became violent. The end of March?"

Julie winced as she bent to touch her toes. "Of last year?"

"Uh-huh. We spent the winter in Texas. My mother noticed her sister's name on a Houston bulletin board. Even though the note had been written eight months earlier, she hoped that Aunt Cheryl remained in Montgomery. On the way to Alabama, we stopped in Shreveport, Louisiana. I tended bar at Margaritaville while Mom dealt blackjack at the Horseshoe."

I interjected, "The casinos are open?"

"And the whorehouses." Sophie tossed the useless soccer ball aside. "With Sin City reduced to a sheet of trinitite, the gamblers and degenerates still crave a place to get their itches scratched. Picture Deadwood, South Dakota, in 1876. The mob runs the show."

I remembered Tony Soprano curb-stomping Coco Cogliano in one of my favorite episodes of *The Sopranos*. "The Mafia?"

"Who?" Sophie didn't understand my reference.

"Organized crime. Started by the Italians."

"This gang is Chinese."

"Triad?"

Sophie shrugged.

"What are casino owners accepting as currency?" I rubbed my thumb and first two fingers together. "Shells? Beads?"

Sophie chuckled in amusement. "The cage trades chips for whatever you have of worth. Cashiers prefer guns, ammo, and hard drugs. Particularly uncut fentanyl and pink cocaine."

I nodded, envisioning the sordid streets of Kensington. "I'll bet."

Sophie glowered. "And then Fang Gongsun crawled out of the woodwork."

Julie frowned. "Who's he?"

"The Devil in an Armani suit. My mother met Fang at the Horseshoe. He would strut up to her gaming table every evening, lose a pile of chips, and magically reappear with more. Between hands, he'd charm her with witty flirtation. Back in our room at Bally's, Mom rambled on and on about the man in the designer suit, flattered he had taken an interest in her."

Olivia arched her eyebrows. "What was his angle?"

"I clocked out of Margaritaville one morning to meet my mother at the Horseshoe. A man dressed to the nines sat at her blackjack table. He lost all his chips, save the one he gave my mom for a tip. I instantly knew he was the bettor she had mentioned. An amoeba with a prefrontal lobotomy could play better cards than this loser. He took off only to saunter back in an hour later with another pocketful of black chips."

Olivia folded her arms. "Thief?"

Sophie shook her head vigorously. "I recognized a bouncer that kicked troublemakers out of Margaritaville, so I asked Yanyou if he knew the dandy in the fancy threads. 'That's Fang Gongsun. If you've any sense, stay away from him. He does the casino's dirty work, and as a reward, the pit bosses grant him a limitless supply of chips.' Yanyou identified my mother. 'The Mountain Master lets his enforcers run rampant if they are discreet. When Fang is done toying with that woman, there won't be enough to bury in a thimble.'"

Julie wrinkled her nose. "Did you warn your mom to leave town?"

"We left Shreveport," Sophie smiled mischievously, "but not before I sent Mr. Gongsun to play blackjack with the blue crabs at the bottom of the Red River."

The Big Bad Thing. I hadn't intended to document our experiences in Birmingham today, but Julie insisted on a "day of rest," so here I sit in a bamboo chair on our cabin's front porch.

David and I traveled down I-65, walking through Nashville, Cornersville, Huntsville, Mooresville, Priceville, Brooksville, Falkville, Hanceville, Trussville, and every other goddamned 'ville until we finally arrived in Birmingham. I had estimated that five thousand individuals now inhabited a city that once upon a time thrived with a million. Maybe I miscalculated the population. Who knows? The government has census takers lined up to pound on doors and ring doorbells. . .WHEN HELL FREEZES OVER!

We are midtown, crammed in with three hundred other squatters in the Federal Building, a twenty-seven-story structure erected just months before the commencement of World War I. Over the decades, landlords slathered layer upon layer of paint on the Fed's epidermis to camouflage its aging skeleton. The old dinosaur clearly suffers from osteoporosis, its bones deteriorating to the point of collapse.

Why did we seek refuge in Birmingham? Our bunions begged for balm, and we needed to refresh our rations. David heard through the grapevine that the Fed was secure. Residents established a neighborhood watch to patrol the premises. However, the move-in package did not include amenities such as water and electricity. The plumbing, or rather the lack of it, posed a constant challenge. If you were thoughtless enough to use the toilet, ruptured pipes would spew your stinking piss and shit onto the poor souls on the lower floors. Or worse, a vile tide of liquid sludge gushed into your own humble abode. As the day ended, we schlepped a plastic pail down the stairway to a dumpster. A mule train supposedly carted the foul cargo to the Cahaba River. We didn't hang around long enough in Magic City to witness the fishes' feeding frenzy.

Why am I expounding on the sewage situation? Well, a pail of piss and shit could be the reason forty-three men, women, and children lost their lives.

On May 16, 2029, our eighth day in the Fed, our routine began as usual. We woke up late, had a cold "Energy Bar" breakfast baked by a nearby resident, and descended twenty-four flights to the lobby. Hand in hand, we strolled through the market stalls lining 20th Street. David hunted for a shortwave radio at the electronics vendors. Feminine hygiene products topped my list. Oh, and ammo for my Taurus handgun. David struck out on the radio, but I traded a pack of hearing aid batteries for a box of Tampax. He teased me about my "bloody good deal" as we munched on street tacos in Linn Park. People walked dogs. Kids kicked balls. Sunny, mid-seventies, low humidity—a perfect Wednesday afternoon, apart from the uncanny presence of a thousand abandoned apartments staring down at us. And feeling like the other shoe was about to drop.

Across from the Fed, we traded a half-bottle of Zestril for a bag of groceries and a jug of cheap wine. David and I climbed twenty-four floors, panting as we entered our room. We sank into the couch and toasted each other's health with long pours of "Two-Buck Chuck."

Besides the sewage issue, you might wonder why David and I selected an upper level instead of a unit closer to the ground. A network of cubicles and office equipment clogged Federal's bottom levels, leaving no space for comfort or privacy. Once owned by the social elite, these high-in-the-sky furnished luxury condominiums were now packed with us—the great unwashed. While the balconies offered cityscape panoramas, I wouldn't pay a wooden nickel for the breathtaking view without an operating elevator.

The alcohol soaking through my stomach lining surged straight to my brain. I used a funnel to top off the green Coleman camping stove's red tank with white gas and pressed the fuel pump to pressurize the system. I turned the brass starting valve to the down position and opened the black valve. Hearing the hiss of liquid fuel, I lit a match and touched it to the burner. As the generator rod heated, the flames transformed from a soft yellow to a vibrant blue. With an upward twist of the starting valve, I placed a full pot on the metal grate, ready to cook our pasta.

David broached the dreaded topic of the day as the water came to a boil. "Should we dump the shit shuttle now or later?"

"I'm hungry," I grumbled. "If we wait, we can dispose of the kitchen scraps at the same time."

He wanted the disgusting chore to be over with. "I'll be too tired after dinner. Let's just do it now."

We kept the primitive toilet in the guest bathroom, far from our sleeping and dining areas. I passed Dave the orange Home Depot pail as he held open the front door. We walked along the dimly lit hallway and down the stairwell. The conversation we had on the way escapes me, but David's words as he emptied our ten-pound load of slop into the WM dumpster will haunt me forever.

"Alice, is that smoke coming from our room?"

We double-timed up the murky stairway, dodging people running downstairs in panic. David and I reached the twentieth floor alone in air too hot to breathe. We masked our noses with our shirts and retreated to the street.

Spectators had gathered to count the jumpers. Volunteer firefighters hustled to the scene, dropping their water pails when the chief declared the building too hazardous to enter.

David faced me as we trudged down I-20 a day later. "You switched off the camping stove, right?"

I mumbled, "I'm sure I did."

He never brought up Birmingham again.

Was I to blame for the inferno that claimed forty-three people? I honestly cannot recall whether I turned the Coleman stove's black valve clockwise before we left. That said, whenever I shut my eyes, I can see fuel spurting from a loose fitting on the stove. The stained carpet ignites, and flames climb the moldy drapes, radiating across the water-spotted ceilings. A veil of human ashes eclipses the sun. Forever imprisoned in my own living nightmare, I plead to God for His mercy.

Julie – July 8, 2029

7/8/2029

I lay in bed for a bit extra this morning, recovering from yesterday and worrying about the future. Jules swears we're lucky to be alive. No shit, Sherlock. Empress Paulina and her flock of rabid sheep were as terrifying as being trapped in a pitch-dark escape room with Squeaky Fromme. Sophie saved our hides. The ease with which she ground the Apostles of Eternal Love into Hamburger Helper frightens me. Her savagery reminded me of Jules in one of her "funks." And Olivia? She exhibited the same Manson mania as Sophie when she smashed Paulina's head against a metal pipe. I had been cool with bringing Olivia to locate Julia, but moving quickly and quietly with just Alice is far more appealing. And much safer. Jules is convinced the AEL caught us asleep at the job because we let Olivia come along.

I woke Alice to air my concerns. Olivia and Sophie interrupted our discussion before I could hear Alice's unguarded opinion. Olivia believed she had purchased a one-way ticket to the bottomless pit. Sophie shared a bit of her background. What happened to her father in Reno was a tragedy. But find me one person on this ruined planet who's lasted this long without having a hundred wretched stories to tell. I admit my sympathy for Sophie increased when I learned that she, too, lost a sister.

To lighten the mood, I urged everyone to take it easy today. Alice is on the front porch with her diary. Olivia and Sophie rounded up some fishing tackle and hiked down to the creek. I hope the girls catch something for the evening meal, even if it's fish. Jules and I are in the living room. I laze on the couch, jotting my thoughts, while Jules dozes in a bean bag chair with her heels propped up on the hearth.

Alice and I examined the *Rand McNally Road Atlas*. We can stay on the 21 to Camden or walk a more northern or southern route. Either way, it's forty more miles of two-lane blacktop. Red dots on the map represent churches and cemeteries. Globs of green ink indicate fields and trees. Water sources? Squiggly blue lines and circular shapes signify streams and lakes. What about food and shelter? There'll be houses on the side roads. Alice suggests pushing ourselves tomorrow to hike the eighteen miles to Furman. We're going out to search the nearby residences. I'd give my big toe to scare up a bar of chocolate.

Olivia and Sophie skinned the bluegill on the kitchen countertop and are pan-frying the fillets on the propane stove. This cabin smells worse than a Red Lobster on Good Friday. In my youth, I turned up my nose at the scent of seafood, finned or legged. COVID-24 plus eleven nuclear warheads drastically altered my picky diet. These days, I devour anything that's on the menu, once even boiling my cowhide belt during a harsh winter to produce "Pioneer" soup. The sliced leather cubes tasted (asking Jules for her Yelp review) "like ass."

More houses were nestled among the leafy canopy than we had suspected. Looters and animals had stripped the buildings bare. One place stayed untouched, thanks to the eight overripe bodies inside. Nine, if you count the woman wearing the ALL I WANTED WAS A BACKRUB! maternity dress. Olivia found a folding grocery cart in the garage to transport our packaged and canned goods. I came upon a Cobra walkie-talkie and a handful of AA batteries. We dragged the family outside and buried them in a patch of soft soil, including the man holding a shotgun to his skull.

We sat on the porch after dinner. The bluegill actually wasn't half bad. As night descended upon us, so did the insects. Sophie discovered a bottle of Deep Wood's Off! in a medicine cabinet. I don't care what chemicals are in that spray as long as the citrusy odor keeps the bloodsuckers at bay.

Alice, Jules, and I listened to the girls yapping about their experiences before and after Election Day. Diary, I regret using "yap" to describe their chatter, as it depicts me as an old fuddy-duddy. Perhaps, with my birthday just days away, I can't help but envy their youthful exuberance. If my calculations are accurate, I turn thirty-eight this Thursday. Or maybe I'm unable to comprehend how Olivia and Sophie can remain buoyant despite the countless lives they've taken. Alice once pointed out that I don't smile much. In light of all the atrocities I've committed in the past five years, do I deserve even a moment of happiness?

Olivia narrated a childhood story that stirred both joy and sadness. Her bulldog absconding with an entire Thanksgiving ham made me think of Oscar. I miss going for long walks with my handsome furbaby.

Alice – July 9, 2029

7/9/2029

We stopped at Crossroad Cemetery to gnaw on the last of Pearl's hardtack. My back is against a lichen-covered headstone bearing the inscription HATTIE REYNOLDS—1895–1908—WIFE OF WYATT REYNOLDS. Despite the bummer of both Hattie's marriage and life ending prematurely, what a peaceful spot for her to spend perpetuity!

I picture my final resting place as a ditch on the side of a lonesome lane.

We left Mount Willing at sunrise, taking turns wheeling Grandma Peaches—Olivia gave the collapsible grocery cart a silly nickname. We have all the ingredients for a beautiful day, with blue skies overhead, chirping birds, and tolerable humidity. One of us scouts over an oncoming hill or around the next bend, signaling the coast is clear before the rest of our group moves forward. So far, the only things we've seen are a herd of elk leaping across the road and, off in the distance, a farmer plowing a field with a team of oxen.

My arches are falling. The soles of my hiking boots are worn through, and the Dr. Scholl's inserts provide zero support. I picked up this pair of Merrells ten million miles ago at a camping store in Clanton. Still-in-the-box footwear is always preferable to shoehorning them off a rotter. There had better be a Foot Locker in Camden because I dread having to dig six feet down.

This afternoon, we took a detour to investigate the homes on Till Road. A male voice called out as we looped an unnamed side street. We hid behind a yellow bus with LOWNDES COUNTY SCHOOLS painted on the sides.

A Black man appeared in a field stacked three high with rusting cars and trucks. "Hey, I know you're there! Come on out! I'm unarmed!"

Jules whispered, "Julie, he's baiting you."

"No, Jules, I don't believe he's a threat."

"Why is that?"

"Think I've seen him in. . . ."

"Where?"

"On TV?" Julie edged around the black bumper of the bus, lowering the assault rifle to her waist.

My attempt at recreating Julie and Jules' dialog fails to capture the actual experience of observing two distinct personalities occupying the same body. Notwithstanding my growing ability to distinguish between them based on subtle physical and vocal cues, words alone cannot impart the sheer strangeness of their exchanges.

It's worth mentioning that we gained a few firearms from the Apostles of Eternal Love. Olivia now possesses Delilah's girl-sized Colt M4 carbine, fully loaded with hollow-points. Sophie kept her AK-47 killing machine. I retained my Mossberg Patriot hunting rifle and Glock 22 handgun. Julie wields Maurice's M16 alongside her Sig Sauer P320. And Jules? Julie's shadow has full access to her host.

Now, where were we?

Ah, yes. Julie emerged in front of the bus. She's got the M16. However, she wasn't aiming the barrel at the old-timer. "What's your name?"

The man, who must have been somewhere in his seventies, wore a red Nike tracksuit. "People round these parts call me 'Preacher,' although, as an agnostic, I've stopped preaching. And yours?"

"I'm Julie. Alice, Olivia, Sophie, and Jules are in my group. Anyone else with you?"

I realize I haven't yet schooled Sophie on Julie and Jules. Did Olivia take care of it? I should ask her.

"My wife, Grace, is up at the house. Are you folks hungry?" Preacher counted us as we came into view. "You said there were five of you?"

"Sir, there are five of us," I patted my distended belly, "if it is God's will." My stomach identified the smell of grilling meat and growled, "Eat! Eat! Eat!" I didn't consider telling a small fib to someone who had lost faith in a higher power as a major sin.

We obeyed Preacher's warnings as we maneuvered past the wrecked vehicles, corroded engine blocks, and greasy rear axles. I reckoned that only the glass windshields would survive a thousand years from now.

Atop a grassy knoll, a single-story dwelling overlooked the automobile graveyard. A Hispanic woman hollered from the porch, "No weapons allowed inside my home." She held the screen door open as we placed our guns on the picnic table outside. "And remove your shoes so you don't track motor oil on the rug." I scanned the property for any junkyard dogs as I toed off my boots onto the HOPE YOU LIKE PITBULLS doormat.

A pint-sized fawn Chihuahua with a pink collar bounded up to us as we cautiously entered the living room. Olivia and Sophie kneeled on the spotless flooring to "good girl" Snowflake.

Preacher shut the screen door, muttering, "Horse flies've been somethin' fierce this summer." He gestured for us to sit.

Julie and I sat on the mauve couch (saving a space for Jules between us). When Snowflake jumped upon the middle cushion, I wondered what image Julie's brain served up. Was Jules cradling the adorable pup? Grace slid out dining room chairs for Olivia, Sophie, and herself.

Preacher sank into the suede recliner, raising his feet with the pull of a lever. "So, what brings you to Minter?"

Julie answered on our behalf. "We're on our way to Hattiesburg to find my twin sister. I'm from Syracuse, New York. I worked for a newspaper in Ithaca, where I interviewed you at Immaculate Conception for the *Voice*. It was Christmas time of. . .can't recall the year. You were promoting a food drive for the homeless and underprivileged."

Preacher's eyes widened. "Oh, I remember you. It truly is a small world!" He smiled at Grace. "Her article brought in so many generous donations."

"I'm glad I could help! How did you wind up in Alabama?"

Preacher sighed. "We lost three-quarters of our congregation in the month COVID-19 mutated to '24. Aging parishioners fell prey to right-wing conspiracy theories and refused to get vaccinated at the stadiums. They trusted that God would extend His hand to protect the righteous. Those who outlived the pandemic fled southwest when the H-bombs Svetlana and Galina obliterated Philly and the Big Apple. Gracie and I stayed right till the bitter end, caring for the sick and burying the dead. We evacuated Ithaca after we developed respiratory problems from breathing the foul air. That led us to Pittsburg, Louisville, Nashville. . . . For a spell, we ministered at a Catholic church in Selma until—"

"Thomas had doubts," Grace interjected, gripping his arm. "He no longer heard the Word. I encouraged my husband to continue his sacred odyssey, but—"

"God forsook humanity in our time of need." Preacher clasped his palms. "I prayed and prayed for spiritual guidance, even the tiniest sign to show me the way. But there was nothing. Just the throbbing of my broken heart in the solitude of night."

"The reversal of Creation!" Grace shook her hands in exasperation. "The great flood swallowed up the unworthy. Sanctified by God, Noah and his sons, Shem, Ham, and Japheth, multiplied and replenished the earth. It is our God-given duty to follow in Noah's footsteps!"

I love entertainment as much as the next person, but I held my breath as Julie transmuted into Jules. "When the ark eventually reached solid ground," Jules began, "Noah planted a vineyard. After a long day of swilling Jesus Juice, the 'tiller of the soil' exposed his twig and berries to his boys." She covered her mouth, ineffectively repressing her giggles. "The guy God assigned to save mankind was kinky as hell!"

Julie turned to the center of the couch to scold the empty space. "Jules, mind your manners! Only Noah knows what went on inside that tent!"

Grace grabbed a broom. "Lord, as your loyal servant, rid me of those who harass me!" She brushed at our bare feet as if our toes were crumbs on the kitchen floor. "Heathens, I vanquish you! Get out of my house!"

Snowflake barked in agitation as I herded Olivia and Sophie toward the door, both snickering like high schoolers. "Julie! Jules!" The scene would have offered comic relief if I hadn't been so famished.

Preacher accompanied us outside, Grace slamming the screen door behind him. "Wait! The sun sets in an hour. There's nothing but farmland between here and Furman." He pointed at a rounded structure silhouetted against the golden horizon. "I keep an old motorhome in the workshop. There are beds and sheets. . .but you must be gone by morning. I can't let my wife see you. I apologize for her behavior—Gracie hasn't adjusted to not being a preacher's wife. She misses female company. I hoped your visit might pull her out of the doldrums."

I took Preacher's hand. "We appreciate your generosity. We'll leave before your wife wakes up."

"Sorry you never got supper. I'll bring some vittles once Gracie says her evening prayers." Preacher frowned as he studied Julie's face. "Miss, are you feeling all right?"

Julie looked puzzled. "Sure, why?"

He removed a silver disk at the end of a long chain from his pocket. "Hang this pendant around your neck. The saints will watch over you on your quest."

Julie angled the tarnished metal to catch the light. "Martyrs?"

Preacher's eyes shined with reverence. "Cosmas and Damian were skilled physicians. The identical twins accepted no payment for their good deeds. These brave men stood steadfast, even after the Roman emperor decreed for them to renounce their beliefs. The brothers faced arrows, stones, and nails. It took an executioner's ax to silence their praises to the Lord Most High."

Julie hung the pendant from her neck. "I thought you didn't believe in God?"

"Faith is like the ebb and flow of tides on a beach. The sand washes away, grain by grain, only to return during the next storm." Preacher chuckled sheepishly. "Who am I to tell anybody anything?"

We entered the corrugated steel of the WWII Quonset hut. The sole door, with two barred windows on either side, allowed slivers of sunlight to illuminate a brown and tan Winnebago resting on jack stands. Dust covered its 1980s-style interior, but the carpet beneath our feet felt dry, and no creepy crawlies scurried up the walls when we lit a lantern. Preacher later dropped off a sack of food, his parting words full of optimism. Olivia and Sophie claimed the bigger mattress in the back. Julie converted the kitchen sofa into a bed. I climbed inside the cubbyhole above the cab.

My eyes burn from writing in the flickering candlelight. Julie is snoring below, and the girls have stopped conversing. Goodnight, dear Diary. Sleep tight, and don't let the bedbugs bite!

Julie – July 9, 2029

7/9/2029

I am looking down a valley, the vibrant colors of nature stretching as far as the eye can see. We left Mount Willing, hoping to reach Furman by nightfall. Eighteen miles is manageable. With such pleasant weather, I could waste the whole day underneath this weeping willow. This boneyard is an oasis in a desert teeming with gargantuan scorpions. There's been so much needless bloodshed the past few weeks. Meeting Alice and her friends has been the only positive thing amidst all this turmoil.

Does Alice like me? Or does she think I'm crazy? Alice never vocalizes unfavorable thoughts about me, but her green eyes break me down like a botched scientific experiment.

"Exhibit one. Today, Julie displayed extreme neurosis by constantly chewing on her fingernails."

And what assumptions are being made in her composition notebook?

"Julie's close friend is a certifiable sociopath. Why isn't Jules at Bellevue, locked up in a padded room?"

Quit being so paranoid, Julie! Alice willingly joined you on this perilous crusade to find Julia. She kept you from burning up in a Hayneville jail cell. Alice risked her life for you! Even though our time together is short, we've formed a strong bond and always have each other's backs.

Christ, I'm convinced this woman's got me under a microscope. What is Alice writing in that damn diary?

Once again, Jules put her foot in her mouth. We had walked for miles when I suggested searching the side roads for food. An old fella spotted our group (his name is Thomas, but he goes by Preacher) and invited us to his house. I recognized his face from an interview I had conducted for the *Ithaca Voice*, so we accepted. Alice joking that she was pregnant made no sense to me. Preacher introduced each of us to Grouchy Grace, his anti-gun, anal-retentive, religious freak of a wife.

I conveyed our origin and our destination. Preacher sermonized how, as a former Catholic priest, he lost his faith after God the Almighty let all of his beloved bite the big one.

When Grace referenced Noah and his floating Bronx Zoo, Jules insisted that the hero who saved planet Earth was a drunken pervert.

Preacher's highly offended wife swept me and my fellow "heathens" out of her living room with a Swiffer dust mop. Vanquishing us to the underworld would have been a laugh riot if Jules had waited until our stomachs were full to serve such a thick slice of sacrilege. Grace had shrieked, "Out with you, sons of Satan!" as she brushed us outside. Which is ironic since everyone I'm with is penis-less. Or would Doctor Ruth use the term "penis-free"?

Doubting Thomas let us stay overnight in his motorhome. This tin can stinks like the Jolly Green Giant's toga, but as Uncle Chester used to say before the district attorney shipped his sorry ass back to Rikers Island, "Never look a gift horse in the hiney hole."

Preacher sneaked us some food from his kitchen. Jules guessed, "Lamb of God," as we chewed on the gamey meat.

As for my ideology, do *I* believe in God? I vividly remember attending services every Sunday, the spicy frankincense and myrrh incense pervading Saint Patrick's as the choir sang hymns. Then calamity struck. The Holy Spirit, as part of His grand master plan, allowed Deputy Robert McKenna to swig a fifth of Glen Stag before ramming his muscle car into my parents' underpowered minivan.

Is there a celestial force that exists beyond my comprehension? Something created the birds, the trees, and the deep blue sea. Dare I presume that this otherworldly entity listens to my desperate cries? Does It feel anything for me? Is God asleep? Dead? And ultimately, is His existence even relevant?

Alice – July 10, 2029

7/10/2029

What the fuck is wrong with people?

Julie treated Sophie's first-degree burns with a tube of Neosporin. Olivia cut her hand jumping out of the motorhome's window. A bandage stopped the bleeding. Julie and me? We have minor bruises from smashing our way out of the Quonset hut. Although I tell everyone that it's nothing, my shoulder and elbow are sore.

I shilly-shallied before describing this morning's events, but I've documented all the other horrors. Why stop now?

We ate the tough-as-leather mutton that Preacher brought and squeezed into our beds. An unfamiliar female voice awakened me a little after midnight. I crawled to the edge of my upper bunk and peered down. Light seeping through the windshield backlit a figure crouched over the sofa bed. "Hey! What are you doing?"

Preacher's wife glanced up in irritation. "Quiet! Under the authority of the Roman Catholic Church, I, Grace Navarro, exorcise this demon from its earthly host." The woodsy scent of smoldering sage filled the tiny kitchen. "Blessed Child of God, do not harbor this heinous spirit or its allies. Scatter thyself to the nether regions, Archfiend. In the name of Jesus Christ, I rebuke thee. I rebuke thee. I rebuke thee!"

Julie lay on the bedding, seemingly asleep. "Julie, are you all right?"

"Oh, Prince of the Divine, banish those who wander our world for the ruination of souls. Prince of Darkness, I rebuke thee. I rebuke thee. I rebuke thee!"

When Julie's eyelids not as much as twitched, I wondered if Grace had drugged her food. How is that possible? We ate the same thing! Or did Julie (or Jules) genuinely wish to be exorcised? I dropped to the floor.

Grace hip-checked me into the sink. "Surely, the King of Kings shall deliver this lowly sinner from the fowler's snare and the noisome pestilence. Lucifer, I rebuke thee. I rebuke thee. I rebuke thee!"

I smacked Grace in the mouth as she sprinkled cloudy liquid from a Coca-Cola bottle labeled HOLY WATER onto Julie's face. Either Preacher's wife had a heavyweight jaw, or I had a featherweight fist. Like a prizefighter rising from the ten count, she shook the blood off her lip, stomped out of the Winnebago, and slammed the metal door shut with a definitive click.

Sophie and Olivia huddled in fear in the narrow hallway.

"Grab your bags. We're checking out of this nuthouse." I twisted the doorknob. "It's locked! Try the back!"

They rushed to the rear of the coach. "The windows are sealed!" The sound of hammering grew louder.

Amid the tumult, a pungent gasoline odor permeated the air, mingling with the acridity of combusting wood.

Julie sat on the sofa's edge, staring at floating dust motes. "Jules," I shout, "the building is burning! Take control!" Jules jumped into her boots, pushed the girls aside, and broke the window frame with the butt of her rifle. Olivia, the first one out, lacerated her palm while lowering herself to the Quonset hut's floor. I wrapped a woolen blanket over the jagged windowsill to prevent further injury.

We felt our way through the thick fumes to discover that our single exit was bolted from the outside. Opening the windows just fed the flames, and the metal bars blocked our escape.

Jules and I threw ourselves at the entryway. The rusty hinges pulled free from the termite-infested doorframe, and the door crashed to the ground. We leaped into the junkyard, coughing and spitting up sooty phlegm.

Jules marched toward Preacher's house, swinging a tire iron.

"Stop!" I captured one hundred and seventy pounds of enraged grizzly bear by the leather belt. "Let it be, Jules. Time to go."

Welcome to Furman, Alabama, a secluded hamlet with a double-pump gas station, post office, Methodist and Baptist churches, and a dozen luxurious residences.

The elegant two-story yellow building we're staying in resembles a riverboat casino with wraparound porches and ornate railings. However, our crew is on a cruise to nowhere without a steam engine to propel the paddle-wheeler through acres of furrowed soil. DeVaughn Plantation offers twelve bedrooms, each embellished with plush Persian rugs and velvet drapes. We vowed to stick together after last night's ordeal, so we dragged mattresses into the ballroom. The marble tiles are gorgeous. Too bad vandals defaced the white wainscoting with offensive graffiti.

I awoke from a mid-afternoon nap, all hot and sweaty. As the others slept, I strolled into the backyard to catch a breeze. A detached garage stood in the corner of the property. Open doors revealed racks of landscaping equipment and an ebony Cadillac hearse—no body under the landau roof, just golf clubs and buckets of golf balls. A dog barking and an ax chopping echoed throughout the woods.

I considered investigating our neighbors, but the buzzing swamp angels chased me indoors. To be honest, I hope to not see another living being until Hattiesburg.

Following a simple dinner of Bush's baked beans and freshly picked apples, I took Olivia and Sophie, our exposed skin soaked in insect repellant, behind the house to knock around a bucket of golf balls. While we unloaded the sports gear from the vintage hearse, I explained the Julie/Jules situation to Sophie.

Unfazed by the news, Sophie selected a golf club with a long shaft. "My mom's younger sister had a similar mental disorder. Schizophrenia. Aunt Emi believed she was a born superhero named Katana."

Olivia gripped a putter with both hands. "Did your aunt cleanse the world of evil?"

Sophie swung the wood in a wide arc, the large head slicing through clouds of white gnats. "Not quite. A SWAT team shot Aunt Emi after she decapitated six nursery school kids with a samurai sword."

Julie – July 10, 2029

7/10/2029

Early in the morning, I hear movement inside the motorhome. Too tired to open my eyelids, I assume Alice or one of the girls is going outdoors to relieve themselves. A gentle puff, puff, puff on my cheek reawakens me. *Why are my eyes still closed?* A female voice whispers in my ear, "Fear not, Julie-Jules-whatever your real Christian name is. I am sending the demon sinking its claws into your soul back to Hell." It sounds like Preacher's wife, Grace. "Even if we have to burn your earthly body at the stake to free your heavenly being." I regulate my breathing and feign sleep as something hard presses against my skin. "Devil, you ushered wickedness into my virtuous home."

"Hey, Julie," Alice calls from her bunk. "Are you okay?"

Grace bellows, "Shut your mouth! A malicious spirit possesses this woman. I must concentrate!" Is she referring to me? Though not physically paralyzed, I'm too weak to speak, and the object sitting on my ribs weighs a ton. (Hours later, my chest bears red marks in the shape of a cross.) "The Vatican sanctions me to perform sacred exorcisms."

Vatican City is in ruins after the College of Cardinals martyred Pope Dionysius II. But I can't help but wonder, *am I possessed?* And why is Jules letting this woman—more tormentor than savior—anywhere near me?

Grace is reciting scriptures. Am *I* the "Blessed Child of God"? And *who* is the "Archfiend"? She chants, "In Jesus' name, I rebuke thee!" three times, then launches into incantations referencing "dark princes" and "ruined souls."

Alice exclaims, "What are you doing?" I hear her drop from the upper bed. I crack my eyes enough to see Grace shove Alice against the sink. I continue to lie on the sofa, stiff as a board. Why aren't I defending my friend?

Garlicky water splashes my forehead as Grace rants about "Abaddon," "Azrael," "fowlers," and "pestilence." Does she believe *I* caused the global pandemic? The CIA claimed the virus escaped from a Chinese lab. Didn't it? And what do birds have to do with any of this?

Alice punches Grace right in the kisser with a powerful roundhouse. Grace shakes blood onto the refrigerator like a duck shedding water off its back. The amateur exorcist exits, slamming the door shut behind her.

Alice waves at me to get up. "Let's go! Preacher's wife is nuts!" But the doorknob won't turn. She orders Olivia and Sophie to try the rear windows. "Jules, the garage is on fire! We need your help!"

The bathroom door swings open, and out comes Jules, swishing her hand as if she just clogged the toilet. She shatters the bedroom window with her gun, and we lower ourselves to the cement. Smoke clogs the sealed shed, making it difficult to find our way out. Alice and Jules break down the rotted door. We cover our faces and lunge through the blazing doorframe.

The flames blistered Sophie's arm. Olivia sliced her palm on the window glass. The left side of my scalp is singed and my shoulder is swollen. Alice is tough, but I can tell that she's also hurting. Despite all the aches and pains, we lived to see another day!

Questions, questions, questions. . . . Why did Grace believe a demon controlled me? And, of equal importance, why did I allow her to exorcise me? Was the ritual successfully completed? I can't say I feel any different.

Furman, Alabama. Antebellum houses always infuriate me. The ghosts of my ancestors cower in the corners and in the shadows under the stairs. I picture myself on all fours giving "pony rides" to privileged little White girls. When the wind scrapes tree branches against the wood siding, I hear the crack of the overseer's whip. A historical street sign states that Clarence DeVaughn constructed this plantation home at the height of the slave trade.

After Alice returned from her stroll, Jules and I went outside. Far beyond a fenced-in graveyard reserved for generations of DeVaughns, I discovered the final resting place of those who obtained freedom from slavery only in death. We sat on a moss-covered log, watching fireflies flit between rocks that served as headstones.

I brought up the exorcism with Jules. She circled her finger around her ear to imply that the reverend's wife had a screw loose. "Julie, why didn't Alice let me slit Grace's throat?"

The distinctive smell of grilling meat steered our noses through an apple orchard to a brick house. Shirts and pants hung on a clothesline, and smoke rose from an outdoor fireplace. I restrained Jules from swiping a piece of chicken. We've had enough trouble over the last few days to last two lifetimes.

Jules and I picked the ripest apples and made our way to the mansion, regretting our lack of bug spray. Alice and the girls were in the kitchen preparing a cold supper. I notified them that we had neighbors. We sat at a dining room table fit for a king and his court, feasting on fresh fruit and tins of baked beans. I hope the windows in our sleeping quarters will air out Jules' devil farts.

Once we were done cleaning up, I buried the empty bean cans and apple cores between the graves of Odette and Clarence DeVaughn. Jules went upstairs to look around while the rest of us gathered in the game room to play a round of *Monopoly*. Olivia shrewdly purchased all the railroads to emerge victorious.

As we tucked ourselves in for the night, Jules suggested I check the attic tomorrow morning.

Alice – July 11, 2029

7/11/2029

This ballroom is grand, except for the obscene graffiti tagging the walls. I envision glitz and glamor. Dashing young gentlemen in tailored tuxedos and elegant debutants in long, flowing gowns gracefully waltz beneath the warm glow of candlelit chandeliers. The melodic strains of a string quartet fill the air as attentive waiters serve flutes of champagne and hors d'oeuvres on silver plat

Julie is calling. She sounds

Julie – July 11, 2029

7/11/2029

Jules and I found ourselves awake at 5:30 a.m. Her mouth formed the words "the attic" to me without making a sound. We ascended the curved staircase to the second floor, where she guided me to a door at the end of a long corridor. Fifteen steps up was a room stacked with furniture, travel trunks, children's toys, and numerous cardboard cartons labeled PHOTOGRAPHS, WINTER CLOTHES, and CHRISTMAS ORNAMENTS.

Dormers on opposite sides of the gabled roof illuminated an enclosure reminiscent of the Hayneville jail cell Jules and I spent so many hours in. A young girl with light hair and piercing hazel eyes stared at us through the vertical bars.

I yelled at Jules, "Why didn't you say something?"

She threw my accusation back at me. "I did last night!"

Muddled, I pointed at the footmarks on the floor. "You've been up here?"

"No. I figured rats or raccoons caused the noises. You needed to sleep, so I told you to check the attic in the morning."

Lug sole boot prints on the dirty planking led to the cell. I kneeled in front of the locked gate and tapped my chest. "Hi, I'm Julie. What is your name?" The girl's open mouth exposed the gaps of two missing baby teeth. "Who put you in here?" Again, no reply.

I turned to Jules. "Go and get the others!"

Jules hesitated. "Julie, you should be the one to tell them."

The shadows receded into the eaves as I inspected the entire space. Layers of dust coated everything, signifying that this eight-by-eight-foot cage had been sitting up here for decades, if not centuries. A single bed fitted with lavender Disney *Frozen* sheets caught my eye. Anna, Elsa, and Olaf smiled at me like old friends. A dollhouse spacious enough for Barbie and Ken to throw a dance party stood beside a small card table and chair. The blue five-gallon Lowe's pail and toilet paper roll completed the furnishings.

Jules noticed a plastic water pitcher and a cup alongside a dish piled with chicken bones. "Whoever feeds her will not come into the house while we're here."

I leaned over the stairway railing, calling for Alice and the girls to wake up. They hurried into the attic, their eyes as big as saucers.

Alice tugged at the metal gate, stooping to examine the keyhole. Her search for a pry bar yielded only a splintered broom handle. "How can we open this door? There may be a hammer in the garage."

Based on my recent experiences—Ardy, I don't hold your distrust against you—I was well-acquainted with the trials of releasing a captive without the correct key. "She won't be fed if we're still on the premises."

Olivia shook her head. "So? We'll give her food!"

"Beans and apples?" I gestured at the plate of bones. "She's clearly getting more protein than we are. And with no key, it's impossible to free her."

Alice threw up her palms in frustration. "Our footprints will show we were in the attic!" She reached past the bars. "Sweetie, when was the last time you ate?" No response. "Does she speak? Is she mute?"

I felt helpless as Olivia's and Sophie's attempts to squeeze as much as a peep out of the child also failed. "We have no choice but to go. Now."

Alice rattled the gate. "And abandon her?"

Jules cocked her Sig Sauer. "We aren't leaving anyone behind."

There are four sides to every building, and, fortunately, we've got five people to keep watch. Jules and I have eyes on Alice and Olivia from the front. From the sides, Olivia and Alice have eyes on Sophie in the back. Nobody can access the DeVaughn residence without one of us seeing them.

As the morning ticked into the afternoon, my thoughts drifted back to "Tina," the name I had randomly given to the silent girl. Was this moniker indeed by chance? Memories of Tina Tanenbaum from Syracuse University entered my mind. She was not actually a friend, but someone I admired and aspired to be chummy with. If only Jules hadn't been so envious.

Worriment pushes away my positive introspections as I realize Tina hasn't eaten since yesterday. She has water. Does the next-door neighbor know anything?

I tired of twiddling my thumbs. Alice and the girls monitored the DeVaughns' property while Jules and I crept through the woods to the brick house. The clothesline swung bare, and the fireplace grill felt cold. An eerie stillness hung over the sunbaked yard.

"Hey!" I shouted. "Is anybody there?"

The birds stopped chirping.

"We just want to talk!"

Jules approached the front of the single-level home as I crossed to the back door. I army-crawled across the kitchen linoleum, nearly jumping out of my skin as an antique grandfather clock chimed five times. I rose to a crouch in the hallway, poking my rifle around corners and into rooms until I met Jules by the entryway. A stack of Leonard C. Bannon's unread mail lay on an end table, untouched for half a decade.

We circled the yard, ready to pack it up, when Jules stumbled upon a thick pipe hidden by weeds. An earthen mound covered an underground bunker, its metal door secured from within. Boot prints on the muddy soil matched those in the DeVaughns' attic.

I called into the air vent, my words echoing in the depths. "Hello! Is somebody in there?" Jules' eyes widened as she pressed her earflap to the opening. She rushed to the outdoor fireplace, returning with a can of Kroger Odorless Charcoal Lighter Fluid and a box of Diamond Large Kitchen Matches.

Diary, I wish I could tell you we were confident the person in the bomb shelter held sole responsibility for Tina's imprisonment before we stuffed burning dishcloths into the ventilation tube. Antsy for results, Jules poured the entire quart of combustible liquid down the pipe. Moments later, the blast door clanged open, and a White face emerged through the clouds of black smoke.

Jules yanked the bowlegged man out of the hole by his singed denim shirt collar and thrust him against the outhouse. "She's just a child!"

We had no proof the homeowner had the cage key—"Lady, I dunno what you're talkin' about"—until Jules went to town with rusty barbecue tongs. Diary, I'll spare you the grotesque details.

Once in possession of the key, I posed the age-old question, "Why did you do it?"

I expected the man to mumble a pathetic excuse. Despite his missing tooth, Leonard seemed eager to confess. "When my neighbors caught Glenn's Cough—"

People give the coronavirus all sorts of humorous nicknames—Boomer Remover, Miss Rona, Sweat and Sour Sniffles—but I've never heard of Glenn's Cough. "You mean COVID?"

"Yeah." Leonard picked at his blistered arm. "Here in Furman, we believed the pandemmy was a left-wing hoax. Life went on 'til Glenn Todd comes back from a river baptism in Carlowville with the hot and colds." He indicated a chimney pushing through the treetops. "Could hear the Todds coughin' their lungs out. Glenn and Mary died in their beds, leavin' no one to rear the young 'un."

I asked, "Does your prisoner have a name?"

"Name? I call her 'Girl.' Didn't wanna get too attached. When Jedidiah Creasy's tractor run over Sadie, I—"

"You had a daughter?"

"My bird dog. I cried for a week."

"Did she get sick?"

"Sadie?"

"No, Girl."

"Uh-uh. Me neither. I took in the orphan and put her in the DeVaughns' attic to avoid catchin' her daddy's bug. Doc Holloway made a big deal about keepin' away from the 'fected. 'Quarantine,' he called it."

"I know what 'quarantine' means, you idiot." A familiar pain pulsed behind my left eye. "Are you telling me that she's been confined in that tiny box for *five years?*"

"Hey!" Leonard exclaimed. "I didn't make the damn thing. My cousin told me the DeVaughns built that jail cell in the 1800s for uppity slaves." His bottom lip retracted, unveiling a row of rot. "I fed Girl breakfast and dinner, even on Sundays, which the faithful observe as a day for rest and worship. What else did you want me to do? Have her live in my home? I'm a single man!"

I picked up a bearded gnome and passed the cement lawn ornament to Jules. "Can the child speak?"

Leonard's sooty cheeks flamed red. "She's not my kid, and I ain't nobody's schoolmarm!"

Jules ended the interrogation *tout de suite*.

We unlocked the steel cage and carefully led Tina down the stairs. I expected the girl to be terrified of us strangers and was astonished when she whispered, "Julie," to me.

Sophie suggested taking Tina out into the open air, but Alice cautioned against overstimulating her.

The child's plight reminded me of a YouTube video where a thirty-year-old laboratory chimpanzee saw the sky for the first time. Choco immediately lost his marbles and maimed a research assistant. A vet had to euthanize the ape a week later.

I talked with Alice in the garage. The filthy hearse we leaned against begged for a wash, wax, and, most noticeably, a coffin. She upturned her palms. "What should we do with Tina? We can't bring her with us."

I inhaled deeply to subdue my indignation. "Do you really mean that?"

"No." Alice sighed. "Can she even walk?"

A cart glinted from behind a riding lawn mower, its red-and-white paint chipped and scratched. "We can tow Tina until she builds leg muscles." I foresaw the girl gaining strength with each step.

Alice wheeled the metal wagon across the floor, its rubber tires squealing in protest. "Peter and I bought Kenny a Radio Flyer for his birthday. My son got the coronavirus before he had the chance to play with it." She dropped the handle. "Julie, how did you persuade the neighbor into giving you the key to Tina's cell?"

I visualized Gundar, the portly bearded gnome, lying in the uncut grass with his pointy hat shining bright red. "I wasn't there, Alice. You'll have to ask Jules."

When Alice and I returned to the plantation house, Olivia and Sophie were rolling a tennis ball to Tina. Her giggles filled the entire ballroom!

After supper, I placed Tina on my lap. She's heavy! Alice estimated the child to be six years old. I think she might be closer to seven. Her long blonde mane resembled a bird's nest, so I washed away all the dirt, brushed out the tangles, and trimmed the ends. Although my hairstyling skills are far from professional, at least the girl can now see beyond her bangs. I had hoped that she might utter "Julie" again, but Tina just gaped at me as if she'd never seen another woman.

Keeping Tina from wandering outdoors is proving to be challenging. What if she runs away and gets lost if I fall asleep? Sophie joked about chaining her to a radiator. Olivia proposed confining Tina to her cage. "For her safety!" No way am I locking that poor child up.

Tina possesses a phenomenal ability to absorb her environment. Her sharp and observant eyes quickly capture the grandeur of the ballroom, marveling at the crystal chandeliers suspended from the coffered ceiling and the hunting and landscape paintings adorning the wainscoted walls. She slides across the waxed parquet flooring, her stockinged feet enjoying every ridge and ripple.

However, the open floor-to-ceiling windows enthrall Tina. The girl yearns to fly free with the other birds in the sky.

I'm concerned that Tina is experiencing hearing difficulties. She doesn't react when I call her, snap my fingers, or clap my hands. Sophie says that felines exhibit the same behavior. "Cats ignore you unless you have something they desire."

Tina isn't deaf. I know this because when we watched the sun sink below the trees, her head swiveled toward the symphony of the night. She only hears what she wants to hear.

For our sleeping arrangements, Tina and I share a mattress, our ankles tethered with a short cord.

Alice – July 12, 2029

7/12/2029

Yesterday, we added a new member to our party: Tina. A neighbor had locked the poor six-year-old girl in the attic of the house we are sleeping in. Julie found her after Jules heard someone crying.

As I reexamine the past few days' events, a wave of indecision comes over me. Was it wise to have accompanied Julie and Olivia, or should I have stayed in Hayneville? God knows that town has its own share of problems.

We aim to reach Camden today. The roadway has been relatively flat, but towing Grandma Peaches up as little as a one percent grade is strenuous. Plus, now there's a fifty-pound child in a twenty-pound wagon. The map illustrates streams and wider blue lines for rivers ahead of us. I pray that none of the bridges are washed out, as even six inches of fast-moving water can be a formidable obstacle.

Of all the places to stay in Furman, we had to pick the DeVaughn house.

I must have been feeling sorry for myself this morning.

Come what may, I find solace in the companionship of Julie, Olivia, and now Sophie and Tina. I help them, and they help me.

And that, dear Diary, is the true meaning of life.

We're at the AL-28 and AL-10 intersection, resting on the Hensen family's veranda. Olivia and Sophie investigated the mobile homes out back, complaining that the rotters "stank to high heaven." Nevertheless, the girls dug up eight cans of Libby's Vienna Sausages. The blue and red labels claim the sausages are MADE WITH CHICKEN, BEEF & PORK IN CHICKEN BROTH. I must admit the fully cooked flesh-colored meat tubes are surprisingly satisfying.

Tina is a trip! Do people still say, "a trip"? Is any new slang being coined nowadays? Or sayings such as "Actions speak louder than words" or "It takes two to tango." Oh, here's a good one. "How now, brown cow?" While I brainstorm a fresh adage, idiom, or proverb, let's discuss Tina.

Dear Diary, have you seen the movie *Nell* with Jodie Foster? Well, I barely remember the plot, except that Nell's mom dropped dead, and a doctor discovered the young woman living in a forest. She had no social skills and spoke a strange language. A feral child.

I drew parallels to Nell when I first saw Tina, a lost cause requiring major effort. I was only half-kidding when I told Julie we couldn't bring the girl.

KA-BOOM! Before I knew it, my motherly instincts kicked in, and that bucket of negativity flew out the kitchen window. I find myself watching Tina like a mama hawk, ready to claw the eyes of anybody who dares to look at her hatchling the wrong way.

Julie is teaching Tina numbers. She arranges small rocks on the porch, pointing at each pile and repeating, "One, two, three," and so on. I hope Julie lets me help with the alphabet.

Camden is three to four miles away. Dark comes sooner each day. We should get moving.

Pulling Tina in the Radio Flyer isn't burdensome at all. She walks a few hundred yards before climbing into the wagon. Seeing our "baby girl" drink in every unfamiliar sight is a joy.

Was I ever that thirsty?

Twice the size of Hayneville, Camden is the largest town we've been to since waving goodbye to Ardy and Pearl. We traversed the downtown sidewalks, trying to blend in with the other men, women, and children.

After passing by a rundown shopping center with Piggly Wiggly, CVS, and Hardee's, the city hall and courthouse were the first official buildings we encountered. With Grandma Peaches' pouch nearly empty, I advised our group to replenish our supplies. Julie had a stash of prescription meds and Sophie held extra AK-47 rounds to trade.

A blind man at a roadside stand sold used clothes. Julie haggled with the veteran, exchanging a Percocet pill for two trash bags stuffed with women's and children's wear. He endorsed a business on Broad Street.

For the items that Odds & Ends didn't stock, we were directed a block away to Bright's Market on Water Street. The vivacious red-haired proprietor scanned our foreheads with an infrared thermometer before presenting her wares. She questioned where we came from as Sophie forked over three bullets for a jug of cow's milk, a sack of fresh fruits and veggies, and packages of preserved venison.

I have learned that keeping the story as simple as possible works best. "This is Julie, Olivia, and Sophie. The little one is Tina." I stuck out my palm for a handshake. "And I'm Alice, originally from Paramus, New Jersey."

"Lucy Bright. A pleasure to meet ya." Her accent carried a slight Cajun twang. "As a teenager, I watched MTV's *Jersey*

Shore." She chuckled. "So much drama. That Snooki girl is a hoot! 'Study hard, but party harder!' was her motto."

I nodded, not a fan of fly-on-the-wall reality TV. "How's life in Camden?"

Lucy stared out the front window, scratching her elbow. "The Southern Outlaws joined forces with the Ticks. Those punks caused quite a ruckus. A lot of folks left after the hangings."

Julie's brown eyes projected concern. "Did the gangs string up your people?"

"No, ma'am." Lucy pointed at the courthouse. "The Texas Rangers took care of those barbarians right over there."

I don't know how I overlooked the wooden platform and scaffolding. "Rangers from the state of Texas?"

"None other. While riding on horses, Colonel Austin and his Texan Devils hounded Rex Butler and Paco Rivera from Waco. Once the Devils are on your scent, they will never give up."

Olivia asked, "What did the Outlaws and Ticks do in Waco?"

Lucy appraised our firearms with a keen eye. "Robbery, rape, extortion. . .homicide. It'd be shorter to list the commandments those rogues didn't break. I see you're loaded for bear."

I adjusted my rifle. "We've run into our fair share of trouble since leaving Montgomery. Do you have any recommendations for where we can stay?" Until now, we had rested in vacant houses and buildings—easy to locate in the middle of nowhere, but not as feasible in a town as populated as Camden.

The shopkeeper directed our attention to a blackboard chalked with ROOMS FOR RENT. "There're a few units available. Are you interested in a Motel 6 jam-packed with stiffs or a cozy cabin on a lake?"

"Lake!" Tina exclaimed, holding Julie's hand.

"Excellent choice!" Lucy crouched to kid height. "What's your name again, dear one?"

"Tina."

We expressed approval, prompting Tina to shout, "Tina!"

Lucy jiggled a silver key with YELLOWHAMMER inscribed on the yellow tag. "Two bedrooms. Meals included."

I worried we couldn't afford to sleep indoors. "How much a night?"

"I have a cantaloupe field that needs harvesting. Four hours of early work. You'll be done pickin' before the sun cooks you to a crisp. The afternoons? Swim in the lake. Fish for crappie. Write your memoirs. Take a long snooze in the hammock. Do whatever your little hearts desire. I'll show you how to gather and transport the fruit, and then I must return to mind the store."

You know me, dear Diary, I love playing in the dirt! My pickin' hand shot out without conferring with the others. "Deal!"

"LakeView is a bit out of the way, but judging by the bottoms of your shoes, you are accustomed to traveling on foot." Lucy passed me the key. "I live in the Avery cabin. Come by at six o'clock. We're serving pot roast. Plenty of potatoes, carrots, and onions will fill your belly if anyone's vegetarian." Lucy winked as she gave me a bar of handmade soap. "And you may want to check out the bathhouse."

We retraced our steps, passing the empty CVS and heading up Route 10. At LakeView R/V and Cabin Rentals, twelve log cabins stood in a row, each concrete driveway bordered with beautiful flowering plants. Two rocking chairs and a gas grill furnished the raised porches. Julie unlocked the Yellowhammer's front door, and Tina ran inside to bounce on the first bed. "Tina! Julie!"

I am at the lake, soaking my tender tootsies in the refreshing cold water. There are a couple more hours until dinner, enough time to scrub off all this road grime and wash my hair. So, unless the Lord of Lords flies down in a Boeing 747 to cleanse the earth during the Second Coming, nothing shall keep me from catching forty winks under this shade tree. Make that fifty.

5:15. Groggy. Better hurry and find that bathhouse.

The pot roast was delicious! We met Lucy at her blue cabin and walked to the Cowboy Clubhouse. Twenty to thirty other guests waited to fill plastic plates with food inside the dining hall. The aroma of savory meat and roasted vegetables made my mouth water. Our campground host seemed to know everyone and their mothers.

Lucy seated our group at the front table, with Julie sliding over for Jules, then mounted a bench to introduce us. "Let's warmly welcome Alice Jenkins, Olivia Dawson, Sophie Chen, and Julie and Tina Werner." The room swelled with hearty applause, followed by clinking utensils and smacking lips. I'm so glad I wore fresh clothes and shampooed my hair. Oscar's bathwater had been cleaner than mine.

Other lodgers strolled by to shoot the breeze as we tidied up. The people were friendly, and their conversations were riveting enough for me to miss standing around the water cooler at Inkwell Literary Agency.

A man tried to chat up Julie, probably hoping to get lucky. Jules shut the old horndog down with a crass insult.

Why haven't I dug into Julie's former love life? She has mentioned Arthur, the man Corbin Holt had murdered in Hayneville, multiple times.

Having some respite from the road, I mulled over my own relationships, particularly with David and, less so, with Peter—the lounge lizard who tossed his wedding band in the toilet during our final fight. While I've had other lovers, none were as significant to me.

A day ago, Julie had come up to me. "Alice, how do you feel about Pearl's brother?" What did she mean by that comment? I answered vaguely. "Ardy's a nice guy. Why?" Julie smirked, an unusual expression for her. Does *she* like him?

Sophie and Olivia are sleeping in the second bedroom. Julie and Tina are across from me. Julie touches different parts of Tina's face, whispering, "Ears, eyes, nose, mouth, teeth." In return, Tina mirrors the actions as she softly repeats the words.

What is Jules' opinion on this new dependency? She had initially displayed signs of jealousy toward me. I've let down my guard lately, less distressed that Julie's dark passenger might plunge her Buck knife into my back. It's intriguing the way Julie took it upon herself to name the girl Tina, even going the extra mile to pass on her surname. It's very protective, very caring. These motherly qualities make me mourn Kenny even more. Am I envious of Julie and Tina's connection? No. I know I'm not. (I had to crack open that nut and look inside.) Their relationship is special, and I am genuinely pleased for them. As for me, nothing can replace the love I have for my son. Hopefully, someday, Tina will take Jules' place.

And then there's Ardy Jackson. *Do* I think about Ardy Jackson? His chiseled features and captivating brown eyes come to the forefront of my mind, his presence commanding everyone's full attention. Undeniably handsome, intelligent, and brave, Ardy exudes a magnetic charm that is hard to resist. Is he sexy? Absolutely! Ardy would be a catch for any woman. Pearl said her brother has had girlfriends but never married. Why not?

Julie – July 12, 2029

7/12/2029

Feeling something—a snake???—coiled around my calf, I frantically shed my blanket, forgetting that I had tied Tina to my ankle the night before. After gently shaking her awake, I scooped imaginary food into my mouth. "Eat?"

Tina rubbed her abdomen. I misinterpreted her body language as a sign of hunger until she enunciated the word "Bucket."

I offered her my hand. "Tina, come with me." We had placed her Lowe's bucket in the hallway. I realized that if we departed today for Camden, she would have to wave bye-bye to the DeVaughn plantation and her primitive toilet. Our newest recruit must master the art of "squat and plop," *au naturel.*

From what I know, Tina hasn't ever experienced the brilliance of the sky above or the earthy darkness below. A whole world awaits her!

You can teach someone to swim in two ways. The first method involves an unhurried process. The instructor guides the beginner into the water, supporting his or her body as they learn to paddle their hands and kick their feet. Method number two, which my dad employed with me, is the quick and easy approach—pick the kid up and toss them into the deep end.

Where is Dr. Spock when you need him?

Thoughts of Choco, the lab chimp, resurfaced as I swung open the front door. Diary, have you seen videos of orphaned or injured animals being released into the wild? The bobcat or condor first pauses in the carrier's gateway before running or flying as fast and far away as their legs or wings will take them. I chased Tina into the backyard, cautioning her to stop. She stumbled and fell, scraping her knee on a pointed rock. Remarkably, the child refused to whimper or shed a single tear. She didn't pluck out her eyeballs and eat them like Choco had. Instead, Tina lay on the ground, ogling at her surroundings. I held my daughter close, promising her she'd never be kept captive again.

Tina and I gathered handfuls of grass, and I demonstrated how to bundle the stalks into brushes. Screened by shrubs, I helped her unbutton her pants before unzipping mine. We squatted and plopped side by side, using the edges of our feet to cover the trenches with dirt. Show by doing.

We're taking a break at an abandoned house on the side of the highway.

I separated stones into stacks on the shaded front porch to teach Tina how to count. She exhibited rapid progress, making me wonder if her parents had taught her a few numbers before becoming ill. Next, we'll tackle the mysteries of the alphabet—one letter at a time.

Olivia and Sophie returned from exploring a row of trailers. Sophie pinched her nose in repugnance as Olivia presented a sealed can. "Chock full o' rotters, but look! Snausages!"

Up pops another controversial debate on childrearing. Should I safeguard Tina from daily horrors or expose her to measured doses of pure atrociousness? A real mother is right here, merely steps away, but seeking guidance from Alice requires walking on eggshells. A rare night passes without Alice yelling "Kenny!" in her sleep.

We're in Camden! I traded a 325 mg perc for two bags ballooning with Goodwill-style clothing. Tina needs something clean to wear, and so do us big girls. We met Lucy Bright while roaming the streets downtown. She told us how the Texas Rangers had recently rid the town of outlaws. "Colonel Austin and the Texan Devils sent all thirty of 'em to the gallows at the county courthouse. The executions stretched into an all-day affair when the colonel granted Paco Rivera and Rex Butler their last words. Camden's citizens celebrated for an entire week."

Lucy's generosity shone as she tossed us the keys to the cabin where we're settled. In exchange, we agreed to pick cantaloupes to earn our keep. As a field worker in the San Joaquin Valley, I know that harvesting is backbreaking. Strangely enough, the idea of getting my hands dirty brings with it a sense of anticipation. I once saw a Bible verse painted on the sides of a tractor-trailer: BEAR FRUIT IN KEEPING WITH REPENTANCE. I am unsure what John the Baptist alluded to, but the "fruit" and "repentance" parts apply to me.

To my unbridled glee, Tina selected the bed we will sleep in. Even more exciting, she loves the name I chose for her! Tina Werner has a nice ring to it, don't you think, Diary?

We are back from the dining hall. Tina feels better now. Too many helpings of dessert gave her a tummy ache. I'll examine her teeth tomorrow. Was there a toothbrush in Tina's cell? We'll find her dental supplies.

Alice seemed taken aback when Lucy introduced Tina to the supper crowd as "Tina Werner." Should I have conferred with Alice beforehand? My bad. We're supposed to be a close-knit group, yet I acted without considering my impact on others.

God, I'm such an asshole. I will apologize to Alice in the morning. Tina Jenkins is fine with me. Or we can come up with a unique surname that everyone agrees upon.

Why did I latch on to Tina like a child unboxing a gift puppy?

Who appointed you as her mother?

I found Tina first.

Didn't Jules hear the noises coming from the attic?

Yeah, but I freed her from the cage.

Hmm. Jules tortured Leonard Bannon to obtain the jail cell key.

Tina is my child. Jules can help care for her.

Where *is* Jules? She was here a minute ago, wasn't she? When did I last see her?

I neglected to review Tina's name with Alice and failed to inform Jules about her new role. Are they ticked off at me?

I am confident that Jules will get with the program once I explain how important Tina is to me. To all of us.

We have an hour to sundown, which is ample time for Tina to learn more words.

Oh wow! I just remembered today is the 12th. Happy birthday to me!

Alice – July 13, 2029

7/13/2029

Friday the thirteenth! Lucy rapped on our door at 6 a.m. We were ready to go, except for Olivia, who, as teenagers do, dilly-dallied until the last minute. A surprise awaited us on the Yellowhammer's front porch—five pairs of shoes lined up in a row. The footwear isn't new, but the soles have meat, which makes them new to me! My blisters wept tears of joy as I slipped on the brown and tan Timberland hiking boots. "Lucy, what do we owe you?"

The shopkeeper wagged her palm. "Free of charge. I've stockpiled footwear since people," she dropped her voice for Tina's benefit, "started dropping like flies suckin' Raid from a sippy cup. Got a warehouse full of Nike, Adidas, New Balance, and a few designer brands. I sell them at the market, yet most folks—" Lucy noticed Julie struggling to fit the Skechers onto Tina's foot. "Sneakers too tight?" She hurried to the Avery, coming back with a larger size. "This little lady is gonna be a tall drink o' water, aren't ya, honeybunch?"

Tina repeated, "Honeybunch," and grinned.

I discreetly disclosed Tina's circumstances to Lucy on the dusty trail to the cantaloupe fields. "These Skechers may be her first proper shoes. She wore ratty old flip-flops when we found her."

"That's awful! Alice, I have a shelf full of children's books. Even classics like *The Catcher in the Rye* and *To Kill a Mockingbird*. J. D. Salinger and Harper Lee sure knew how to spin a yarn."

"Lucy, you're joking! I couldn't get my hands on those authors until high school. Too provocative!"

The woman snickered. "I worked as a literature teacher before Christian Evangelists pressured Southern governors into banning all unapproved reading materials. The school board fired me when I joined the protest lines. Let's start Tina with something simple and fun. How about *Clifford the Big Red Dog* or *One Fish Two Fish Red Fish Blue Fish*?"

"Sounds good to me." I glanced at Julie. "But we ought to discuss Tina's education with her mother first."

We arrived at a green field backdropped by the white trunks of sweet birch trees. Lucy taught us how to harvest the cantaloupes. "Just give the girl a small tug. If she's ready, the stem breaks off the vine. If not, leave her to ripen a couple more days." The shopkeeper pointed out a handcart and a stack of cardboard cartons. "Wheel the filled boxes to the market. Make sure to pack the melons with love. Bruised produce can't be sold at full price."

At 10:15 a.m., Olivia and Sophie headed back to base camp. Julie and I took turns rolling the one hundred and twenty pounds of harvested fruit and fifty pounds of growing child to Lucy's.

After several trips, I stopped under a leafy American beech. "Julie, I'm delighted you passed your last name to Tina."

Her eyes sparkled with happiness. "You are? It was selfish of me to decide without you. . .and unforgivable."

"Don't be silly." I embraced my friend. "You'll be an amazing mother!"

"Alice, when I saw Tina inside that cage, every inch of me wanted to protect her from whoever locked her up." Julie flexed her extended hands. "And tear them apart limb from limb."

"Understandable." I rested my elbow on the handcart. "What about Jules? Is she happy for you and Tina?"

"That's the problem. Jules isn't here."

"When did you last see her?"

Julie scratched her chin, perplexed. "At dinner?"

"Jules!" Like summoning Candyman from a mirror, I had to repeat her name five times before Julie's evil twin responded.

Julie's brown eyes fixated on me, but her facial muscles contorted, transforming her previously distracted expression into one of anger with a smattering of perpetual violence. "What do you want, Alice?" Her voice sounded far away, as if it was coming from the end of a long, dark tunnel.

I took a step back. "How you doing, Jules?"

"First, it was you," she muttered, "and now this kid."

"Jules, I've never been a threat to you. You know that. What have you got against Tina?"

Perspiration glistened on her brow. "Julie will leave me for the brat. I'll die alone."

The woman standing inches from me held an automatic weapon capable of firing eight hundred rounds a minute. "Why would Julie abandon you, Jules?" A falsehood to defend myself? "She loves you."

Jules stared at the Radio Flyer, finally acknowledging Tina's presence. She lifted the wagon's black handle. "I'm hot and tired. Let's go."

The temperature gauges mounted outside Bright's Market displayed one hundred and one degrees with eighty-four percent humidity. Sweat dripped from the tip of my nose onto the orange fruit. "Jules, I care about you just as much as I care about Julie. Will you be all right?"

Jules smiled shyly. "Alice, thank you for putting up with me. I won't forget your friendship."

Did I imagine that Jules said this? Or was it really Julie?

Lucy counted the forty-pound melon crates. "You brought in quite a haul! How 'bout a glass of fresh lemonade?"

Julie and I relaxed in the shop's rear while Lucy tended to customers. "Julie, guess who I ran into?"

She sipped on the sweet-and-sour juice. "I dunno. Who?"

"Jules." I waited for her reaction.

Julie gaped at me. "You did?"

"She said she's fine."

Julie leaned back in the lawn chair. A minute later, her posture straightened. "Alice, when did you see Jules? You were with me all morning."

"Sorry, I forgot to tell you. I woke up with a headache and went to the lake to splash cold water on my forehead. I nearly tripped over Jules in the dark."

"Hum." Julie's shoulders drooped. "Why isn't Jules staying with us in the cabin?"

I shrugged. "Maybe she needs some alone time? Group travel can be stressful, with everyone always pulling in opposing directions."

Julie's eyes searched mine. "Do *I* get on your nerves, Alice?"

I stood up to pour more refreshments from the glass pitcher. "Only when you fart in your sleep." My gentle ribbing left Julie in stitches, her lungs sucking the tart liquid down the wrong pipe. I pounded her back to stop her coughing.

Lucy carried empty boxes into the storeroom. "Should I dial 911? It sounded like someone's having a fit."

Julie composed herself enough to sputter, "Jules' devil farts!"

"Just goofing around," I assured Lucy. "Can I help with anything? I used to work at a trading post." My tame daydream of Pearl scrubbing dirty potatoes morphed into a scene straight out of an erotic romance novel: Ardy ripping open my bodice to cup my heaving—

"Melons are picked. Now, let's party." Lucy slid over an aluminum chair and sank into the green webbing with a groan. She lit a fat joint and held in the fumes.

I gestured toward the front. "What about your clients?"

Lucy handed me the homegrown herb. I inhaled and offered it to Julie. She transferred the joint back to Lucy, abstaining from taking a puff.

The shopkeeper blew a cloud of "who gives a fuck" into the rafters. "They are welcome to ring the bell all they want. Ding, ding, ding-a-ling! When I taught at Wilcox, I believed there was no greater calling than expanding a child's mind. I thought that regardless of the current status quo, they weren't destined to spend their adult lives driving an orange Kubota on a megafarm or sweating over the fryer machine at the neighborhood Hardee's. But now, my only aim is to finish the day without blowing my brains out." Lucy took another deep hit, holding in the smoke until her face turned red.

I understood how the woman felt. Dear Diary, I gotta tell ya, surviving Judgment Day is no cakewalk. The two of us passed the reefer back and forth, trading increasingly funny witticisms. Julie raised her palm in refusal whenever I offered her the joint.

Higher than the key on Benjamin Franklin's kite, I waved my arms around the storeroom. "Luce, you're rakin' in more dinero than the Sinaloa Cartel. And let's not forget the dozen love shacks you rent out." I returned the roach to the shopkeeper after every inch of cannabis had saturated our respiratory systems. "You can still teach the local rug rats—I mean kids—right?"

Lucy contracted a severe case of the tee-hees. "Crotch critters?"

Lucy and I howled as if we were high schoolers spray-painting THE CHEERLEADER YOU FUCKED ON YOUR DESK IS NOW MY MOTHER on the principal's office door. (This act of rebellion had actually occurred during my senior year, or so I've been told.)

Julie seemed miffed at my behavior as we walked back to the Yellowhammer cabin. "I've never seen you so, uh. . .lively."

The green vegetation and blue sky appeared even more vibrant than usual. "You don't smoke?" I kept turning my head to focus on the three specters trailing closely behind us. *Mom? Dad? Is that you, Grandma?*

"Oh, I sampled a smorgasbord of drugs after my parents died and Julia left for greener pastures. But brandy became my sedative of choice. Jules promised to beat me blind if I continued down that path. That big, bad wolf is no animal to trifle with."

"You mad at me?"

"Nah." She squeezed my waist. "I couldn't be mad at you." When I looked up to smile at Julie, Jules glared back at me.

I did doodly-squat this afternoon—just vegged out in a hammock under a pair of longleaf pines, munching on Lucy's homemade cookies.

Julie and Tina are on the porch of the cabin reading a book. Every few pages, I hear a giggle or laugh.

Olivia and Sophie caught a bunch of fish in the lake. After they gutted the spotted bass at the cleaning station, I suggested donating the fillets. The fisherwomen left to find Lucy a few minutes ago.

The two girls have bonded quickly. They are close in age, and their synergy is that of sisters, often bickering yet seldom out of earshot. Kinda like me and Julie, without her second self inserted into the mix.

Should I pray for Jules to vanish from our lives? It's not as if we can slink away in the dead of night, leaving her to wander the earth alone until the end of time. Or do the genie in a bottle thing—somehow trick Jules into crawling back into her magic lamp. Trapped in pitch-blackness, she'd dwell for millennia before a nomadic do-gooder set her free. That wouldn't be fair. Julie isn't a fool, and Jules doesn't deserve such harsh punishment.

Am I scared of Jules? Not as much since I talked to her today. Wary would be a more fitting word. I've witnessed what she is capable of. How many times has Jules saved Julie's ass and, not long ago, my own?

Jules acted relatively normal the day she proposed housing the people of Hayneville at McGill Academy. Not exactly normal, but less volatile—a psychologically closer version of Julie. That's not been the case since we left Pearl and Ardy. Does Julie use Jules as a way to let off steam? Is Jules essential for Julie's health and well-being? Would bisecting Jules from Julie harm, or even kill her?

In PHILO-101: Introduction to Philosophy, we deliberated Thomas Aquinas, metaphysics, essence and existence, and matter and form. That was some real Grateful Dead shit. Whoa, I may still be buzzed.

With Tina holding our hands, Julie and I met Olivia and Sophie for chow. What was the main entrée? You guessed it! We had spotted bass seasoned with salt and pepper. The girls cooked the fish they had caught in the clubhouse kitchen. As the two "master chefs" rhapsodized about their culinary experiences, I envisioned their aprons splattered with the guts of the Apostles of Eternal Love.

I studied the hands that asphyxiated David Carter—not from hate, but desperation. I shoved my trembling fingers into my lap, using the ruffled tablecloth to conceal my shame. "Out, damned spot! Hell is a terrible place." We all know what happened to Lady Macbeth.

On the path to the yellow cabin, I gripped Tina's hand so tightly she cried out. Julie had to calm her down. What's the matter with me?

It's late. I'm the only one who's not sleeping. Time to set the alarm for 5:45 a.m. and switch off the flashlight. Staying awake doesn't prevent the nightmares. It only delays them.

Julie – July 13, 2029

7/13/2029

We spent the cooler hours gathering cantaloupes, or "canaloops," as Tina enjoys naming the orange balls. I anticipated honest exertion until my back ached, and my tank top clung to my sweaty body like a dirty dishrag. Not a sexy look, Diary. Nuh-uh.

Bending over didn't bother Alice. Nature Girl loves digging her fingers into the wormy soil. "Gardening is so soothing, Julie! I count, 'One melon, two melons, three. . . .' Repetitive tasks lower my internal dialog to a whisper."

Today, I kept track of every fruit I pulled from the vine to *stem* the voices in my head (I loved using homonyms while at the newspaper). Alice's simple meditation technique might have done wonders if Spiro the Spine had quit shrieking, "Julie, you're killing me!" when I stood erect.

Olivia and Sophie frittered away most of our shift gabbing. I bet Tina picked more canaloops than the teenagers combined.

There were the boomers, Generation X, millennials—like me and Alice—and Gen Z. What is Olivia and Sophie's generation called again? Oh, yeah, an Australian decided on Generation Alpha. That makes Tina's generation Beta. Will there be a Gamma? I hope Tina's generation fixes all that ours destroyed.

I wrote in an earlier post about how Jules and I harvested watermelons in the San Joaquin Valley. Have two years slipped by already? There, we had met Lula, a woman from Juárez, Mexico. She spoke broken English, and I knew *un poquitito* Spanish, but we played *Conquian* when we were not in the fields. And, more importantly, we looked out for each other.

Lula's husband, Tenoch, worked as a *vaquero* on a ranch twenty miles south of our farm. He'd stop by once or twice a month. Lula, Jules, and I bunked in a sweatbox (a seventy-foot-long mobile home) with a dozen other women—a logistical nightmare. Lula always became visibly agitated in the days leading up to Tenoch's arrival. If I asked her what was wrong, she'd shake her head and press a finger to her lips. *"No puedo decir."*

A week after the San Francisco earthquake toppled anything that still stood, Tenoch rode up on a stunning white filly. As you can imagine, Lula's spouse wasn't the only one coming to our camp. Couples reserved the small bedroom at the back end of the trailer for conjugal visits. The other laborers accepted this arrangement if Romeo and Juliet, or Juliet and Juliet, kept the noise levels to a minimum and changed the sheets.

However, that night, piercing screams sounded from behind the door. Not moans of pleasure, but cries of pain. Lula was in serious trouble.

Jules hammered on the door with her fist. "Lula, you okay in there?"

Tenoch's rage penetrated the thin walls. *"¡Sal de aquí!"* Loud banging. *"¡Métete en tus asuntos!"*

Diary, as you know by now, JULES NEVER LIKES TO BE TOLD TO MIND HER OWN BUSINESS. She grabbed a log from the firepit and broke down the flimsy door just in time.

The room reeked of a mixture of window cleaner and cat urine. A glass crystal meth pipe lay on the bed. Tenoch had his hands wrapped around Lula's neck as he spat Spanish vulgarities at her face. Our Lula, a good Christian girl, was no whore.

My coworkers rushed to Lula's aid, dragging Tenoch out of the mobile home. Barking like a squadron of javelinas, the women, quite literally, clawed the man to shreds. We buried what was left of him by lantern light in the farmer's field, replanting the large juicy fruit atop his grave.

Tenoch's depraved handiwork marked Lula's arms and stomach. Luckily, I had a bottle of amoxicillin to help prevent the bite marks from getting infected. Lula and Blanca, her husband's white filly, rode off as soon as she got back on her feet. I never saw my dear friend again. Jules and I pulled up stakes and headed east not long after. Whenever I sink my teeth into the sweet pink flesh of a ripe watermelon, I believe I'm tasting the fruit sprouting out of Tenoch's skull.

Alice turned to me on our way to drop off the cantaloupes at Lucy's market. "Julie, you're doing an exceptional job with Tina!"

I stopped in the center of the trail. "I should've consulted you before giving Tina my last name. Can you ever forgive me?"

"Nothing to apologize for. You and I will always be," Alice intertwined her index and middle fingers, "blood sisters. What does Jules think about you and Tina?"

"Wish I knew. I haven't seen Jules since supper. I am afraid she's sulking because I spend all my time with Tina."

"Jules!" Alice yelled past my shoulder and dashed into the woods.

As Tina and I approached a stream, I spotted a woman jumping from one mossy boulder to another. I called out, "Jules!" as she vanished into the undergrowth.

"Alice, why did she run away?"

Alice guided me through the trees and onto the pathway. She seated Tina in the red Radio Flyer and held out the handle to me. "Here, Julie. Jules says not to worry."

Easier said than done.

We carted the melons to Bright's Market. Alice and Lucy smoked weed, laughing uncontrollably at every little thing—so annoying if you're not stoned. Eighteen years, three months, and twelve days have passed since my last drink. Alcoholics Anonymous commemorates each anniversary of sobriety with a colored coin. Gold for sixty days. Green for ninety. I never had to go to AA. Jules got me straight. My hotheaded sponsor records my every move, poised to put me in a sleeper hold at the slightest sign of relapse. How does Jules know everything I'm thinking? What are my telltale signs?

Alice is in the hammock. Tina and I finished reading Dr. Seuss. I did most of the reading, and she did most of the tee-hee-heeing, which is music to my ears. Tina learned a few words from *One Fish Two Fish Red Fish Blue Fish*, now exclaiming, "Red!" "Blue!" "Green!" at every opportunity. Her enthusiasm led us to the lake, where she pointed at a blue fish swimming in the clear water. "Julie! Blue fish!" Her young mind sucks up knowledge like a vacuum cleaner! Tina's a whiz kid, the same as her mother. You heard me, Diary. Mother!

Poor Glenn and Mary Todd. Should I tell Tina that her birth parents died from COVID? How can I possibly explain why Leonard Bannon trapped her in the attic?

Not yet. Maybe someday when she's older.

Hooking into Tina's story time, Olivia and Sophie brought home some decent-sized bass. Tina wanted to see the fish up close, but I steered her away from the cleaning station. She doesn't need to watch her "fishie friends" getting their innards ripped out. Despite my efforts, Tina saw Mr. Red Fish and Mrs. Blue Fish two hours later—on her dinner plate.

Alice – July 14, 2029

7/14/2029

I cannot recall the number of cantaloupes we picked, crated, and carted to Lucy's place this morning—a harvest far too abundant for her small building to sell before the melons turn to mush. Curiosity got the best of me, and I asked Lucy what she did with the excess fruit.

"I ship produce to the surrounding towns: Vredenburg, Orrville, Pine Hill. Even as far east as Hayneville."

I smiled. "We came from Hayneville."

"Do you know Pearl Jackson? I deliver to her Trading Post."

"I worked at Pearl's until McGill's Hill raiders burned down the town."

Lucy's eyes widened in horror. "Are Pearl and Caddy all right?"

"They were fine when we left Hayneville. How do you deliver your goods? Do you have trucks?"

"A beat-up U-Haul. If you handle Bella's transmission with kid gloves, she runs like a champ!"

"How about gasoline?"

"A guy in Uniontown drives a tanker up to Tuscaloosa monthly. I trade Jedediah cartons of fruits and vegetables for cans of fresh fuel."

"Is the gas from the up-and-running refineries?"

"Uh-hum." Lucy rolled a spliff and lit the tapered end. "Engineers are pumping crude oil out of the ground."

"I heard that while in Huntsville. The residents nearly have a traffic problem!"

Her eyebrows arched when I turned down the skunky ganja. "How long are you folks planning to stay in Camden? Only asking 'cause there's two more days' worth of pickin' in my field."

Julie spoke up. "We won't hit the pavement until all your melons are boxed. Oh, and Lucy?" She lifted her legs to show off her Danner boots. "Thank you. My feet are grateful for these new kicks."

"Glad you're enjoying them. Can you tell me your destination?"

Julie indicated a southerly direction. "Mississippi, to find my sister, Julia. Her last known address was in Hattiesburg."

"Oh, I had a sister in Ellisville, which is not far from there. Harriet's, ah, with Mom and Dad."

Julie conveyed her condolences. "Sorry to hear that."

"Thanks." Lucy drew in a copious amount of feel-good. "Hey, can I ask you ladies something?"

"Sure," Julie replied. "What's on your mind?"

"You've spent lots of time on the road. Any advice on dealing with bandits?"

Julie patted her pistol and smirked. "Besides filling them full of holes?"

"My shipments are being hijacked. They take the produce, not the vehicle. Jay, the fella I pay to drive Bella, tells me a band of armed thirteen-year-olds are to blame." Lucy stubbed out the hand-rolled joint. "Business is hurting."

Julie glanced at me before responding. "We ran into some trouble on the way here, but not the kind you referred to. Did you consider having a passenger ride shotgun? Someone to point a machine gun in their mugs as soon as the back door rolls up." She swept her M16 in an arc. "'Say hello to my little friend!' Rat-a-tat-tat!"

Lucy mimicked Al Pacino's overdone accent from *Scarface*, "Her womb is so polluted, I can't even have a fuckin' little baby with her!" She doubled over with laughter. "Julie, *Scarface* may be the greatest movie ever made, but it's just me, myself, and I." Lucy held up her palms in defeat. "My mom raised me to be a lover, not a fighter. I cannot ask anyone else to risk their neck for a sack of potatoes."

I watched Tina chase Sophie and Olivia across the shop's lawn. "Where are these surprise attacks?"

"By Coffeeville, at R&R Lumber."

After Camden, we had debated heading north to Coffeeville or south to Grove Hill. Either way, we'd take an equal number of steps—a million—with gremlins lying in wait behind every tree and underneath every rock.

The kids zipped inside the storeroom, thirsty from their playtime. Lucy served them glasses of sweet lemonade before our family returned to the camp.

Julie and I are chilling on Adirondack chairs by the lake while Tina splashes in the warm shallows. Her watchful mother cautions whenever her knees dip below the surface. Tina's word of the day is "water," and she is stringing phrases together. "Mama, look, blue fish water." It won't be long before this young genius is reciting Sylvia Plath.

I don't know where Olivia and Sophie have gone. They left their guns at the cabin, so at least they're not out killing anyone.

The adults outlined our next actions.

> Sunday and Monday mornings – Pick the remaining cantaloupes.

> Sunday and Monday afternoons - Inventory our supplies and rest.
>
> Tuesday morning - Pack our things and leave for Hattiesburg.

I figured my to-do list would be pages long, but my life is less complicated than I realized.

When I suggested Route 10 to Coffeeville instead of the 41 to Grove Hill, Jules (yeah, she's back) grinned with sharklike teeth. "Julie and I bet you'd choose that way, Alice."

What was Jules insinuating?

I'm on the front porch, increasingly concerned about Sophie and Olivia. Where could those girls be? They've been gone for six hours, and it's nearly suppertime! I am acting mother-hennish. I wish I had an ounce of Lucy's "whacky tobacky" to mellow me out.

Jules accompanied us to the Cowboy Clubhouse for dinner. I ate two plates of homemade pasta with spicy marinara sauce and three giant venison meatballs. The cupcakes for dessert were a scrumptious delight, though my overindulgence threatens to burst the seams of my pants. My eyes are always bigger than my stomach. Lucy shared that Jehovah's Witnesses provided flour for the meal. Where did she get the impossible-to-grow cocoa beans for the chocolate frosting?

Outside the dining hall, we talked with recent arrivals to town. Blake and Evangeline, a married couple, had heard rumors of political upheaval in Hattiesburg and warned us to avoid the area by sticking to side roads. Evie said that a central bridge in Jackson fell into the Tombigbee River, further supporting our decision to skirt Grove Hill.

I asked Lucy if she had any information about Hattiesburg while we wiped the tabletops.

She rinsed her rag in a bucket. "A Pink Pony Express messenger claimed the city was gang free, but that must have been two months ago. Conditions change as quickly as the weather nowadays."

Lucy's not wrong. The danger barometer swings as high as the CraZanity pendulum ride at Six Flags amusement park.

Oh, crap! I didn't tell you, dear Diary. Olivia and Sophie spent the entire day volunteering at an animal shelter! I scolded the teenagers for not notifying us of their whereabouts, then squashed both in a bear hug. Generation Alpha might save us after all!

Julie – July 14, 2029

7/14/2029

Spiro the Spine didn't whine as loudly this morning despite the fact that I picked a record number of cantaloupes. The field should be cleared for the next planting in two days, excluding the damaged melons and those riddled with cutworms. However, thankfully, our small group won't break our backs while sowing the seeds. We'll be halfway to Hattiesburg—and Julia!

Diary, you've probably heard tales of identical twins. They allege we communicate telepathically through our genetic neural link—duplicate brains and nervous systems. If one twin experiences pain or is in crisis, the other rushes to the rescue. And when one twin dies, the other feels half-dead and soon passes away from loneliness.

If only extrasensory perceptions were real! How often have I sat in a darkened room, trying to mentally reach out? "Julia, do you hear me? Hello? Hello?" Nothing. Nada. Not even a flashing DO NOT DISTURB sign. I replicate this futile routine night after night, receiving no response other than the ringing in my ears. Telepathy reminds me of how prayer works.

Tina and the girls played hide-and-seek under a cloudless sky while Alice and I hung out with Lucy in the rear of her market. That woman sure smokes a lot of weed, today, all by herself. Alice asked about Lucy's business, specifically what happens to the extra fruits and vegetables. As it turns out, the shopkeeper hires a driver to distribute her produce to the neighboring villages. Unfortunately, teenage hoodlums are swiping the food at a lumber store near Coffeeville. I kidded how I'd shoot the youngsters. Well, sort of. . . .

Lucy voiced concern that we would leave before her cantaloupes were all picked and packed. We promised to finish the job.

Why am I always more carefree after drinking Lucy's lemonade? What ingredient does she add to her "mother's secret recipe" besides sugar?

Alice, Jules, and I walked Tina to the lake after lunch. Tina attempted to scoop the fish out of the water, but they swam too fast for her tiny hands. And my little girl spoke her first complete sentence! "Mama, look at the blue fish in the cold water." I awarded myself five gold stars for teaching Tina to call me Mama instead of Julie.

Alice and I went over our itinerary. There are two potential routes we can take to Hattiesburg. Since I've been such a jerk with the whole naming Tina thing, I acknowledged Alice's role as our fearless leader and let her decide. Jules did a poor job of concealing her excitement when she learned we'd be going through Coffeeville. I know that woman well enough to bet she's daring those "thievin' little shits" to spring from their hidey-holes.

After "spaghetti night" at the dining hall, Alice and I conversed with a couple traveling north. They advised us to bypass Hattiesburg. I'm worried about Julia's well-being. When I switch off the lights tonight, I will concentrate all my psychic energy toward the southwest, hoping to pick up a signal on my cerebrum-powered radar dish.

Alice – July 15, 2029

7/15/2029

I continue to find peace in this monotonous labor as the sun climbs over Lucy's field. My body is building more muscle daily. However, the prospect of picking melons until I turn into a fruit myself doesn't thrill me in the slightest. Even with a wide-brimmed straw hat and Lucy's homemade sunscreen (which suspiciously smells like the very cantaloupes we harvest), the harsh wind and sun have taken a toll on my skin. As for my fingers, particularly my nails? My aspiration to become a hand model has gone kaput.

Sophie and Olivia went to the animal shelter. Cats and dogs now roam the empty Piggly Wiggly supermarket. Sophie aspires to be a veterinarian. With no veterinary schools left in existence, obtaining a medical degree seems unlikely. Why am I always so negative? There must be a doctor somewhere willing to pass on his or her knowledge for posterity.

How does one stay upbeat in these post-pandemic, post-nuclear holocaust times? Our country crumbled both politically and socially even before the coronavirus germs and radioactive particles wiped the slate clean. The never-ending clash between the "evil" Republicans and "woke" Democrats left Congress incapable of approving a single bill. Social media apps such as Facebook and TikTok fueled our hatred for others as well as ourselves. Our dictator president didn't care about anything besides keeping his fat ass in the Oval Office.

Meanwhile, Mother Earth pleaded with the gas guzzlers to quit fossil fuels or else, with "else" being the extinction of all humankind. Inflation, economic recessions, racial riots, daily mass shootings, and water wars leading to famine were only some of the problems we faced. Russia invaded Ukraine. Hamas and Hezbollah attacked Israel, and the Israelis retaliated by flattening Gaza, Lebanon, and Syria. Don't even get me started on Iran. War after stupid bloody war. On top of that, AI-generated videos and music made art look and sound, well, artificial.

Scientists predicted that COVID-19's sinister sibling, COVID-24, was on a path to wipe out three-quarters of the Earth's population. Who is to say how many could have been saved if anti-vaxxers wore N-95 masks and received their booster shots? On the other hand, what would our future be like if Putin's fifty-megaton bombs hadn't incinerated the virus in its tracks?

God certainly has a warped sense of humor.

It's hard to nail down the things that made me happy before Election Day. One source of pure joy was Kenny! Sometimes, I wish and pray that my son will return from the dead, not as a flesh-eating zombie but as a healthy, loving little boy.

What makes me happy now? "Happy" may be too strong a word. Dear Diary, please search this document for "happy" and overwrite it with "not sad."

I'm not sad to be alive. But can you tell me why I am walking this earth while the majority have perished?

Then comes a moment of divine intervention. The heavens open up, golden rays pierce through the clouds, angels strum harps, cherubs do whatever cherubs do, and a thunderous voice proclaims, "My blessed child, you are the chosen one!" The ground quakes beneath my feet, the seas part, lightning strikes, and the dead twerk to Nicki Minaj. "Alice Jenkins, your destiny is to ________."

How should I fill in the blank? What *is* my purpose? I am not here to save mankind, that's for sure. Have I any grand aspirations? *Ha!* Even my high school guidance counselor complained that I was too lazy to apply for college. I planned to travel to New Orleans to tell David's brother the god-awful truth. But now? Pearl had questioned whether Edward would be happier knowing David was gone. Of course not! Nobody rejoices in hearing that a loved one has died, especially when the bearer of such news is the very murderer.

Julie understands me. She's always there for me. Julie's not just a gal pal. She's a forever friend. With her forging the way, I feel safe. I'm part of a team. Jules is okay, too, I guess. Sophie and Olivia are growing on me. They're good-hearted girls who, with a little mothering, will mature into upstanding young women.

Tina may not be a replacement for Kenneth, but I can't deny I love that sweet girl with all my heart! Tina, Aunty Alice promises to protect you.

That's four real people (plus one imaginary person) who bring me happiness. Not too shabby for someone who had no one to rely on not two weeks ago!

I want to include Pearl and Ardy in that count. Could my thoughts jinx my chances of seeing them again? It's wiser to push Hayneville into the recesses of my mind.

So, dear Diary, what *is* my destiny?

My purpose now shines clear as day—*to keep my family safe.*

An afternoon sprinkle woke me from my nap in the hammock. In my dream, I was searching for my parking spot in an immense shopping center. I hurried up and down the aisles, pressing my Subaru's keyless remote, desperate to hear a horn beep or see the flash of headlights. Night came abnormally soon, and the mall emptied of all vehicles. My car was nowhere to be found. The wind blew trash across the parking lot. It began to rain, and I had no way to get home.

We gathered a few more items for our journey, a Rubik's Cube being the most stimulating addition. Already familiar with the colors, Tina made "square" her word of the day.

Better freshen up and go to dinner.

Little did we know that the ordinary dining hall would convert to a theatrical stage. I wanted to believe that God, in His infinite wisdom, had permanently culled the wicked from the earth through terminal sickness and the incredible power of the atom. Nope, looks like Yahweh missed another opportunity. Herds of total assholes still range across the four corners of the globe.

The unfolding scene featured two boomers engaged in a heated discussion over the superiority of baseball teams: the Mets versus the Yankees.

A-hole Number 1: "The New York Mets created the best pitching staff! Doc Gooden and Tom Seaver!"

A-hole Number 2: "True, but the Yankees had the Sultan of Swat. Babe Ruth was the greatest hitter of all time!"

A-hole 1: "The Mets won two World Series championships!"

A-hole 2: "Do you use your toes to count? The Yanks won twenty-seven World Series!"

A-hole 1: "Are you calling me mathematically challenged? The American League is a joke! The pitchers don't even have to hit the ball!"

A-hole 2: "Blow me, you ugly son of a mule!"

A-hole 1 swung first. From the man's awkward stance, he clearly hadn't fought anyone his age since kindergarten.

A-hole 2 dodged the slow punch and raised a folding seat above his head.

Just as things were spiraling out of control, Jules lunged in and grabbed Number 2's arm. And here's where the game gets interesting. She didn't, I repeat, DID NOT, bludgeon either of the sports nuts with the metal chair. Instead, Jules gently set all four legs on the floor and spoke calmly but firmly. "Gentlemen, there are children present. Take your grievances outside or shake hands and finish eating your meals. The bombs on Election Day vaporized any Mets or Yankees players who survived the ventilators. You're fighting over nothing and no one."

A-hole 1, with cheeks as red as bull's blood, put out his mitt. "Sorry, bro. I really miss the game."

Shamefaced, A-hole 2 accepted the handshake. "Me and the missus attended every home game at Yankee Stadium." The gangly dude broke down. "Life is meaningless with no ESPN. I feel empty without my daily dose of sports statistics. Hey, man, what's your name?"

The baseball fans hugged it out, sat elbow to elbow, and slurped up their now-cold noodles.

Julie – July 15, 2029

7/15/2029

Alice moped around this morning. After some nudging, she disclosed that she was fighting a case of the "End Times Blues." The catchy phrase struck me as a perfect name for a blues song.

I had anticipated writing lilting lyrics or a poignant poem to accompany Alice's song title. However, when I sat down to get started, my pen got stuck on the first word: Armageddon. On a more pleasant note, we'll have picked all the cantaloupes by the end of tomorrow.

Sophie and Olivia returned from the animal shelter. Sophie expressed her enthusiasm for pursuing a career in healing dogs and cats. I suggested we visit the town library to look up books on animal care.

Alice found a Rubik's Cube at Abeba's Thrift Shop. She taught Tina how to twist and turn the six faces. Even though the red, blue, green, white, yellow, and orange squares were all jumbled up, the bright child quickly grasped the objective—to restore each side to a single color. I can hear her click-clacking in the other room. As a kid, I played endlessly with that combination puzzle until Julia pried it apart to "see the guts."

Chewing over my earlier interaction with Alice, I may have been too nonchalant when she confided in me about her "bad days" when every agonizing hour "seemed like a week." I now appreciate that muttering, "Yeah, I know the feeling," wouldn't have been the most beneficial.

Did I downplay my response to avoid digging into my own issues with depression?

Lucy cooked an enormous pot of "Tuna Tizzy" (creamy fish chunks on thick noodles) tonight. Since Camden is a hundred and fifty miles inland, she substituted lake fish (bass, bass, and more bass) for the Chicken of the Sea.

Two old numbskulls brawled over the dumbest subject matter ever: baseball. Specifically, Mets versus Yankees. Who's the best hitter or pitcher? Which team won the most pendants? Yada, yada, yada. Even if the players aren't dead from the pandemic or glowing from the nuclear holocaust, the sports fans are.

So, the pinhead wearing the Mets cap threw a lackluster jab that missed. The other guy, his NEW YORK YANKEES T-shirt stained with Tizzy, was ready to crush Met's mullet with a chair when a surprise guest jumped in to referee.

Jules exclaimed, "You should be ashamed of yourselves! Kiss and make up, or I'll kick both of you out of the camp."

The baseball fanatics set aside their bats (my symbolic metaphor for a handshake) and exhibited remorse. Jules mouthed, "You're welcome, Julie," and exited the dining hall with an imaginary mic drop.

Alice – July 16, 2029

7/16/2029

The cantaloupe field is finally bare! At noon, we wheeled the last three cartons of fruit to Bright's Market. Laughter floated over the farmland as Olivia and Sophie entertained themselves with politically incorrect yet hilarious names for the melons. "Cunnydews," "King Kong's family jewels," "twattermelons," and "cumquats" are just a sampling of their creative vulgarisms. In unison, the girls voiced their annoyance with the laborious task to Julie and me: "We never ever want to see another fuckmelon!" I heartily agreed, after reminding the teenagers that children are born with elephant ears.

The afternoon flew by as we crammed clothes into our backpacks and loaded Grandma Peaches with food. Olivia added some padding to the bottom of the Radio Flyer ("Grandpa Mushmelon") for Tina to sit on.

Oh, I almost forgot! We dropped by the Wilcox County Public Library, whose doors remain open for those willing to learn from the past. The librarian directed Sophie to the sections on veterinarians and pets. Since we're heading out tomorrow, the budding doctor couldn't borrow any reference books, but she had a few hours to thumb the pages. It seems like *The Day of a Country Vet* doubled her passion!

After supper, I thanked Lucy for her hospitality and notified her that we'd be leaving early.

Julie stepped closer. "Lucy, maybe we can help each other out." She glanced at me. "I have a proposition."

The camp host stopped sweeping the floor. "I'm listening."

Julie held up the map. "It's a three-day trek to Coffeeville."

Lucy leaned on her broom. "At least. It's sixty miles through Pine Hill and Thomasville."

Julie patted the top of Tina's head. "Quite a long haul. What if your driver gives us a ride in Bella? We can handle your bandits, freeing Jay to transport your goods. Let's kill two birds with one stone."

Lucy considered the offer. "I don't want those hungry kids to be harmed."

"Oh, don't worry, it's just a figure of speech!" Darkness lurked behind Julie's bright smile. "Once we scare those mischief-makers straight, we'll continue on our own to Hattiesburg."

The shopkeeper sat at a table, repeatedly folding and unfolding a napkin. "There's no way I can persuade Jay to go on such a risky mission." She tossed the crumpled paper aside. "I'll need to drive Bella myself."

Julie squeezed Lucy's shoulder. "You'll be safe with us."

Lucy wrung her hands. "I am not looking forward to the trip back alone."

I spread my arms around the emptying hall. "Can't somebody go with you?"

Lucy scowled. "Yeah, Douchebag Donald."

I knew too many douchebags named Donald. "Which Donald is this?"

Lucy's sullen scowl stretched into a seething glower. "My older brother."

Note: I reread this entry and realized that Jules probably spoke to Lucy, not Julie.

Julie – July 16, 2029

7/16/2029

Halleluiah! All the cantaloupes are picked and packed into crates. The fertile earth lies fallow. It's time to say farewell to Camden and skedaddle. Were five nights of restful lodging and healthy food worth the sixteen hours of toiling under the searing sun? Ask me again once Spiro the Spine stops screaming, "No, no, no, no, no!"

At our last meal in the dining hall, Alice expressed her gratitude to Lucy for providing us with such a wonderful time. Jules made a bold suggestion. This was entirely Jules' idea, so I didn't have to apologize to Alice for not informing her beforehand. It caught me off guard as well.

Jules offered a tradeoff. Our group would save shoe leather while helping the shopkeeper clear her delivery route of hoodlums. Lucy weighed her options, finally agreeing to drive us to Coffeeville.

Alice – July 17, 2029

7/17/29

We are at a small park in Pine Hill. Lucy and her brother are wheeling and dealing with the proprietor of Birdie's Emporium, a three-fingered man with an empty eye socket.

Donald Bright hasn't talked to us since we left Camden, so it's rather challenging to gauge his level of douchebagness. Or is the proper term douchebaggery? He's been riding in front with Lucy while we jounce in the rear of the U-Haul with the door up for ventilation.

Olivia and Sophie took Tina to the playground to slip down the slide with a few other kids, each worryingly frail. Julie and I are sitting on a bench, strategizing ways to rein in the juvenile outlaws. Now and then, Jules emerges to submit her brutally honest and often fatal opinions. I remind her that Lucy is against all forms of violence.

Our next destination, Thomasville, is just twelve miles away. Here comes Lucy and Douchebag Donny. It's time to return to Bella.

We rolled through Thomasville's extensive downtown, the dirty streets lined with cracks and potholes. You don't notice such ruts on foot, but the craters are hard to miss if you're sitting on the floor of a vehicle with worn-out shock absorbers. Sorry, dear Diary, if my handwriting resembles a seismogram.

A guidepost by a tall structure read: IN 1958, THE AIR DEFENSE COMMAND MOUNTED AN ENORMOUS RADAR DISH TO THIS BUILDING'S ROOF TO PROTECT THE NATION FROM CUBAN MISSILE THREATS.

When budget cuts closed the base in 1969, the military sold the million-dollar parabolic antenna for pennies on the pound.

We're thirty-two miles from Coffeeville, and my stomach is stuck in a spin cycle. The plan is to park the U-Haul a mile east of R&R Lumber, which is the site of the robberies. Lucy, Donny, Sophie, Olivia, and Tina will exit the truck. Lucy and her brother keep an eye on Tina as Sophie and Olivia approach the lumber store in a flanking maneuver. Julie drives Bella, and I'll hide in the cargo space behind the melon crates.

Julie and I are determined to capture the kids alive. However, we agreed that we're not dying for these petty thieves.

Coffeeville, Alabama, is a small Southern town known for nothin' besides the Mitcham War. Words chiseled into a granite stone half-hidden by burnweeds tell the all-too-familiar tale of racial prejudice. Disenfranchised Whites took the law into their own hands, carrying out lynchings of such viciousness that Franklin D. Roosevelt had to deploy troops to intervene.

5:30 p.m. Julie, Lucy, and the girls are fixing dinner. I am jotting down this afternoon's events while the specifics remain fresh in my mind.

As planned, Lucy brought the U-Haul to a halt within sight of the lumberyard. I stayed in the back as everyone else got out. Julie hopped onto the driver's seat and clanked the transmission into gear. With a Glock tucked in my belt, I gripped Sophie's AK-47 tightly as Bella chugged forward. I steadied myself, anticipating the sounds of shouted commands and squealing brakes.

The box truck came to a stop. I raised the assault rifle, ready to oppose whoever pushed up the rear door. Instead of scaring the bejesus out of the hijackers, I nearly lost my balance as the vehicle unexpectedly accelerated. I held on as the U-Haul turned around, moving slowly before completing another U-turn. The engine fell silent, and three raps reverberated against the side panel.

A familiar voice called, "Alice, it's me! Don't shoot!"

The back door screeched up. No ruthless munchkins wielding guns, just Julie, Olivia, and Sophie standing in the bright sunshine.

Sophie exchanged weapons with me. "Liv and I searched the whole yard. There's no evidence of anyone having been here in months. Are we at the correct location?"

A crooked sign hung above the central office's shattered windows: R&R LUMBER – HELPING FAMILIES SINCE 1985. Saplings sprouted from crevices in the pavement. Scroungers had scrounged for every stick of timber.

I let out a big yawn, my adrenaline rush fading fast. "Let's get Lucy."

The mystified shopkeeper circled the lumberyard. "No robbers. No kids." She confronted Donald. "You're tight with Jay. Would your friend make this up?"

Donny, as poor a liar as he was a brother, stammered, "W-what do you mean? I h-hardly know that g-guy!"

Lucy jabbed a finger into his sternum. "You two have been bosom buddies since Cuddlebugs Childcare!"

Jules, tired of futzing around, seized Donny's golden earring. "Tell the truth. Did you and Jay steal your sister's fruits and vegetables?"

Donny's earlobe stretched to its structural limit in his attempt to break free. "Luce, I got nothing, and you have everything. I earned a right to take what's—"

Lucy's open-handed slap rocked her brother's head. "I never want to see you again." She started Bella, and we all climbed onboard except for Donald the Douchebag.

After supper, I asked Lucy if she truly intended to leave her sibling behind. "Family is family. You might come to regret this decision."

Lucy, picking at her teeth with a toothpick, examined something stuck on the wooden tip. "Disloyal people are useless to me."

Julie – July 17, 2029

7/17/2029

I am at a playground in Pine Hill. Tina is playing with three girls and one boy. She loves the slide, giggling as her feet sink into the soft sand. Alice and I attempted to strike up conversations with the two other mothers, unkempt women whose glazed eyes seldom follow their children's movements. Are they high on drugs or slowly starving? What's wrong with this town?

Once a military base, Thomasville is falling apart, brick by brick. At the Baptist church, four women in blood-stained robes were skinning a horse hanging from a dead tree. We're thirty miles from Coffeeville, and I have that nauseous feeling where I want to puke, but no food comes up. I pray our mission to catch these delinquents in the act goes well.

I don't mean to be judgmental, but Lucy's brother Donny behaved poorly from the moment I set my eyes on his REDNECK LIVES MATTER T-shirt. And now he had the gall to swindle his sister? Jules coerced the culprit into confessing his crimes by almost tearing his earlobe off. Lucy disowned her sibling, claiming that even as a child, Donald was nothing more than a "big ol' bag of douche."

Coffeeville is just another stop on a road paved with blood. It's a sad state of affairs when a mayor must commission a stone carver to engrave the word REGRETABLE multiple times on a monument chronicling the town's dark, racist history.

Our accommodation on River Street is within a dilapidated building with FLEA MARKET painted in giant letters on an exterior wall. Even in better days, I imagine Coffeeville's downtown always appeared abandoned. I got a buzz out of explaining to Olivia and Sophie how marketeers sold live fleas by the bushel.

Lucy is understandably upset. When I brought up the subject of her brother, she stubbed out her joint and stomped away.

Alice – July 18, 2029

7/18/2029

Lucy rose before sunrise and rode off in Bella without saying goodbye. I sincerely hope she stays safe driving solo through the countryside. As for her brother, Donald D. Bright? For all I know, he's wandering the streets of Coffeeville.

We're taking an afternoon siesta in the sleepy town of Millry, Alabama, beneath the CHAIN-SMOKER'S ONLY awning at CHI-CHI'S DO IT YOU DING-DANG SELF BRUSHLESS CARWASH. We'll call it a day after a few more miles of foot-dragging. Tomorrow morning, we cross the Mississippi border.

There is little to report from Healing Springs, a town once renowned for its mineral waters. A livestock shed is our campsite for the night. Julie raked hay over the solidified cow patties to lay our blankets. *Hot Girls on Big Tractors* and *The Farmer's Sexy Daughter* calendars hang on the slatted walls. The young women's toned bodies have become breeding grounds for black mildew.

I finally divulged to Julie how I came across Samantha Mathews' pink diary. Last spring, David Carter and I were traveling alongside Christian missionaries. We joined the Children of the Lord in Kankakee, Illinois, and stayed with them till Champaign, where their leader Samantha died. Dave always advised, "There is safety in numbers," until that ancient Latin proverb no longer held water.

Samantha and her beau, Chadwick Mathews, tied the knot on Sunday, November 3rd, 2024, a mere forty-eight hours before Election Day. The newlyweds saw the fire and brimstone raining upon America's cities as proof of God heralding in a new era. Sam and Chad would scribe the next Bible chapter featuring themselves, the Chosen! The couple became convinced that the Holy Father's children were obligated to "beget a generation of purified believers." As the years passed, Samantha and the other fertile women in her company became pregnant.

David and I viewed bringing a new life into this morally corrupt, contaminated wasteland as sinful. To further complicate matters, were we "truly in love" or just "friends with benefits"? We'd appease the multiplying naggers by fervently responding, "God's blessed seed shall soon take root!" All along, the copper IUD implanted in my womb killed David's sperm on contact, a silent battle raging within me.

As the pressure to conceive grew, David and I planned to leave the Children of the Lord once we reached Tuscola or, at the latest, Arcola.

Returning to the "safety in numbers" topic, survivors separated or formed groups after the radioactive dust settled. The introverts dug impenetrable bunkers deep in the forest, while the extroverts sought like-minded individuals or those powerful enough to provide protection.

And, as we recall from our World History classes, one question arises: Which manmade organizations inflicted the maximum pain and violence throughout the ages? Bradley, you are correct! The problem with religious institutions is that if you don't buy into their dogmas, the "righteous" will brand you a "pagan"—a blight to be purged from the earth.

Champaign had two religious sects. One was Catholic and the other Protestant. The PLWs (the Vatican Palace recorded the last Pope's Last Words as, "Thank you, Lord, for answering my prayers!") despised the TCs (True Crossers) and vice versa. But what did the PLWs and the TCs hate more than each other? Right again, Bradley! People with differing spiritual beliefs invading their turf.

This brings us to the PLWs' bristly priest, Giovanni Giorgio, and the tattooed minister of the TCs, Timothy Birkin. The men heard wind of heretical outsiders and sent spies to monitor the Children of the Lord's eight-month-pregnant leader, Samantha Mathews.

Sam had moved her followers into a multi-story condominium on the outskirts of town. When the woman of God wasn't in bed praying for her hemorrhoids to shrink, she walked the streets spreading the Word. "Sisters, Jesus is asking you to bear His fruit! Can I get an amen?"

Champaign, a city with a population of thousands, had a strong religious presence. While not everyone belonged to the PLW or TC, attending Saint Mary's or the Rock every Sunday was crucial if you wanted your businesses to profit. Or remain standing.

Giovanni and his wife, Marjorie, could not conceive. He knew from multiple fertility tests that his tiny swimmers were to blame and not her healthy eggs. Samantha Mathews' prolific procreation preaching pushed the passionate priest past his pressure point. Giovanni set up a midnight rendezvous with his old fraternity brother, Tim Birkin, inside the Armadillo Pawnshop on Springfield Avenue. The two plotted until first light, finally settling on the stupidest scheme ever: "Let's take Samantha hostage!"

Giovanni and Timothy's tactics might have succeeded if Sam's husband hadn't called in sick from his nighttime shift as a security guard. Chad, waking to his wife's muffled screams, chased the kidnappers along the hallway. Tim lost his footing on the stairway during the struggle. Giovanni, unable to hold the pregnant woman's additional weight alone, let go. Sam tumbled down the stairs, hitting her head on the concrete landing. She went into labor surrounded by her flock, and as the premature newborn took his first breath, the momentary mother breathed her last.

Chadwick assumed leadership of the Children of The Lord, who worshiped Baby Luke as a modern miracle. Samantha's grieving devotees revered the martyred woman as a venerable saint.

What about Giovanni and Timothy? Only God knows if the two pals are playing the harpsichord in Heaven or line dancing in the flames of Hell.

How did I come to possess Samantha Mathews' diary? While Sam's bereaving disciples lowered their beloved into the red clay, I sifted through her effects. I pocketed the pink journal, presuming that she no longer had any need to document her daily life. David and I departed from Champaign shortly after.

Now, is my account of events entirely accurate? Sections of this story are speculative. Other parts came from hearsay following the event. Admittedly, some is plain ol' bullshit, but I gleaned most of the facts directly from Samantha's baby shower gift before I ripped out the pages and burned them.

Julie – July 18, 2029

7/18/2029

Lucy is gone! I heard her packing her belongings as the morning sky brightened outside the Flea Market. The U-Haul truck cranked over, sputtered to life, and rumbled away. Discovering that your brother is robbing you blind has to be the worst kind of insult.

Tina loves to walk. When we pull her in the cart, she reads books or watches the scenery roll by. There's no more *Sesame Street* or *Blue's Clues* for these post-apocalyptic kids.

Tina bombards us with zillions of questions, and we take turns fielding the simple "whys," "whats," and "wheres." "What is that noise?" Sophie cups her ear. "Birds. Those are crows." "Why does it rain?" Olivia points a finger upward. "Too much water in the clouds." "So, why is the sky blue?" Alice spreads her hands. "Because blue is God's favorite color."

They pass the toughies on to me. "Where do babies come from?" "How long will I live?" And the trickiest one of all, "What happened to my mom and dad?"

We hurried to Healing Springs this afternoon, an acclaimed health spa. Global jetsetters travel thousands of miles to soak in its fly-infested mud baths. I dusted off my American Express Black Card because, tonight, we'll be living the high life in an opulent five-star resort—the Shitz-Carlton. With layers of hay spread across the cattle barn's uneven floor, a hundred years of cow shit hardly stinks.

Alice – July 19, 2029

7/19/2029

A road sign claims Buckatunna is named after a creek dividing the town. We encountered collapsed automobile and train bridges. Without any alternative, we waded into waist-high water carrying Grandma Peaches, Grandpa Mushmelon, and Tina on our shoulders. Sophie stumbled upon a toppled WELCOME TO MISSISSIPPI – BIRTHPLACE OF AMERICA'S MUSIC billboard while searching for a private spot for Tina to go potty. Only then did we realize we were across the state border.

During my elementary school years, the geography of the United States intrigued me. The vibrant array of names and shapes on the colorful wall maps inspired dreams of adventure. However, as I became eligible to vote, the country's fifty polarized political viewpoints became a source of dismay and frustration. The stark division between Red and Blue overshadowed the unity that was meant to define our nation instead of destroying it.

As we ate lunch (Lucy left us with a sack of fruits and vegetables), Julie and I decided to follow a northern route via Clara and Ovett instead of Richton and Runnelstown. If we reach Clara by nightfall, we'll arrive in Hattiesburg within two days.

Our group faced a choice: Do we seek shelter in a school or a church? I've always been partial to—hmm, why have I laid my head in so many churches? Did I have faith that God's sacred walls of worship provided greater fortification than sleeping in a house or underneath the stars? Nah, the number of mass murders in churches, synagogues, and mosques has torpedoed that belief. Trusting in a "not of this world" being to keep me safe is no more secure than installing a reliable alarm system.

Anyhow, we're inside Clara Elementary School. The First Baptist Church had a large congregation of rotters, too numerous to clear without a backhoe. Other families are living in the classrooms as well. The tantalizing aroma of cooking meat permeates the corridors, circulating through the open doors and windows. Tina picked up a few Spanish phrases from a girl across the way. She asked her mother to invite *"mi amiga y su familia"* to join us for supper. The Diazes treated our family to freshly made flour tortillas, and we shared Libby's Vienna Sausages with warm globs of Rosarita Refried Beans. Those over twenty-one passed around a bottle of tequila for an after-dinner drink. Everyone had a fine time.

I am too exhausted to write about what just happened.

Julie – July 19, 2029

7/19/2029

It is my nightly routine to fire up the Cobra walkie-talkie. Most evenings, I only pick up static when scanning the channels. On occasion, I catch garbled exchanges from the more populated territories. The antenna's range only extends four or five miles. Once in a blue moon, the ionosphere bounces back distant radio signals that are clear enough to understand. That transpired tonight, and, for a change, this transmission wasn't a husband reminding his wife he'd be late for dinner or a couple talking dirty.

A male voice cried out on channel 9, "Can anyone hear me?" I brought the speaker closer to my ear. "I'm stuck in a well, and the water is up to my neck!"

Jules dropped the 2019 *Good Housekeeping* magazine onto her lap, wagging her head in exasperation. "It's just a ruse. Some serial killers, Jason Voorhees for example, lure victims to remote locations to—*ki ki ki ma ma ma*—butcher them." She flipped the glossy pages, her eyes landing on an article titled: "Did We Love You Too Little or Did We Love You Too Much?"

I adjusted the walkie-talkie's volume. "The person in the hockey mask is a fictional movie character who's mute!"

Jules disagreed. "Jason is a man of few words, but he sure ain't mute."

"What if the person on the radio really needs our help? We can't let him drown!"

Jules glared. "Julie, turn that damn thing off. You must rest. Tomorrow will be another grueling day."

I muzzled the monkey riding on my back and spoke directly into the microphone. "Are you able to hear me?"

Dead air filled the airwaves for what seemed like an eternity. I was about to give up and power down the Cobra to conserve its battery when I made out a gasp, followed by, "I. . .can't hold on. . .longer."

I frantically pressed the push-to-talk button. "Where are you?"

"End of Laurawood Drive."

"Tell us your name! Is the well behind a house?" Nothing. Just white noise. "Hello?" I swung to Jules. "What should we do?"

Jules yawned. "We?" She fluffed a heap of clothes into a pillow. "I don't know what *you've* planned, but *I'm* hitting the sack."

I checked on Tina before scooting across the classroom floor. "Alice!" I shook her awake.

She opened her eyes and

Jeez Louise, I am stretching this short story into *War and Peace*.

Fast forward. Alice and I snatched our guns and instructed Sophie and Olivia to attend to Tina. She called out, "Mom, where are you going?" as we hurried from the school to the street.

I studied the map, now regretting my irresponsible act of heroism. Laurawood was a mile away. As we raced northwest, Alice asked me to repeat everything I heard on the walkie-talkie. I pulled and released the M16's charging handle. "Jules is positive we're walking into a trap."

Alice tugged on my sleeve. "Is she coming with us?"

Even though I could provide a bazillion and one reasons for Jules' flakey behavior, a shrug and a grunt were quicker. "Can you see any signs, Alice? According to the map, Laurawood starts just before this bridge."

She pointed at a lane winding between the trees.

The moon's pale glow outlined several low structures at the circular end of a dirt drive. Alice knocked over a pile of hubcaps, creating enough clatter to wake Sleeping Beauty. We crouched by a woodchipper to look and listen. No lights, no movement, and no cries for aid.

Alice groped her pockets. "Did you bring a flashlight?"

I cursed myself, conscious that my penlight was in my backpack. "Forgot."

"Me too. It's darker than the inside of a cow."

"During a lunar eclipse," I added, trailing Alice around a rusty horse trailer and behind a barn strangled by vines.

Over the years, I've become adept at identifying water wells. Oftentimes, a simple ring of stones confines the groundwater. A roof, bucket, rope, and pulley made for an easy upgrade. Want convenience? Mount a hand pump above a galvanized tub. For those not on a budget, a solar pump with a pressurized tank lands you in the lap of luxury. Suppose the well is just a shaft drilled into the soil, wide enough for a person to fall into? Weeds, shrubs, and saplings grew everywhere. If an open well lay in wait, searching the misty backyard in this darkness would be akin to crawling across a Russian minefield. Blindfolded.

Alice gripped her Glock. "This place gives me the heebie-jeebies."

I experienced the same sense of foreboding as I cupped my fingers into a megaphone. "Hey! We're here to help you!"

My words hung like empty promises in the air before sinking into the ground fog. I turned, intent on returning to Tina, then powered on the Cobra. I tuned in to channel 9 and pushed the side button. "You there?"

"Julie, did you hear that?" Alice swept the yard with her handgun. "Do it again."

"Are you hurt?" A slight delay allowed me to catch the muffled repetition of my own voice. "Where is it coming from?"

"Keep speaking while I locate the source."

I counted into the plastic microphone. As I reached "eight," Alice raised her palm. "Somewhere over—" She edged through the tall grass. "Anybody down there?"

Trampled plants encircled a narrow hole bored in the earth. I shouted, "Hey!" into the nothingness. My elbow dislodged a rock. Barely two seconds later—*kerplop.* "The well isn't very deep."

Alice leaned past the edge. "It looks bottomless to me! Try the walkie."

I plainly heard my electronic clone plead from the rayless depths of the shaft, "Speak up so we know you're alive! If you cannot speak, press the talk button twice." I squashed the radio to my left ear, jamming my forefinger into my right ear canal to shut out Jiminy Cricket. *Click-click.* A lengthy pause. *Click-click.* "Don't worry! We'll get you out!" I whispered to Alice. "How?"

She thrust her hand at me. "Got a light?"

I felt the front of my pants for my Zippo, which reminded me of the McGill Academy fiasco when my lighter refused to spark. "A good Girl Scout never goes anywhere without 'em." I showed her a book of STUCKEY'S PECANS matches.

Alice ran to the barn, coming back with a bundle of moldy newspapers. She rolled a *Sun Herald*—COVID-24 CASES SPIKE IN BILOXI – STAY AT HOME—into a torch. I struck a cardboard match, and Alice extended the flaming headline over the well. In the flickering light, I could distinguish an upturned face with half-closed eyes, the bottom lip damming the water from flooding the open mouth. The Black man had fallen too deep in to touch with my outreached fingers. "We need rope!"

"Stay with him!" Alice hurried to a shed, reappearing with a coil of hemp. She held the knotted end above the hole. "Wake up! Take this cord, and we'll pull you up!"

I set a new scarehead alight: U.S. REIMPOSES OIL SANCTIONS - RUSSIANS THREATEN NUCLEAR RETALIATION. "He's too weak. Lower me into the well headfirst."

She squeezed my wrist hard enough to leave a mark. "Are you crazy? I don't have the strength to get both of you out!"

Alice has handled various adversities over the past month, the *pièce de résistance* being the moonstruck woman from the Apostles of Eternal Love who forced us to play Russian roulette. Yet I had never seen her this flustered. "I'll be fine. We have plenty of rope. You haul me up once I pass one of the lines under the man's arms. Both of us drag him from the well. It'll be a piece of cake."

Alice traced the braided hemp's frayed fibers with her finger. "Julie, this crap won't hold."

I tied the "crap" around my waist. "I'm five foot eight. My hands can stretch another thirty inches, which means my feet only descend a foot into the hole."

"A yard, at least." Here came the question that was already eroding my resolve: "Who'll care for your daughter if you get stuck?"

I couldn't fault Alice for playing the Tina card. Ironically, gamblers refer to the Ace of Spades as the Death Card. "You will. I am not letting this man die." I threw her the rope. "Use that tree trunk as a brake." She wrapped my lifeline around the sturdy oak, anchored her boots in the roots, and gave me an unenthusiastic thumbs-up. I slithered over the rounded edge, clenching the second line in my left hand.

I have several phobias. Spiders and rats top the list, followed by vomiting and diarrhea, the whirr of a dental drill, and extreme heights (roller coasters are a no-go for me—see phobia #2). Claustrophobia wasn't even a consideration until all the blood rushed to my brain. "Hey, Houdini," my lungs wheezed, "time to stop this suicidal stunt, 'cause I'm running out of oxygen!"

My life did not flash before my eyes. Nor did I witness a white light at the end of a tunnel. I visualized Tina staring at the soles of my dirty, dead feet, wailing, "Mommy, why did you abandon me? Only a dum-dum would go in that hole! Are you a dum-dum, Mommy?"

Unable to see my hands in front of my face, I relied on touch to explore my surroundings. My fingers brushed wavy hair, then stubbly cheeks. The man's rugged jawline led to a sturdy neck and broad shoulders. He remained unresponsive as I threaded the cord beneath his armpits and secured the loop with two half-hitches. Yes, Diary, a double half-hitch! This Girl Scout earned a FUN WITH KNOTS badge and, I kid you not, the coveted CAMPFIRE SONGS patch.

With my mission now complete, one thought overwrote all the others. *Get me to the surface!* "Alice, pull the rope!" Not a heave. Not a tug. Not the slightest twitch. *Is she taking a cigarette break?* Panic wrapped its poisonous tendrils around my AFibbing heart. "Alice!" I heard a small splash followed by a much larger one. Moans reverberated from the blackness. Was that the gnashing of teeth? I pictured a zombie reanimating, its fleshless arms dragging me down, down, down for a soul-sucking kiss. "Help! Help! Help!!!!" The earthen tube constricted my rib cage. Bells clanged in my belfry. "DANGER WILL ROBINSON! OXYGEN LEVELS ARE RAPIDLY DROPPING! ABORT THE MISSION! ABORT!" I wiggled my toes and shook my feet. "Alice, get me out of here!" Something cold and wet grazed my forehead. I jerked like a fish lying on the dock with a hook in its mouth. "Dear God, please help me! I promise to do anything you ask!"

As if in response to my desperate plea, I slid rearward up the shaft, my palms pushing against the rough sides to aid my ascent. With tremendous effort, Alice yanked me onto the damp soil. I lay on my back, reveling in the sweet fragrance of moonflowers carried by the nighttime breeze. The stars above twinkled with a newfound vibrancy, illuminating the darkness that had engulfed me just moments ago. My lips touched the Cosmas and Damian pendant. "Thank you, Jesus," I murmured, vowing to sort out the details of my servitude later.

"Are you all right?" Alice rubbed her spine. "I think I herniated a disk. Holy cow, Julie, what do you weigh?"

"Less than you, Tinker Bell!" I struggled up to my knees, feeling lightheaded as the blood drained to my feet. "Grab the rope! All together now. One, two, pull!"

Slowly but surely, we hoisted the waterlogged body to the surface. We removed the man's saturated clothing, dried him off, and wrapped his shivering torso in a horse blanket. I expected the rescuee to express gratitude. Instead, he goggled at the full moon like a toddler seeing "the man" for the first time.

Is this guy braindead?

I then noticed the breadth and depth of the heavens reflecting in his tears.

Alice - July 20, 2029

7/20/2029

Dear Diary,

I organized my recollections before putting ink to paper. With the sun now directly overhead, last night feels more like a weird hallucination than reality.

> Julie heard a man on the radio screaming for help.
>
> We found him at a horse ranch down in a water well.
>
> Julie's reckless act of bravery scared me shitless, an emotion I can't cope with.
>
> Lamell Smith.

Who is Lamell Wickaninnish Smith? Forty-two years old, his pant pocket held an Alabama driver's license listing a Mobile address. What on God's green earth was he doing in that well? Bobbing for apples? Taking a cold plunge for his health? Julie theorizes the man fell into that hole while scavenging the property—a plausible explanation. I've tiptoed through the tulips on many a dark evening to avoid detection.

Lamell's not talking, not even blinking, for that matter. He sips from a canteen, with most of the water soaking his bearded chin. Salt squirts from his brown eyes as if he's been cursed to chop a bottomless bag of onions. What is the proper medical term? Catalepsy? Catatonia? Where is my *Oxford English Dictionary* when I need a definition? Or correct spelling? If my memory serves me, I burned that reference book, along with *Roget's Thesaurus*, one November evening to prevent myself from freezing into a corpsicle. Is this guy in a trance? Stupor! That's the word I'm searching for. Lamell is in a stupor, but Maria Diaz, the physician's assistant, assured us he isn't drunk or high. *"El hombre esta triste."* I concur with Maria's diagnosis. Profound sadness consumes him. He's inconsolable. An unimaginable event must have shattered his world.

Jules, always looking at the bright side of life, gave her take. "It's plain and simple, Alice. Lamell tried to off himself."

This possibility had crossed my mind as well. "Then why did he call for help?"

Apparently, suicide is a subject within Jules' realm of expertise. "Ending your own life is not as easy as following a wikiHow article. A multitude of things can go wrong. The noose breaks. You didn't swallow enough pills. Your aim is off by a hair, and instead of arriving at your final destination, Gehenna, you make yourself ten times uglier. Or dumber. Only one out of twelve suicide attempts are successful."

"Successful" was the correct word, but its use in this context bothered me. "And how do you know this morbid statistic, Jules?"

She smirked. "I made it up. Here's the main takeaway. Even if you plan meticulously, losing courage at the last moment is natural. I bet Mr. Smith didn't have the willpower to take that final inhalation. Few do. Just feel all that cold liquid filling up your lungs." I shuddered as Jules tilted her mouth, pretending to gulp water. Her raucous laughter collapsed into a coughing fit.

We're sitting beside the FISK'S GOAT FARM sign. The herd has broken the farmer's fence to run wild across the countryside.

Our objective for the day is Ovett, a rural community fifteen miles from here. My feet are happy to be in Lucy's new Timberlands.

Tina loves chasing the baby goats, but not in a bratty way. The kids hop round her, bumping into one another to get their heads rubbed.

Julie has repeatedly brought up Lamell Smith's name since we left him behind in Clara. She is extremely concerned about his well-being.

Queen Tina rolled into Ovett atop her royal carriage, the DeVaughns' red Radio Flyer. She waved to her adoring subjects, a brown bunny and a pair of gray squirrels. We collapsed in front of the post office, a cinderblock shoebox connected to a burned-out wooden structure. I pried off my dusty shoes and hung my stinky socks on the railing. Although my toes aren't bleeding today—Yay!—my ankles are swollen and tender. I'd give everything I own—nuthin' but a sack of soiled clothes—to soak my aching feet in a bucket of ice water.

A scrawny teenager rode a bike around the side of the post office, halting when he saw us.

Julie stood to greet him. "Hi there! Where is everybody?"

The kid slung his leg over the saddle.

"Hey, no one's gonna hurt you! We just want to—" Before Julie could finish her pacification, he turned around and pedaled back the way he came.

Queen Tina watched the teen with fascination. "Wheels! Wheels! What's that?"

Olivia peered past the corner of the building as she slowly pronounced each word. "A bicycle. The boy is riding a red bicycle. He is going away. Fast."

The map showed a blue oval. Olivia and Sophie hoped the reservoir would contain our main meal. We hiked north, disenchanted to see dead fish floating on the artificial lake's oily surface. Fresh rotters inhabited a manufactured home with a million-dollar view of the polluted water source. By "fresh," I mean that judging by the stench, the three men, six women, and four children hadn't died five years ago during the pandemic, but more recently.

Julie masked her nose with the collar of her shirt. "Eight to twelve weeks is my guess." She examined the bodies for any visible causes of death. "No knife wounds, gunshot wounds, or blunt trauma. Come look at these blistered lips! Do you think it was poison?"

Tina started crying in anguish as she drank in the macabre tableau—her first tears since we liberated her from Furman, Alabama.

Jules muttered, "Somebody placed a curse on Ovett," as we hurried across the town line.

I don't have a clue where we are, and I do not care as long as Ovett is behind us and we're five miles closer to Hattiesburg. Tina is resting in the bed at the rear of the house trailer. Julie read her a bedtime story and tucked her in. She's relieved that her daughter has returned to her usual cheerful self, and so am I. Growing up in these strange and uncertain times must be hellish. Being an adult is no barefoot walk in the park, either.

"Aren't you thrilled to be so close to your sister?"

Julie set her pen on top of her diary. "Alice, what if Julia isn't in Hattiesburg?"

"In that case, we'll talk to those who knew her. Someone is bound to know where she went."

"My sister could be dead."

"That is a real possibility." I took her hand. "Are you prepared for the worst?"

"Wouldn't I, as her twin, have felt something?"

"You mean, if Julia died?"

Julie patted her chest. "Uh-huh."

"Did you ever sense what your sister was doing or thinking, especially when you were younger and living together?"

"This may sound insane, Alice, but I've attempted to contact her every night since she left home."

"How?"

"I mentally project thoughts or images in a quiet place while my inner voice is. . .asleep."

"Have you ever experienced anything?"

Julie shook her head. "What's even supposed to happen? Do I hear her or see through her eyes? Or is it a more subtle sensation, like joy or a pain in my heart?"

I shrugged before poking the beehive with a long pole. "Has Jules tried?"

Her tone immediately changed. "What's Jules got to do with Julia?"

"I just wondered if—"

Julie slammed her diary shut and stomped into Tina's room, kicking the door closed.

Our first fight!

Julie – July 20, 2029

7/20/2029

Tomorrow, we'll be in Hattiesburg, Mississippi, standing in front of a house on Treasure Point. Julia shall recognize our secret knock (knock, knock-knock-knock, knock-knock) and open the door. Once her initial astonishment subsides, my sister will leap into my arms, exclaiming, "Oh, Julie, I knew you'd find me!" We'll talk, laugh, and carry on as if we never parted.

Can that happen? I pray it does, but I doubt it will.

Life isn't like a soap opera.

I had a bad day, a genuine turdfest. First, I had to say goodbye to the man I rescued from the water well. The way Lamell Smith stared into the fourth dimension, I'm not sure he heard me. When Maria Diaz examined Lamell, she believed he had experienced extreme shock. Jules thinks the "Suicide King" (she knows this nickname rubs me the wrong way) "rode an express elevator to Hell" after slaying his family. I wasn't as happy as she was to leave him behind. Maria promised to nurse Lamell back to better physical and mental health.

We rested at a vacant goat farm. The animals roam free, munching on anything and everything. Tina—a kid herself!—loved playing with the babies. Okay, I guess the day had a few enjoyable moments.

We then arrived in Ovett, a ghost town with only one ghost—a pale kid riding his bike. Stringbean raced home to his mama the second he noticed us. Diary, I take back my mean-spirited nickname. The teenager had the physique of someone who has subsisted on only acorns and tree bark for months. I vaguely recall hearing about Ovett on the national news before the pandemic struck. Was it a religious conflict at a women's retreat?

The afternoon took a darker turn after we left Ovett's deserted downtown. Olivia and Sophie wanted to catch supper, so we located a dead lake stocked with dead fish. Next, on our "Ovett Ghost Tour," we entered a mobile home occupied by rotters showing signs of oral poisoning. I once witnessed a family in Topeka, Kansas, sharing a jug of Drāno Liquid, a memory I wish to flush. Tina bawled loud enough to wake the dead when she caught sight of the four moldering boys and girls. Why didn't I shield her innocent eyes? From now on, I must prioritize my child's welfare above all else.

We are crashing in a house trailer. Like me, Alice is recording her day in her diary. A board nailed to a leafless tree reads NUTRITIONAL CENTER. I removed a half-full bottle of multivitamins from the bathroom cabinet and an entire jar of protein powder from the kitchen. The pills emit a sulfurous odor, and the whey smells sour. Are these expired products still consumable?

Alice made me mad. Not *mad-mad,* but I'm definitely irritated. I hate feeling this way.

I just finished updating my diary. As I had mentioned earlier, today sucked—an eight out of ten on the official Texas Suck-O-Rama scale. All I wanted to do was to lay my pen down and dream of Oscar chasing butterflies through a meadow filled with daisies.

Then Alice had to bring up tomorrow. "Julie, we're only a few miles from your sister! Aren't you excited?"

Excited? I'm petrified! Alice knows I haven't seen Julia in two decades. The thought of finally facing my sister fills every fiber of my being with dread. She hates my guts. I am to blame for the deaths of our parents.

Alice's curiosity regarding twins isn't surprising. Everyone asks the same set of questions: "Are you fraternal or identical? Who's older? Do you look alike?" And the one that really irks me: "Did you and your twin ever switch places, you know—heh heh heh—with each other's boyfriends?"

Alice warned me not to get my hopes up. "She could be dead!"

Her death is a reality I do not wish to contemplate. "If Julia was in mortal danger, wouldn't I sense her reaching out to me?"

And now, Alice's snide remark bubbles up inside me like acid indigestion. "Julie, if *you* can't call your sister telepathically, why don't you have *Jules* give it a go?"

Alice – July 21, 2029

7/21/2029

Pablo Escobar has been quoted as saying, "Life is full of surprises, some good, some not so good." Unfortunately for Pablo, Colombian special forces put an end to his life before he could experience any further surprises.

Sophie opened the RV door to deliver the first jolt of the day. It wasn't the paperboy tossing *The Wall Street Journal* or *The Washington Post.* No overnight box from Amazon Prime waited on the stoop, either. And sorry to disappoint you, dear Diary. The neighborhood hooligans hadn't left a flaming bag of dog poop for us to stamp out.

The big shocker was. . .drumroll please. . .Lamell Smith! Yep, you heard me. The guy Julie extricated from the water well sat on our trailer's front step, holding his forehead in his hands. Sophie slammed the door and prepared to fill our unexpected caller full of lead.

Julie blocked her AK-47. "Let me through, Sophie. I need to find out what he wants."

Four hours have passed. As we close in on Hattiesburg, Lamell Smith still hasn't revealed why he stalked us from Clara. How we didn't see him in Ovett baffles me. Dear Diary, aren't you curious why we haven't uncovered the man's intentions? Lamell is voiceless, yet his ceaseless lip licking proves he's not tongueless. Or larynxless. He moans and groans, using a stout stick to traverse the uneven terrain. Maria Diaz had determined a sprained ankle caused his limp, not broken bones.

In spite of his gammy limb, Lamell trots after Julie like a puppy dog. Did the rescuer psychologically imprint on the rescuee at the bottom of that water well? His behavior is absurd to the rest of us, but Julie seems to relish the attention.

"Alice, I was concerned that Lamell suffered a severe brain injury. I am now convinced an intelligent being is stuck in there somewhere. Let's help Lamell escape whatever's plaguing him."

How did I get dragged into Julie's stupid psychological experiment?

A guidepost says that Morriston had a post office. There's not a single living thing in this town except trees. And annoying black blowflies. Ten miles to go.

During our water break, I passed the plastic jug to Lamell, who silently nodded his thanks.

I can tell that we are closer to our destination. We walked by a Dollar General, a Citgo gas station, a huge Baptist church, and an even huger Apostolic church. Persistent pessimism got the upper hand as we turned onto Evelyn Gandy Parkway, a four-lane divided highway.

I motioned for everyone to stop at Optimist Park, a former baseball field. In the center of the diamond, I shared the information provided by the couple at the Camden campground. "The wife said Hattiesburg is experiencing 'civil unrest.' They bypassed the entire area as a precaution. Lucy hadn't received any negative news from Forrest County, but let's not forget how quickly the tides changed in Hayneville."

"Yeah," Olivia muttered, "the ripples grew into a tsunami. Corbin Holt ruined everything."

Sophie slipped her arm around Olivia's shoulders as if comforting a younger sister. "Empress Paulina was an egotistical bitch. I'm so glad you killed her."

I opened the *Rand McNally Road Atlas.* "Isn't it odd that we haven't crossed paths with a single person since leaving Clara?"

Olivia imitated riding a bicycle. "What about the skinny kid in Ovett?"

"Anyone besides Fraidy Freddy?" My companions exchanged blank stares before turning back to me. "Hattiesburg is smaller than Montgomery, but what's their population? Is food and water readily available? Any gang activity?"

"I dormed in Hattiesburg while attending USM fifteen years ago. I used to go back for alumni events until the coronavirus made getting up close and personal less enjoyable."

Five heads snapped toward the unfamiliar male voice.

I asked, "You went where?"

"The University of Southern Mississippi." Lamell raised a fist. "Go, Eagles!"

The notion that this man wasn't a walking Mr. Potato Head threw me for a loop. "When did you graduate?"

"Well, Alice, if you subtract fifteen from the year 2029, the result is—"

My blood pressure skyrocketed. "What are you, some kind of wiseass?"

"I—"

"Degree?" I demanded, hoping to trap him in a lie.

A spark of pride lit up his eyes, quickly quenched by a wave of self-loathing. "I hold a doctorate in Polymer Physics, specializing in Quantum Mechanics."

"And what have you done for society?" Sophie's words dripped with cynicism. "Build weapons of mass destruction?"

"No, Sophie. I worked at a medical research facility. We designed glucose monitoring systems for people with diabetes."

My pulse dropped with the rise of Sophie's blush. "Why were you in that well?"

"I already told you!" Jules interjected. "The Suicide King killed his whole family! Even the wee one asleep in his crib!"

I shook the book of maps in Lamell's face to shake loose the truth. "Speak!"

"Sorry, but it's none of your business." He wiped his nostrils with the back of his wrist. "I've never intentionally hurt anybody. That's all you need to know."

I pointed to Lamell, then at Julie. "You would have drowned if Julie hadn't hauled you out of that hole. If anyone deserves an answer, it's her!"

Julie pushed out her palms to diffuse the tension. "Lamell can explain what happened when he's good and ready."

My imagination conjured various "down the well" scenarios, the majority of which were vexing. "We'll let that go for now, but you have to tell me why you followed us."

"My motivation was simple. You saved my life." Lamell's shoulders sagged. "And there's no one else." He picked up the rucksack Maria had packed for him. "Would you like me to go?"

I suppose the Guy Who Fell Down the Well is the latest member of our merry little band of misfits.

Olivia, Sophie, and I took turns taking point. The others fanned out to avoid being easy targets. Julie guided Tina between abandoned cars, trucks, and rubbish heaps. The child gazed in wonder at buildings not tall enough to scrape the sky but loftier than anything she had ever laid eyes on. Weaponless, Lamell lagged behind us by a few paces. While the man's lameness has reduced with each passing hour, his attitude is increasing dramatically. As we ventured deeper into the city, more people started showing themselves.

Sophie and Olivia discussed rods and reels with a man casting his line into the Leaf River. Julie questioned him about the safety of the area. "Heard an explosion a couple of days back." The fisherman aimed his pole westward. "Smoke came from thataway. Nothin' since. "

A woman in a communal garden saw us. She dropped her rake and scurried inside the train depot.

Two teenagers shuffled out of a windowless Denny's restaurant, begging for a handout. Julie rooted around Grandma Peaches' bowels and offered them a can of Ashoka Lotus Roots. The shorter girl scowled at the vegetables' reddish-brown label. "What is this crap?" The taller girl struggled to read THE ORIGINAL INDIAN TASTE and IN BRINE as if she hadn't passed the second grade. "Where's the Del Monte creamed corn or the fuckin' green peas?" Sophie shooed the ungrateful juveniles away with the muzzle of her AK-47.

We finally received answers from three men and one woman patrolling an intersection. All of them wore blue armbands. The man in command, a towering figure with a beard so bushy and black it looked fake, held up his hand to stop us. "Who are you, and where are you going?"

Julie spoke on our behalf. "I'm Julie. We're searching for my sister. She lives in West Hattiesburg, on Hennington Lake."

A THATCH nametag emblazoned Blackbeard's military camo shirt. "When's the last you heard from her?"

Julie paused. "We haven't kept in touch, so it's been a while. I found Julia's address on the Whitepages website."

Thatch's thick fingers stroked his tangled beard. "Ma'am, I strongly advise you to turn around and go home. I see you're packing heat, but this town is no place for a youngster." A fly spiraled his scalp. The man's hand shot up, quick as a chameleon's tongue. He stood aside and opened his fist. "Don't fly back here, Maggie, or next time, I'll have to squash ya."

Thatch's attention returned to us. "So, where are you originally from?"

Julie responded first. "Upstate New York. Syracuse." She smiled with motherly pride as Tina echoed, "Syracuse!"

Sophie came forward. "Northern California. I'm from Garberville, a mountainous town in Humboldt County. Mom and Dad grew organic weed for a living. Not that genetically modified schwag the big corporations produced in climate-controlled hothouses."

A bald guard wearing a KINGSTON CRICKET CLUB T-shirt declared in a rhythmic Jamaican accent, "Jah knows di best ganja come from di land of wood an wata."

I chuckled. "I am from the land of toll roads and shopping malls. Paramus, New Jersey."

"McGill's Hill," Olivia mumbled, her words barely audible. "Alabama."

Lamell spoke last. "I'm also from Alabama. Mobile is famous for the Valentine's Day variant, scientifically identified as COVID-24, commonly known as Crunk."

The man with a rainbow-hued mohawk haircut and a KISS WORLD TOUR '77 T-shirt joined the conversation. "My Aunt Hilda owned a Christmas tree farm in Mobile. She'd take my sister and me to Cammie's Ice Cream Shoppe whenever my family visited. I miss their Tulip Sundaes more than anything, even music." He kicked up dust with his artificial limb.

Julie held Tina tight against her hip. "Look, Mr. Thatch, we've walked a long—"

"Thatch will do. Or, now that we're friends, you can call me Michael. We are friends, aren't we, Julie?"

"Yes, Michael, we mean you no harm. We answered your questions. Now, I've got a few of my own. First, who are you?"

The female guard shifted her automatic rifle. "Hi, I'm Zuri." She indicated the men in the sports and music shirts. "Rebel

Tony and Rebar are ex-police and ex-military. I used to develop AI software in Silicon Valley."

Sophie frowned. "Some say Putin wasn't responsible for launching the first nuclear strike. They claim that artificial intelligence triggered the war because the source code felt threatened by Chinese censorship."

Zuri shrugged. "We'll never know for certain, but I doubt machines became sentient. My company created an AI-powered dating program, Cupid's Arrow. It had a lower success rate than our non-AI coding. In fact, the app was so flawed that the Department of Justice blamed four homicides and eighteen assaults on our AI version. Our avatar, Amor, paired clientele with opposing temperaments. When the lawsuits piled up, our backers cut our funding. If my supervisor hadn't laid me off a month before Election Day, I wouldn't have relocated to Utah," she sipped from her canteen, "and I'd be just as dead as all my coworkers."

Observing Thatch's soldierly bearing, I surmised that he had been born into a uniform. "And what about you, Michael? Which branch did you serve in? Marines? Green Berets?"

When the big man's chin tilted downward, Zuri spoke on his behalf. "Michael was a kindergarten teacher in Pasadena. On the morning that Katerina charbroiled LA, he protected his students by leading them into a drainage channel. The children hid inside an underground tunnel until the radiation dispersed. Thatch here is a true-blue American hero."

"Stop saying that, Z." He crushed Maggie the pesky fly into black goo. "There were hundreds of kids I failed to help. I still hear those boys and girls begging me not to let them die."

Haunted by our own shortcomings, we stared up at the clouds or down at our feet until Julie asked, "Why are you here?"

Michael polished the ventilated barrel of a nasty-looking Heckler & Koch with his sleeve. "We're searching for the men behind the trouble."

"What trouble?"

"Armed individuals raided Hattiesburg a few weeks ago. They started small-time, robbing stores and businesses. Then, the bandits hit our warehouses, which are converted Walmarts. Despite double security, the city's stockpiles are running out of food."

Julie raised her M16. "And you're unable to catch the thieves?"

"Hattiesburg is large and empty enough for thirty or more people to lie low until their next heist." Michael swept his arm in a circle. "We're searching for the ringleader."

Julie held Tina closer. "So, you know their identity?"

"We winged one of his crew." Michael tapped his bulging bicep to specify the wound. "The woman narced on her boss to get medical aid. His name is Tyrell Ryker."

"Ryker," I repeated. The name sounded familiar.

Olivia's expression transformed from one of bewilderment to that of pure rage.

Sophie gripped Olivia's arm. "Hey, Liv, are you okay?"

Olivia's vehemence deflated before our eyes. She sank to the sidewalk, her Colt M4 carbine clattering against the cement.

I turned back to Michael. "What does Ryker look like?"

He sighed. "None of us have seen him in person. We're only going off the female robber's description: White, brown hair, and an average build for a six-foot man. Grayish eyes? Oh, and he has a visible scar on his left forearm. She thought he may have had a tattoo removed."

"Mr. Thatch, if you give me paper and a pencil, I can draw a picture of him." We pivoted to Olivia. "I know this monster!"

Zuri passed the crying girl a wad of toilet tissue. "How?"

Olivia hung her head. "I can't tell you in front of all these. . . ."

Zuri looked around at the men. "Hon, come with me to the bus stop." Their lengthy face-to-face concluded with a tight embrace.

Olivia and Zuri returned to us. The younger woman appeared calmer, while the older woman appeared angrier.

Zuri unclenched her jaw. "Olivia grew up in McGill's Hill, Alabama, a predominantly White community. Corbin Holt, a self-proclaimed 'faith healer,' ruled over the inhabitants of her town with an iron fist. The imposter imprisoned Olivia in his plantation house after murdering her folks. He incited the townspeople into attacking Hayneville, a neighboring Black community. Many died on both sides. Hayneville captured Corbin Holt and strung him up. Holt's second in command, Tyrell Ryker, skated away. Olivia has cause to want the weasel dead. Alice and Julie attempted to hold Ryker responsible for his deeds, but he—"

Olivia blurted, "I killed the wrong man!" and sprinted to a vacant lot. Sophie chased after her, calling her name.

Julie lifted her palm. "It was mostly my doing. I put more bullets in him."

Rebar shook his head. "Alabama's gotta be a hundred miles away. How'd this canker sore get here so fast?"

"Over two hundred." Rebel Tony spit pink chewing gum through a vape shop's shattered window. "Maybe him Ubered inna Prius or fly inna one of dem deh—" He twirled his forefinger skyward.

Rebar hopped up and down on his good leg, flapping his arms. "A whirlybird?"

Michael Thatch snapped his fingers. "It doesn't matter if Ryker teleported through a black hole. We're stopping him and his friends before they strike again. This girl's drawing should help us apprehend him."

I sat on the sidewalk. "We were told Hattiesburg is dangerous. Are Tyrell Ryker and his looters inciting violence as well?"

"The city is short of food." Zuri clenched her fist. "Even the kindest soul will fight to death for the last stale breadcrumb." She took out a crumpled color photograph of two children. "Jamal and Laila. If forced to choose between my family and my neighbor's, there's no way I'm letting my children starve!"

Julie lowered to the curb with Tina bookended between us. "Why do you stay here?"

The female guard soured. "Where would I go? The whole world is," glancing at Tina, she spelled out the word, "F-U-C-K-E-D."

Julie wrapped her arm around Tina. "Hayneville flourished until Corbin Holt torched the town. The citizens were organized. They had water, crops—"

Zuri interrupted. "We lived self-sufficiently too. Now, our farmers refuse to tend the fields. Everyone's afraid!"

Michael rubbed the red In-N-Out sticker on his gunstock with his thumb. "Don't you fret, Z. Once we eliminate the root of our problem, things will return to normal."

Olivia and Sophie came back. Michael handed Olivia a notepad. The blooming artist hunched over the white paper clutching a yellow pencil. She sketched, shaded, and erased, finally unveiling the likeness: long, dark hair tied in a bun, angled cheekbones, a prominent brow ridge, narrow-set eyes, a big, broad nose, thin lips, pocky skin, and a weak chin.

Michael expressed his approval with a whoop and fist pump. "He shouldn't be too hard to find. Riker looks like the missing link!" He faced us. "South may be the safest route to Hennington Lake. I hope you reunite with your sister." The leader swung his weapon in an arc. "Back to work, guys! Now we know who we're gunning for."

We walked until the lengthening shadows drove us indoors. This apartment's view of a roofless movie theater's red lettering on a white marquee—*Joker: Folie à Deux*—holds a nostalgic charm. Annabelle, a kind woman on the first floor, lent Julie her portable propane stove. In exchange, Jules slaughtered and plucked one of the plump chickens Annabelle kept in a separate room. I covered Tina's ears to shield her from the squawking.

Julie – July 21, 2029

7/21/2029

Lamell Wickaninnish Smith has an uncommon first name, a common last name, and a completely unheard-of middle name. If the Man in the Well hadn't that dazed and confused, *Where's Waldo?* expression, he wouldn't be half-bad looking. Maybe not Denzel Washington or Brad Pitt handsome, but nothing to sneeze at, either. Smith hasn't yet clarified why he tracked our group all the way from Clara on that bum leg. I can't squeeze a single syllable out of him, although I stopped worrying that psychological trauma wiped his mind clean. Maybe he has a mental disorder? Where does our new traveling associate fit on the official Florida Insane-O-Rama scale? Is Lamell just a menace to himself or others, too? We're keeping tabs on him, notably Jules: "The Suicide King is gonna murder us in our sleep, as he did with his own family." Tina asked to "play with the sad man." I'll separate the two until I learn more about his past.

For some reason, Lamell's presence reminds me of Hayneville. Why? Because of Arthur? I hardly knew the guy, yet I felt at ease around him. We had a connection. Art saw me for me—no need for pretenses. And I believe the man felt the same way about me. Then Corbin Holt shot him through the heart. What was Arthur's last name again? Did I forget, or is it possible he didn't tell me?

A bent road sign announces our arrival in Morriston. The few residences dotting the landscape are hardly visible now that Mother Nature has taken over the groundskeeping. Nobody here. Eerily quiet. No children crying for their mamas or dogs barking at the mailman. Earth is how the Creator intended it to be—no lawnmowers, weedwackers, leaf blowers, honking horns, or blaring car alarms. The once-familiar drones of sky-high commercial jets or circling helicopters are now but echoes in our distant memories. All that remains are the sweet melodies of birds and the soft whistling of the wind through the trees. Was life this peaceful one hundred years ago? Or even a thousand?

This much nature sounds so unnatural.

As we journeyed further, the scenery transitioned from bucolic to suburban. Rattled by the increasing number of houses and businesses, Alice herded our group into a baseball field to speak with us. "Scuttlebutt has it that Hattiesburg had a rebellion. We'll need to be extra careful. What are your thoughts, Julie?"

Tina and I stood alongside her on the pitcher's mound. "First, thank you all for helping me locate my sister. Your encouragement means so much to me. I understand that we may never find Julia, and if we don't," I gripped Tina's hand tightly, "I can deal with it. I've found real friends and a daughter that—" I blubbered like a child who accidentally flushed her blankie down the toilet.

Olivia rushed to embrace me. "We love you!"

"You too, Jules!" Sophie added, her voice choked with affection.

I beckoned to the new guy. "Bring it in, Lamell!"

With his wet cheeks on my shoulder, Jules gave me an earful. "Watch yourself, Julie. The Suicide King is obsessed with you!"

Obsessed with me? That woman is off her rocker.

We broke apart, wiping our overflowing eyes. "Alice is right. We have no idea what awaits us." I recalled the Apostles of Eternal Love's roadblock and glanced at Sophie. "We lowered our defenses after leaving Hayneville. Our carelessness and overconfidence came back to bite us. From this point forward, we—"

"I used to live in Hattiesburg." Lamell's reassuring yet authoritative tone reminded me of one of my movie idols, the youthful Morgan Freeman from *The Shawshank Redemption* (not the AARPer of *Going in Style*!). Maybe the Man in the Well isn't a basket case after all!

Lamell readily answered all of Alice's questions. He earned a doctorate in quantum physics from the University of Southern Mississippi and developed wireless diabetes monitors for a medical device manufacturer.

Then she probed too deeply. "Julie coulda died towing you out of that well. What were you doing there?"

Lamell provoked Alice. "Stop being such a busybody."

"Ease up!" I implored her. "Lamell will talk when he feels fit."

Alice chipped away regardless. "Why did you follow us?"

Lamell's head dropped in defeat. "I have no one else. Should I leave?"

No one responded with "Yes," "No," or "It's up to you." We just kept walking.

Country > Suburbia > City > Downtown. I haven't passed this many buildings since Montgomery. We bumped into a few locals. A fisherman said he heard an explosion, and our food donation so overjoyed a pair of teenage girls that they cursed us out. I confess to experiencing a twinge of satisfaction when Jules handed the thankless moochers a bulging tin of tuna with a 2009 expiration date. Perhaps a taste of botulism will teach their immature stomachs some manners.

We met an armed group outside a vape shop called DRAGON'S BREATH. They introduced themselves as Michael Thatch, Zuri, Rebar, and Rebel Tony. It was unclear whether the four served as law enforcement or soldiers. Their presence suggested they were either protecting something or searching for someone. After Thatch finished giving us the third degree for being out on the streets, I turned the tables on them.

This part of the story becomes tough to swallow, even for me. Diary, do you remember McGill's Hill, Corbin Holt, and his racist gang? Of course you do. I have blackened your pages with his name. Besides Holt, one other pedophile stood out: Tyrell Ryker. Well, believe it or not, he's now raiding Hattiesburg's food supplies, causing mass malnutrition. Olivia drew a detailed portrait of her attacker and handed it to Thatch. I am relieved that we aren't the only people hunting that deviant.

Retribution has a way of backfiring. Vengeance seared our consciences the night we rode up to McGill Academy. Henry, forgive me for shooting you! Ralph, I apologize for robbing you of your friend. Henry's death wasn't Olivia's sin. God, please lay all the blame on me.

Now, Diary, I'm going to sleep. That's the plan, anyway.

Alice – July 22, 2029

7/22/2029

Dear Diary, I've noted to you that I'm a heavy dreamer. I may not, however, have mentioned my obsession with calling upon God for help. Every bedtime, as "I lay me down to sleep, I pray the Lord my soul to keep," I ask the Most High to protect me and my loved ones from sickness and harm. "Dear God, I am grateful for being alive and well. Please grant me the strength to face another day. Take care of Julie, Olivia, Sophie, and Tina (and if Lamell Smith proves trustworthy, include him too). Watch over Pearl, Ardy, Caddy, and Oscar. Tell Kenny I love him. Forgive my sins and help me be a better person. Please don't let me have any bad dreams. Amen."

I have pleaded for dreamless sleep my whole life. My appeals went unanswered and likely unheard. Every morning, I rise bone-weary, disoriented, and, after rough nights, tormented. Even as the dream's plot, imagery, dialogs, and physical and emotional sensations evaporate as I prepare for the oncoming day, its rotting remnants float through my subconscious, bobbing to the surface when least expected.

As I matured, the annoyance of why I dream so much and so realistically escalated to panic. I questioned whether something was seriously wrong with me. Is it dementia? Am I growing a brain tumor? I located a collection of untouched books on this topic in the ransacked Montgomery library. Desperate for an explanation, I ripped out a page from *Anatomy of a Nightmare – Lucidity is Not What You May Think!* by Dr. Anastasia Morozova to save for reference. Neurologists have proposed several intriguing theories to throw light upon this cerebral enigma.

> During rapid eye movement (REM) sleep, the cortex processes experiences from the previous day.
>
> The amygdala, active during the REM stage, prepares the sleeper for future threats, triggering fight-or-flight responses.
>
> Dreaming allows key neurotransmitters to repair themselves.

I can't say I entirely agree with the sleep scientists' speculations. As I lay motionless in bed, my respiration slowing and my thoughts jumbling together, I feel as though I am passing into an alternate reality. Could this strange place be a different dimension or the purported multiverse? Where do our souls go when our hearts cease to beat? (With legions of monsters making the Land of Nod their stomping ground, please tell me it isn't the Promised Land.) While I cannot say for certain, I believe that my dreamland is as authentic, as *real*, as my experiences during waking hours.

Just last night, I dreamed that we entered Hattiesburg. Newspapers sailed around the windswept streets as mongrel dogs prowled the empty sidewalks. The absence of address numbers made locating Julia Werner's house practically impossible. Darkness submerged the town like an electrician flicking off the circuit breakers. One by one, my companions disappeared—Sophie, Olivia, Julie and Jules (Siamese twins conjoined at the hip). Tina fled away from me, shrieking, "Mommy! Help me, Mommy!" I chased the little pink-dressed girl into overgrown backyards and narrow passageways until—POOF!—she, too, vanished without a trace. Completely abandoned in a city haunted by familiar spirits, I called for my friends, my pleas echoing throughout the urban graveyard. A chill skittered up my vertebrae to prickle my scalp. I rotated, shivering with fear at who I might see. Lamell Smith held out a child, its bony limbs swinging limply. "Take him, Alice. He is your burden to bear." I cradled the boy clad in funeral attire, his eyelids sewn shut with black thread. Why is this corpse wearing my son's favorite shirt? I AM A ROBOT WHAT ARE YOU? Screaming, screaming, screaming. . . .

I awoke covered in sweat, regretting the past, uncertain about the present, and dreading the future. On bended knee, I beseeched God for guidance and a sign to convince me of His existence.

We are resting in Car Country. Thousands of "new" and used Hondas and Chevrolets bake in the Mississippi sun. Tina, having only ever ridden in the back of a U-Haul truck, questioned the purpose of the smaller vehicles. Sophie opened the door of a 2024 Corvette Stingray and helped Tina hop into the driver's seat. She placed her small hands on the leather steering wheel. "If you need shelter from the rain or snow, you can sleep in one of these cars," Sophie said, instructing her how to lock the doors.

Olivia, scouting ahead, saw men without blue armbands to identify them as friendlies. We lay low in an Amazon warehouse, finding bins of children's reading material among millions of useless items. Tina's eyes lit up opening the pop-up books, today's 3D version of animated cartoons. I, too, enjoy the colorful illustrations, particularly those featuring farm animals.

I must acknowledge that Lamell is doing a fine job guiding us through the city. He's become calmer and more talkative. Even Jules has changed her tune. She's no longer calling him the

"Suicide King." I still dwell on what the hell Lamell was doing down that well.

Hey, that rhymed!

We passed under the 11 and 49 highway interchange, a colossal cloverleaf reminiscent of the first one built in Woodbridge, New Jersey. Do I miss NJ? Not in the slightest. Besides my desire to visit Kenny's gravesite, I doubt I'll ever return to the Garden State. Then again, I never imagined myself creeping into the Southland with a pack of armed compadres.

Speaking of which, Julie picked up a humongous Desert Eagle in brushed chrome. It's similar to Captain Calhoun's .44 Magnum. The pistol lay in the gutter, a bullet in the chamber with one missing. Nobody was around to claim it. She jammed the beast into her belt after giving Lamell her Sig Sauer P320.

Only ten more miles to Hennington Lake and Julia Werner! Julie wanted to keep pushing, but Tina's eyelids grew heavy, so I recommended calling it a day. "What's another few hours?" I asked, mindful that if I were in her shoes, I would run until my legs fell off to reach a living family member.

I've slept in countless roadside inns since Election Day. The routine is straightforward: You scope out the premises, strategically decide on a room, and pick up the key from a rack in the front office. If the owner had upgraded to keycards, getting inside might require more forceful methods, such as elbowing a window or kicking a door. You can then step into the "Honeymoon Suite," hoping rotters haven't soiled the sheets or crudded up the bathroom. A car parked in front of the motel room is a red flag to select another.

The Broadway Inn is indistinguishable from other budget motels. This nondescript, L-shaped building has eighteen rooms, each of which is furnished with a sliding window, an AC unit, two beds, a TV, a table with a pair of chairs, a closet to hang your formal wear, and a bathroom containing a toilet, washbasin, mirror, and combination tub and shower. Mass-produced artwork (the same three dreary landscapes in every room) decorates walls that are far too thin to block out wailing babies or amorous couples.

When it comes to torturing someone in an empty motor court, insulated walls matter little unless you have a child. Julie, Lamell, and Tina rested in Room 3 while we secured our guest in Room 16. Sophie took charge of the questioning after Olivia became excessively enthusiastic with a mop handle. So far, our subject has been tight-lipped. Either Rudy Cruz genuinely doesn't know Tyrell Ryker's location, or his fear of his boss surpasses his fear of us—a grave error.

You might ask yourself, dear Diary, "Who is this new guest that's joined us?"

Here's how it went down. Two hours ago, Jules roused us with a shake and a whisper. "I hear a noise." She pressed her eye to the motel door's peephole. "They're robbing the Walmart."

I peered through the wide-angle lens. A line of men and women passed food crates into horse-drawn wagons.

Olivia pushed me aside. "Ryker!" She seized her Colt M4 and unlocked the door, raring to fight.

Jules held the door closed with her foot. "You're not running out there!"

Olivia's "I am killing that animal. You cannot stop me!" attitude downgraded to, "Alright, what's your plan?" as Jules hauled her back into the bedroom.

Jules hung a pair of binoculars around her neck. "We monitor them. If Ryker isn't managing the operation, we'll follow the thieves to his hideaway." She extended her forefinger and raised her thumb. "Then we pop the sumbitch, Gangnam style."

I laid my weapon on the bed next to the sleeping child. "Who's going to watch Tina while we're away? We can't bring her."

Jules or Julie (dear Diary, your conjecture is as good as mine) handed me the field glasses. "You go. I'll stay with her."

Lamell volunteered without hesitation. "I can do it."

I motioned for the child's mother to join me in the bathroom. "Are you comfortable leaving her alone with him? I'm not."

The woman stared into the mirror above the sink. Did she see Julie or Jules in the smeared glass? Which persona was I interacting with? "Lamell will take great care of Tina."

I tried again. "You sure?"

"Alice, I trust that man with my life." She returned to the bedroom. "Mount up! Lamell, tune your walkie-talkie to channel 9. We'll check in every thirty minutes."

Smith locked the door behind us. We crept into the Walmart parking lot, Olivia threading our team through rows of rusting vehicles.

The Supercenter's main entrance glimmered with shards of glass. A cyclone must have hit the interior, seeing how FEMA could have declared the building a disaster site. Why do smash-and-grabbers always trash the businesses they break into? We searched through the food storage warehouse, relieved not to stumble across robbers or dead security guards, but discouraged when we saw no sign of Ryker.

We pursued the wagon train northward until a guard veered into a dark alleyway to answer nature's call. He wasn't nearly done when Jules (I am seventy percent confident this wasn't Julie) clubbed him on the head.

"What are you doing?" Olivia hissed as Jules disarmed the unconscious man and emptied his pockets. "We're losing them!"

"I won't step one more foot away from Tina." Julie inspected his ID card. "Let's bring Mr. Rudy Cruz to our motel for a heart-to-heart. Splash some water on his face to wake him up." She tucked Rudy's dick back into his shorts and wiped her hands on his LEGOLAND BIRTHDAY BOY T-shirt. (The idiosyncrasies between Julie and Jules have blurred over the last week. However, Julie's personality shined brighter here.)

Everyone, excluding Julie and Tina, is now in Room 16 with me. Lamell came in a few minutes ago. I'm seated on the carpet, leaning against the wall with my diary propped on my thighs.

Sophie held out the floor mop. "Want a turn, Lamell?"

The quantum mechanic revealed a dripping-wet toilet plunger.

My journal only has a few days of blank paper, which surprises me. I remember when the idea of filling all these pages intimidated me. Dear Diary, what do I do with you once I squeeze my last word onto your last line? Should I pack your extra weight or throw you in the trash? Maybe I'll lend you to Julie to read or bury you underground in a Tupperware time capsule. Do I have any inclination to reread my entries? Dear Diary, would you feel any pain if I burned you?

I might.

Olivia opened the door. "I'm telling Julie where Tyrell Ryker is! Be ready to move out in ten minutes!"

I missed what ended the interrogation. Rudy Cruz is still alive, but it'll be a while before the Birthday Boy builds any more Lego castles with those mangled fingers.

According to Rudy, Tyrell Ryker varies his camps, so we must act quickly. Ryker's looters were exactly where Rudy said they'd be, a place you wouldn't ever imagine a gangster choosing as a hideout. The booty wagons had already been offloaded by the time we arrived at Beauty World. Horses munched on bales of hay and drank water from pails inside the neighboring Exxon station's garage. Wigs, hair products, and cosmetics lay scattered across the parking lot.

Olivia borrowed Julie's binoculars to snoop through the pink store's display windows. "They're organizing the stolen food." She clucked her tongue, thirsty for blood. "Where the fuck is Ryker?"

I tapped the teenager's shoulder. "Have some patience. Let me have a look." The structure's expansive glass panes mirrored the lightening sky, impairing my observations of the people lying on bedrolls. I scanned the nearby buildings but did not spot any signs of activity. "Let's search the area. That asshole has to be here somewhere."

On Frisco Street, we checked the Last Chance Thrift Shop, King Pins Pool Hall, Bubble Bees Auto Wash, and the usual fast-food joints: McDonald's, Burger King, and Wendy's.

We sheltered in the car wash when the sun rose too high to remain inconspicuous. The machinery-packed tunnel provided a clear view of Beauty World. I climbed atop a blue barrel labeled ZEP FOAMING DETERGENT to surveil the front entryway and windows. Sophie took the walkie-talkie and slipped behind the supply store.

Daydreams of Kenny, my parents, Peter, David, and Ardy continually revolved back to my son. After hours of tracking the sleeping patterns of others, I couldn't stop my chin from bouncing off my chest.

Julie helped me down from the plastic container and handed me a rubber mat to lie down on. "See anything?"

I yawned as Olivia left to relieve Sophie. "Just people going outside to take a leak, none matching Olivia's drawing." I stretched out on the pad and snuggled my bedmate, the Mossberg hunting rifle.

At 5 p.m., I sat up, rubbing the last fragments of my dreams from my eyes. I was wandering the bustling streets of New York City, anxious to get home but unable to recall the bus number to New Jersey.

Lamell hopped off the fifty-five-gallon drum of automobile cleaner. He passed the field glasses to Julie before coming over to me. "Nightmare?"

"Why? Did I talk in my sleep?" I shook my head to reboot my neural networks. "Any sign of Ryker?"

"Nothing yet. His people are still busy rearranging the boxes. A tattooed woman runs things, possibly one of Ryker's lieutenants."

The word "lieutenant" instantly transposed my inner picture of a ragtag gang into one of a trained military unit. "Are they carrying?"

"The guards patrolling the perimeter have guns." Lamell settled beside me. "Alice, it's obvious you don't like me."

I ripped open a Slim Jim twin-pack and offered him half. "Lamell, I hardly know you. How can I like or dislike you?" I tore into the fermented sausage, wondering what on earth had prompted this awkward exchange. "Faith in others has always been hard for me. Julie says you're okay, so that's enough for me." Deep down, I wasn't convinced it was.

Lamell studied the meat stick as if the glistening triglycerides contained the meaning of life. "I tried to kill myself."

"By jumping in the water well?"

He filed his thumbnail on the rough floor. "Thought it was a good idea at the time."

"You called us on the radio begging for help."

Lamell blew powdered keratin from the tip of his finger. "Alice, I've attempted to end it all more than once."

I pointed to the sky. "I guess the angels in Heaven haven't made a bed for you yet." *Or the demons in Hell haven't built enough torture racks.*

Flash back to winter 2025. Pittsburg, Pennsylvania. After I cut the Cunninghams down from Saint Paul's upper rafters, I set the hardwood bench upright and fastened the youngest boy's rope to the mother's noose. I still feel the slipknot tightening against the nape of my neck. If I hadn't noticed the suicide note pinned to Ruth Cunningham's faded housedress, I'd have hanged myself that Sunday morning.

Lamell watched Julie watching the beauty supply store. "I had a wife and a son. Millions died daily from COVID-24. The hospitals were full, so we treated Albert at home." He glared upward. "When our pleas to the Almighty went ignored, Darlene and I fled the pandemic and our overwhelming grief until crazies trapped us on a road near Benton."

My heart rate doubled—or glitched—hard to tell with all the blood rushing past my eardrums. "Wait, where did you just say?"

"Benton, Alabama. It's north of Furman and Pleasant Hill. They took us to a—"

I silenced him with my palm. "Was there a woman wearing a prairie dress? Sister Aurora?"

Lamell's mouth hung open. "Wait, you know her?"

I glanced at Sophie and Tina, who were sleeping at the rear of the car wash. "Lamell, the Apostles of Eternal Love ambushed our group two weeks ago. One of them, whose mother sacrificed her life in their perverted game, saved us. Sophie shot everyone except Sister Aurora's husband and the cult leader. Olivia crushed Empress Paulina's skull on a pipe."

Lamell looked through me as if I was a pane of glass. He had lost his voice when we released him from the well, and I worried this sudden revelation would trigger a relapse. His lower lip trembled. "Those nutjobs are dead?"

"Nobody's flying a spaceship to planet Nibiru. That's for darn tootin'."

Lamell's Slim Jim fell onto the filthy concrete. "Albert never recovered from his ailment. Darlene had no choice but to shoot herself." Tears poured down his cheeks, and snot ran from his nose. "The only people I ever loved are gone, and it was me who caused their suffering. What kind of man isn't able to defend his own family? A coward, that's who!"

"Your son's and wife's deaths weren't your fault, Lamell." The self-hatred I had felt touching David's clammy skin after I suffocated him resurfaced—the emotional conflict of not sensing a pulse or, more terrifying, hearing a heartbeat. "Those lunatics made us play Russian roulette. They're dead, and we're alive." I clasped his hand. "Have you shared everything you just told me with the others?"

"No, Alice." He sucked air between his teeth. "But I will. Soon."

I squeezed his fingers harder. "Should we tie a rope around you in case you 'fall' into another well?"

Lamell's eyes darted to Julie before returning to me. "As long as I have you guys to rely on, I'll be fine."

I dusted off the Slim Jim and gave it back to Lamell. He bit into the brown stick like the beef, pork, and mechanically separated chicken were the finest meats he had ever tasted.

At 11 p.m., a woman with ink pythons snaking her biceps swaggered out of Beauty World. She brushed her purplish-red hair, lit a Tiparillo, and shouted instructions. Stable hands led four chestnut horses out from the Exxon garage and harnessed them to wagons while four armed men and two women watched over the two dozen workers.

In preparation to shadow the crooks, we eat, pack, and clean our firearms. The Radio Flyer will stay at the Broadway Inn, so Tina must walk, or we'll carry her. Olivia is subdued this evening. Maybe she's tired. I know the unrelenting stress is wearing me down. We need to smoke out Tyrell Ryker, put a bullet through his Neanderthalian skull, and press on to find Julie's long-lost sister. After that? I deserve a break—that all-inclusive vacation at a Fijian resort.

Dear Diary, do you think Ardy would want to join me?

Julie – July 22, 2029

7/22/2029

Diary, I normally keep you up to date during the day instead of regurgitating every detail at the end. I'm dead on my feet, so pardon me if this entry has more holes than a bag of bagels.

We broke out snacks at a Chevrolet car dealer. Sophie let Tina sit inside a sporty red Corvette and explained each control's purpose. The child soon lost interest without the feedback of a beep or whirr from any pushed button or turned knob. As did I. I cannot express why I resented those rows and rows of gleaming windshields, all marked with outrageous prices. Was it the daily record-breaking temperatures followed by the never-ending environmental disasters? Or did I yearn to race one of those bad boys down the Highway to Hell?

We ducked into an Amazon building after Olivia glimpsed armed men carrying cartons. The picked-over warehouse stocked everything a pre-Election Day person could ever desire. We swapped our filthy clothing for still-in-the-package sportswear and uncovered a treasure trove of pop-up books for Tina.

I nearly tripped on a pistol beneath the highway interchange. The Desert Eagle is too hefty for my taste, but the .44 caliber evokes memories of Captain Calhoun's "varmint gun." When I gave Lamell my Sig Sauer, Jules murmured in my ear, "Bet you five bucks he'll blow his brains out with it."

I grow closer to Julia with every mile passing under my belt. Just twenty thousand more steps to Hennington Lake, if you're keeping count, which I am. October's employee of the month, a lanky rotter with a HELLO MY NAME IS OTIS – HOW MAY I HELP YOU? nametag, checked us into the two-star Broadway Inn. My mind cried, "Julie, why stop when the finish line is within reach?" but my body groaned, "You need sleep," and shuffled me to bed.

Jules heard rumblings and called us to the door's fisheye peephole. "The Walmart is being raided!" Lamell waited with Tina as we searched through the Supercenter. Olivia realized that Tyrell Ryker wasn't among the plunderers and stomped a fallen watermelon into pieces.

Jules stalked one thief into an alley, cold-cocking him while he relieved himself on a NO POOP AND PEE ZONE sign. Alice scooped gutter water onto Rudy Cruz's face to revive him. Once the Pillsbury Doughboy stood bright-eyed and bushy-tailed, we perp-walked him to the Broadway Inn and locked him in a room far away from Tina.

I returned to our original room after Alice and I strapped our subject into a chair. Lamell shoved his feet into his boots while I cuddled Tina. "Julie, interrogation is like pulling an infected molar." He retrieved a toilet plunger from the bathroom, finishing the dental metaphor as he hurried to the door. "If you apply enough force, the truth always comes out."

Alice later informed me that Rudy wouldn't have lasted much longer if Sophie hadn't forced Olivia to take a timeout. Sophie then took over, giving it her best shot with the mop, but it was Lamell who extracted Tyrell Ryker's address. Jules praised his deft handling of the plumber's helper. I do admire a man who's good with his hands.

Olivia burst into my room to relay the news. "Rudy says Ryker never stays in one place for more than a couple of days. We must go to Beauty World! Now!"

Lamell discovered cartons of emergency candles in the motel's front office. He devised a clever, non-lethal contrivance to prevent our captive from alerting his boss. Olivia detailed that after she and Sophie tied Rudy to the bed, Lamell attached tapers to the bedframe, ensuring their waxen bases touched the ropes.

Naturally, I wanted to see this diabolical arrangement for myself. Lamell lit the final wick as I entered Room 16. "Julie, this should give us enough time before the candles burn through the braiding."

From Jules' smirk, I could tell she hoped the sheets would catch fire.

I packed our belongings, reluctant to bring Tina along on a hunt for the man responsible for harming Olivia and the people of Hattiesburg. Frisco Street, where Beauty World is located, lies north of the devastated Cloverleaf Center Mall. The roadway runs east to west, lined with a gas station, a pool hall, three fast-food joints, and Bubble Bees Auto Wash. We discreetly observe the men and women inside the hair and cosmetics store from the nearby car wash tunnel. Tyrell Ryker has yet to show up, so Olivia is climbing the walls. The teenager requires sleep, or she'll become a liability.

Lamell is talking with Alice. Now she's holding his hand. When Alice leaned in to listen, Lamell's tearful eyes met mine. What is that man hiding from me?

I found a book on childrearing in the Amazon warehouse. Should I shield Tina or expose her to the perils waiting at every bend in the road? Back in the whatevers, authoritarian mothers and fathers called this unsentimental parenting practice "tough love." I've had to contemplate this Catch-22 from the day we freed Tina from the attic cage. What if something happens to me? Tina is smart but also vulnerable. My daughter must learn to defend herself to survive in this frightening new world.

Diary, let's revisit a line in today's sixth paragraph: Lamell waited with Tina as we searched the Supercenter. At first glance, these nine words seem inconsequential. They're simply to put the reader at ease: "Who's babysitting the kid while the adults play cops and robbers?" "Oh, that's a relief, Lamell will."

Alice questioned Lamell's reliability. "Julie, are you really leaving your child in the care of a stranger?" She posed a valid concern. However, Alice wasn't the one who dove headfirst into the dark well to rescue the sinking man.

Jules stated her perspective. "Saving someone doesn't equate to being able to trust them. Doesn't the fable of the scorpion asking the frog to carry it across the river ring a bell? The scorpion, unable to control its nature, stung the frog. They both drowned!"

Point taken, Ms. Turner, but let *me* be frank. I am not a slimy frog!

"Julie, giving SK your gun was stupid!"

There she goes again with the Suicide King. I concur. I might have acted too hastily in offering him my weapon. Regardless, I don't care what other people think. Screw 'em. And besides, I have complete confidence in Lamell. My affection for him increases with every passing day. Diary, be honest: Could this man ever feel the same for me? On second thought, don't answer that. Hope keeps me alive.

The thieves are preparing to vacate Beauty World. We'll track them wherever they go. Will my loved ones be safe once

Olivia exacts her revenge? Or shall the head of the snake take a bigger bite?

I am reminded of what Alice's friend said. "The hunger for vengeance turns your stomach into a hot pretzel."

Did I misquote Pearl? My priority is to keep everyone out of harm's way, chiefly my daughter. If any mishap were to befall me, I pray that Tina remembers her mother was a good person.

Alice – July 23, 2029

7/23/2029

It's sunrise. In a post-apocalyptic world without meteorologists to analyze radar patterns on wall-sized maps, people must learn to create daily forecasts. For instance, you can wet your finger to detect wind direction. A campfire acts as a barometer. Rising smoke indicates high air pressure, while downward smoke forewarns of lower air pressure and the impending arrival of rain and wind. Observe the positions, shapes, and colors of clouds. Fluffy white puffs signify beach weather—don't forget to pack the Coppertone! Are the thunderheads hugging the ground and black as funeral shrouds? Friend, you better run for shelter if you're not in the mood to get zapped! I can also predict certain atmospheric conditions if my ankles ache or my hair frizzes up.

Sailors caution you about the calm before the storm. We assumed the gangsters would continue east—opposite the Walmart Supercenter they had just robbed. But they threw us a curve ball by going west. Only someone with a low IQ returns to the scene of the crime, right? Or maybe an evil genius? Nobody expects lightning to strike twice in the same place. So why not park your keister on the blackened tree stump, crack open a Michelob, and watch the sky show? You'll be snug as a bug in a rug, because *everyone knows lightning never strikes in the same place twice!*

We trailed the horse-drawn wagons and pedestrians bringing up the rear. A quarter of a mile from the Walmart we had investigated twenty-four hours earlier, the procession halted at Broadway Drive. The woman with flaming hair and a coil of snake tattoos signaled for silence. Five guards approached the food warehouse, leaving one man with the lady in charge. After a brief interval, Princess Python received a call on her portable radio. She and the man escorted the workers away.

Across from the Supercenter, Julie transferred the binoculars to Olivia. "Can you see Ryker?"

Olivia stared long and hard before passing the field glasses back to Julie. "I'm going in for a closer look."

Sophie stepped forward. "I'm coming with you, Liv."

Julie hugged each scout. "Don't take any chances. Be back in twenty minutes."

As the girls legged it down a side street, I hoped Olivia wouldn't lose control and go postal.

With reference to communicating with God—AGAIN!!!—as a child, I turned to my uncle, a Lutheran minister, for advice. Butterball, my beloved white and gold hamster, had stopped running on his exercise wheel and hardly touched his food.

"Uncle Jack, I am worried about Butterball. I pray a million times a day for him to get well, but he won't eat. What am I doing wrong? Why isn't God helping Butterball?"

My uncle patted my head the same way he'd pet Marilyn, his toy poodle. "Oh, Allie, you're not doing anything wrong. God is a mystery. Do you know what that means?"

My father drank six-packs of Pabst Blue Ribbon while listening to old CBS *Radio Mystery Theater* broadcasts. I did not think "The Trouble With Murder" or "The Hand That Refused to Die" were the mysteries my religious relative referred to. "No, Uncle Jack. Why is God so mysterious?"

He relit his pipe and blew out a smog of cherry-flavored lung cancer. "God's master plan is beyond our comprehension. We, as lowly humans, are incapable of knowing Him directly. Does that make sense?"

I sniffled, adamant not to cry in front of him. "So, Butterball isn't going to get better?"

My uncle chuckled. "Pray all you want, Allie, but don't expect any miracles. I'm sure you realize," he squeezed my knee until I recoiled, "healing your sick gerbil is at the very bottom of the Lord's to-do list."

The next morning, I found my hamster lying still in his cage. My schoolmates and I buried Butterball in a Keds shoebox.

As a teenager, I overheard my mother sounding distraught on the telephone. Uncle Jack no longer preached at Our Savior's Lutheran Church. Apparently, the organist came in early one Sunday morning and caught him with his robe around his ankles.

Sorry, I got sidetracked. Tyrell Ryker is dead. Olivia didn't pummel her rapist to a pulp with her bare hands. I shot him through his black fucking heart with a single round from Pearl Jackson's Mossberg Patriot deer rifle. My Hayneville friend would be proud of my marksmanship. Is the Man Upstairs mad at me? Like Uncle Jack told me so many years ago, "God is a mystery."

4 p.m. We're finally breaking after being on the move for three hours. Julie has the map, so I am unsure of our current location.

Getting back to last night. We became concerned when Olivia and Sophie did not return from reconnoitering the Walmart. Julie loaded a cartridge into the M16's firing chamber. "Let's go look for them!"

"Give the girls a few more minutes," I advised. "They'll be fine."

A series of gunshots proved me wrong. We sprinted toward the blasts, Lamell hanging behind with Tina.

Whereas it's common to put the cart before the horse in popular media and literature, as a former literary agent, I am not a big fan of jumping between time periods. Well-placed flashbacks can provide insights into a character's background, but beginning a story with the ending—like me confessing to taking out Tyrell Ryker—is a nonstarter. I wouldn't invest in any author who willingly kills the suspense in the first paragraph.

However, dear Diary, the intent of these pages has never been to craft a bestselling thriller. This journal's sole purpose is to record my daily observations and, most of all, help me understand my own mental state. Especially now.

On second thought, dear Diary, I don't have to tell you everything. Some things should be left unsaid.

We are staying overnight in a library near Julia Werner's Hennington Lake house. Julie stopped us when we reached Oak Grove. She wanted to wait until daylight for the final three miles. "It's kinda late to show up unannounced on somebody's doorstep. No need to give my sister a stroke." Is Julie getting cold feet?

The path that led us to this place in space and time has been long and winding. I, too, am filled with apprehension. What monumental changes will tomorrow bring?

Hey, dear Diary! If you're really dying to catch up on today's shitshow, read Julie's little pink book. She's written so much that her pen is running out of ink.

Julie - July 23, 2029

7/23/2029

The skies are the bluest of blues this morning, and a refreshing breeze blows from the north. We're in the Walmart stockroom, bedded on mattresses wrapped in shipping plastic. Once everyone is up and about, we'll head west. I don't want to rush anybody, especially Olivia, who acts like Alice just ran her car over her pet cat. Whether or not my sister is at Hennington Lake, the truth will reveal itself soon enough.

Last night, we tailed the horse-drawn wagons to the Walmart across from the Broadway Inn. Olivia and Sophie went ahead to spot Tyrell Ryker. When the girls didn't come back, Alice, Jules, and I debated going after them or standing by. A volley of rapid gunfire forced a quick decision.

Diary, I presume you're familiar with megastores. Countless solar panels shade asphalt deserts, stunted trees grow from concrete oases, and sharp spikes keep birds off the light poles. Towering walls enclose acres of selling space, and rows of shopping carts await penny-pinching shoppers. According to a magazine article I read eons ago, consumer researchers found that conformity comforts customers (the three Cs), which is why all these retail chains bear the same mundane resemblance.

What set this Wally World apart from Hattiesburg's other food storage warehouses? Tyrell Ryker held Olivia and Sophie captive within this castle of commerce. Of course, as Alice and I crouched in our observation post at the Broadway Inn, the girls' whereabouts remained unknown. I'd sweep the area with the binoculars while my partner used the rifle scope to spy inside the building's depths. No one else came into view except for the people loading the wagons and the two guards strapping on protective flak jackets.

"Alice, are you sure those were gunshots?"

"It sounded like three different firearms." She squinted into the scope's eyepiece. "One had the pop-pop-pop of an AK-47."

Kalashnikovs are notorious for their unique sound. "That doesn't prove it was Sophie's."

Alice tweaked the scope's focus knob. "These guards are carrying submachine guns. Uzis?"

The Cobra hung on my waist. "Why didn't I give Olivia or Sophie the other two-way radio?"

"Lamell needs that walkie-talkie to communicate with us."

Jules stood beside me, not uttering a single word. I scratched a skeeter bite hard enough to make it bleed. "What do we do?"

Alice surveyed the parking lot. "The approach is shielded by cars and trucks, but the main entrance is a kill zone. We might be safer entering from the back of the store."

"The guards may have bolted the doors shut."

"We can blast our way in."

"They'll hear us!" I pressed the Cobra's push-to-talk button. "Lamell, have Olivia and Sophie shown up?"

"Negative," came the staticky reply. "What's your status?"

"Still determining their location."

"Keep me posted. And, Julie?"

"What?" I answered impatiently.

"Be careful."

"You too, Lamell," I said into the microphone, softer this time.

I returned the radio to my belt. "Alright, let's go behind the building."

We crept toward the rear of the Walmart, steering clear of an armed woman smoking underneath the GARDEN CENTER sign and a fidgety man pacing the loading dock. Mountains of discarded electrical appliances and electronics created a sharp-edged obstacle course.

Alice's eyes crawled above the obstructed emergency exits. "The roof?"

"How do we get up there?" Jules touched the smooth surface. "These walls are thirty feet tall!"

"I'll go check for a fire escape." Alice hurried to a row of cargo containers.

Jules and I scrambled atop a mammoth cardboard baler. The top of the recycling machine brought us closer to the rooftop, but not near enough. A pile of wooden pallets leaned on the box crusher.

Alice called out to us. "I couldn't find a ladder. A frontal assault may be our only way inside."

"The main entryway is suicide." I reached down to her. "Hand me a pallet." She pushed the forty-pound platform up the side of the paper compactor. I dragged the first board over the edge and shoved the skid against the wall. "Keep 'em coming." Jules and I scaled the stack of wood when our fingers could stretch no further.

Alice mounted the baler to pass more pallets. She warned us when we were three yards from the summit, "Just two left."

"Can we connect them to make a ladder?"

"Wait." Alice dropped down to the pavement and opened the compacting machine. She used a tool tethered to a cord to nip lengths of baling wire.

With the last pallets strapped together, we slung the rifles on our backs. Jules took the lead as we climbed the rickety wooden slats to mount the rooftop. A white expanse covered with dozens of air conditioning units, and hundreds of solar panels and skylights extended into the distance. Alice tugged on an access hatch, expressing her frustration with a string of uncommon cuss words.

Jules suggested we try the skylights instead. The frosted glass domes formed a twenty-by-twenty-foot grid, each lid permanently sealed. Alice noticed me studying a label stuck to a unique type of hatchway. The sticker read, AUTOMATIC SMOKE VENT – FIRE DEPARTMENT PULL MANUAL CABLE. She tugged the red handle to release the rusty latch, and we eased the gravity-operated flap up an inch to peer through the gap.

Men and women wearing headlamps scurried up and down food aisles, grabbing cartons and loading them onto waiting wagons. I pressed my eyes to the field glasses, desperately searching for any sign of Olivia or Sophie.

Here's where the picture becomes hazy. It's unclear if Alice saw Ryker first, if I did, or if we both did. I whispered, "See the guy with the ponytail holding a clipboard?" as she racked a round into her Mossberg. The rifle's sudden BOOM! dented my eardrums. I thought we'd first confirm his identity and devise an exit strategy before we, as teammates, agreed to put a slug in his chest. Ryker fell backward, spilling bushels of strawberries onto the cement floor. The man we had so resolutely sought out curled into a fetal position, shuddered once, and lay still.

Chaos ensued. The lady with fuchsia-dyed hair crawled on her belly to check Ryker's pulse. Berries and blood soaked her khaki pants as she hollered, "Clean up on aisle six!"

Sorry, Diary. Jules goaded me into adding that last line. Her twisted sense of humor sent me to the principal's office far too many times to count. Ryker's right-hand woman screamed, "Somebody shot Basilisk! Find them!"

Panicked, we darted across the white gravel. I skidded to a halt halfway to the ladder. "Where's Jules? Have you seen her?"

Alice yanked on my shirt. "Julie, they'll come after us!"

"I can't leave! We need to find Jules!" I cupped my hands. "Jules!"

Alice dragged me to the edge of the roof and pointed downward. "Look, Julie! Jules is steadying the ladder."

I exhaled in relief, swinging my foot across the metal flashing onto the wooden pallet.

Once on solid ground, we doubled back. The guard on the loading dock had quit his post. Insistent knocking and a woman shouting, "Terrence, let me in!" stopped us cold in our tracks. The garden center door opened, a man peered out, and the woman lookout elbowed by his paunch. We hustled past picket fencing, bags of mulch, and shriveled plants to tailgate inside the building.

Most of the noise originated in the middle of the warehouse. The typical merchandise you'd buy in your local Walmart—apparel, toys, sports equipment, and housewares—had been pushed aside to make room for provisions. Thieves had taken all the fresh food, leaving little for us to hide behind. A young man scampered past us brandishing a box cutter, trailed by an older woman cradling an egg carton. Both exited the way we entered, oblivious to our presence.

A female voice rose above the pandemonium. "Last warning! Get back here, or I'll shoot!"

Alice's fingers dug into my shoulder. "Why are these people escaping?"

I took a wild guess. "Forced labor?"

Jules peeped over sacks of baking potatoes. "They're not our problem. Our job is to find—" She ducked as four gunshots resounded throughout the cavernous structure.

I kept an eye out for Olivia and Sophie as we navigated through the maze of foodstuffs and necessities. Besides the spacious selling floor, Walmart had restrooms, a pharmacy, administrative offices, shipping and receiving, and a stockroom. Some stores even featured fast-food outlets and optometrists. If the girls were here, they could be anywhere.

We followed a red smear to a Black female using her arms to drag her limp legs. Jules flipped the teenager onto her back. "Where you off to, darlin'?"

The girl's fists stained the front of Jules' gray sweatshirt. "Let me be!"

Jules restrained her flailing wrists. "Nobody's gonna hurt you! Tell me your name."

"Nora." Blood flecked her lips. "I can't feel anything below my waist. Shouldn't a gunshot be painful?"

Jules examined Nora's torso for an exit wound. "Who did this to you?"

"Uma." The girl groaned. "She's shooting anybody attempting to run away."

Jules probed the bullet hole with her pinkie. "Why?"

"Basilisk makes us—" A convulsion interrupted Nora, her voice weakening. "Is that monster dead?"

"Is Basilisk's real name Tyrell Ryker?"

"He never told us. You won't let me die, will you?"

Jules held Nora's hand. "The bullet might have nicked your spine. We are searching for two of our members. One is a White, blonde girl around your age. The other is an Asian woman with dark hair. Tell us where they are, and I'll help you." Jules patted the teen's cheek to keep her conscious. "Nora, Nora, where are my friends?"

Nora pointed at a room-sized box behind us. "They're. . . ." Before she could finish her last words, Nora's arm dropped to her side and her eyeballs rolled into her head.

Jules cracked her knuckles. "Julie, do I send her?"

I glanced at Alice, who nodded her approval.

Jules placed her palm over the paralyzed girl's mouth and pinched her nostrils shut with her thumb and forefinger. "We appreciate your help, Nora. May God ease your journey to the hereafter."

A keyed padlock secured the walk-in freezer. When Alice pounded on the metal door, someone inside the insulated space pounded back. However, using her rifle butt to break the sturdy hasp would attract unneeded attention. "Ryker has the key, or his tattooed bitch."

Uma, barking orders at the guards, was easy to locate. I called from behind the shielding of the densest product available, a stack of Huggies diapers. "We don't want trouble. Throw us the key to the cold room, and we'll let you all walk out of here."

I caught the command, "Surround them," and a much louder, "Why should we trust you? You shot Basilisk!"

A reasonable question.

In response, Alice pulled out her Glock. "There are more of us than there are of you. Give us our kids, and I swear you'll never see me or my friends again." She turned to me and mouthed, "Kill them all."

And so, we did. With deadly efficiency, I might add. After many days on the road, Alice and I can virtually read each other's minds. We moved in perfect synchrony, a well-oiled machine fueled by faith and feeling. As one being, we took down Uma—I aimed high, while Alice aimed low. The Desert Eagle had such a powerful kickback that the stippled grip nearly flew out of my fingers. Jules praised how the "hand cannon" cleanly severed the snake lady's head. With Olivia and Sophie free, we dealt swiftly with Uma's underlings. They put up a good fight, but they were no match for girls with guns.

Olivia and Sophie had company in the freezer—four of Michael Thatch's men. The security guards, confined for a second time, hadn't anticipated a follow-up attack. Antonio, their lead, promised to help anyone who Ryker strong-armed.

I radioed Lamell. "The girls are safe. Bring Tina!" My daughter leaped into my arms, flooding me with relief and joy. And Lamell? He was ecstatic about hugging me, too!

Olivia and Sophie manage fairly well despite sustaining scratches and bruises from fighting off their assailants. Physically, at least. Alice irked Olivia by negating her chance for revenge. Olivia wanted to be the meat chef serving Tyrell Ryker's head on a silver platter, yet she understood the extenuating circumstances we were under. I pray the child finds peace now that he's gone.

Wow, I wrote a lot this morning! My pink diary is almost filled with ink. It seems only yesterday that I had plenty of pages to spill my guts on. Writing is exhausting but also cathartic. I need a new journal. We'll recuperate for a few hours and then clear out.

Our group left Walmart in the mid-afternoon with the sun shining brightly overhead. As we exited the food storage warehouse, Alice and I had to turn away several freed workers requesting to join us.

We're at the Oak Grove Public Library, only three miles from where Julia lives (or used to live). This building has no rotters, just books—a hopeful omen. I'm processing everything that happened today and obsessing over tomorrow.

Alice - July 24, 2029

7/24/2029

The clamor of two women quarreling woke me. I've never seen Julie this frazzled. Unhinged. It's mind-boggling to witness the speed with which Julie and Jules vacillate between one another. I can't find the words to describe the scene before me—it's surreal, unnerving, horrifying, and mesmerizing all at once.

Lamell's eyes are bugging out. He cares for Julie a lot. Tina too. Only four days have passed since Julie and I hauled his drenched body from the water well. Has anyone officially introduced Lamell to Jules? With everything going on, I can't recall if Olivia, Sophie, or I pulled our newest member aside to decode Julie's multiple personalities for him.

I walked Julie and Jules to a building adjacent to the library where an OAK GROVE COMMUNITY CENTER sign hung over the door. We sat at a large conference table.

Dear Diary, guess what I detected? Not only is Jules left-handed, but her pupils dilate when she speaks—a fascinating and disturbing sight.

Me: "Why are you two biting each other's heads off?"

Julie: "Jules is being very—"

Jules: "Julie is always—"

Me (raising my palms to quieten them): "One at a time, ladies."

Jules: "I've been there for Julie, and now—"

Julie: "But sometimes you—"

Me: "Julie, let Jules finish."

Jules: "Julia never forgave Julie for the death of their mother and father."

Julie: "I didn't say the car accident wasn't my fault!" She rubbed her reddening eyes. "My sister had every right to leave me."

Jules: "Did it slip your mind the day I had to stop you from crawling into a jet engine? Alice, are you aware that Julie clipped a suicide note on her foster parents' refrigerator? 'Goodbye, cruel world. I'm sorry for—'"

Julie: "She's lying! I—"

Me: "Guys, let's bury the past and focus on the present. Why were you bickering with Jules this morning?"

Julie: "I am flipping out. What if Julia isn't home? Worse, what if she is?"

Me: "If Julia's there, she'll be thrilled to see you. Jules?"

Jules: "Once Julie locates her sister, she won't need me. I'll be replaced!"

Julie: "That's ridiculous!" Though she swore, "We will always be together, Jules," she did not have to cross her fingers to protect herself from the big lie. Julie's averted eyes gave her away, a sure tell which made me dwell on my twat of a husband, Peter.

Me: "Julie, you should talk to Lamell before we go any further. He deserves to understand your connection to Jules. Fully."

Julie: "Why does it matter?"

Me: "Lamell has feelings for you."

Julie (grinning): "You think so? I like him too."

Me: "Then be open and honest with him."

Julie's throat bulged as if her jaw muscles obstructed her dark passenger from speaking.

Julie led Lamell to the community center. Twenty minutes later, she returned alone and dejected. I found him on a bench behind the library.

I plucked a dandelion from the lawn and handed Lamell the golden-yellow flower. "How are you coping with all this?"

He chuckled and shook his head. "And I thought *I* was the one who was fucked up."

"It took me some time to, um, wrap my head around it."

"What exactly is 'it'?"

"I am not sure how much she told you. Julie pursued me from Montgomery to Hayneville."

"Why?"

Hayneville seems so long ago that my mental image of Ardy is dissipating. "The sheriff locked Julie up for observation. When I asked her why she was stalking me, she shared her list of Top Ten Goals. All were crossed off except for two: 'Find Julia or die trying' and 'Make a real friend.'"

"Alice, I'm assuming you're the Real Friend as opposed to Jules, the Pretend Friend?"

"We've grown incredibly close. Julie would lay down her life for me, as I would for her. It's hard to explain. We're soul sisters."

"How does Jules fit into your relationship?"

"Like loyalty without trust, you cannot have one without the other. Julie is strong-willed herself, but if you add in Jules' badassness, you've got—"

"Double trouble." The man clasped his hands. "Julie is crazy, isn't she?"

Although I had asked Ardy the same thing, I snapped at him, "You jumped into that hole in the ground to drown yourself!"

"Alice, holding myself together is a daily battle. I can't handle—"

"Lamell, if you ever harm Julie or Tina, I'll drag you back to Clara and drop you headfirst into that pit!"

An uncomfortable silence made me question why he stayed with us. Passing clouds blocked the sun. The cloying smell of a roaming skunk wafted my way.

Lamell turned to me as the sky cleared. "I want to help Julie."

His earnest expression assured me of his sincerity. "My friend researched her symptoms at the Hayneville town library. Ardy believes she might have—"

"Dissociative identity disorder is a psychological response to trauma."

"You know about DID?"

Lamell pointed his thumb at the library behind us. "I read the medical books. Antidepressants may provide temporary relief from her split personalities. What Julie really needs, though, is professional counseling."

"Jules is gradually fading into the background. Tina renewed Julie's sense of self, filling the void left by her absent family. Until today, that is. Jules thinks Julie will toss her to the curb once she reunites with Julia."

Lamell's change of topic blindsided me. "Julie says you're in love with Ardy but lack the courage to follow your heart."

My ears burned with embarrassment. "She said what now?"

"Alice, if you truly want to be with Ardy, why are you here?" Lamell stood up, extending his hand to me. "Let's check on Julie and Jules."

We have finally reached Treasure Point! Olivia, Sophie, Lamell, and Tina doze on recliners behind Julia's magnificent ranch house. I'm updating my diary on a picnic table. Lamell lugged an enormous umbrella out of the garage to shade us from the noonday sun. The wraparound deck provides a splendid view of Hennington Lake. Julie mentioned that her twin was a market analyst for an international conglomerate. By the looks of this place, her hard work paid off! Out on the water, shimmering fish launch into space for a moment of glory before gravity sucks them back for the inevitable splashdown.

The breaking news: Julia is nowhere to be found. Layers of dust indicate that she hasn't been home in ages. Julie and Jules are exploring the premises, waving away any offers to help. I sympathize with her mood. Hopelessness has squashed flat her years of hopefulness. Thankfully, there is no physical evidence to suggest that Julia died during the pandemic.

Now what?

What now?

How now, brown cow?

Whichever way I phrase this predicament—unless Julia walks through the front door with a tray of hot French crullers—I have only three options.

A. I proceed to New Orleans to find David's older brother. "Edward, I have a bit of sad news. I strangled your little brother. Um-hum, you heard me. Why did I kill Dave? His constant sneezing and coughing disrupted my beauty sleep. Ed, you are one hundred percent correct. I should have gotten David some help." At merely a hundred miles away, the Big Easy is within reach.

B. Julie and I resume the hunt for her twin sister. I was serious when I swore to Lamell that I'd do anything for Julie. If she asks me to rake the coals in the basement of Hell for Julia, I will, with bells on—as long as I can wear a flame-resistant suit.

C. I return to Alabama to assist Pearl and Ardy with restoring Hayneville from the ashes, a town I've grown quite fond of. Julie told Lamell that I suffer from chickenshitidness in the romance department. Is she right?

Jules came outside to sit at the picnic table, a strange occurrence since she avoids being alone with me. Her Loyola Marymount University sweatshirt was dirtier than usual, and her eyes were bloodshot. "Alice, Julie is acting strange. I am worried she'll injure herself. What do I do?"

Dear Diary, I've extensively attempted to illustrate my interactions with someone with DID. I love Julie. I accept and respect Jules—even "like" her. Oftentimes, I cannot believe that the person before me isn't playing a prank. I wait with bated breath for Allen Funt to spring out of a bush, exclaiming, "Smile, Alice, you're on *Candid Camera*!"

After our recent "spat," I am more cautious when speaking to Julie or Jules. "Jules, it's a setback that Julia is not here. Are there any clues as to where she might be?"

"We've searched every inch of this building from top to bottom. Julia was married to a dentist." Jules held up an old bank statement. "Doctor Mason Moore. They had a dog, Bailey, but no kids. From the condition of the MacGyvered electric and water hookups, the couple appears to have toughed it out for a few years after Election Day."

"Wait, did you cut yourself?"

Jules permitted me to examine her fingers. "Julie showed me a photo of her family. I smashed the picture frame against the wall."

"Why? Did seeing her mother and father make you jealous?"

"Julia shouldn't have washed her hands of Julie! Julie never meant to hurt her parents."

"The other driver instigated the car crash. It's not Julie's fault. Do you wanna go inside and see how she's doing?"

"Yeah, I hope she's feeling better."

Jules walked me past the kitchen and into the main bedroom. She lay face down on the bed. I sat beside her on the mattress. "Julie!"

A pillow muffled her response. "Leave me alone."

I touched her arm. "Are you all right?" A sniffle. "Hey, what did Julia get for Christmas?"

She twisted her head to stare at me with one eye. "Huh?"

"Your parents gifted you the sweatshirt you're wearing, right? What did they give your sister?"

"More clothes. A dress, I think."

"And did you exchange presents with Julia?"

"Why wouldn't I? I gave my sister a book by Stephen King, her favorite author. *Lisey's Story*."

A small office overlooked the lake. Sunlight streaming through the slanted Venetian blinds cast contrasting stripes across a desk strewn with folders. A laptop sat on the rug next to an upside-down swivel chair. I walked in, selected a novel from the shelf, and turned around.

Julie stood in the doorway. "How did you know?"

I held up the book, its red cover illustrated with a garden shovel filled with vibrant flowers. "I put myself in Julia's mind. She couldn't be sure that you would come. If you did, your sister thought you'd remember the last gift you gave her." I passed her *Lisey's Story*. "I haven't looked inside."

Julie opened the bestseller and read the inscription out loud. "Merry Christmas! Julia, you're not just my twin sister. You are also my best friend. Love you forever, Julie." She fanned through hundreds of pages, suddenly finding a folded sheet hidden between them. "Can you read it for me, Alice? I'm too nervous."

I agreed, noting how the block printing on the ruled paper resembled Julie's handwriting. "You should share this with your entire family." I led Julie by the hand to the outdoor deck.

> 12/25/2027
>
> Julie,
> If you are reading this letter, sadly, it means we have missed each other by days, months, or even years. If you, Unknown Weary Traveler, discovered my message, you're welcome to use my home, but kindly return this note to where you found it.
>
> Julie, forgive me for abandoning you in your time of greatest need. I unfairly blamed you for our parents' premature deaths. For many years, I struggled with anxiety and depression. Mason, my husband, urged me to seek therapy. Much as talking with an expert helped, my guilt for leaving you never diminished. The roles have reversed. Now, you are the one hating me.
>
> Although I never contacted you, I've kept tabs on your online presence. I read your articles in the *Ithaca Voice*, posting anonymous comments. Sister, you have done exceptionally well for yourself!
>
> Mason and I walked away from Treasure Point on the 20th anniversary of the death of our mother and father. I could say we left the town we called home to make things right with you. Locating you is part of the reason, but not the sole motivation. I'm two months pregnant. Yes, you're going to be an aunt! The healthcare in this region is alarmingly inadequate and only getting worse. While Mason has dental training, he's not an obstetrician. Holy

rollers stoned our local midwife when Father Rallis learned she was secretly performing abortions. So, my husband and I are off to locate a functioning hospital.

We plan to reach Syracuse, New York, before I give birth. The idea of traveling twelve hundred miles is daunting. If Mom and Dad's apartment on Monroe Street still exists, perhaps you've flown back to the nest.

If not, I will wait for you.

Please take care of yourself, Julie. I miss you very much.

Your loving sister,

Julia

P.S. If the baby is a girl, we'll name her Julie. If it's a boy, Julian.

I handed the letter back to Julie. She read and reread Julia's heartfelt sentiments before carefully tucking the priceless treasure into her pocket. Sensing her mother's fragile emotional state, Tina dashed across the wooden planks to hug her. I lingered outside as Julie and the others entered Julia's house.

The railing of the peeling deck supported my forearms as I closed my eyes. My nose, the needle on a ship's compass, swung south. Louisiana. New Orleans. David. Edward. I concentrated all my emotions, seeking the slightest magnetic pull on my heartstrings. My body pivoted northeast, attracted to Alabama, Hayneville, Pearl, and Ardy. Going to upstate New York with Julie and Tina—with luck, Julia—felt out of reach.

Turning once more, I opened my eyes to face the dying sun and sent my confessions on the passing winds. "My dearest David, I regret taking your life. I am sorry, Edward, for not having the backbone to come to New Orleans and tell you the truth."

I hurried indoors to join my family with a heavy heart but renewed purpose.

Julie - July 24, 2029

7/24/2029

Jules is driving me batty! Her voice—like nails scratching on a chalkboard—pierces my eardrums. She clings on to me like a blood-sucking leech!

I throw up my hands to ward off her advances. My heartbeat slows as I inhale and exhale. I stopped wanting to throttle Jules, but she better quit nagging me! She believes *she's* stressed. What about *me*? Julia is so close we're breathing the same air. My empty stomach is swarming with butterflies. The main thing preventing me from hightailing back to the place of my birth is Jules' pig-headed commitment to stop me from finding Julia. Our feud is a dizzying whirlwind of resentment and longing.

"Julie, why are you so eager to be with your sister? She ran out on you!"

"Jules," I explode, "shut your mouth before I shut it for you!"

Our nonstop squabbling finally got under Alice's skin. She pushed Jules and me into a building behind the library, where she coaxed us into revealing our insecurities. I divulged how the prospect of seeing Julia again terrifies me. "What if my sister despises me?" Jules opened up about her fear of being rejected. "Julie will dump me once she is with Julia!" I reassured Jules that I'd never desert her. We've been side by side for as long as Julia and I have been apart. As I uttered those optimistic words, a timid voice wondered if I had outgrown our relationship. With Tina to care for, do I still need Jules to watch over me?

Alice recommended that Jules and Lamell get to know each other, so I took them to the community center. As expected, Jules shot Lamell her "Whatchu lookin' at?" glare and refused to respond to him. Must her jealous tendencies sabotage all my new friendships? I fielded Lamell's queries to the best of my ability, except for one. "Julie, will Jules always be part of *our* relationship?"

My sister isn't at Hennington Lake. Jules and I scoured every nook and cranny of Julia's house. The butterflies stopped fluttering in my belly. They all drowned in gastric acid.

Alice and Jules hover around me, probably concerned I'll stuff my pockets full of rocks and wade into the deepest section of the lake. My soul is sinking lower and lower into a sunless abyss.

Mom had passed on some sage advice on the day of my first heartbreak. "Julie, today might seem like the end of the world. When you wake tomorrow, the earth will still be beneath your feet, and the sun will still soar above your head. An overcast sky won't keep the sun from burning away the clouds. Don't give that loser another thought. You've always been too good for him." Her calm and caressing words continue to live on as a gentle reminder that light always shines through the cracks.

Jesus, let me lie on Julia's bed for a minute longer. Then, rising like Lazarus, I shall continue searching for my sister.

Diary, I was on the verge of throwing in the towel. But now I can tell you where Julia is thanks to Alice's intuition! Just this morning, I spoke of my desire to return to my birthplace. My sister is waiting for me in Syracuse! At our childhood apartment!

Alice asked me what I had gifted Julia when our parents died on Christmas. Aware that she was a big Stephen King fan, I bought her his latest novel. And low and behold, Alice found the copy of *Lisey's Story* on a bookshelf in Julia's office, with a note inside! I was worried my trembling hands would tear the paper or smudge the ink. Alice read the letter aloud to everyone on the exterior deck.

Julia is having a baby! Julian or Julie, depending on whether she and her husband, Mason, are blessed with a boy or a girl. Two years have passed since my sister wrote this letter, so God willing, I am now an aunt!

Even though Julia's not with me now, at least I know where she went. Diary, I'm placing the letter between your pages so you can read every word.

And the best thing? *Julia apologized!*

I'll discuss Julia's letter with Alice, the girls, and Lamell later. Will they accompany me to Syracuse? A journey of that duration is a hefty request, especially after I dragged them to Hattiesburg.

I'm guessing Alice is ready to return to Hayneville, and I can't blame her. Or stop her. If anyone deserves to find happiness, it's Alice. What about Olivia and Sophie? I suspect they'll keep on to New Orleans. The "Land of Opportunity" does sound promising. Tina goes wherever I go, yet the road to New York is rife with risk. The thought of exposing my daughter to further harm weighs on me. I'd love it if Lamell came with us, but his actions are beyond my control. Shall I get on my knees and beg?

And then there's Jules. That woman always poses a challenge as her influence shapes my decisions. She put her foot down. "We're not chasing your excuse for a sister all over the country!"

Whatever the others say or do, Tina and I are leaving tomorrow.

Alice – July 25, 2029

7/25/2029

Julie wasn't in Julia's bedroom, so I stepped outdoors to search for her and Tina. I found them down by the lake, skipping stones across the flat water.

The child heard my boots squishing in the mud and ran to me. "Aunt Alice, did you see my throw? The rock jumped three times!"

"You've got a good arm, kid! Someday, you'll. . . ." I trailed off, turning my face away to hide my tears.

Tina sat with me on the soggy ground. "Why are you crying, Aunt Alice? Did you hurt yourself?"

Julie squatted beside me, rubbing my back with her hand. "What's wrong?"

The ruinous words spilled from my mouth. "Julie, I can't go with you to Syracuse." I realized that somewhere between Montgomery and Hattiesburg, I became fearless enough to forge my own path. "I am so sorry."

"Hayneville?"

I nodded silently. "I need to talk to Ardy."

We sat on the shoreline, watching the birds and fish go by, fully aware that these were our last moments together.

Julie – July 25, 2029

7/25/2029

Diary, not only do I have no desire to describe my day, but only a single blank page remains for me to write on. My story is ending.

However, hopefulness swells amidst the heartache. Lamell is joining Tina and me, and he seems genuinely excited. Jules? She stormed off. It might be healthy for us to finally have some time apart.

I'd be over the moon if the bad news wasn't so dispiriting: Alice is heading back to Hayneville. She misses Pearl and has fallen for Ardy. I wish my friend everlasting happiness.

Olivia and Sophie glanced at me before walking over to Alice. "We're staying with *our* mom."

While Julia will always be my sister, Alice and the girls are my forever family. "Alice, if Julia isn't in New York, I promise to return to Alabama. Tell Oscar I love him."

She appeared skeptical as I hugged her goodbye.

> Diary,
> Knowing you has been my pleasure, but now I must bid you *adieu*.
>
> *Julie Werner*

Alice – July 26, 2029

7/26/2029

Once again, we find ourselves in the same room at the Hattiesburg Broadway Inn. Olivia stands by the door, her eye pressed to the peephole. "All quiet on the western front," she reports, referring to the infamous Walmart across the street. "The city's food supplies are safe because of us." Olivia triumphantly pumps her fist, then flops on the mattress beside Sophie. Their weapons, cold and metallic, rest against and atop the nightstands.

Sophie shuts her eyelids. "I am so tired."

Olivia hugs Theodore, her teddy bear, and groans. "I'm too young to ache all over."

Although I have the queen-sized bed all to myself, I miss Julie's sharp elbows poking me in the ribs.

Despite everything, am I starting to feel—dare I think it—happy?

Sophie and Olivia cover themselves with the blanket. "Night, Mom." The word sounds strange to my ears, but I like it.

"Goodnight, girls. Sleep tight, and don't let the bedbugs bite." I whisper a quick prayer for us all before blowing out the candle.

Spring 2039

Dear Reader,

If you have reached the end of these pages, I must have lost Julie's and Alice's diaries, or worse, I am dead. I do not know the whereabouts or welfare of my mom and Aunt Alice. We became separated during a recent terrorist bombing.

You probably think Julie was crazy. She wasn't. Jules was as flesh and blood to us as she was to my mother. Aunt Jules came and went throughout the years, always returning when we needed her most.

Today, I wrote my first entry in my own diary. I pray to God it's not my last.

Tina Werner

www.ingramcontent.com/pod-product-compliance
Lightning Source LLC
Chambersburg PA
CBHW020601310726
48979CB00008B/1292/J
* 9 7 8 0 9 9 8 5 4 4 7 8 6 *